PRAISE FOR CATHERINE ASARO AND
The Saga of the Skolian Empire

"Asaro has once more produced an entertaining yarn with a stronger emotive content than one usually sees. The fans she has won with her previous Saga volumes will be pleased, and even though this one is part of a series, it stands well enough on its own to bring more fans to the bookstore counter. Watch for it, and for the rest of the "Triad" subsaga it introduces."

—*Analog* on *Schism*

"This is the tenth installment in Asaro's nonlinear history of the Skolian Empire and also the first in a subordinated series the Triad. There are elements of space opera, romance, military SF, and high adventure . . . which should more than satisfy her very diverse readership. This is shaping up as one of the major series in the genre, and unlike many other similar sequences, it hasn't become diluted with the addition of more volumes."

—*Chronicle* on *Schism*

"*Schism* is a fine addition to Asaro's saga of the Skolian empire. The romance and royal intrigue add depth to the space-opera plot. The characters are real people . . . overall, an excellent book that leaves the readers begging for more." —SciFi.com

"O lucky, lucky readers. Catherine Asaro adds another glittering gem to her Skolian collection. . . . Ms. Asaro continues to grow in both depth and complexity, seamlessly integrating characterization, plot and scientific conjecture into elegantly developed concepts that both challenge the mind and please the heart. Another knockout display of superlative storytelling! Thank you so much for such a glorious read."

—*Romantic Times* (4½ GOLD MEDAL Review)
on *Ascendant Sun*

"*Ascendant Sun,* the fifth novel in Catherine Asaro's fabulous Skolian Empire saga, is an exciting and enthralling work of science fiction. . . . Ms. Asaro continues to rise in ascendancy to the apogee of the science fiction universe with this triumphant novel."   —*The Midwest Book Review* on *Ascendant Sun*

"*Skyfall* gets started with a blood rush and never slakens the pace a notch. . . . It's the perfect hook to get readers caught up in the Skolian Empire saga. Enjoy the non-stop action, adventure, and danger in *Skyfall.*"   —*SF Site*

"With a mixture of technology, physics, action, romance, and characters you can't forget, Catherine Asaro's *The Radiant Seas* offers an insightful look at human nature, a rollercoaster of emotions, and most engrossing read—far better than the vast majority of books sold as 'great' hard science fiction."
                    —L. E. Modesitt, Jr. on *The Radiant Seas*

Schism

Tor Books by Catherine Asaro

Schism

Catherine Asaro

A TOM DOHERTY ASSOCIATES BOOK
NEW YORK

This is a work of fiction. All the characters and events portrayed in this book are either products of the author's imagination or are used fictitiously.

SCHISM

Edited by James Minz

A Tor Book
Published by Tom Doherty Associates, LLC
175 Fifth Avenue
New York, NY 10010

www.tor.com

Tor® is a registered trademark of Tom Doherty Associates, LLC.

ISBN 0-765-34837-3
EAN 978-0-765-34837-1

First edition: December 2004
First mass market edition: September 2005

Printed in the United States of America

0 9 8 7 6 5 4 3 2 1

To my family,
John and Cathy,
with all my love

Acknowledgments

I would like to thank the following readers for their much appreciated input. Their comments have made this a better book. Any mistakes that remain were introduced by small, pernicious gremlins bent on mischief.

To Jeri Smith-Ready and Aly Parsons for their excellent reading and comments on the full manuscript; to Aly's Writing Group, for insightful critiques of scenes: Aly Parsons, Simcha Kuritzky, Connie Warner, Al Carroll, J. G. Huckenpöler, John Hemry, and Ben Rosenbaum.

A special thanks to my editor, Jim Minz, for his insight and suggestions; to my publisher, Tom Doherty, Priscilla Flores, Irene Gallo, Jodi Rosoff, Nancy Wiesenfeld, and to all the other fine people at Tor and St. Martin's Press who did such a fine job making this book possible; to my excellent agent, Eleanor Wood, of Spectrum Literary Agency; and to Binnie Braunstein for her enthusiasm and hard work on my behalf.

A heartfelt thanks to the shining lights in my life, my husband, John Cannizzo, and my daughter, Cathy, for their love and support.

Contents

1

Sky Ship

Today, Soz's world would change forever.

Born Sauscony Lahaylia Valdoria Skolia, she just went by Soz to most everyone. She had spent her first seventeen years of life in an idyllic existence, but she was determined to leave it behind. Today she would leap for the sky—with or without permission.

Soz stood outside, on a walkway that topped the massive wall surrounding her home. The house was a small castle of pale bluestone with turreted towers at its four corners. The muted calls of children and the whistling of lyrine in their stable came from below, in the courtyards. Beyond the house, the village of Dalvador rose like an island in the plains, beneath the lavender sky of the world Lyshriol. She loved this land and she loved her family. Her father, the Dalvador Bard, recorded the history of his people in ballads. The days passed in pastoral beauty, warmed in the golden haze of two amber suns. But she couldn't stay. Just as someday that binary star system would perturb Lyshriol out of its orbit, so Soz would soon leave her tranquil life here.

By interstellar standards, the house was primitive—but only on the exterior. Over the years, Soz's mother had arranged subtle modifications to this ancestral home of her husband. The optical, electrical, and superconducting systems were hidden; mesh networks were accessible only by discreet consoles; mechbots cleaned when no one was around; and the self-repair nanobots in the building's structure were too small to see. The improvements never marred the beauty of Lyshriol.

The Dalvador Plains extended in all directions around the

village. Far to the northwest, they lapped against the Stained Glass Forest, a jeweled swirl in the foothills of the Backbone Mountains. Beyond the forest, the Backbone raised its spindled peaks into the sky; beyond that, the massive range called Ryder's Lost Memory rose up, so distant it was no more than a violet haze. To the east, a cluster of rustic buildings stood at the edge of a broad, flat field. Except for the paved area, it could have been a tiny village.

But it was far more.

A ship was landing on the tarmac of the minuscule starport, its roar obliterating the sounds of children and lyrine in the courtyard below. Beautiful and deadly, glowing like alabaster against the sky, a Jag starfighter set down on the paved area.

Soz hadn't expected this unscheduled visitor, but she intended to seize the opportunity. She would convince the pilot to take her off planet—away from this smothering paradise.

Shannon Valdoria ran through the plains.

He raced through the swaying, supple reeds, his passage teasing iridescent bubbles off the tips of stalks. The filmy spheres floated into the air and popped, spraying him with glitter. He ignored them, running hard.

The whitewashed houses of Dalvador interrupted the plains, their blue or purple roofs like blossoms turned upside down on the houses. Shannon had never seen a flower, except in holobooks his tutors gave him about other worlds. Today he had escaped his studies and wandered in the plains until he fell asleep in the sea of reeds, drowsing beneath the suns.

The roar of the ship had awoken him.

Now he ran toward the starport, and his white-gold hair whipped across his face. Just into adolescence, he had yet to reach his full growth, but it was already clear he would never achieve the towering size of his older brothers. No matter. None could match his speed; he ran like the wind that rippled the reeds around him.

Exhaust billowed into the sky as the starfighter landed.

* * *

Eldrinson Valdoria sat in his dove-tail chair, the one his wife called a work of art, molded as it was from purple glass-wood and set with white and rose brocaded cushions. He was composing a ballad to record events of the past year, the weddings, births, and deaths in Dalvador. He held his drummel, or drum-harp, on his lap and plucked its strings, evoking a cascade of notes that sparkled like clear water in a creek. Today he sang in his tenor range, and his voice swelled in the air. As the Dalvador Bard, he recorded the history of his people in ballads.

He had left the lights off, avoiding the technological marvels his wife had brought into his life. Even after being married to her for three octets of years, he still wasn't used to it all. He could have lit an oil lamp, but he enjoyed the shadows that pooled here. The stone floor remained cool. All was quiet, though a few minutes ago a great wind had roared outside, unusually loud. Across the room, the four-poster bed stood solidly, its posts carved in totems of bubbles. The downy quilt was puffed like a blue and rose cloud. He contentedly strummed the harp while he thought of the children he and Roca had made in that bed, an octet plus two more. Eldrin, their oldest, was gone from home seven years now, a father himself with a young son.

A knock came on the door.

Eldrinson smiled, thinking of his wife. "Roca?"

A man answered. "It's Del, Father."

Eldrinson tensed as Del's unease came to him. In a family of empaths, they tended to keep their moods private behind mental shields, but Del's concern was strong enough to reach him despite those protections. He set down the drummel and went to the blue glasswood door. Opening it revealed a man of twenty-four, or twenty in the decimal system of counting that Roca used. Del had features that Roca called "edgily handsome," though Eldrinson didn't really know what she meant. Del looked like him, and no one called him edgy. They both had violet eyes and shoulder-length hair the color of burgundy wine. He supposed it was true Del did have a fiercer aspect about him. Long and leanly muscled, he stood taller than most men of Lyshriol, his height inherited from his mother.

The title of Bard would go to Eldrinson's oldest son if he ever returned to Lyshriol, but if not, Eldrinson thought he would choose Del to follow him, though Del's songs tended toward a driving beat and hard lyrics rather than the softer ballads his father composed. Eldrinson had never understood Del's angry, tangled music, but it fascinated him.

"What's wrong?" Eldrinson asked.

"A Jag has come." Del must have been singing too long again; his deep voice sounded hoarse.

"Jag?" Eldrinson asked. "What does that mean?"

"A starship," Del said, shifting his weight, taut with contained energy.

"Oh. Yes." Eldrinson stepped out into the antechamber. "A military ship, isn't it?" His son Althor had spoken about them.

"I think so." Walking with him, Del reached across to his hip for the sword he wasn't wearing. He stiffened when his hand closed on air. Then he just stalked at his father's side.

It relieved Eldrinson that the ship didn't thrill his son. Del had never shown any inclination to leave Lyshriol. In that, he took after his father; on the rare occasions when Eldrinson had accompanied Roca offworld, he had been acutely uncomfortable. Why would a warship from her people come here now? She had mentioned no visitors.

They headed down the hall outside his suite. Del had a longer stride, but he held back for his father. The tension felt almost tangible in this restless, moody son of his.

"Where is your mother?" Eldrinson asked as they descended the curving staircase to the lower levels.

"I think she went to see Vyrl and Lily."

Now that Eldrinson thought about it, he did remember Roca saying she might visit the grandchildren. It would give Vyrl, their fourth son, a chance to study for his college placement exams. The boy had already delayed them a year, caught up in his young family and the new farm. Eldrinson didn't have a good feel for this business about Vyrl being a "virtual" student who would attend an offworld university through the mesh; he was just glad the boy wouldn't leave Dalvador.

The impetuous fellow had run off with Lily, his childhood sweetheart, four years ago. Although Vyrl and Lily had been a bit young, it hadn't seemed that unusual to Eldrinson. Couples in Dalvador often married around the time they reached two octets in age. Vyrl and Lily hadn't been that much younger. He had never understood Roca's shock, as if they were two children instead of a young man and woman in love. It gratified him to see his son happy, grown into a man now, a husband and father.

A door slammed below, followed by the pounding of running feet. Eldrinson and Del came around the curve of the stairs into view of the Hearth Room, which stretched out to a large fireplace. Eldrinson's youngest son, Kelric, was just dashing into the room.

"Father!" Kelric jolted to a stop at the stairs, his face flushed. He looked so much like his mother, with her gold coloring and spectacular good looks, though on him it was boyish rather than angelic. He was only one octet of years, yet already he stood almost as tall as his father and had more bulk. He stared up at them, his thick curls tousled over his collar, his eyes lit with excitement.

"It's a Jag!" Kelric waved his hand in the direction of the port. "Can I go look? Do you think they would give me a ride?"

Del stopped on the stairs and crossed his arms. "How do you know they haven't come here to blow you up?"

"It's an Imperialate ship! They're supposed to protect us." Kelric turned his eager gaze on his father. "Can I go?"

Eldrinson exhaled, calming his pulse. He wished he could share Kelric's zeal. Yes, the Skolian Imperialate, his wife's people, protected this world. But their military was an enigma to him, a great dark machine. Their ships usually stayed in orbit; he didn't see how this one could be bringing anything but trouble.

He started down the stairs. "Kelli, let's wait until we know more."

"Father." Del drew him to a stop. "Maybe you shouldn't go out there. It might be better if we contact the port from here. This building has safeguards."

Eldrinson squinted at him. "I don't know how to make them work." Roca had arranged the security system, and every year strangers updated it, but he had never been clear on exactly how it protected the house.

Del scratched his chin. "I think it has to be activated from the console room."

"Do you know how to do it?" Eldrinson asked.

"I could figure it out."

"It's easy," Kelric said impatiently. "I can do it."

Del scowled at him. "This isn't something for a little boy. You would probably end up inviting them to shoot at Dalvador."

"I would not! And I'm not little." Kelric sped up the staircase, easily taking the steps two at a time. As he passed them, he added, "We can watch from the Blue Tower. If they do anything bad, I'll go turn on the security system."

Eldrinson glanced at Del. His older son shrugged, then lifted his hand, inviting him up the stairs. They returned the way they had come, following Kelric.

The tower looked out over the massive wall that surrounded the house. The circular chamber at its top was made from bluestone, with a domed ceiling and a blue glasswood door. Eldrinson stood with his two sons at the arched window, watching the port. The Jag had settled onto the tarmac and fumes drafted around its alabaster body. Out in the plains, a slender figure was running toward the port, a cloud of drifting bubbles in his wake. Shannon. Eldrinson would have recognized his sixth son anywhere. With his pale hair and slight build, the boy resembled the half-legendary Blue Dale Archers from the northern mountains.

Closer by, Soz stood on the walkway outside that topped the wall, her back to them as she gazed out at the port. Atypically, she wore a dress today, one of the bright, swirling affairs most girls in Dalvador adopted. Usually she preferred breeches and shirts. He had never fathomed why such a beautiful girl wanted to dress like a boy, but arguing with her never achieved anything. This daughter of his was a force of nature that couldn't be denied.

Eldrinson didn't understand Soz. He loved her, but she was a mystery. Offworld technology fascinated her. As a child, she had taken apart her brother's laser carbine and put it back together before Eldrinson even figured out what she was doing. He couldn't keep up with her razor-sharp mind. Most of all, he dreaded the distant look that came into her eyes when she gazed at the night sky with its brilliant, cold stars. She was slipping away from him and he didn't know how to bring her back.

Kelric pushed open the window and leaned out, crowding Del. "Hey, Soz!"

Eldrinson hauled him back inside. "Careful. You could fall."

The boy flashed him an intense look, half apology, half frustration. Then he turned back to the starship. It tore at Eldrinson to see his rapt expression. How long before the wanderlust took Kelric away, too?

"Look!" Kelric waved at the ship. "People are coming!"

Eldrinson peered where he pointed. Two people in dark clothes had left the Jag and were crossing the tarmac. A woman came out of a port building holding some object, probably a holofile, though he couldn't be sure from so far away. She conferred with the visitors, handed one of them the file, waited while he did something with it, then took it back and returned to her house.

"That looked routine," Del said.

"They don't seem to be threatening anyone." An odd feeling tugged at Eldrinson, an anticipation he didn't understand. Why? Perhaps he was picking that up from Kelric.

The visitors headed toward Dalvador, walking through the thigh-high reeds, except on them, the reeds barely came above their knees. One was an unusually tall man, but Eldrinson wasn't sure about the other. A woman possibly, given the curves of her body, except she was as tall as the man. He had become used to such women among his wife's people; Roca was his own size, and he was above average for a man on Lyshriol. But this person would tower even over Roca.

"Are those soldiers?" Del asked.

"They're Jagernauts!" Kelric said. "Real ones."

Eldrinson hesitated. "Skolian warriors, you mean?"

"Fighter pilots!" The boy beamed at him. "Like Althor will be someday."

"Ah." Eldrinson nodded. His second oldest son, Althor, had gone offworld three years ago to study at a military academy.

Althor had never had trouble with Skolian disciplines. It gratified Eldrinson, because he couldn't learn to read and write. His people had only oral traditions. He picked up spoken languages without thinking, and Skolian "base ten" numbers came easily to him. He could even see why they counted that way instead of in octets. They had five fingers on each hand instead of four. Their hand structure was odd, with no hinge that let the palm fold lengthwise, so two fingers on each side could oppose each other. Instead, they had a fifth digit, a "thumb." So their base ten made sense. But so much else about them didn't—their reading, science, literature. That some of his children learned it so easily never ceased to impress him.

But why did he think of that now? "By Rillia's arrow," he suddenly said.

Del and Kelric turned to him with identical expressions, their foreheads creased in puzzlement.

"Can't you feel it?" Eldrinson asked. Surely they must. They, too, were empaths.

Del tilted his head. "Something . . ."

"Yes!" Kelric cried. "Is it him?"

"Who?" Del squinted at their visitors, who were halfway

to Dalvador now. Then he answered his own question. "Oh, I see."

Eldrinson stood straighter, filling with joy and uncertainty. Althor had come home.

2

Warlord's Legacy

No one saw Soz enter the Bard's Hall. Today she preferred it that way. She slipped behind the stone columns that lined its walls. The ceiling arched overhead, high and vaulted, with stained-glass skylights. Sunlight poured through the tall windows and slanted across the hanging tapestries, which showed scenes of Archers in green tunics and leggings. They sat astride lyrine, animals with prismatic horns and hooves and silver coats. The polished floor stretched out ahead of Soz, tiled in pale blue and lavender stone. At the far end of the hall, two great stone chairs sat on a circular dais.

The Dalvador Bard, her father, stood on the dais, dressed in blue trousers, knee-boots, and a white shirt fastened with thongs. He had donned his ceremonial sword belt with its finely tooled sheath, the leather worked with gold and gems. Amethysts glinted in the hilt of his sword. Sunlight lit up his clothes and hair and surrounded him with a nimbus. But he wasn't the only sight that enthralled the people gathered around the hall, the staff of the house and Soz's family.

A gold giant was kneeling before the Bard.

The man went down on one knee with his head bowed, his elbow resting across his bent leg. His stark black uniform contrasted with the jeweled colors of the hall. Conduits threaded his pullover, gleaming rings of silver circled his huge arms, metallic studs packed with components glinted on his trousers, and the heavy gauntlets on his wrists glittered with lights. The black bulk of a Jumbler hung low in a holster at his hip.

Althor had come home.

One moment Soz longed to throw her arms around the brother she had always admired; the next moment she wanted only to hang back. It had been three years since he had gone offworld, and she no longer felt at ease with him. His skin and hair were metallic gold, inherited from their mother, but he had their father's violet eyes, though metallic lashes fringed them. His massive physique and great height not only dwarfed the men of Lyshriol, it made him large even among Skolians. He exuded power, authority, and menace. Her brother had become a stranger.

Her father drew his sword and it glittered in the sunlight. When he raised it over Althor, Soz tensed. Even knowing he would never harm his son, she felt her pulse leap as the blade came down.

Had a Lyshrioli warrior knelt before him, Eldrinson would have cut off a lock of the man's shoulder-length hair. Althor had cropped his hair short, so their father only razed off one gold curl. It fell to Althor's shoulder and floated to the ground. This was the Ritual of the Blade, where a Bard accepted or refused the fealty of a warrior. By drawing his sword, he challenged the man's courage. If the Bard refused a lock of hair, he spurned the supplicant. Nor did the warrior always survive; a Bard could kill with impunity during the ceremony.

In reality, Althor served Imperial Space Command, not a supposedly barbarian king on a backward planet. When Althor graduated next year from the Dieshan Military Academy, he would become a fighter pilot in the J-Force, one of the four branches of the Skolian military, along with the Imperial Fleet, Advance Services Corps, and Pharaoh's Army. Nothing required him to swear fealty to Eldrinson. That he did so anyway spoke eloquently, for all to see, of his esteem for his father.

Soz couldn't hear them, but the Bard must have spoken, for Althor rose to his feet, towering over their father. Someone drew in a sharp breath, and Soz glanced around to see several housemaids watching Althor, their violet eyes wide and appreciative. Even through the shields she raised to protect her empath's mind, she felt their desire, how much he impressed and attracted them. Pah. The concept of her brother being the object of female desire was just too much. Not that he had ever seemed interested in Dalvador girls.

Her father and brother embraced. Soz suspected Eldrinson had tears in his eyes, but he would hold back, too proud to cry in front of everyone. To have his son descend from the sky in such a dramatic display and then kneel before him had to feel incredible. It touched her heart that Althor chose to greet him this way. If only that could take away the pain. Although their father had always encouraged Althor's dreams, he refused to hear the same from her. It wasn't Althor's fault, but it made being around him difficult. Would he be willing to take her offworld? Her hastily conceived plan had become even more complicated.

Two men were coming forward from the columns behind the dais. No, one was eight-year-old Kelric, already as tall as an adult. Del walked with him. The woman who had come with Althor stayed behind, unobtrusive, half hidden by a column.

Kelric took the six stairs of the dais in two big lunges and ran to his brother. Althor pulled him into a hug. Even from here, Soz could see Del's grin as he slapped Althor on the shoulder.

"He's even taller," a voice said, with a chime on the second word.

Startled, Soz turned. Her brother, Shannon, stood next to her, slender and supple, his eyes level with hers. She had always wondered what it was like for him, living in the shadow of such giant brothers. He had the silver eyes of a Blue Dale Archer. Somewhere in the distant past, one of their ancestors must have had a child with an Archer. The traits could lie dormant for centuries and still run true when they manifested. Shannon might be one of the few Archers left; no one had heard from them in centuries.

"My greetings, Shani." She had been so absorbed in the scene on the dais, she hadn't felt his pensive mood earlier, but now it came through to her.

He tilted his head toward Althor. "He is magnificent." His words flowed like clear water in a stream.

Soz smiled. "Hero worship? Surely not."

"You feel it, too."

It wasn't how Soz would have put it, given her conflicted emotions toward Althor. "I admire what he has achieved."

"Do you envy him?" Shannon pitched his words low, so only she would hear.

"Envy? Why?"

"Father won't let you become a warrior. Women cannot."

A familiar anger stirred in Soz. "Of course we can. ISC has more women in the military than men." Dryly she added, "It used to be a matriarchy, Shani."

"That may be." His voice had a singsong quality. "But not here. Father will never let you go offworld."

"How is he going to stop me?"

"I don't know," he admitted. "He wants you to marry Lord Rillia."

"Oh, for flaming sakes." Soz put her hands on her hips. "I'm not marrying anyone, let alone a man more than twice my age who can't read or write."

"It doesn't bother Aniece."

"She's eleven years old. She doesn't know what she wants."

"Thirteen," Shannon murmured, giving their sister's age in octal instead of decimal.

"Eleven. And no matter how you count it, she's too young to marry Lord Rillia and I've no intention of doing so."

Shannon's lips curved upward with that otherworldly beauty of his. "Gods help Lord Rillia if Father did make you marry him."

"Very funny." Soz turned to watch Althor, who was talking with Del and Kelric. Her brothers never stopped lamenting poor Lord Rillia's dire fate, destined to marry her.

Soz had other plans.

Eldrinson entered the Hearth Room flanked by his sons, Althor on one side and Del on the other. Kelric came, too. A sense of light filled Eldrinson. Althor's arrival had been a fine moment, a fine moment indeed.

A flurry of motion erupted across the room as Roca swept into the hall, surrounded by people. Tall and vibrant, she riveted his attention even after all these years. Her creamy skin had gold highlights and her eyes resembled liquid gold. Her hair fell down her shoulders, arms, and back, gold, bronze, and copper, all those curls he loved to play with at night. Her face and body had inspired an uncounted number of literary works, symphonies, and other art across the Imperialate. During her years as a dancer with the Parthonia Royal Ballet, she had dazzled audiences. Now she dazzled him.

One of their other sons arrived with her, Vyrl. Roca said the name Vyrl should be pronounced *Vahrielle,* with an Iotic accent. Eldrinson had never mastered the accent; he drawled *Verle* just like everyone else in Dalvador. His son's mane of hair curled to his shoulders, gold and bronze, with metallic glints, but he had the Lyshrioli violet eyes. He was a good head taller than his father, with a muscular, graceful physique honed by years of dance training.

It bewildered Eldrinson that Vyrl loved to dance. Mercifully, for now the boy had chosen Lily and farming over going offworld to become a performer like his mother. Men in Dalvador never danced. Although Eldrinson understood that no one looked askance at a male dancer among Roca's people, here it would be a terrible scandal. People would consider such a man female. Well, supposedly. Lily knew and she didn't seem to mind.

In any case, it warmed him to see the young couple. And they had brought the grandchildren. Hallie, their three-year-old, skipped through the room, her curls flopping around her shoulders, her eyes bright, her cheeks plump and rosy. Lily carried the two-year-old, and Vyrl cradled the baby in his arms.

"Althor!" Roca threw her arms around her son. He gathered her into a hug, both of them glimmering in the light from the lamps in the Hearth Room. Then they separated and Roca tilted her head back to look up at him. "Honestly, you've grown again."

He grinned at her. "Ten more centimeters."

Roca's laugh sparkled. "You will increase the gravity of Lyshriol."

Eldrinson slapped Althor on the back. "So he will." He motioned everyone toward the end of the hall, where sofas and chairs stood around the bluestone hearth. Hallie ran away giggling, chased by Kelric, and the rest followed, Vyrl bouncing the baby.

One discord jangled in their harmonious gathering: Tahota, the woman who had accompanied Althor, a tall Skolian with gray-streaked hair. She stayed in the background, silent. Her clothes had a military aspect, dark blue tunic and trousers with gold insignia on the shoulders and chest. He recognized only the symbol of the Imperialate, an exploding sun within a circle; the other markings meant nothing to him.

Tahota seemed bemused by the commotion. Was she a romantic interest for Althor? Surely not. On Lyshriol, a woman of her appearance would be about five octets in age. Given how Skolians could delay getting older, though, she could be any age. Regardless, she was much too mature in years for Althor. Besides, she was obviously inappropriate. A female warrior? No. It was too much. Althor epitomized the military ideal: strong, intelligent, powerful, imposing—and male.

He did wish Althor would marry, though. Two octets plus five more years in age and still his son had no woman. Roca seemed to think this was normal; indeed, she claimed he hadn't reached the "age of majority" among her people. Absurd. Althor was well beyond the age when a man started a family.

They all settled around the hearth while a maid lit the fire. She peeked at Althor, her lovely face glowing. He smiled at her, but his response was polite only, nothing more. Eldrinson sighed. Maybe the boy had a girlfriend somewhere else.

Althor glanced at him sharply. Eldrinson supposed he wasn't shielding his mind as well as he might. Well, he had no objection to his son knowing his father wished he would settle down and make grandchildren.

Everyone was talking at once. Vyrl, Del, and Kelric pumped Althor for news about anything offworld, from technology to sports. Roca asked about his classes at DMA. Eldrinson sat back, content to listen. It gratified him to have them gathered like this, all so healthy and full of life. His family.

Except they weren't all here. Chaniece, Del's fraternal twin, was visiting another village, which could explain why Del was even less settled than usual today. Aniece had fallen asleep upstairs, worn-out from growing; lately his youngest daughter was moody and irritable, a contrast to her usual amiable nature. After seeing so many of his children through adolescence, Eldrinson recognized the signs. She was less a child every day. Denric was probably off somewhere reading and didn't yet realize Althor had come to visit. How the boy could spend so much time with holobooks, Eldrinson didn't know. It pleased him, though, that Denric read so well.

What he didn't understand was why neither Soz nor Shannon had come to greet Althor. They had both seen him arrive.

They should be here.

Soz stood on a balcony of the third story in the house, her arms folded on the bluestone wall that came to mid-torso. She gazed out at the plains. Wind played with her hair, throwing curls around her face. Unlike other girls in Dalvador, who wore their hair long, she kept hers at shoulder length. It was black most of the way down, then shaded into wine-red and turned gold at the tips, bleached by the sun. Her mother called it "sunrise hair."

A rustle came behind her. With a start, she turned to see an imposing woman in the doorway of the balcony, a military officer in a dark blue tunic and trousers. The gold studs on the woman's shoulders and the insignia on her chest indicated she was a colonel in the Imperial Fleet. Why a high-ranking naval officer would show up with Althor, Soz had no clue. The J-Force and Imperial Fleet were completely different branches of Imperial Space Command.

The woman nodded formally. "My honor at your presence, Your Highness." She used Iotic, an ancient language spoken now only by the antiquated Skolian noble Houses and the Ruby Dynasty.

Soz winced. She so rarely heard her Skolian titles here, she tended to forget she had them. "My greetings, Colonel." The Iotic came naturally to her. She spoke Trillian more often, the language of Dalvador and Rillia, but she shifted easily between the two.

"May I join you?" the colonel asked.

"Yes. Certainly." Excitement jumped in Soz. She wanted to ask a million questions. *How does it feel to fly a starship?* But her bluntness could annoy people, and she didn't want to ruin this opportunity to hear about ISC.

The colonel came over to stand with Soz. Her gauntlets glittered, alive and active, monitoring the surroundings. She was a good head taller than Soz and had a lean build with well-defined muscles under her uniform. Soz had always considered herself fit, but she could blow away on the wind compared to this woman.

Subdued, Soz turned back to the view. The house was on the edge of the village. The plains made her think of a silvery ocean with an iridescent sheen on its waves. The suns were low in the sky, behind the house, and long shadows stretched out over the land. Clouds of shimmer-flies drifted across the countryside.

"It is an uncommonly lovely world," the colonel said.

"It's all right." Soz actually thought it rather boring, except when the rare storms swept across the land.

The woman motioned at the sky. "I've never seen blue clouds."

"It's from an impurity. Like food dye." Soz smiled. "It's most concentrated in the water, but it's everywhere."

"Can you see it in the air?" The colonel sounded intrigued.

"Sometimes. It comes from the glitter that plants use to reproduce." It seemed mundane to Soz. "The dye isn't dangerous, just an irritant, but it can cause problems. We have nanomeds in our bodies to break it down. They're passed from mother to child."

"It's amazing," the colonel mused. "Humans can adapt to so many variations in their environment."

Soz glanced at her hands, with their four fingers and thumb, so different from most everyone else on Lyshriol. "In people, too."

The officer smiled at her. "I should introduce myself. I'm Starjack Tahota, from HQ City on Diesha."

"My greetings, Colonel Tahota." Soz offered her arm and Tahota grasped her elbow while Soz grasped hers. After they separated, Tahota said, "Your father was looking for you earlier."

Just thinking about him made Soz tense. She couldn't talk to Althor about leaving if Father was present. She said only, "I was waiting until I could have Althor to myself."

"He expected you might."

"He did?" That sounded perceptive for Althor. "Amazing." Tahota laughed. "Brothers can be insightful, too."

Soz regarded her doubtfully. "Why does he have a starfighter? He doesn't have his commission yet."

"He's learning to work with its EI brain."

"Why are you with him? Aren't you Fleet?"

"That's right." Tahota was watching her closely. "He isn't cleared to take a fighter out on his own."

"Shouldn't his instructor be a J-Force pilot?"

Tahota studied her with that unsettling intensity. "J-Force works with all branches of ISC."

Although Soz knew DMA drew its instructors from all

four branches of the military, she wouldn't have expected an officer with such a high rank to accompany a cadet on a training exercise. Nor would she have thought they would let him come all the way to Lyshriol. "He's lucky to have a colonel to train with."

"I also had another reason for coming here," Tahota said.

Soz felt a nervous tickle in her throat. "What is that?"

"I coordinate admissions for the ISC academies."

Soz froze. Admissions. Including the Dieshan Military Academy? She had already taken the preliminary exams, but it would be another year before she could submit an application, and that assumed she passed the prelims. It wasn't a given: she couldn't even openly train or study for the tests here, and she had no referent to judge her abilities.

That was her least problem, though. She had taken the exams in secret, without telling her parents, but she couldn't apply without their permission. Soz could handle her mother; Roca would resist the way she had with Althor, dismayed at the thought of her children in combat, but she wouldn't stop them if they felt they had to go. However, Soz had absolutely no doubt her father would forbid her to apply. It would start a quarrel between the two of them that would make their others pale in comparison.

"I oversee the various academies," Tahota was saying. "My job is what we call 'behind the desk.'"

"I see." Soz didn't, though. She tried to pick up clues from the colonel's mind, but Tahota knew how to guard her thoughts well.

"I'm here to discuss your application to DMA," Tahota said.

Soz squinted at her. "I haven't made one yet."

"But you were planning to, I assume."

"If I pass the prelims." Soz grimaced. "And if my father doesn't hit the sky."

"Yes, your brother said there might be problems. A student your age cannot enroll without parental permission." Then Tahota added, "Except in certain cases."

Soz had never heard of such. "What kind of cases?"

"That depends on the discretion of the admissions committee."

"That must be some discretion," Soz said, "if they send a Fleet colonel all the way to a backwater planet as the instructor for a boy who hasn't finished his own studies and to talk to a girl who hasn't qualified yet to apply."

To her surprise, Tahota laughed. "Your brother was right."

"About what?"

"You don't tiptoe with words."

Apparently sometimes Althor did know her as well as he had claimed when they were younger. "It's true," she admitted.

Tahota pressed a stud on her gauntlet. A chip snapped out of it, elongated into a thin rod, unrolled into a sheet of holofilm, and stiffened. Soz wanted to ask how it worked, but she held back. This didn't seem the time to indulge the insatiable curiosity that people told her could be truly maddening.

"Here." Tahota handed her the holosheet. "Take a look."

Wary, Soz scanned the sheet. Glyphs floated above it, along with charts and symbols. She recognized the J-Force symbol, the silhouette of a Jag in flight. She made out her name near the top of the sheet. The glyphs were in Skolian Flag, which she spoke but rarely used, so it took a while to decipher the rest. She wasn't certain, but it looked like the graphs referred to her preliminary exams.

"Are these my scores?" Soz asked.

"That is correct."

Soz tried to speak with nonchalance, though her heart was racing. "Looks like I did well."

Tahota made an incredulous noise. "Looks like?"

Soz indicated a chart above the sheet. "Well, this doesn't make sense. It says I did better than one hundred percent of the people who took the test. That isn't possible."

"Why not?"

Soz frowned. The colonel had to be testing her; she couldn't be that dense. "Because the percentage specifies how many people you did better than out of every hundred.

Obviously I couldn't do better than one hundred out of one hundred. That would mean I did better than myself."

"The numbers are rounded off." Tahota flicked a holicon, or holographic icon, that floated above the sheet. The numbers changed to show more digits after the decimal place. The 100 percent changed to 99.99999 percent.

Soz whistled. "Good gods. If I didn't know better, I would say this means I had the top score out of ten million."

Tahota answered quietly. "That is exactly what it means."

Soz stared at the holos and a roaring began in her ears. She looked up at the colonel. "I take it this means I qualify to apply."

Tahota gave a startled laugh. "More than that. I've been in my position for three years and I've never seen scores like yours. They're brilliant across the board, as well as in the dossiers ISC and the Assembly have on you."

Soz stiffened. "ISC and the Assembly keep records on me?"

"On every member of your family. Surely you knew that."

"Because we're the royal family?"

"That's right."

Soz knew it made sense, however much she disliked it. Technically, the Ruby Dynasty no longer ruled in this age of elected government; they hadn't for centuries. But they controlled the star-spanning meshes that tied Skolia together into an interstellar empire, and that gave her family a great deal of power. Of course the Assembly kept dossiers. But even that couldn't dim her mood now. Inside, she was singing. One out of *ten million?* Surely her father couldn't tell her *no* after this. Althor was an honors cadet, but he didn't burn with the fire that consumed her. How could her father beam with such pride for Althor and begrudge her the same dream?

Tahota was watching her face. "When someone ranks as highly as you've done, their admission is automatic."

"You mean *I'm in?*"

"I'm authorized to bring you back when Althor and I return to Diesha."

Soz's thoughts whirled. Everything she wanted was within her grasp, but it was happening too fast. "My father will never say yes."

"We don't normally accept a student without parental consent." Tahota had that careful quality to her voice again. "However, these are extenuating circumstances. DMA will admit you without their permission if you decide to go that route. We would prefer you had their blessing, but it won't be required."

"Good gods, why?" Soz waved the sheet at Tahota. "Just for this?"

"Yes." Tahota's gaze never wavered. "How familiar are you with the work of your brother, Imperator Skolia?"

That caught Soz off guard. She found it hard to think of Skolia's mighty Imperator as her brother. Half brother, actually. Kurj was her mother's son from a previous marriage. A Jagernaut in his youth, he had risen in the J-Force until he reached its highest rank, Jagernaut Primary. From there he ascended to command of the entire J-Force.

Then he became Imperator.

Kurj commanded ISC. All of it. He was in charge of all four branches, the entire armed forces of Skolia. Soz knew the rumors, that people called him a military dictator, that with the loyalty of ISC, he had more power even than the Assembly. Althor resembled him, but Kurj was more metallic, and even larger than Althor, his physique so massive that he had trouble visiting a heavy gravity world. It was why he rarely came to Lyshriol. Or so he claimed.

Unlike most people, Soz had never feared Kurj. She liked his taciturn style, besides which, he appreciated her interest in the military. She never let him know how she felt, though. She remained on constant guard with him—for Kurj hated her father.

Eldrinson Althor Valdoria, a folksinger from a primitive culture, was seventeen years younger than his stepson. Good genetics, modern medicine, and cell-repair nanomeds gave Roca an apparent age in her twenties, but she had a good half century on her husband. As far as Soz could tell, though, Kurj would have considered his stepfather the scum of the universe regardless of their ages. She didn't understand why. For all that her father exasperated and annoyed her, he was also one of the finest people she knew. She loved him deeply and she had never doubted he felt the same about his children, no matter how much he struggled to understand them.

Whatever the reason, Kurj's antipathy toward her father remained strong. If she went to DMA this way, it would wreak havoc within her family. "If Kurj is offering this just to get at my father, I don't want it."

Tahota pushed her hand over her head, pulling back hair that had escaped the roll at her neck. "I don't claim to understand relationships in the Ruby Dynasty. But I can say this: Imperator Skolia has far more important concerns here than his personal life."

"Such as?"

"He has no heirs."

Soz snorted. "I'm sure he does, somewhere." Kurj's penchant for beautiful women was well known.

"No legitimate heirs," Tahota amended.

"He has to marry a Rhon psion." It was why the Assembly hadn't opposed Roca's marriage to Eldrinson, despite his being otherwise completely inappropriate in their view. He was Rhon.

Soz knew the drill. Empaths and telepaths, or psions, resulted from the Kyle complex of genetic mutations. The more Kyle genes a psion carried, the greater their abilities. The Rhon had them all. But the traits were recessive; both parents had to give them to their children. As Imperator, Kurj could dally with whomever he pleased, but he had to marry a Rhon woman. Unfortunately, the Rhon were rare almost to extinction; the only ones known were related to him. The Assembly had coerced the Rhon to intermarry once, forcing a union between Soz's oldest brother and his aunt, the Ruby Pharaoh. The resulting turmoil had nearly destabilized the government. They weren't likely to try such again.

So Kurj remained single. She doubted he cared. He liked his freedom. He was almost sixty, but he looked thirty and he could father children until he was old and doddering if he wanted.

It wasn't anything she wished to discuss with Tahota, though. She said only, "I'm not sure what this has to do with DMA."

"Imperator Skolia inherited his position."

That was tactful. Better than saying, *Your brother assassinated your grandfather.* It might not be true, after all. It could have been an accident. Soz had no idea; it had happened before her birth. The previous Imperator had been Roca's father.

Roca was a politician, not a military leader, but nevertheless, she should have inherited the title. Kurj had taken it instead, by forcing his way into the Dyad ahead of her. The Assembly had found him kneeling next to his grandfather's body. They ruled the death an accident, but that could have been because they were terrified of his immense power. By that time, he commanded the loyalty of Imperial Space Command, the massive Skolian military.

Soz said only, "Yes."

"He needs heirs. They must come from your family."

"I doubt it." Going for the greatest understatement of all time, Soz added, "Kurj doesn't like my father."

"I wouldn't know." Tahota's cautious tone made Soz think the colonel knew far more than she admitted. "But his heirs must come from your family."

This visit began to make more sense. "He picked Althor, I take it."

Tahota said, simply, "Yes."

Soz tried not to grit her teeth. Of course he would choose Althor. Why not? Shannon had said it this afternoon. Althor was magnificent. He even looked like Kurj. Why the blazes this colonel came all the way here to tell her this news was a mystery Soz could have done without.

Then, suddenly, she saw. It was a courtesy. Kurj wanted her to know before he made the announcement. Letting her attend DMA would ameliorate the blow. She had never expected anyone in her family to become the Imperial Heir, but in her more audacious moments she had imagined it, that she would rise through the ranks as Kurj had done and someday command ISC. Damn it all, they hadn't even given her a chance to prove herself.

She spoke coolly. "I'm sure Althor is pleased."

"He doesn't know yet."

"Oh." Soz folded her arms. "Why tell me first?"

And Tahota said, "You are Kurj's other choice."

Soz froze. "What?"

"You are his other choice for the Imperial Heir. Possibly your brother Kelric, too, though it is too early to tell yet for him." Tahota leaned against the wall. "Of all the Valdoria children, only the three of you show sufficient ability to succeed the Imperator. Going by seniority, Althor would be the first choice. By aptitude, you would be first."

Soz barely heard anything past the first sentence. Gods all-flaming-mighty. Tahota had showed up out of nowhere and dropped an antimatter bomb. She took a deep breath. "You have to slow down."

"All right." Tahota waited, giving her time.

Soz spoke slowly. "You're saying that Kurj wants Althor and me to be his heirs. To succeed him as Imperator." She reeled at the words. "He hasn't decided who will be first in line, but Althor and I are the heir and the spare?"

"That about sums it up."

Soz struggled to reorient. Although she had always known she was in line for the Ruby Throne, she had never expected to be Kurj's heir, too. Her Aunt Dehya was the Ruby Pharaoh. Their ancestors had ruled a matriarchal empire, but now an elected Assembly governed Skolia. The dynasty still existed, however. The pharaoh had broken with tradition and named her son and only child as her heir, followed by Roca and Roca's children, both the daughters and the sons. Soz was eighth in line, too far down to expect anything. Nor had she ever thought Kurj would choose his heir from among the children of the stepfather he so deeply resented. She didn't know whether to shout, laugh, or blanch.

"It's—unexpected," Soz said.

Tahota smiled. "But deserved."

"Wait until I tell Denric." At sixteen, he was nearest in age to her of all her siblings, and they were close despite their different interests. "He won't believe it."

"We would rather you say nothing," Tahota said. "Not until the new line of succession is announced."

"This is a lot to think about." Soz squinted at her. "I'll bet it isn't a usual part of your duties, telling prospective DMA cadets they might become Imperator."

Tahota gave a startled laugh. "No, it isn't."

"Why couldn't Kurj tell me himself?"

Tahota went into careful mode, so obviously choosing her words with caution that she could have been walking through a minefield. "The Imperator thought my presence here might be more conducive to a peaceful visit."

"That was tactful," Soz said. "You could have just come out and said my half brother hates my father's guts and wouldn't go near this planet if you gave him another half a galaxy."

Tahota cleared her throat. "I wouldn't know."

I'll bet. Kurj had chosen Tahota well; she knew how to be discreet. "You know, it's funny," Soz said. "When I saw the Jag landing, I thought it would end this idyllic life I have here."

Tahota raised an eyebrow. "Why would a Jag endanger your family?"

"It wasn't danger." Soz looked toward the port, which was just barely visible around the edge of the castle. Althor's Jag waited on the tarmac, gleaming like alabaster. "I was going to ask the pilot to take me to Diesha. When I got there, I was going to apply for status as an emancipated minor, so I didn't need parental consent for DMA." The alternative would have been to wait eight more years, until she was twenty-five, an adult under Skolian law.

Tahota spoke quietly. "That's a big step."

"I know. I don't want to hurt my family. I just can't be what I'm not." She waved her hand at the plains basking in the golden sunlight. "This is beautiful, but it's not me. I can't marry Lord Rillia and settle down having babies. I would go crazy."

"Your aptitude tests say as much."

"I didn't expect to get support from DMA."

"Why not?"

Soz shrugged. "I'm sure you have hundreds of good applicants."

"Thousands," Tahota said. "For about thirty positions."

It didn't surprise her. Academies for the other branches of ISC were larger than DMA. Jagernauts not only had to be empaths, which were rare, they also had to survive one of the most psychologically grueling jobs in ISC.

"I have to talk with my father," Soz said.

The colonel nodded. "I want to tell Althor first, though."

"Oh. Yes. Of course." Soz hesitated. "Do you think he has any idea?"

"I think so. I'll talk to him this evening and let you know after I do." Tahota regarded her with understanding. "I'm here for your support and to answer any questions your parents have."

"Thanks." Soz hesitated, not wanting to jinx any of this but unable to contain her questions. "Why are you offering to take me now? I'm a year too young."

"Your scores say you're ready."

"Even so." Although Soz couldn't pick up much from Tahota's well-guarded mind, she sensed gaps in the colonel's answer. "I'll be more ready next year."

Tahota's face turned grim. "Hostilities between Skolia and the Trader Empire are escalating."

"That isn't in the broadcasts."

"No. It isn't." Tahota exhaled. "Will we go to war? No one knows. But ISC is pushing its best cadets through as fast as possible."

It made sense to Soz.

She just didn't know how she would tell her family.

3

Blue Dale Moons

Shannon stayed away while his family celebrated at dinner. He knew his behavior puzzled them. Their thoughts brushed his mind. He didn't hide; if they believed he was lost or in trouble, they would come looking for him. But he kept to himself.

He had known before the Jag landed that Althor was coming home. His brother's luminous mind warmed his like a sun. It had always been that way with the two of them. It had devastated him the day Althor left home. He understood little about why his siblings or parents did what they did. He loved his family, but as he had grown older, he had felt more apart from them. His life here left him restless and empty, and he didn't know how to fill the gaps. Although lately he always thought of girls, it was never those in the village. He imagined girls like himself, with white-gold hair and silver eyes, slender instead of voluptuous, ethereal and misty. In Dalvador they were too robust, too much the daughters of farmers. He wanted to ride in the wind, never stopping, never settling. To be chained to a farm, trapped by the land—he could never bear such a life. It baffled him that Vyrl wanted it so much, enough even to study agriculture at the university. Shannon loved his brother and his sister-in-law and their children, but that life seemed hell to him.

While the family dined, Shannon stayed in the stable. He sat in a stall next to Moonglaze, his father's massive war lyrine. He understood lyrine in a way he couldn't fathom people. Lyrine never analyzed. They lived in the moment, with no emotional barriers between them and the people they loved. It made sense to Shannon. Humans analyzed too much.

One of his biology texts claimed lyrine descended from horses and had been genetically engineered for Lyshriol. Shannon didn't care. They weren't horses now. Moonglaze's prismatic hooves and his two horns splintered light into colors that sparkled and danced. Even in the dim light, hints of rainbows flashed on the amberglass stall as Moonglaze shifted restlessly. The great lyrine would have kicked most people who intruded on his privacy, but he tolerated Shannon and Eldrinson.

Shannon sat in a trance. He felt the minds of his siblings and parents questing for him, puzzled by his absence. Several times someone came into the stable seeking him, his scholarly brother Denric once, his mother later, then Vyrl's wife Lily. He didn't answer when they called and they didn't intrude, though they knew he sat in Moonglaze's stall. Eventually they returned to the house.

Moods swirled throughout the night, the joy of his parents in Althor's visit and the excitement of his family. Other moods stirred below the surface like eel-streamers in a lake. Tension, uncertainty, sadness. A sudden spike of shock from Althor. Shannon absorbed it all like a sponge soaking in water. He just took it all in. The causes would become clear later, or not.

So he sat.

Finally he sensed what he had waited for the entire day. Althor was alone. Shannon could tell by the change in his brother's mood.

He left the stable then.

Soz paced through the outskirts of Dalvador, following a cobbled alley that meandered behind a row of shops with all sorts of goods: glasswood place settings, furniture, and tools; delicacies sold by merchants who traveled to Dalvador from Rillia across the mountains; finely worked metal goods from the blacksmith; glitter to grow bubble crops. To her right, the fields of her father's farm spread out under the night sky, the reeds heavy with bagger bubbles. The crescent of the Blue Moon hung above the horizon and the gibbous Lavender Moon shone higher in the sky.

Tahota had shaken the foundations of her life. Surely Soz could make her parents understand. She just needed to present it right, in a manner that would convince them she couldn't pass up such an incredible opportunity. Realistically, they would be upset no matter how great she considered this news. But if she talked to them enough, stayed calm and enthusiastic, surely she could soften their resistance. Her mother would be easier, so Soz would approach her first. If Roca came around, she might ease her husband's opposition.

"I thought you were a ghost," a voice said. "A ghost haunting Merchant's Lane."

Soz whirled around, her back to the wall of a bedding shop behind her. A youth stood lounging against a glasswood pole that held up the roof of a bubble-sculptor's shop. The moonlight made his eyes look black and silvered his burgundy hair. He smiled, slow and languorous. "You going to knock me over and carry me off, Soz?"

Soz put her fists on her hips. "Not a chance."

"Too bad. It might be fun."

"What are you doing, sneaking up on me, Ariquil?" She deliberately used his full name instead of Ari, the nickname she had called him when they went swimming in Blue Potter's Lake a few octets ago.

He ambled over to her. "How come you're wandering down here?"

Soz crossed her arms. She had liked him last year, then she hadn't, and then she had again. By the time she had untangled her confusion, he had gone off with some other girl. Soz hadn't known whether to be angry at him or at herself.

"I asked my question first," she said.

"I was bored. I went for a walk." His voice had deepened recently, with that vibrato that adult men among the Lyshrioli possessed. He was taller now, his eyes level with hers. He touched a lock of her hair where it curled on her shoulder. "You look good, Soshoni."

She pulled her hair away from him. "Don't call me Soshoni." She should have never told him the affectionate nickname her parents had given her. "And where's your girlfriend?"

He was all innocence. "What girlfriend?"

"Oh, I don't know. Maybe that girl you were all *over* a few octets ago."

He shrugged. "I don't see her anymore."

"Why not?"

"She's not you." He hinged his hand around her cheek, cupping her face. "Remember that time we went swimming and lay on the shore afterward?"

Soz remembered every detail. He had kissed her that day, which had scared her off, only for a few days, but he had grown tired of waiting. Or maybe he just didn't believe in fidelity.

She nudged away his hand. "I'm trying to forget."

"Why?" He smirked. "You're jealous."

"Go away, Ari."

"You want me to stay."

She glared. "Not a chance."

"Yes, you do."

"Pah."

"You love me, Soz." Laughing, he grabbed her hand and pulled her toward him. "Come on, Soshoni."

Caught by surprise, Soz reacted on instinct, as she would do when training in the hand-to-hand combat she wasn't supposed to learn, but that she had practiced for years with her brothers. She yanked him forward, rolled him over her body, and swung him down on a pile of pillow-sacks stacked by the wall. He landed with a thud, his breath going out in a whoosh.

With an explosion of breath, Ari sat up. "What the hammer-hell was *that* for?"

Soz's face flamed as she dropped next to him. By Rillia's Arrow, she hadn't meant to do that. It had been a reflex, prodded by her tension today and her anger over that other girl. "I'm sorry, Ari. You surprised me."

He scowled at her. "You know, Soz, your approach with men leaves a lot to be desired."

Maybe that was true, but she was still mad at him. "You approached me."

"At peril of my life."

She glowered. "But of course it was all right for you to run off with whatever her name was after you kissed me."

He rubbed his side where he had hit the sacks. "You disappeared. I thought you were trying to get rid of me."

"No I wasn't." Her face heated as they stood up together. "I was confused."

He smiled ruefully. "I thought you were going to slap me silly that day I kissed you."

His kiss had inspired far different thoughts. Embarrassing thoughts. To cover her flush, she said, "If I recall, we were having an argument about who could swim faster." For good measure, she glared at him.

"You've never seen yourself mad." His lashes lowered halfway over his eyes, sensually sleepy. "It makes you look like a goddess on fire."

She wished he would quit looking at her like that. He made it hard to think straight. "Listen, Ari, I can't—I mean, it's not that I don't want to be with you. But I may be going away soon."

His expression cooled. "Right."

Soz knew she was bumbling this. If she hadn't been so uncertain about the rest of her life, she would have liked to go back with him to Blue Potter's Lake. They could swim in the secluded hollows formed by blue glasswood trunks in the water and lie together where no one would find them. Then they could explore this kissing business more.

She had to explain, make it clear she hadn't meant to reject him. Conversations about emotions had never been her strong point, though. She didn't have the words. She couldn't tell Ari about going to the academy yet, not when she hadn't told her parents. It wouldn't be right to let him know first, besides which, he had never been any good at keeping secrets.

Instead of trying to talk, she took his hand. He regarded her warily, but he didn't pull away. She tugged him until they were nose to nose. Then she kissed him, once, uncertain and awkward.

"Ah, Soz." He put his arms around her waist and pulled her forward. "That knocks me out, too." Then he kissed her more deeply, making tingles start in her stomach.

"See," he murmured against her lips. "It's not so bad."

Their first kiss had been nice, but these second and third ones were even better. "Not bad at all."

He kissed her again. "We could go swimming."

Soz wanted to say yes, but she couldn't. Besides, if her father caught her swimming at night with a boy, he would throw Ari in the dungeon and lock Soz up in her room for fifty years. Not that the castle had a real dungeon anymore, just storerooms underground, but she had no doubt the Dalvador Bard would make one in honor of any boy who snuck off with his daughter to Blue Potter's Lake.

"I can't, Ari. Not tonight. I have to talk to my parents."

"You can talk to your parents anytime."

"It's important."

His face stiffened and he let her go. "Sure, Soz. Fine. Go talk to your parents."

"Ari, don't."

"Go on. Go away."

"This is important."

He shrugged and made a show of not looking at her.

Soz regarded him with exasperation. He always acted like this when he didn't get his way. It reminded her of why she had been uncertain about their friendship. "You really want me to go away?"

"You're the one who said you had to go."

"Let's not argue."

Finally he looked at her. "I think you should go away. I can't take all this, 'I don't know what I want' from you."

"You know, a little patience never hurt anyone."

"Go on. Go home."

"Fine. I'll go home." She stayed put, though.

"Aren't you going?" He hadn't moved either.

"Ari—"

"Yes?"

"I'll see you tomorrow."

He regarded her warily. "You want?"

"Yes. I do." Tomorrow, after she had told her parents, she could explain more. Maybe she and Ari weren't all that compatible, but he was the first boy who had ever kissed her and she had known him for years. That counted for a lot.

He grinned, wicked now instead of sulking. "I'll be around."

"Me, too." She could think of nothing clever to say, so she just added, "I better go."

"Sure." He touched her cheek, and his finger lingered. "See you." Then he sauntered off as if nothing ever bothered him. Part of that was a cover, she knew, so she wouldn't see how he felt. But she had known him long enough to realize he really did see life in those terms. You worked in the fields in the day, spent time with friends in the evening, had fun, and avoided anything that made you worry.

Soz wished her life were that simple.

It was dark in the entrance foyer to Althor's suite. Shannon walked through shadows up to the gold glasswood door. He laid his palm against its surface and closed his eyes while he searched for his brother. Althor's mind glowed like a star. And he was alone. Reassured, Shannon opened the door.

Althor was standing with his back to the door, pulling off one of his boots. He dropped it on the ground, then sat on the bed and tugged at the other boot. Shannon watched, uncertain. For so long he and Althor had shared kinship, so close in their youth. Althor had been a hero to him, the older brother he idolized. He had let his mind blend with his brother and never realized it. But in the days before his brother left home, Althor had become distant, withdrawing as he focused on the upcoming changes in his life. It had bewildered Shannon, who could never imagine leaving this world.

Then Althor had gone away.

Shannon had been three years younger when Althor rejected them. Yes, he had known his brother was going to school, not discarding his family. But Shannon had felt ripped in two as if he had lost half of himself.

"Can I come in?" Shannon asked.

Althor jerked, looking up. Seeing Shannon, he inhaled sharply as recognition flooded his mind. Astonishment. Joy. The emotions burst from him, overwhelming in their intensity.

"Chad?" Althor stood up, a brilliant smile on his face. "Good gods, Chad, how did you—"

Then he stopped, his surge of pleasure fading into confusion and no sign of recognition at all.

Suddenly a different smile warmed Althor's face, this one relaxed and familiar. "Shani, is that you?"

Relief washed through Shannon. He came inside and closed the door. "Didn't you recognize me?" He heard how musical his voice sounded next to Althor's rumble. He was a tenor: Althor was a bass. Shannon knew many people wondered if he felt lacking next to his powerful brothers. With Althor, the opposite was true. Shannon felt safe with him. Protected.

"You've grown," Althor said. "A lot."

"Some." Shannon went over to him. Althor had to be more than a head taller and at least twice his weight. "You have, too."

Althor grimaced good-naturedly. "Sometimes I feel my legs getting longer at night." He hesitated. "Shani, I'm not sure you should be here."

Of all the responses Shannon had thought possible, this was the one he had feared. He understood; Althor was angry because Shannon had never answered his letters, either by holo or the web. "It never bothered you before."

"Father is troubled because you didn't come to dinner. You should go talk to him."

"Do you hate me now?"

"Good gods, no." Althor seemed bewildered. "Why would you say such a thing?"

"I should have written you."

His brother's posture eased, though he still seemed as tight as a wire. "It's all right. I know reading and writing don't come easily for you. Mother and Father keep me in touch."

Shannon didn't know what to make of that. Did Althor really believe him illiterate or only offer it as an excuse? Although some of their siblings struggled to write, it had never bothered Shannon. Althor knew that. And he felt his brother's strain now. Something had jolted Althor when Shannon first entered the room.

It was his fault. After Althor had left home, Shannon had grieved. He couldn't accept that his brother wanted to go. Wrestling with that rejection, he had estranged himself from Althor while he came to terms with the knowledge that the brother he loved didn't want to stay, that for some inexplicable reason Althor wanted to fly Jag fighters. Shannon would never understand but he didn't want to be estranged anymore. If Althor hated him, better to find out now than to agonize for three more years. Or longer. Since he never intended to leave Lyshriol, he would rarely see Althor. He meant to stay here, tonight, until he put right the strain between them or Althor convinced him it was impossible.

He sat on the bed. "What did I do to make you angry?"

"Angry?" Althor looked down at him. "What do you mean?"

"You left Lyshriol." He wished Althor didn't tower over him so much.

Althor sat on the bed, bringing his eyes closer to Shannon's level. "Is that why you didn't write? You thought I was angry?"

"Weren't you?"

"Only that you didn't write."

Shannon tried to read his mood, but Althor was shielding his mind. "When I first came in here tonight, you were different."

Althor answered awkwardly. "You looked like someone I know. It startled me. That's all. You've changed. Grown up."

Shannon remembered his brother's surge of recognition. Althor had responded to him in a way Shannon had never known, even imagined. He didn't mind that Althor had thought he was someone else. It intrigued him. He wanted to explore it, understand this new reaction, swirl it into the sea of his emotions.

He touched Althor's cheek. "Yes. I have grown up."

Althor gently pushed his hand away from his face. "Don't."

"Why?"

"Shani, I'm an empath. I feel what you want."

Wryly he said, "Then perhaps you will tell me." He wasn't certain himself.

Althor thought for a moment. "Maybe it has to do with the Blue Dale Archers. You are so much like them, and they are so unlike other humans." He spoke as if he were still working it through. "I wish I knew more about that part of our heredity. I think you have no barriers in your emotional responses to people."

Shannon wasn't certain what he meant. When you loved someone, you loved them in all ways. It permeated your life. If you hated them, you cut them out of your life. "Why would I want barriers?"

"Most humans make them between different types of loving."

Shannon set his hand on Althor's arm, feeling the muscles beneath his black pullover. "Tell me about Chad."

"Shani, don't." Strain crackled in Althor's voice. He pulled his arm away.

Shannon felt cold. Bereft. "You act as if I am your enemy."

"You don't understand—"

"I can't, not here, not in Dalvador." Shannon struggled to express what he barely knew himself. "It is about loving, somehow, but I never understand. It blends into confusion. I think only of Blue Dale girls, silver and ethereal, but here all the girls are—too much. I don't know if I will ever find someone like me." Loneliness poured into him, but it filled nothing. "I feel empty."

"Do you mean empty with girls?"

"I wouldn't feel safe with the daughter of a farmer."

Althor spoke carefully. "Tell me something. How many children would you like to have?"

"Children?" The question perplexed Shannon. "I don't know. It will depend on my wife."

"In Dalvador, most boys your age have begun to consider marriage and a family."

"Girls here aren't like me." Althor was searching for an answer, but Shannon couldn't figure out the question, and Althor was guarding his mind too well. It didn't bother Shannon. Emotions were better absorbed than studied. It would become clear in time. "Someday I will search for the Blue Dales and find a wife there."

Althor rubbed the back of his neck. "Then the reason you hesitate is because you haven't met a girl you like."

"Yes." Shannon waited.

"You seem lonely," Althor said.

"I probably repulse Dalvador girls." He couldn't keep the hurt out of his words.

"Shani, no." Althor touched Shannon's hair as if he were brushing a treasure. "You are incredibly beautiful."

Shannon exhaled, then moved closer and put his arms around Althor's waist. When Althor hugged him back, he felt as he had in Moonglaze's stall, content to absorb affection. It permeated his empath's mind. Remorse filled him at his coldness these past years. His brother had rejected Lyshriol, but not him, Shannon, after all.

Althor laid his cheek against the top of Shannon's head. "You aren't repulsive."

"Stay with me tonight." It would heal so much.

"Good gods, Shani."

What had he said wrong? "I would like to stay."

Althor let him go, gently but firmly. "I don't think that would be wise."

Shannon closed his eyes. The loneliness saturated him.

"Shani—" When Shannon opened his eyes, Althor spoke with tenderness, though he seemed to ache inside. "You won't always be lonely. Someday you will love a woman, marry, have children."

Shannon wondered at Althor's sadness. He felt it now. Loneliness also wrenched his brother, and Althor believed he would have to live with it for the rest of his life.

"You will find someone, too," Shannon said.

"No. I won't." Althor seemed to wrestle with his answer. "I've tried to be what Father wants. I've taken women as lovers, tried to consider marriage. But it isn't going to happen."

"Why not?"

"It doesn't matter." He spoke quietly. "I am deeply sorry that it hurt you when I left. I never meant for you to feel rejected. But I have to do what is right."

"I won't hurt you."

"Shannon—"

"Listen." He splayed his palm on Althor's chest. "You're going away tomorrow. I will only see you every few years, if that often. You are an empath like me. A Rhon empath. It tears me apart when you leave." Softly he said, "Give me this night to remember you by."

Lines of strain creased Althor's face. "I'm sorry. But no."

Shannon lowered his hand. "Why?"

"Things might happen that—that shouldn't."

"I don't care." Shannon's feelings swirled. How could Althor love him but not love him? "Is it the tall woman who came with you?"

"Colonel Tahota?"

"Why is she here?"

"She just told me an hour ago. Kurj has chosen his heirs." Althor sounded stunned. In shock. "Soz. Me."

Kurj? Althor must mean their half brother. The Imperator. Shannon had little interest in offworld affairs. "Is that good, that he chose you and Soz?"

"Yes. I think." Doubts about his suitability for the title infused Althor's mood.

"You can do it." Shannon had no doubt.

"I hope so."

"But it changes nothing with us."

Althor brushed Shannon's hair back from his face. "I can't bend and blend my feelings the way you do."

Shannon had no idea what he meant. "I won't try to make you stay here. It would be wrong for me to try." He wished more than anything that Althor would, but he would no more try to force it than he would try to pull a moon out of the sky. Perhaps Althor believed his offer fickle or insincere. "I would neither ask nor wish such company from anyone else."

His brother's face gentled. "I know."

"But you will not let me stay?"

"I can't." Althor's voice softened. "But know always that I love you, above and beyond all others. Will that be enough?"

It wasn't enough. But it seemed to be the most they could have. Shannon answered in a low voice. "Know it for me, too."

"Take care, my brother."

"I will." He didn't see how. Althor had rejected him in yet a new way. Shannon reeled inside. But he knew now that Althor did it for him, not as a rejection. He had also absorbed the truth; if he stayed tonight, it would hurt his brother, and the reason was because Althor did love him. In his own confusing way Althor would always act on his sense of honor. Shannon loved in too many ways for Althor, who needed to put what he felt into compartments. His brother couldn't let his emotions run in a river while he went to wherever they would take him.

"Do you want me to go?" Shannon asked.

"No." Althor's voice caught. "But perhaps it is better that you do."

"Be well," Shannon said softly.

"And you."

After Shannon left, he returned to the stable and sat with Moonglaze. He was beginning to wonder if he, Shannon, was fully human. The emotions of people, even his own family, made so little sense to him. He felt painfully out of place here, until at times he thought he would die from a lack of air, or not air, but something more vital. He was suffocating and he didn't know how to make it stop. He wanted to saddle Moonglaze and ride away, fly across the world until he escaped the hurt he never understood.

Eldrinson stood in the window of his room on the third story of the house and looked toward the starport. Copious light from the Blue and Lavender Moons poured across the plains, their ghostly radiance silvering the Jag that crouched on the tarmac.

"It is so strange," he said.

Roca came up behind him and put her arms around his waist, her front to his back as she looked over his shoulder. "What is?"

"That my son should come out of the sky with flames and thunder." He leaned his head against hers. "A war god, eh?"

"Well, a fighter pilot, anyway."

"I wish he didn't have to leave tomorrow."

Roca sighed. "I also. Part of me wants to keep them with us all the time. But we have to let them go, Eldri. They grow up and live their own lives."

"Vyrl stayed." Eldrinson smiled. "All those fine grand-children he and Lily have given us."

Her voice warmed. "They are beautiful indeed."

"Do you think Althor has a girl?" He had noticed his son's silence on the subject.

Roca turned him around so he was facing her, the two of them standing with their arms around each other's waist. "Would it bother you if he didn't?"

"I suppose he has much to occupy his time."

"Yes. He does." Roca hesitated. "What I don't understand is why Colonel Tahota came with him. She isn't an instructor at DMA."

Eldrinson didn't know what to think of this female warrior. She showed impeccable courtesy, but she made him uneasy. "Women shouldn't fight wars, Roca."

His wife frowned at him. "And what will you do next year when your daughter insists on enrolling at DMA, hmm?"

He rubbed his eyes, feeling his more than five octets of age despite all the "nanomeds" the Skolian doctors gave him to keep his body young. "I don't know, love. I'm hoping she will change her mind."

"Eldri." Roca cupped her palms around his cheeks. "She isn't going to change her mind."

"She cannot go." The thought alarmed him even more than when Soz had challenged him to sword practice a few years ago—and bested him. That was the last time he had parried with her. "Lord Rillia plans to ask for a marriage with her."

"Our children don't take well to arranged marriages. Look what happened with Vyrl."

"But, Roca, this is different. We wanted Vyrl to marry an offworlder. It's no wonder he ran off with Lily. Besides, they've been in love practically since they were born. Soz has no young man, unless you count that scoundrel, Ari, who ought to have his backside paddled. Lord Rillia is a mature man of Lyshriol, a leader of our people. He will be good for her."

His wife had that look he dreaded, the one that meant he would never get her agreement. Roca said, "She won't do it. Soz wants to go. We can't hold her here. She will only hate us for it."

Panic at losing his daughter to an interstellar war swept over him. He covered it with anger. "She will do as I say. And I say she will stay here and marry Lord Rillia."

"Eldri—"

"No!" He couldn't bear to think that another of his children would leave for the stars, especially not Soz, his beautiful, brilliant, headstrong daughter. Gods only knew what would happen if she became a warrior. "My decision is final. I will hear no more."

Roca didn't look the least bit cowed by his statement. "If I know Soz, I suspect that when the time comes, you will hear a lot more."

He winced. "She is rather formidable."

"That she is."

"We have time. She hasn't applied anywhere yet." He moved his hands up Roca's back, a smile coming to his face. "It occurs to me that we might occupy ourselves with other concerns tonight."

Roca laughed. "What, you want more children? Ten isn't enough?"

"Twelve." In octal, of course. Eldrinson drew her into an embrace. "I can't help myself, with such a beautiful wife."

"Flatterer."

He hefted her up in his arms, with one arm under her knees and the other around her back. Then he grunted. "Wife, you are not the lightest person in the world." She was beautiful, yes, curved and statuesque, but she was no slip of a girl.

"I could walk." She sounded miffed.

Eldrinson pressed his lips against her cheek. Then he carried her over to the bed on the other side of the room. With a grin, he dropped her onto the quilt, making all the pillows bounce. "See?" He folded his arms, doing it the way he knew made his muscles flex. "I am not so old that I can't carry my wife."

Roca laughed, pulling her hair out of her eyes. "Come here." She grabbed his hand and yanked. He sprawled next to her on the bed, laughing, his hair flying. Then he pulled her into his arms, savoring her body against his. Even after three octets of years he loved to touch her, perhaps even more now than when they had first met. They nestled together in the quilts, kissing, her mouth soft against his, her lips parting for him.

Sometime later, after the oil lamps had burned down, he and Roca drowsed in the blue moonlight. Their clothes lay somewhere on the floor. Contentment filled him. Today had been good. His children often bewildered him, especially Althor and Soz, but he loved them all, those lights Roca had given him. He wished they would stay near home, as Vyrl had done. But Roca was right. When the time came, he had to let them go. That included Soz. But not offworld. Kurj would destroy her. Imperator. Eldrinson could never leave his daughter in a universe overseen by a man who had murdered his grandfather and hated his mother's husband. It was bad enough Althor chose ISC. He couldn't let it happen to Soz.

Eldrinson had a plan. He would spend this coming year getting Soz accustomed to the idea of marriage with Lord Rillia. This daughter of his was formidable, yes; as Rillia's wife, she would be well suited to help the Rillian Bard lead the people of Rillia and Dalvador.

He just needed time to make her agree.

4

The Decision

Soz paced Althor's room. "I don't know how to tell him. He will explode through the roof."

Althor was stuffing clothes into his duffel. "Just don't lose your temper."

Soz stopped and glared at him. "I never lose my temper."

Althor laughed. "Right. Never." Sunlight slanted through the window and made his gold skin shimmer. He was perfect in every way, physically, mentally, intellectually.

"Don't you ever get tired of being a hero?" Soz grumbled.

"What hero? Why does everyone say that?" He lifted his hands, then dropped them. "I've never done a damn thing except pass my exams at the academy. Real heroic."

"It's the principle of the thing. You look and act the part so well." She resumed pacing. "Father will never accept my going to DMA. He wants me to marry Lord Rillia and have lots of yelling, crapping babies."

Althor went back to packing. "Gods help Lord Rillia."

Soz glowered at him. "Why does everyone say, 'Gods

help Lord Rillia' when the topic of our purportedly incipient nuptials comes up? Why doesn't anyone say, 'Gods help Soz'?"

Althor laughed good-naturedly. "Purportedly incipient nuptials? Soz, no one talks that way."

"I do. And you're changing the subject."

"All right." He crossed to the window and motioned at the view. "See that?"

She went to peer out. The plains outside rippled in swells, as on an ocean. "What about it?"

"You're the wind, Soz. Or a storm. You rush across the land and leave everyone hanging on to their hats."

"Are you getting poetic on me?" Although she admired artists, she herself had the artistry of a stone block. Not that Althor had shown any particular interest in poetry before. Rocket engineering was more his style.

He leaned against the window frame. "You have to talk to Father."

"Perhaps I should tell him first, rather than Mother."

"Do you want me to be there?"

"No. I have to do this myself." She hesitated, worrying her lower lip with her teeth. Then she said, "If Tahota hadn't come and I had asked you to take me with you when you left here, without Father's permission, would you have done it?"

"Ah, Soz, that's a hell of a question." For a moment he regarded her. "Yes, I think so. But you don't know how grateful I am that I don't have to make that decision."

Her face eased into a smile. "You know, you're all right."

His grin flashed. "From you, that is a towering compliment."

Soz laughed, relieved, and glanced out at the plains. A youth was running through the reeds, his head thrown back, his blond hair streaming. "Look. There's Shani."

Althor went unusually still. "So it is."

"I'm sorry about last night. I don't know why he wouldn't come inside for dinner." Soz couldn't believe the way Shannon had refused to greet his own brother. "He gets odder all the time."

"It's all right. He came to talk to me later." Althor turned back to her. "He's changed so much. I didn't even recognize him at first."

"He's lonely. He can't seem to connect with anyone."

Althor hesitated. "For an instant I thought he was someone else."

Something in the way he spoke gave her pause. "Someone who hurt you." She didn't need to make it a question.

He leaned his back against the wall, his arms folded as he stared across the large room. "Have you ever given up something you wanted so intensely it hurt? You knew you had to do it, that it was the only choice, but you also knew you would regret it for the rest of your life?"

Soz wondered what brought on this pensive mood. "Not yet. I would feel that way if I married Lord Rillia."

"Don't give up your dreams." He looked at her. "You have a gift. It deserves a chance to develop."

She grimaced. "A gift for what? Annoying people?"

"For military strategy."

She finally asked the question that filled her thoughts now. "Do you think we're going to war?"

"Gods only know. From what I've heard, the Traders have been preying on our ships lately even more than usual. They either kill the crew and passengers or sell them as slaves."

"How can they get away with that?"

"They claim our ships go into their territory."

"Do they?"

"No."

Soz felt cold. "Can we prove it?"

"No. They keep or destroy the stolen ships, with all their records." His gaze darkened. "They get more and more daring, baiting us, trying to goad us into attacking first. That would make us the aggressors and help them win allies."

Her anger sparked. "They are the ones that sell and torture people. They've already 'attacked.'"

"Slavery is legal for them." He regarded her intently. "None of this has to do with heroics, Soz. Never forget that. Being a Jag pilot is one of the worst jobs in ISC."

She could barely hold still. "I know."

"It's why the academies are so tough on their cadets."

"An academy is a place. It's people who are tough on other people." She put her fists on her hips. "You going to give me a hard time at DMA, you being a senior when I'm a novice?"

His cocky grin came back. "Upperclassmen get to help train the new cadets."

She snorted. "Right. Make our lives hell."

"You'll do fine."

"What time are you and Tahota leaving today?"

"Probably this evening."

"You going to fly that Jag?"

His gaze smoldered. "Hell, yes."

Soz made a show of looking dubious. "Is it safe for me to ride with you? What if something happens? Maybe I need to know more about the ship. Just in case."

Althor laughed. "I'm not going to let you fly my Jag, Soz."

Oh, well. Althor knew her better than she wanted to admit. "I'll sit in the copilot's seat."

He answered amiably. "Give yourself a few months before you take DMA by storm. You don't have to do everything the first day."

"I know that." In truth, Soz was impatient to get on with matters. She wanted to fly a Jag so much, it felt tangible in her life. "Ah, hell, Althor. Just let me sit in the pilot's seat for a few minutes."

His smile crinkled his eyes. "All right."

"Hey." Soz beamed at him. "Great."

But first she had business to take care of here.

Shannon ran for over an hour. He fell into a trance, his feet beating a rhythm on the plains, reeds brushing his thighs, clouds of filmy spheres in his wake. He wished he could ride Moonglaze through these plains, never stopping, never feeling. It hurt too much to feel.

Lately the girls in the village giggled at him all the time, playing flirting games he couldn't fathom. Maybe he wouldn't fathom Blue Dale girls, either, but at least he wouldn't feel so out of place. Except the Archers no longer existed. They had all vanished in the high northern mountains. The youths his age were always going off to hunt, sneak around alehouses at night, or generally get into trouble. His brother Denric used to understand, before books took him away. Now all Denric thought about was literature and going to college. No one else just wanted to run in the wind.

After a while Shannon slowed down. Finally he stopped and flopped on his back, reeds bowing over him, their stems supple and translucent, silvery green. They resembled the glasswood columns of the trees in the Stained Glass Forest, except these were much thinner and more flexible. Bubbles drifted off their tips and popped, showering him with glitter. Soon more reeds would grow from that sparkling dust.

Shannon closed his eyes. He didn't know why he stayed in Dalvador. No, he did know. It would sadden his parents if he left. The Valdoria children were dispersing like glitter on the wind. Eldrin, the firstborn, had gone offworld and married the Ruby Pharaoh. Althor had gone to DMA. Soz probably would, too. Vyrl had married and moved to a farm outside of Dalvador, but at least he stayed here. Denric would go offworld to the university. Aniece wanted to marry Lord Rillia and become an accountant by attending an offworld university as a virtual student, like Vyrl. Kelric already talked about seeing the stars. If Shannon left, too, what would that do to his parents? He couldn't desert them.

But the loneliness would starve him.

Eldrinson sat in the alcove of the master suite on a cushioned bench. Windows reached from the bench to the ceiling. Outside, a golden day graced the plains, and Dalvador basked in the amber sunlight. He picked a melody out on his drummel, composing a song for a festival that had been held in Starlo Vale an octet of days ago:

The planters jumped high,
They jumped so high.
They sang their news,
Sang their news.
Sang their news.
Three times they told,
Three times they sang
Three times they sang
Their tales of plenty;
Their crops of twenty.
Twenty bushels, piper-reeds ripe and true;
Twelve only, bagger-bubbles so few.
Thirty-four sure, sweet-spheres, gold and blue.
Six octets total, bubble squash full and clean,
Every color, red, yellow, orange, blue, and green.

He stopped, frowning, unsure about the rhymes. Usually for a rhyme scheme, he kept the number of syllables equal in the rhyming lines, but that didn't work here. Still, he liked the way the harvest tally fit the music. It worked.

A knock came at the door. He lifted his head. "Come."

The door opened, revealing a familiar, beloved, exasperating sight, Soz in the blue leggings, gray tunic, and soft gray boots of an archer. Boy's clothes. It wasn't that they weren't lovely on her. But they were for *boys.* Not girls.

Still, it gladdened him to see her. He beamed, pleased she had sought him out. They argued so much lately. He wished he could find a way to talk with her, to regain the easy warmth they had shared when she was young.

"My greetings, Soshoni," he said.

She stood awkwardly in the doorway. "May I come in?"

"Of course." He set the drummel on the bench next to him. "Come sit with me. Tell me why you look so pensive."

She came to the alcove and sat on the cushioned bench near his drummel. "I wanted to talk to both you and Mother."

Her strange mood unsettled him. These past few years as she had turned from a girl into a woman, she had become more distant, but he could usually judge whether she was happy, angry, sad, or full of energy. Right now, he couldn't tell, and that made him uneasy. He didn't intrude on her privacy as an empath; it would have been like entering her room without knocking.

"Would you like me to get her?" he asked.

She shook her head. "It's best if I talk to you first."

Eldrinson felt a chill. "What is wrong, Soshoni?"

"A few months ago, I took the preliminary exams for the Dieshan Military Academy."

He froze. No. *Not now.* He needed more time. He spoke more stiffly than he intended. "You know how I feel about that."

"Father, listen, please." She watched him intently, her eyes so green, so unlike Lyshrioli eyes. "I passed the tests. I even did well. Really well."

"Why do you waste your time with such things?" He didn't want to hear. Couldn't hear. "It serves no purpose. You cannot go to Diesha. I won't sign the forms."

She regarded him steadily, not angry, not growling, different today, composed in a way that frightened him. "If I stay here, my spirit will wither and die. Surely you see that. I have to go." Her voice caught. "You have to let go."

His thoughts whirled. "Why does it matter? It will be a year before you need to worry about it."

"I've already been accepted."

No. *No.* He had to barrier his mind from this news. But he couldn't do it; he lived in the moment, unable to cut himself off from those he loved. He could only say, "That cannot be."

"It is."

"But you said you took only preliminary exams."

She nodded in that quiet way she had today, so odd, so unlike her usual fire. "I did better than I expected. They want me to enroll now."

"Now? NO!" He rose to his feet, filled with the fear of losing her, of her death, of the violence she could meet out there in a harsh universe beyond his ken. "I will not allow it! You cannot go."

"You can't stop me." She stood up as well, defiant now. "They will accept me without parental consent."

"What? No! They can't do that." Skolians claimed young people didn't reach their majority until three octets plus one year of age. Eldrinson thought it absurd; in Dalvador and Rillia you became an adult at two octets. It didn't matter. By their own definition, Soz was a child. His child. They couldn't take her away from him. He wouldn't allow it.

"I don't want to go without your consent." She was using her quiet voice again. "I would ask you please, Father, give me your blessing. Please understand."

A terrible foreboding settled over him. "Who gave you permission to do this?"

"The DMA admissions office."

"I see. And who let them do such a thing."

Soz hesitated. "I don't know."

Eldrinson barely kept his anger in check. "Could it by any chance be your dear half brother, Kurj, the Imperator, who tried to shoot me dead the first time he met me? Who would see me in my grave rather than acknowledge I am his stepfather? Is that who gave you permission to defy his own laws and turn your back on your family?"

Soz drew in a deep breath. "Father, listen."

"I have heard too much."

"Kurj chose his heirs."

"I don't care what Kurj has done. You will not leave."

"Listen to me!" Her eyes blazed. "Kurj designated Althor and me as the Imperial Heirs. Don't you understand what that means? Someday one of us will be Imperator."

Eldrinson was dying inside. He had spent years trying to make peace with his warlord stepson, to no avail. It was painful to live with Kurj's scorn, his barely disguised contempt, even hatred, but he had never expected this, that Kurj would rip his children away. He could live with Kurj's loathing because Kurj was in another place, distant, unable to affect his life. Now Skolia's mighty Imperator reached out his long arm to take what Eldrinson valued above all else, even above his own life—his children.

"No." He was whispering now. "You cannot do this." It was a betrayal beyond his ability to comprehend.

"Ah, Father." Soz's anger vanished, replaced by a pain she didn't hide. "It isn't what you think. He has to choose heirs. The Assembly has insisted, regardless of his feelings about your marriage to Mother. He has all of Skolia to worry about, nine hundred settled worlds and habitats, hundreds of billions of people. He *must* train Rhon psions to assume his position."

This couldn't be true. Kurj couldn't take his daughter and send her to die in war. Or worse. "You cannot go." He would repeat those words a million times until she heard them.

"It's the information networks that stretch across the stars." She spoke as if urging him to see what she meant. "Only the Rhon can control them. Without them, interstellar civilization as we know it couldn't exist."

"It makes no sense." Roca had told him this, that instantaneous interstellar communications were possible only through some universe outside spacetime, someplace where light speed had no physical meaning. It meant nothing to him. Light was light. It had no speed. They expected him to believe this bizarre place existed that only people with Rhon minds could tolerate, a place that made speech among the stars possible? It was stories, fables. That Kurj would use this insanity to take his children—no, he couldn't accept this betrayal.

He spoke slowly, measuring his words. "If you leave, you are no longer my daughter."

"Father, don't." A tear ran down her face, so unusual for this daughter who hid her gentler side. "Don't ask me to make that choice."

Somehow he kept his voice steady, though surely it would break soon. "My daughter is a woman of Lyshriol."

"But it is all right if your sons leave?" Bitterness edged her voice. "Althor is your glorious son, coming down in a pillar of flame, but I am betraying you?"

"Is it not bad enough that he leaves? Must you go, too?" He despised himself for his bewildered tone. "If you go now, Sauscony, do not come home again. You will have no place here."

Another tear ran down her face. "Neither Althor nor I are what you think, Father. We may break your heart, but remember this—always, for both of us, we love you. You gave me a wonderful childhood, one full of love. You can disown me when I leave tonight on that ship, but I will always love you."

With that, she turned and left the room. For a moment he simply stood, frozen. Then his shock cracked open like a dam breaking, water flooding, rushing, bursting through the cracks and past the jagged edges of his thoughts.

Eldrinson crossed the room in a few strides. He yanked open the door and strode out to the hall that stretched the length of the house. He was running by the time he reached the top of the main stairs. He pounded down them, coming around their curve—and collided with Roca.

"Eldri, what's going on?" She caught her balance. "Soz told me you just *disowned* her. Then she went off. She won't talk to me."

"Your son never gives up, does he?" He couldn't stay calm. "You stopped him from killing me. You stopped him from having me declared incompetent. You stopped him from having me caged in a lab while they studied my brain. Now he retaliates by taking my children."

Roca stared at him. She didn't try to deny his words; they both knew the extremes Kurj had taken in his attempts to end their marriage. "That was a long time ago. He's changed."

Eldrinson struggled to breathe. "Apparently not much."

"Listen. Kurj *had* to choose his heirs. The Assembly voted on it. And his heirs have to be Rhon psions. I'm Deyha's heir. Our children are the only real choice."

Eldrinson stared at her. "You *knew?*" His world was breaking apart. He had nowhere to stand.

"I knew they had voted. I didn't realize Kurj had done anything until now, when Althor told me."

He gripped the banister. "Soz told me."

Her forehead furrowed. "About Althor?"

"No! Herself. Kurj chose them *both.*"

"Gods above. That was what Althor meant."

"Meant by *what?*"

She exhaled. "That it was Soz's decision what to say."

Eldrinson didn't know where to put his dismay, his anger, all this pain. "Where is Althor?"

"Outside, in the courtyard—"

He pushed past her, taking the stairs two at a time.

"Eldri, wait!" Roca caught up with him. "You have to calm down. You'll have a seizure."

He kept going, unwilling to hear, unwilling to acknowledge that he owed his life to the doctors of her people, to hated technology he barely understood, to the Skolians who were stealing his children.

At the bottom of the stairs, he strode through the house until he reached the archway out to the courtyard with the potted plants. Shoving open the doors, he saw Althor talking to Del by the fountain. Arches of blue water spouted into the air and fell in sprays back into the round basin.

Eldrinson walked over to them. "Althor."

His son turned. He started to smile, then stopped. Eldrinson didn't know how his face looked, but given the way Althor stiffened, he doubted it was pleasant. He heard Roca nearby, but he kept his attention on his son. "Soz says she is leaving with you tonight."

Althor let out a breath. "She talked to you, then."

Eldrinson strove to keep from clenching his fists. He wouldn't threaten his own son. "I have forbidden her to leave."

"What did she say?"

"That she will go anyway."

"Father, I'm sorry. But she has to make her own decision—"

"No!" Eldrinson was losing the battle to stay cool. "She is a child. She does not have to make her own decisions."

Althor regarded him, his metallic eyes and face glinting in the sunlight, so much like his mother. *Like Kurj.* "She is seventeen. Twenty-one, in octal. Here that makes her an adult." He spoke quietly. "If she is old enough to marry a man more than twice her age, she is old enough to decide her own future."

"According to Skolian law, she is a *child*. They break their own laws to take my daughter?" He couldn't believe Althor would do this. "If you take her against my wishes, you will violate the basis of every trust I have ever put in you."

Althor spread his hands out from his body. "Father, she is a genius. A technological genius. A military genius. You can't cage her spirit here. She would be miserable."

"Miserable?" He gave Althor an incredulous look. "Miserable to have a happy life with a good, decent man? Instead I should send her to war, to gods only know what violence?" His voice was shaking. "What if she were taken prisoner by the Traders? Could you live with knowing you had made it possible for them to torture and enslave your sister? Are you out of your *mind?*"

"The choice isn't ours to make," Althor said. "It is hers."

Eldrinson ground out his words. "If you take her on that ship tonight, you are no longer my son."

Roca stepped forward. "Eldri, stop."

Eldrinson swung around to her. "You would let this happen? You, my wife? Their *mother.*" His voice caught. "You put your loyalties with a man who once sought my death?"

A tear ran down her face. "It isn't that way. We need time to talk. Soz will be in school for four years, perfectly safe. A lot can happen in that time."

"That's right." He wanted to smash his fist into the wall. "Skolia could go to war against the Traders." He swung around to Althor. "I mean it. If you take her, don't ever come back here."

A voice came from beyond the fountain. "Father, no!"

Startled, Eldrinson turned. Shannon stood in an archway of the courtyard with his hair disarrayed from running in the plains.

"Don't send Althor away." Shannon came across the courtyard, his dismayed gaze on his father.

Althor spoke quickly. "Shani, it's all right."

For a long moment Eldrinson looked from Althor to Shannon and back again. Then he said, "Shannon, go inside."

"But, Father—"

"Now!" Eldrinson pointed at the house. "You will do as I say, young man."

Shannon swallowed. He went on, past them, into the house.

Althor spoke in a low voice. "Father—"

"Enough!" Eldrinson clenched his fist. "You have my final word. You will leave your sister here and you will bring back a wife the next time you come home. Or don't you ever come back again."

Althor stared at him. "*What?*"

"You heard me."

His son flushed. "What does a wife have to do with anything?"

Eldrinson knew he should stop, that he should go on doing what he had always done, letting himself believe what he wanted to believe about Althor, loving his son for the good in him, leaving unspoken what he didn't understand. But he couldn't do it any longer, not with so much betrayal. "You think I'm stupid? I'm an empath, damn it. You never look twice at those beautiful girls who vie for your attention. But you can't keep your eyes off your own *brother.*" His voice shook with anger. "Come home with a wife, Althor. Or don't come home at all."

With that, Eldrinson strode back into the house, leaving his sons and his wife in the courtyard.

5

A Harbor Lost

They gathered on the tarmac under a sunset that smoldered red and purple across the sky. Soz stood with Althor, and they hugged their family good-bye. Their mother had come, also Del. Chaniece, too, who had returned when she received news that Althor had come home. Chaniece resembled their mother most of the Valdoria daughters, though she had violet eyes and lavender-streaked yellow hair. It hurt Soz to see her older sister's dismay now, knowing Chaniece had arrived just in time to tell them farewell, possibly forever.

Denric stood with Chaniece. He was a youth of Lyshriol rather than of Skolia, with his yellow curls, violet eyes, and slender build, so much like the people of Dalvador. None of the younger children had come; their father had forbidden it. He also stayed away. Nor had Ari come, though Soz had looked for him in town and his home this afternoon and left messages. She knew the truth; her siblings and friends belonged here and she didn't.

Tears ran down Roca's gold cheeks. Soz's own eyes filled with moisture. This had been so much worse than she expected. For all that she had known her father would be angry, she had never thought it would end this way. She couldn't turn back. No matter how hard she tried, how much she wished otherwise, she couldn't be what he wanted. She would have given almost anything to keep him from being hurt, but if she didn't go now, she might never leave.

Colonel Tahota stayed back while they said their goodbyes. Even through Soz's mental barriers, she felt the colonel's subdued mood. Tahota had the unenviable job of dealing with the aftermath of yet another attempt by the Assembly to control the Ruby Dynasty, in this case by forcing the matter of Kurj's heirs. It didn't help to know they were right.

That night Soz left the home, the place where she had known so much joy and love—and that was now forbidden to her.

Shannon sat in a curtained alcove on the third floor of the house. He pushed into a corner where the stone bench met the wall, pulled his knees to his chest, and laid his forehead on his knees. The roar of the departing Jag had long since faded. Nothing could fix this wound. Father had sent Althor away. Forever.

It was his fault.

Shannon knew the truth. He hurt people and they left. He gave nothing. He had nothing. Loneliness was breaking him apart.

The door of the outer room scraped open, glasswood on stone. Shannon raised his head. He looked through the crack where the curtain didn't quite meet the wall and saw his father shut the door. Eldrinson walked heavily to a table in the center of the room and sat in one of its high-backed chairs. Resting his elbows on its surface, he put his forehead in his hands.

His shoulders were shaking. He was crying. Shannon had known many moods from his father, but never this heart-deep anguish. *It was his fault.* He had seen his father's anger, heard him banish Althor. Because of him, Shannon. He never meant to cause pain. He had simply gone to Althor. It had done so much damage. He couldn't bear to be the cause of this. Nor could he bear more rejection, more anger, more pain.

The door opened again. Roca came inside, but Eldrinson didn't look up as she closed the door. She went to the table and sat in a chair near him.

He lifted his head. "Are they gone?" Tears streaked his face.

Her face was wet as well. "Yes. They left."

His voice cracked. "They are dead to me."

"Eldri, don't do this." Roca reached for his hand.

He pushed her away. "You could have helped me. You didn't."

"It is wrong to make her stay."

Eldrinson stared at her. "But it isn't wrong for her to go? To show so little respect for her parents?"

"She is no longer a child, no matter how we may feel. We must respect her wishes."

"Kurj will destroy us. He will tear apart our family. Gods know, I've never done anything to him. But it will never change his antipathy toward me."

She exhaled. "It is true, he will probably never accept you as his stepfather. But he no longer tries to destroy you."

"No, now he does it through our children."

"He didn't want to name any heirs. The Assembly forced him."

"I was so happy today." Eldrinson's voice caught. "So proud of Althor, so overjoyed to have the family together."

"Eldri, give this time. It will heal."

"That woman, Colonel Tahota—why did Kurj send her?"

"To answer our questions." Relief at his quieter tone showed on Roca's face. "She has much status within ISC. They did honor by sending her."

His anger sparked. "Your son couldn't come himself?"

"Would you have wanted him to?"

"No." Eldrinson grimaced. "When he comes here, I feel his aversion every moment. He loathes Lyshriol. He judges everything I do and say."

Shannon strained to understand their currents of emotion. He felt how much they hurt, but he couldn't interpret their complicated moods. He hardly knew Kurj; it had been over six years since his half brother had visited Lyshriol. Shannon's life had been even more an ocean of moods then. He remembered Kurj as huge and taciturn. Imposing. But not hostile. Shannon had liked him.

"I talked to Tahota this afternoon," Roca was saying. "Kurj intends honor by Althor and Soz."

Eldrinson shook his head, his face drawn. "My children have—" He stiffened, the rest of his sentence lost.

"Eldri?" Roca leaned forward. "What—ah, gods, *no.*"

A strange static crackled in Shannon's mind. His father's gaze turned vacant, a frightening lack of *person.* Roca stood up suddenly, grabbing her husband as he went rigid and sagged to the side. She caught his arm, but his weight was too much. He fell out of his chair, pulling Roca with him, and they crashed to the floor, knocking away the chair. Shannon soundlessly cried out when his father's shoulder smashed against a table leg and his mother's head struck the chair. Roca recovered immediately and leaned over her husband, moving fast, laying him on his side.

Then the demons came.

Terrifying spasms wracked his father's body. He convulsed as if invisible creatures shook him with violence. His arms and legs hit the floor, and his head jerked back and forth.

"Father!" Shannon jumped off the bench and swept aside the curtain.

His mother snapped up her head. "Shannon, good gods, where did you come from?"

Shannon came to them and stood over his father's body, staring in horror, his hands out from his sides.

"Shannon!"

Her voice penetrated his shock. He looked at her, silently pleading with her to make it all right, to fix this new shock. His father continued to convulse.

She spoke fast. "Go to the master suite. Bring me the holotape and air syringe in the top drawer of the nightstand by the bed. Can you do that?"

Help. She needed his help. He focused. The master suite. Air syringe. "Yes."

"Hurry," she said.

Shannon ran outside and down the halls, his hair flying back from his face. It took ages to reach their suite, but finally he was there. He raced through its entrance foyer and slammed open the inner door. Night darkened the room inside. He ran to the stand and rummaged in the drawer, sending trinkets, memory cubes, and disks flying. He found the syringe immediately—but no tape. He searched frantically, throwing a necklace on the floor, a timepiece, a cluster of strings for his father's drummel. No tape!

Shannon dropped to his knees and scrabbled through the debris on the floor. There! He grabbed the glimmering spool and jumped to his feet, the syringe clutched in his hand as well. Then he tore out of the suite and ran back through the house.

He found his mother still kneeling by his father. Eldrinson had gone limp—no, his father couldn't have *died*—

Eldrinson's chest rose, slow and shallow as he breathed.

Shannon crouched next to his mother. "Here." He pushed the tape and syringe into her hands.

"Thank you." Her voice had a gratitude he didn't deserve.

Unrolling the tape, Roca laid it along Eldrinson's neck. Holos appeared above it, diagrams and statistics. For a moment she studied them, her forehead furrowed. Then she released a breath. She adjusted the syringe and dialed in a prescription. Shannon watched anxiously. Had he caused this, too, bringing demons to his father's body?

As Roca set the air syringe against Eldrinson's neck, she spoke softly. "He will be all right."

His voice shook. "Why do they come?"

A hiss came from the syringe. "Who comes?"

"The demons."

Roca glanced at him. "There are no demons, Shani. It's just epilepsy."

He didn't believe her. Yes, he knew his father had epilepsy. He had read about it, as they all had, learning what to do if he had an attack. The Skolian program of treatment was supposed to prevent seizures, but they could still happen. This was the first time Shannon had seen a big one. He knew the truth, regardless of what his mother or any doctor claimed. Spirits of malice attacked his father, probably brought here by Shannon's misdeeds.

Roca set the syringe and holotape on the floor, then eased Eldrinson onto his back and straightened his limbs. With a sigh, he settled back, breathing more naturally now. His eyelashes lifted and he stared blankly at the ceiling. Comprehension gradually returned to his gaze.

"Eldri?" Roca said.

He looked at her, his face tired. Then his gaze shifted to Shannon. "Shani? Where—?"

"I was in the alcove," Shannon said.

"You . . . heard?"

Shame swept over Shannon. "I'm sorry. I didn't mean to. I was already there when you came in. I didn't want to disturb you."

"Ai . . ." Eldrinson closed his eyes. After several breaths, he tried to sit up. Roca slid her arm around his torso. He got onto his knees, pulled up his booted foot, and tried to stand, but he sagged so much, he almost knocked Roca over.

"Shannon," she said.

He slid his arm around his father's waist. With the two of them as support, Eldrinson managed to stand. Then he drew away from them and tried a step on his own. Immediately his legs buckled. He grabbed the table and hung on, his face pale, his jaw clenched so hard Shannon could see the bones against his skin.

Roca reached to help, but he shook his head, sharp and angry. "Leave me." His usually resonant voice was flat and dull. He stared at her with a suppressed fury that frightened Shannon, not because he believed his father would ever hurt any of them but because he feared it would bring on another attack.

Roca stepped back, giving him room. Eldrinson pushed away from the table and walked slowly to the door. Shannon started after him, but his mother caught his arm.

"Not now," she murmured.

He understood. The Bard needed his pride. Eldrinson opened the door and left the room.

"I'm sorry." Shannon's voice broke. "I'm sorry."

"It's not your fault." His mother dropped into a chair at the table and bent her head.

"I should go." Shannon didn't know where, only that he had to free her from his presence.

"Shani, wait." His mother motioned to another chair at the table. "I need to talk with you."

Unease swept over him. He went to the chair and laid his hand on its high back. "Yes?"

"Sit down, honey."

That didn't sound ominous. She called him Shannon Eirlei Valdoria when she was angry with him. He sat slowly, watching her, trying to read her mood. She was tired, very tired, and afraid for his father. Her pain over today went deep; he could skim only its surface.

"This afternoon," his mother began.

"Does he really mean to banish Soz and Althor?"

"I don't know what will happen."

"Tell me the truth," he said in a low voice.

Shadows darkened her eyes. "Yes. I think he means it."

A part of Shannon died inside. "Althor will never come home."

His mother's gaze sharpened. "What did your father mean about Althor looking at you?"

Hai! He couldn't discuss it with his mother. He didn't even understand it himself. "Nothing."

"That 'nothing' contributed to his disowning his son."

"I don't know why." That was the truth.

"What happened between you and Althor?"

"Nothing." He dropped his mental barriers and let her sense the truth of his answer.

Roca's shoulders sagged. "We're frightened, Shani, all of us, your father, me, Kurj, Althor, Soz. War leans on us and I don't know if we can stand under its weight."

Her words poured over him and sheeted off like water that couldn't soak into a dry sponge. "I thought all war had ended."

She looked at him oddly. "What makes you think that?"

"Althor ended it." Shannon knew the story well, how Althor had ridden into battle five years ago with their father, mounted on a great war lyrine, wearing disk mail and leather armor, with his sword at his side, his bow and quiver on his back—and a laser carbine over his shoulder. Two days later Althor had stood on a ridge above the Plains of Tyroll and slaughtered over three hundred of their enemies with one carbine. It had taken only minutes. Men with swords and bows couldn't combat the technology of an interstellar empire. That day, Althor had ended war on Lyshriol.

His mother spoke tiredly. "I wish we could end the wars among my people. More than anything, though, I would wish for my children a gentler life than one of killing." Her voice caught. "But it seems they must follow pipers I cannot hear."

"I'm sorry," he whispered.

Roca squeezed his hand. "I am so very glad some of you stay."

Shannon stared at her drawn face and he knew without doubt that he had failed her, failed his father, failed Althor. That moment last night when he walked into his brother's room, he had started a tragedy. He had hoped the person he trusted and loved above all others would help ease his loneliness, but instead he had caused more trouble than he could bear.

He knew what he had to do.

The stable was dark, but Shannon needed no light. He walked straight to Moonglaze's stall. The lyrine nickered, stepping restlessly behind the green glasswood half door.

"Hai, Moonglaze." Shannon crooned, giving the lyrine sweet bubbles he had picked from a shrub outside. Moonglaze pushed his nose into Shannon's hand and crunched on the delicate orbs.

"Come on." Shannon whispered, though no one was out this late to hear him. He had waited until everyone went to bed. He put a soft pad over Moonglaze's back and settled his travel sacks across the lyrine's haunches. Moonglaze whistled a low protest, and Shannon made soothing noises, all the time scratching in the thick purple hair curling at the lyrine's neck, until Moonglaze quieted.

Shannon strapped his quiver of silver-tipped arrows onto his own back. He was carrying his bow. Then he walked Moonglaze outside and across a courtyard. He didn't leave by the main gate, which had a watchman. Instead he snuck out a small gate no one used, one overgrown by vines and prickly glasstubes. He pushed through the screen of growth and brought Moonglaze out into tangles of bagger-bubble reeds. Light from the Blue and Lavender Moons filtered through the foliage. Moonglaze lifted his great head and shook it with pleasure.

"Good Moon." Shannon fastened his bow to his back, then mounted and guided the lyrine along an overgrown path that wound around the house. They were on the edge of Dalvador, and within moments they reached the stubble that marked the onset of the plains. Shannon gave Moonglaze his head and the lyrine took off. He had never understood why his mother thought the name Moonglaze was too poetic for a war mount. This lyrine flew through the night, fluid and silent, no more visible than a glaze on the moon. The stubbly reeds of the plains brushed his hooves, then his legs, then even higher, but it didn't fetter the lyrine. These plains were his home, just as they had always been for Shannon.

Until now.

He would probably never find the Blue Dale Archers. But he would search all of their legendary territory in Ryder's Lost Memory and the Blue Dale Mountains.

For he had nowhere else to call home.

6

The Empty Stall

Soz had always expected it would thrill her the first time she sat in the cockpit of a Jag fighter. Today she felt only subdued. She and Althor were side by side. Althor slouched in the pilot's seat, dozing, its silver exoskeleton covering him like a second skin. Although she couldn't see its prongs, she knew they had plugged into sockets in his neck, wrists, and at the base of his spine. He also had sockets in his ankles, but his boots covered them.

Tahota was taking her turn in the auxiliary chair crammed into the Jag's tiny cabin behind them. Her seat had enough smart-ware to adjust for its passenger's comfort, and the colonel was sleeping for the first time since they had left Lyshriol, leaving Althor to tend the Jag by himself. He didn't have much to do; its Evolving Intelligence, or EI, could pilot the ship.

They were superluminal now, traveling in inversion. It was one of Soz's favorite areas of study. Light-speed was like an infinite tree limiting the speed of the ship. They could never go over the tree; mass and energy became infinite relative to the rest of the universe at the speed of light. The solution turned out to be simple, at least in mathematical terms. They needed only add an imaginary component to their speed. It let them "go around" the tree by entering a complex universe where mass, energy, and speed had imaginary components. In mathematical terms, the relativistic equations became functions of a complex variable. It let them circumvent the singularity at light speed. Scientists called it inversion because it inverted constellations relative to their subluminal positions.

Now they raced through inversion, headed for Diesha, home world to ISC headquarters and the Dieshan Military Academy.

The cockpit mesmerized Soz. She knew roughly what she would see, but this Jag had more components than she expected. Its full design was probably kept secret from the public, including eager young applicants to DMA. Transparent panels had folded around her body and come alive with holomaps and other displays. She wanted to memorize it all. It kept her occupied; otherwise, she would have nothing to do but brood over what had happened at home.

Althor stirred and pulled himself upright and stretched his arms. He scanned the panels that had clicked into place around his body, but Soz doubted he needed to look. The Jag's EI brain fed data straight into his node. He and the EI were getting to know each other, developing the symbiosis they would need to work together. This fighter would be his when he graduated from DMA. It would fly for no one but him or a pilot he granted permission.

He glanced at Soz. "Did you sleep?"

"I can't." She waved her hand at the controls. "It's like a great big puzzle. I have to solve it."

He smiled. "You probably knew more about Jags than most novice cadets even before this ride. And none of them are coming to Diesha in one."

She wanted to be excited, but her enthusiasm felt damped. To succeed in her lifelong dream meant so much less when it came at the price of losing her home.

Althor settled back and studied views of space displayed on the holoscreens over his head. Soz didn't think he was paying much attention to them. After a moment, he said, "I can't believe he said that about Shannon. He knows me better than that."

Soz knew he meant their father. "He was angry. At me. At you for taking me. He didn't mean what he told you about not coming home."

"Like hell. He meant every word of it." He spoke under his breath. "Nothing like having your father out you in front of your family."

Soz wasn't sure what he meant; she hadn't been there during his argument with Father. Del had told her about it. She wanted to ask more, but she hesitated. She hadn't seen Althor for three years and even before that they hadn't been close enough to talk about such personal matters. Given that they had just been disowned, though, she wanted to understand why. "When he's had time to calm down, he'll realize you would never hurt Shannon."

Althor spoke awkwardly. "Shannon certainly startled me."

"What did he do?"

"Asked to stay with me last night."

Soz gaped at him. "*What?*"

He squinted at her. "I'm not sure he realized what he was saying."

"He likes girls, Althor. I'm sure of it."

"I know. I asked him about it." He rubbed his eyes. "I don't think even he knew what he wanted. The way he experiences life and emotion is different from us. He doesn't separate what he feels into boxes."

Soz glanced back into the cabin. Tahota was sleeping, her mind quiescent. Turning back to Althor, she spoke slowly, unsure what to say. "I don't know him as well as Denric and Aniece do, but I can guess why he came to you. He trusts you. He always has. He loves us all, but he feels closer to you."

"I've always treasured that. Now I feel as if I've ruined it."
Althor's voice quieted. "When he came into my room last
night, I thought for one minute that he was a—a friend of
mine." Then he added, "A former friend."

Soz heard the loss in those words. "Former by your
choice?"

He averted his eyes, his lashes glinting. "It's complicated."

"Maybe Shannon picked up your reaction. That may be
why he thought you would let him stay the night."

"All I know is that I've made a mess of things."

"It's not your fault." Soz wished she could fix it. "I knew
Father would be angry, but I thought he and Mother would
talk to Colonel Tahota, and that she could ease their fears."

"How?" Althor met her gaze. "Skolia may go to war. You
or I could die or be taken prisoner. Maybe Father is right.
Maybe I am insane to take you to Diesha."

Her anger stirred. "Yet it was all right for you to gallop off
to war with Father when you were sixteen?"

"That was something he understood."

"And if we go to war with the Traders?" Urgency drove
Soz, the drive to go to Diesha, to DMA, to combat. To protect her family and her people. "I've read the histories, the
analyses, even the contraband essays. Some of it is propa-
ganda, but gods, even taking that into consideration, the
Trader Aristos are monsters."

He met her gaze. "They don't see it that way. To them,
we're the abominations."

"Like hell."

"In their view of reality, only they should be free. The rest
of us should be slaves. Especially psions." His voice tightened. "That we, the Ruby Dynasty, a family of psions, once
ruled an empire and still have power violates everything they
consider moral and right."

Soz made an incredulous noise. "That justifies kidnapping
psions, selling them, torturing them for pleasure?" She
crossed her arms, cold now. "And what about the rest of their
people, the taskmakers? How can the Aristos justify enslav-
ing billions, even trillions of people?"

"They would say their people have better lives than ours. That the average standard of living for a taskmaker is higher than for a free Skolian citizen."

"I'd rather live in poverty than slavery."

He leaned toward her. "Yes, it is a repressive regime, and yes, those taskmakers are slaves. But it *isn't* a horror, except for psions, and we only constitute a tiny fraction of one percent of their people. Taskmakers live in relative freedom and prosperity." He rubbed his neck through the exoskeleton, working at the muscles. "It's why their civilization is so stable."

"You think it's all right?"

"Gods, no." He lowered his arm. "But be realistic, Soz. The Eubian Concord, what we call the Trader Empire—it's the largest civilization in human history. It has thrived for centuries. Why? Because however much we loathe their methods, they *work*. If you expect their taskmakers to revolt, forget it. Yes, some would like freedom. Some strive for it. But not that many. It isn't only that the Aristos breed them for passivity. As long as they don't make trouble, they have good lives, even better in material terms than they might have under our government."

Soz turned away. "Brainwashing people into accepting a despotic government doesn't make it right."

"No. It doesn't."

Tahota spoke from behind them. "It just makes the despots that much harder to defeat."

Startled, Soz turned around, causing panels to readjust around her body. Tahota was awake, reclined in her seat. The colonel spoke to Althor. "I read your systems as green."

Soz blinked. She saw no outward sign Tahota was communicating with the ship. No, that wasn't true. Lights on the colonel's gauntlets were glittering more than usual. Tahota must have linked to the ship through both hard jacks and remote. She and Althor had become part of the Jag's brain.

"No problems here," Althor said.

Tahota nodded. "Good work, Cadet."

Cadet. Strange to hear her brother addressed that way. Her

incoming class would be called novice cadets, followed by
journeyman, junior, and finally senior, like Althor this year.

Soz regarded Tahota with curiosity. "You know how to pilot a Jag?" It seemed odd for a Fleet colonel.

"I used to be a flight instructor," Tahota said. "I can fly
just about anything."

Soz grinned. "So will I, someday."

Tahota's face relaxed into a smile. "I don't doubt it."

Soz straightened in her seat, gratified by that expression
of confidence. She wished her family could respond that
way. They were the core of her life. They meant everything.
Banished from her home, she felt no satisfaction in her minor accomplishments. It didn't change her drive, that com-
pelling need to *know* that pushed her with relentless force.
But it left a hollow place within her that no Jag starfighter
could fill.

Eldrinson awoke slowly, into sunlight, and drowsed while
his mind cleared. Althor had come home. His contentment
vanished as the rest of it came back to him, the entire day,
ended by his seizure. He opened his eyes. He was lying in
bed on his back. The ceiling vaulted high above him, but its
polished bluestone and gracefully scrolled carvings had no
beauty today, though for years he had loved them. He
wanted to believe it had been a terrible dream, that Soz and
Althor hadn't left. But the day remained. He had awoken. It
wasn't a nightmare.

"Soshoni," he said, remembering the little girl laughing,
her arms outstretched to him, her curls bouncing. Or Althor,
his stubby toddler's legs working hard as he ran across the
courtyard chasing a shimmer-fly.

"Eldri?" Roca's voice came from nearby.

Rolling over, Eldrinson saw her buried under the blue
quilt, just her forehead showing. He tugged down the blankets, uncovering her face. Her glittering lashes lifted to reveal gold irises. He had seen those eyes open almost every
morning for the last four octets of years, but today he felt no
joy in them.

"My greetings," he said, his voice flat. Cold.

Roca pulled herself up, letting the blankets fall around her waist. She wore an old sleep gown, rose silk worn with age. The suns cast early morning light through the alcove windows across the room. His drummel lay on the cushioned bench there, forgotten.

"Are you all right?" Roca asked.

"No." He pulled himself up and rubbed his eyes, wishing he could rub away yesterday. "It really happened."

"Yes."

"Hai, Roca." Is this how he would awake for the rest of his years, filled with grief?

"Talk to me," she said.

"Why?" he asked dully. "You're an empath. Don't you know what I'm thinking?"

"No. You're too guarded right now."

"I'm flat." His tongue felt thick. "Did I do that, Roca? Did I turn them out?"

She spoke with urgency. "Send them a message. Tell them they are welcome in their home."

"I cannot." He loosened the collar of his sleep shirt. It was strangling him.

"You can."

"I meant what I said. They made their choices."

Her hand clenched the blanket so hard her knuckles whitened. "They are my children, too. This is my home as well as yours. I do not want them banished."

Eldrinson leaned over to her. "This has been the house of my family for centuries. It was my ancestors' house, my grandfather's house, my father's house, and now it is my house. This is my world and my land and I shall do as I please with it."

She gave him an unimpressed look. "If I remember correctly, Your Royal Possessiveness, inheritance of land goes through the female line here. To the wife, love. Me."

Eldrinson scowled. It irked him when she was right. "Nevertheless." He wasn't sure what to add to that. The mother usually left the land to the children, but it could be complicated.

"I am going to write Soz and Althor," she said.

He crossed his arms and refused to look at her.

"They will ask me how you are," she said.

He said nothing.

"They will tell me how much they miss you."

"You talk too much this morning," he said.

"They will tell me they love you."

Hai. That pierced like a sword. "Stop."

"Eldri, look at me."

He slanted a glance at her. She was tousled and sensual, her hair spilling over her body, her breasts straining against the flimsy nightdress, her nipples poking the cloth. He sighed and pulled her into his arms. "You are impossible," he grumbled against her neck.

She put her arms around him. "We will deal with this."

He spoke against her hair, his cheek pressed to hers. "I don't know how to deal with it. The ground is crumbling."

"Don't push them away."

He knew what she wanted to hear, that he would rescind his decree. He couldn't. It was hard enough with Althor, but at least his son had grown into a man strong and trained for war. Eldrinson knew, logically, that the skills a soldier needed for interstellar warfare were far different than what Althor had learned here. He even realized Soz could be well suited for them, that physical strength made little difference when they could augment their bodies, and machines did the fighting. But his heart couldn't acknowledge that truth.

"I can't bear to think of Soz out there," he said. "It's killing me."

Roca leaned back to look at him. "She's stronger than you know."

"She's my little girl."

"Not anymore."

He spoke softly. "The rest of the universe may see the formidable woman, but I can never forget how I held her in my arms when she was a baby."

"Althor, too."

"But he is a warrior! A man of power." He hesitated, confused. "I think."

"You think?"

"I don't know what to think," he grumbled. "My children don't seem to know whether they are men or women. Soz acts like a man. And Althor, well. Althor." He had a failure of imagination when it came to Althor's personal life.

Roca took his hands and held them in front of her body. "I ask only this, Eldri, that you think on what I've said. When you are ready, talk more with me."

He looked at their clasped hands. She hadn't asked for promises or retractions. Just that he talk to her. "Very well."

"Good."

He gave her a rueful look. "We should probably get out of bed, too."

She dimpled. "For now."

Eldrinson laughed, soothed by her presence. "For now."

Her smile faded. "You must talk to Shannon. He was upset last night, especially after you had the seizure."

"I will." The boy had grown more and more distant this last year, until Eldrinson no longer knew how to talk to him. But he would do his best.

After they dressed, they went down to the dining room where the cook put out breakfast every morning. Eldrinson didn't know what to expect when he faced his other children. He needed to reassure them, tell them he loved them, but he didn't want to upset them, either. He felt as if Soz and Althor had died, but they thought their brother and sister had only gone away.

The breakfast room wasn't large. A long table filled most of it, made from amber glasswood, warm and luminous. Glasswood paneled the walls in gold, with red accents. The counter along the far wall was set with blue dishes, cups, and utensils. Tanna, a young woman on the housekeeping staff, was setting several platters of food on the counter. She moved with efficiency, and her bright dress, blue and white with rosy ties, swirled around her knees.

Del and Chaniece were sitting at one end of the table picking at their breakfast, yellow bubbles in syrup. Aniece sat near them, her dark hair tousled, her gold eyes sleepy. She wasn't eating. Across the table, Denric slouched in a chair, staring at his plate of yellow bubbles. Next to him, Kelric devoured his meal with gusto, oblivious to the silence.

The children rose to their feet as Eldrinson and Roca entered through an archway in the long side of the room. Eldrinson nodded to them and they settled into their places again. Kelric went back to eating.

"Where is Shannon?" Eldrinson asked.

"I guess he overslept," Denric said.

Tanna looked up from her work. "I aired out his room earlier, Bard Eldrinson. I don't think he slept there last night."

Foreboding stirred in Eldrinson. He looked around at his children. "Have any of you seen him today?"

"No." Aniece poked at the bubbles on her plate. "Maybe he's with Moonglaze."

Eldrinson spun around and strode out of the room. By the time he reached the courtyard outside, he was running. He would know if harm had come to Shannon, surely he would know, and he felt no problems, but that only made him more uneasy. He should have been *more* aware of Shannon in the house if the boy was upset. But he felt nothing.

Eldrinson banged open the door of the stable. "Shannon?" He entered the dim interior, his boots crunching the crushed reeds scattered across the ground. Lyrine stirred in their stalls, pushing their heads over the doors and whistling at him. A stable boy at the other end of the building was pouring water from a bucket into a trough. He looked up as the Bard entered.

Eldrinson strode to Moonglaze's stall. "Shani, are you here?"

The stall was empty.

* * *

"We have no idea where to look." Roca stood by the counter in the breakfast room while Eldrinson paced back and forth. "How will you find him?"

"I'll find him." Eldrinson couldn't stay still. He had to repair this wound he had gouged in his family. He was aware of the other children, of Chaniece standing by the long table, resting one hand on its surface. Denric stood next to the her, tense and alert, and Aniece sat in her chair, her eyes large as she watched her father pace.

"I'll know where he is," Eldrinson said. "I'll feel it."

"He's gone north," Denric said. "To search for the Archers."

"Yes." Aniece spoke earnestly. "He'll go to the Blue Dale Mountains, Hoshpa."

"We can take the port flyer up there," Roca said. "Brad Tompkins is going to help. He's in contact with the orbital defense system."

"Yes. Take the flyer." Eldrinson stopped in front of her. "You search by air. I will search by ground."

"We should be able to pinpoint his location from the global positioning system in orbit."

"Will that really work?" Eldrinson found it hard to believe machines that floated above the sky could locate his son.

"It should. We'll let you know where to find him." She tilted her head toward Denric and Chaniece. "Don't go alone."

"Very well." He resumed pacing, unable to contain his agitation. The world had gone wrong and he didn't know how to make it right. Was he such a monster that he drove his children away? The thought made him wither inside.

"Let me come, too," Aniece said, her voice young and scared. "I can help." Her curls framed her worried face. Dark curls. She had inherited the color from Roca's mother. No one on Lyshriol had such hair except his two girls. Aniece. And Soz. *Soz.*

He sat in the chair next to Aniece, his heart aching at her innocent face. "I thank you for your offer, Nieci. But we must ride hard and go fast. Your lyrine couldn't keep up."

"You will find him, won't you?" she asked.

He took her small hand. "Yes. Certainly." For all that he had never been comfortable with the technology of his wife's people, right now he was immensely grateful for it. Without their help, he could spend years searching Dalvador, the Rillian Vales, Ryder's Lost Memory, and the Blue Dale Mountains.

A rustle came from the archway at the end of the long room. Turning, he saw his son Del striding toward them. Eldrinson rose to his feet.

Del stopped in front of him. "Brad is on his way."

"Good." Eldrinson had known Brad Tompkins for over three octets of years, from even before he had met Roca. Brad had taught him English. For years Eldrinson had thought "Brad" was a misspelling of the English word "Bard," and that the administrator represented a province called "Earth." He eventually realized Brad was a citizen of the Allied Worlds of Earth and that he had come here to administer the port back when Lyshriol didn't matter to anyone. Earth had relinquished its claim, giving Lyshriol to the Skolians, but Brad had stayed on at Eldrinson's request. In the years since, he had become a close friend of the family.

Tanna appeared in the entrance of the hall, escorting Brad. Tall and well built, the administrator had dark skin, a wide nose, and tightly curled black hair sprinkled with gray. He came toward Eldrinson, his gait as strong and steady now as it had been thirty years ago. Except for a few lines on his face, he had hardly aged. It astounded Eldrinson what these offworlders could do. They had even slowed his own aging.

He and Roca met Brad halfway down the hall. As soon as Eldrinson saw Brad's face, he knew they had more trouble. "What happened?"

Brad spoke grimly. "Someone stole a shroud from the port."

"Shroud?" Roca asked. "You mean the jammer?"

Brad nodded. "The one for individual travelers. Its range is limited, but it gives powerful camouflage, more than enough to hide one person."

Eldrinson silently swore. "Do you think Shannon took it?"

"It had to be someone who knew it was in a locker at the port," Brad said. "Shannon does. I taught him the combination to the locker when he worked at the port last year."

Eldrinson felt as if a weight had settled on him. "Does this mean you can't find him?" *Say it isn't true.* The problem with these advanced systems was that offworlders had equally advanced gadgets to counter them.

"With a jammer like that," Roca said, "Shannon could make himself virtually invisible."

"We can still search with the flyer," Brad said. "But you might have more luck on the ground. The jammer hides him from our sensors but it can't make him invisible to your sight."

"Chaniece and I will help," Del said.

Denric came over, with Aniece at his side. "I can ride with you as well."

Aniece looked from her parents to Brad. "Shannon wants to be an Archer."

Eldrinson knew she was right. "We'll ride toward the Blue Dales." He turned to Denric. "You and I can take an octet over the pass through the Backbone Mountains to the Rillian Vales." He glanced at Del and Chaniece, grateful his children could help. "You two take a party north in the Backbone, toward Castle Windward and the Blue Dale Mountains."

Roca spoke to Brad. "Is the flyer ready?"

"Ready and waiting. The *Ascendant* is sending a shuttle, too."

Eldrinson peered at him. "It's what?" He had thought the *Ascendant* was a vessel high above Lyshriol.

"The battle cruiser in the orbital defense system," Roca said. "Its shuttles can do planetary work."

"The flyer is better adapted to working in the atmosphere," Brad said, "but any help is good." He hesitated. "I don't know if this matters, but I noticed something odd yesterday."

"Odd?" Roca asked. "What do you mean?"

"A blip in the energy output of the electro-optic systems at the port. It happened about the time Althor's Jag took off."

Eldrinson tensed at the mention of the ship that had taken his children. "Was it the fighter?"

"The ship took off fine." Brad shrugged. "It might be nothing. Energy fluctuations often occur."

"What made you notice this one?" Roca asked.

"It seemed unusually sharp. But it vanished immediately."

Roca pushed her hand through her hair, disarraying it around her shoulders and arms. "A Jag has some high-powered systems. Many are classified, which means they might affect your systems in ways you can't prepare for."

"Will it affect our search?" Eldrinson asked.

"It shouldn't," Brad said.

Eldrinson spoke quietly. "I apologize if my son sabotaged your port."

"I doubt Shannon would know how," Denric said.

"I hope not," Roca said.

Aniece was watching her father's face. "You'll find him."

Eldrinson managed a smile. "Yes. We will." Despite his words, his heart felt heavy. Of all his sons, Shannon seemed most vulnerable. He could take care of himself, yes; he knew the land and mountains better than most people from the Dalvador Plains. But he was still a boy, no matter how much he considered himself a man.

More than anything, though, he feared Shannon didn't want to be found.

7

The Backbone

Soz woke up when Tahota and Althor switched seats, squeezing past each other in the cramped cabin. Soz had hoped they would let her sit as pilot for a while. If it had just been her and Althor, she might have convinced him, but with

Tahota here, she had to behave. She didn't want to start out at DMA by getting into trouble.

Althor lay back in the recliner. He was even more cramped than Tahota, with bulkheads curving over him. Yawning, Soz stretched her arms. Her seat readjusted, adapting to the stiffness it detected in her muscles.

Tahota was checking the heads-up display above her. "Sleep well?"

"Well enough," Soz said.

The colonel indicated a heavy lever, silver and black, near the pilot's seat. It glittered with smart-threads. "Know what that does?"

Soz had never seen the device on the Jag schematics she had dug up on the interstellar meshes. So she guessed. "It's manual control for navigation, in case something happens to the EI brain."

"Not for navigation. Weapons." Tahota tapped the lever and brought up a menu of small holos that floated parallel to the vertical column. She indicated a miniaturized display of statistics. "You can choose Annihilators, tau missiles, or MIRVs."

Soz's pulse leapt. She hadn't known Jags carried taus. That had to be secured information; it certainly wasn't in any public schematics. She studied the column. "Is the manual control as accurate as the EI?"

"Almost never," Tahota said. "But it's a good last resort."

Soz glanced at her. "Have you ever flown a Jag in combat?"

"Not a Jag. I piloted Starslammers, Thunderbolts, and Ram stealth tanks."

Whoa. "Those are some big ships."

The colonel's gaze glinted. "Yes."

Soz had no doubt she would never want to go against Tahota in battle. "Do you still fly?"

"Not anymore." A hint of disappointment showed on her face.

Based on her first impressions, Soz thought Tahota was wasted behind a desk, directing academy admissions. Perhaps Kurj was grooming her for a higher position.

A shiver went up Soz's back, the sort that came with her rare flashes of precognition. Her thoughts about the colonel evoked it. Why? The Kyle traits involved empathy and telepathy, abilities that resulted from an enhanced interaction of the brain waves of one person with another. The fields produced in the brain fell off rapidly with distance, so the people involved had to be close together. Even then, they usually only noticed the effects if both of them were psions, so that each had the specialized neural structures and transmitters that interpreted the fields created by neural impulses.

Given that precognition involved sensing future events rather than fields, it shouldn't have been among the Kyle traits. Yet in rare cases the strongest psions showed sparks of the ability. It came as a mood, an interaction yet to happen. Researchers believed it resulted from temporal uncertainties in spacetime, especially for a ship in inversion. Soz knew only that she suddenly had a vivid impression: someday Starjack Tahota would do a thing of great importance, something so dramatic it created spacetime ripples that reached her even now.

Then the sensation passed. Soz blinked at the colonel, wondering if she had imagined it all.

"Is something wrong?" Tahota asked.

"No." Embarrassed, Soz changed the subject. "Do you know when we will reach Diesha?"

"It shouldn't be long," Tahota said. "Jags accumulate fewer temporal errors during inversion than other ships. The time it takes us to reach Diesha should be roughly equivalent to our flight time during inversion, plus however long we travel at sublight." Her eyes took on the inward-directed quality of a pilot accessing her internal node. "Redstar says ETA in about one day from now."

"Redstar?" Soz asked. "Do you mean the Jag?"

"Its EI, actually."

Althor spoke from behind them. "Redstar uses that name for both itself and this ship."

Soz turned around. She had thought he was going to sleep. He grinned at her startled expression. "I know my ship."

That intrigued her. "Have you been flying it long?"

"A few months, since summer."

"That late?" Soz had thought cadets began working with their ships in their junior year.

"It's not unusual," Tahota said.

"It took me a while to find the right match." Althor shifted his long legs and settled himself as comfortably as was possible in the restricted recliner. "This is the third Jag I've worked with. I had trouble linking with the EI on the first. The second one didn't like me."

Soz smiled. "How can an EI not like you?"

"Hell if I know," he growled. "It said I was too aggressive."

Her laugh sputtered. "You're a fighter pilot! You're supposed to be aggressive."

Althor crossed his arms. "It claimed I made impetuous decisions based on an 'overly developed instinct to kill without exploring nonviolent options.'"

"What are you going to do, stop in the middle of a battle and say 'Excuse me, can we explore some options first, before we blast each other apart.'"

Althor smiled slightly. "That's how I felt."

Tahota spoke. "Of course in combat, you do whatever is necessary to survive. But a large percentage of battles are fought by uncrewed drones and controlled from standoff platforms. It makes sense that an EI would prefer to analyze its options first."

Althor gave her an incredulous look. "Fine for the EI. If someone blows it up, it can restart from a backup. I only have one life. I can't be reactivated from some copy."

A light on a front control panel lit up and cycled through red, yellow, and green. Althor suddenly laughed.

"What was that?" Soz asked.

His lips quirked upward. "Redstar says if an enemy ever tries to blow me apart, it will reactivate my brain from a copy."

A ship with a sense of humor? Soz could see why Althor was more compatible with this EI. When faced with his fear of dying, the other Jag decided he was too aggressive and this one made jokes to reassure him.

"I never realized how much the personality of your Jag could affect how you work with it," Soz said.

"It's crucial," Tahota said. "It's one of the only reasons senior cadets wash out of DMA. By that time, those who can't cut the academic, physical, or discipline requirements have left. But if you can't link with an EI, you can't fly a Jag."

"I had always assumed you just start flying," Soz said.

"We don't publicize the difficulties," Tahota said. "But if it were that easy, the link wouldn't be so tight nor the pilot-Jag hybrid so effective."

Soz slanted a look at her brother. "At least you found one that will put up with you."

He smirked. "Gods know what will happen when you try, Soz. All the EIs will run in terror."

"Ha, ha. Very funny." She glared for good measure, though her lips twitched upward. She looked forward to starting her studies.

If only this hadn't all come with so much loss.

Night Charger was a huge lyrine, dark violet, with strong legs and a beautifully proportioned body. As much as Eldrinson admired the animal, though, it felt strange to ride him. He had always taken Moonglaze.

He and Denric started out with Del and Chaniece. They brought two octets of men with them. Four extra lyrine carried ISC tents with all sorts of equipment, including comm devices, climate controls, medical syringes, and monitors, and food for both themselves and the lyrine. Denric had slung a laser carbine over his shoulder.

Eldrinson would have rather done without it all; he was happy to camp out by himself, without a tent, and what the blazes would Denric do with the carbine? Threaten Shannon into coming home? Hardly. But ISC insisted they take weapons and his doctor insisted he go with ISC supplies, especially after he had suffered such a serious seizure last night. He had no doubt Colonel Majda and her people were also tracking them from the redoubtable *Ascendant* up in orbit.

Their two groups soon parted, the twins going northward into the mountains with one octet of men while Eldrinson and Denric headed west with the other. They rode across the plains, and their group spread out, searching for signs that Shannon might have come this way. In the sky, Aldan hung to the side of Valdor, but soon the larger sun would eclipse his smaller brother. It took less than four hours for them to orbit each other.

For the octet, Eldrinson had chosen men he had ridden with during the war. They were farmers now, but today they had swords at their hips. He had worn his as well, though it seemed superfluous in a mission to bring home a runaway teenager. Still, they could never be certain whom they might encounter. Rillia lay beyond the mountains and had always been at peace with Dalvador, but they had long fought Tyroll, which lay farther to the west. The chance always existed of a skirmish with wandering Tyroll soldiers adrift after the war.

The ride invigorated Eldrinson. On another day, he would have loved the meditative quality of their journey. They traveled at an easy pace, slow enough to check the countryside for signs of Shannon.

The octet captain, a husky fellow named Jannor, rode up alongside him. His yellow and bronze hair tossed in the wind and his eyes gleamed with mirth. Eldrinson remembered a night on the Plains of Tyroll when he and Jannor had lost touch with the rest of the men. They had crouched in a ditch, stranded and freezing, while Tyroll soldiers patrolled the area. Delirious from a wound, Eldrinson had suffered a grand mal seizure. Jannor stayed at his side throughout the convulsion, tending him, protecting. He had been Eldrinson's strength that night, the light that helped him make it to dawn, when they finally escaped back to their own army.

"A fine morning you brought for us," Jannor said.

Eldrinson smiled. "I can't take credit for the weather."

His friend snorted. "You do for everything else." When Eldrinson laughed, Jannor held up his hands. "Wasn't it you who claimed he had brought the suns down from the sky to deliver him a fine wife and children?"

"I had perhaps drunk too much reed juice," Eldrinson admitted.

Denric was listening with undisguised fascination. "Really? I've never seen you drunk."

Eldrinson scowled at his son. "I wasn't drunk."

Jannor burst out laughing. "You were rolling nose to the stone."

Eldrinson made a rude noise and stared straight ahead. Then his mouth quirked upward. "It was good wine."

"Aye," Jannor said. "That it was."

They rode in silence for a while. Denric gradually pulled ahead, until Eldrinson and Jannor were riding by themselves.

The husky farmer spoke in a more serious voice. "We will find him."

Eldrinson pushed locks of blowing hair out of his eyes. "Yes. We will." He prayed it was true.

The Stained Glass Forest rose up out of the rippling plains before them. The tree trunks were columns of hollow glasswood, translucent, glistening in the sunlight. Smaller tubes branched out from them, and filmy, glistening disks hung from the branches, some a handspan in diameter, others smaller. Each tree was one color, but the forest had many hues: a red as vivid as the ruby necklaces that had come down to Eldrinson from his ancestors; blue like the glass bowls and goblets in the castle; an emerald so deep it brought to mind a lake high in the mountains, under the shade of a rock overhang; yellow and gold like the suns; and a violet as pure as Lyshrioli eyes.

They slowed down as they entered the forest, and Denric fell back to ride with Eldrinson again. As Jannor went on to check on the octet, his shoulder brushed a translucent red disk hanging from a branch. It inflated into a sphere and rose into the air, detaching from the tree. When Eldrinson passed it by, he poked at the sphere and it popped, spraying him with ruby glitter.

Denric smiled at his father, then nudged a yellow disk, making it inflate into a sphere that drifted away through the trees. Stained-glass light dappled in ever-changing patterns on his face and the curls that spilled down his neck.

"I've been thinking," Denric said. "About what Vyrl wants to do, attending the university as a virtual student."

"He seems happy with the idea," Eldrinson said. Vyrl had avoided his studies whenever possible in his youth, but since his marriage to Lily, he seemed to have buckled down.

"I can do that, too," Denric said. "I can study literature here in Dalvador just as well as if I went offworld to Parthonia."

His words made Eldrinson ache with an emotion warm and painful at the same time. He had already alienated three of his children; he didn't want to make another mistake. "You've dreamed about going away for years. I appreciate your offering to stay home, but I would never ask it." He had tried that with Soz and brought on a disaster. "Go to your university, son. Go see the sights." At least no one would be trying to kill a boy whose goal in life was to read books.

Denric's shoulders relaxed from a hunched position Eldrinson hadn't realized they had taken. They rode on in companionable silence.

After a while, Denric said, "I wish I understood Shannon."

"I also," Eldrinson said.

"I thought I did. But I had no idea he would leave like this." His forehead creased. "I knew he was lonely, that he felt out of place. We used to talk about it, but he's kept more to himself this past year. I should have said something, drawn him out more."

"It's not your fault, Denric." Eldrinson thought of the boy's restless spirit. "He wants to find his own kind."

"*We're* his kind." Denric looked up as a blue sphere drifted by them. He tapped it and the sphere deflated, trickling blue glitter. "The Blue Dale Archers don't exist. He's chasing a dream."

"We need to seek our dreams." With difficulty, Eldrinson added, "Even when they hurt us." Soz and Althor had gone after theirs knowing they might die. He couldn't bear the thought of his children in pain. Better not to think of it at all than to dwell on what might happen. An image of Kurj came to him, that giant with his implacable face. Yes, Eldrinson knew Kurj showed great honor to Althor and Soz by naming them as his heirs. But he could hate Kurj for that honor.

They came out of the forest into the foothills of the Backbone Mountains. Here the ground rolled in gentle swells, but ahead it rose more steeply, and beyond that it sheered up in sharp ridges. In the distance, the peaks rose stark against the sky, spindled like the bones of a gigantic skeleton.

They followed well-traveled paths here in the foothills. Except for stops to rest the lyrine, he hoped to ride as long as they had daylight, one octet of hours plus six more. With day and night the same length, they wouldn't need to sleep the entire night and could set off again before dawn.

It bemused Eldrinson that the length of day and night varied on many worlds. His children's tutors claimed night and day lasted the same amount of time here because Lyshriol had no axial tilt. Variations in weather came from atmospheric churning or changes in altitude. The scientists who studied Lyshriol seemed to find these qualities odd. They insisted it supported their theory that this planetary system was artificial, that astronomical engineers had moved Lyshriol into this orbit sometime in the past.

Even having visited other worlds, Eldrinson found it hard to imagine living in a place where the lengths of day and night changed or the climate varied greatly. Surely such an environment would be too chaotic for humans to survive! His children's tutors insisted otherwise, though, and so did Roca and all those scientists.

By the time they reached the mountains proper, the air had cooled. The lyrine picked their way up a well-worn path bordered by blue stones. Swaths of blue snow dusted the outcroppings on either side and crusts of darker blue ice edged the boulders.

Eventually they reached a branch in the path. One fork went north, veering sharply up into the vertebrae of the Backbone. Eldrinson reined in Night Charger and scrutinized the route. He spoke to Denric. "The Mirrored Cliffs are up there." Shannon loved the sheer cliffs, named for the reflective sheets of ice that covered them. "He might have gone that way."

"I can check," Denric said. "It would only take a few hours."

Eldrinson knew Roca would want Denric to stay with him if they split up the group. She always drew family around when she was worried, and his seizure last night had been a bad one. She was one of the few people who knew the truth: in his youth, his condition had been so severe, he hadn't expected to survive. For his first few octets of life, he had lived constrained by his seizures, in partial seclusion, watched over by his cousin Garlin, his only living kin. Each year it had grown worse.

Then the Skolians had come. Their doctors gave him nanomeds that patrolled his body and interacted with his brain to prevent seizures. Even with that, it had taken years before he genuinely believed he could live a normal life. Yet now he took it for granted. So did Denric. His son had no idea about his convulsion last night. Eldrinson didn't think the boy had ever seen him have one that serious. It wouldn't occur to Denric to worry.

Well, I feel fine now. He could take care of himself. Besides, he would have four men with him, and he had packed the air syringe. It had a comm embedded in its stock for emergencies; if necessary he could summon help even while giving himself medicine. Roca had wanted him to wear yet a second comm on his wrist, but Eldrinson had drawn the line there. He agreed to use one in the syringe because it was a reasonable precaution, however much he disliked it, but he wouldn't wear a bracelet as if he were a helpless child unable to care for himself.

He looked up the western trail he would take. It rose gradually to the Notch of the Backbone, a pass visible in the distance as a groove against the sky. Beyond that, the trail would descend the mountains until it reached the lush Rillian Vales. By the time Denric's group reached the Mirrored Cliffs in the north, Eldrinson could be through the Notch.

Denric could take the Mirrored Pass down into the wilds north of Rillia. Shannon might have gone either way; the Mirror trail would take him closer to the Blue Dale Mountains, but the Notch would get him into Rillia faster, where the riding was easier.

Eldrinson made his decision. "We can regroup tomorrow morning," he told Denric. "I'll meet you at the end of the path down from the Mirror."

"I think it's a good idea," Denric said. "We'll cover more area that way."

They divided up the supplies among their two groups, and Eldrinson sent the ISC equipment with Denric. He pulled up next to his son and indicated the glittering mammoth of a gun Denric had slung over his shoulder. "You take the carbine, too."

Denric hesitated. "Are you sure?"

"I wouldn't even know what to do with it." Eldrinson waved his hand at the northern trail, remembering how much Denric enjoyed trekking in the Backbone. "Go on. Get on with you."

Denric grinned, his face alight. "I will see you then!" He wheeled his lyrine around and headed up the trail with his men. Eldrinson sat astride Night Charger and smiled, watching him, this sunniest of his children.

Then he set off for Rillia.

Shannon rode through the glasswood forest of Ryder's Lost Memory, ducking his head under dusty clusters of bubbles. He had never ventured this far north. Ryder's Lost Memory went on in every direction, forever it seemed. He had ridden for over a day now, higher and higher, until the air turned icy. He wore a heavy shirt and double leggings, also a mech-jacket with climate controls, but even with the hood up, cold air cut past its warmth and tingled his cheeks. He hurt everywhere; his feet ached from his heavy boots, which he rarely wore; his legs ached from riding Moonglaze for so long; and his brain ached from lack of sleep.

Moonglaze had plodded through the night, then finally stopped and slept standing up, with Shannon draped over his back. Shannon awoke only when he started to fall. Dismayed at such treatment of his mount, he had tended the lyrine with solicitous care, grooming and feeding him, cleaning his hooves, and scraping glitter off his horns. Then they resumed their trudge northward through the forest.

Multicolored sparkles drifted everywhere, making him sneeze. Bubbles constantly rose from the trees and popped, spreading so much glitter that it covered his trail within minutes after he passed. He had lashed his bow and quiver to his travel bags to keep them from stabbing bubbles and showering him with the damnable stuff. He grimaced; enough covered him to make a tree grow on his clothes.

Shannon exhaled. Running away had made sense last night, after he took the jammer so no one could find him. Now, sagging with exhaustion and hunger, he no longer felt clear on the matter. He longed for a warm bed and a hot meal. Tree-bubbles weren't edible, and he had passed fewer and fewer shrubs with fruit, only the sparse and prickly spine-spheres. It could take days to reach the Blue Dale Mountains. He wasn't sure he would know when he had arrived. He doubted anyone put signs up to welcome visitors.

He slouched in his seat, the reins loose in his hands while Moonglaze picked the way. The rocky ground kept the trees from growing tall, but they remained thick on the landscape. Blue patches of old snow were melting on the ground or gathered in crooks of trees, all mixed into slush with the glitter.

Shannon leaned over Moonglaze's neck. "I'm so hungry." He tugged the reins, drawing the lyrine to a halt. Aching and stiff, he slid off the great animal, taking care not to jostle the travel packs, one of which held the jammer. He hit the ground in a thump that jarred his legs and torso. With a groan, he crumpled to the ground. Moonglaze whistled and pushed at him with his front horn, the larger of the two on his head.

Shannon sighed. "I'm so tired." He lay there, no longer able to avoid the effects of two days without any real sleep. He needed to see to Moon . . . shouldn't leave him . . .

Slumber covered his thoughts like a blanket. . . .

* * *

It was well into evening before Eldrinson and his men found a place to camp. They had easily made it through the Notch, but they weren't far enough down the mountains to reach Rillia before night. Instead they holed up in hollows under a series of overhangs that bordered the trail. Eldrinson wrapped himself in a rug from the travel sack he had slung across his war lyrine.

Night Charger crowded into the hollow, blocking the entrance, holding in the heat. With a grace extraordinary for his large size, he folded his legs under his body and settled in for the night. Lyrine often slept standing up, but this wasn't the first time Eldrinson's mount had helped keep him warm by resting on the ground. He could just see the sky through the open space above the animal's back.

The sounds of the others setting up bedrolls drifted to him in the vast silence of the mountains. He was glad they had sent the extra supplies with the other group; he had always enjoyed camping in the open, without all those gadgets and silly amenities Roca's people insisted they take. Climate-controlled tents with plumbing, for flaming sakes. Might as well stay home. In his youth, before the doctors had treated his epilepsy, camping had been a risk he almost never dared to take. Now, with his family and political responsibilities, he rarely had the chance to go off on his own. He enjoyed this trip, though he dearly regretted the circumstances that had led to the journey.

A head appeared in the twilit patch of sky visible above Night Charger's back. Jannor. He winked at Eldrinson. "What, no music?"

Eldrinson stretched his arms out of the rug into the icy air, then pulled them back. "Even if we had room to build a fire here, it's too cold to sit around one."

"Sing anyway," someone called from nearby.

Eldrinson waved amiably at Jannor. "Go get your tired old self comfortable."

"Tired! Old!" Jannor snorted. "I could haul your backside off a lyrine ten times straight in a tournament."

"Better watch out," Eldrinson said, "I may call your bluff."

"Jan, be quiet so he can sing," one of the other men said.

"You're lucky," Jannor told Eldrinson. "You're saved from ignominy by the demands of your audience."

Eldrinson laughed heartily. "Just in case you believe this notion about knocking me off a lyrine has merit, we will hold a tournament when we get back."

Jannor grinned. "Your challenge is accepted, O inglorious Bard."

"Inglorious!" Eldrinson said. "You will rue your words."

"I rue the day the two of you met," one of the men called from his nook under the cliff. "The one-upping hasn't stopped since."

"Sing, already!" another said.

Eldrinson smiled at his longtime friend. "Go on with you, Jannor. Leave me some silence so I can think of what to sing, inglorious or otherwise."

"Actually, otherwise," Jannor said. He disappeared quickly, before Eldrinson could catch him in the compliment.

Eldrinson sat considering his options. He didn't usually sing without warming up first, but he doubted they wanted to hear vocal exercises. He hummed a low note, testing his voice. It felt full and clear tonight, so he launched into a simple but popular ballad of the suns.

Valdor was born first,
Born first of the two;
First of the two sons,
First of the two suns;
But Aldan came soon after.

Rillia shot the gourd in the sky,
Pierced the gourd in the sky,
Pierced the gourd in two,
And made the moons,
The two true moons,
The Lavender and Blue Moons.

Rillia made the gift moons,
Two gifts for the gods,

The two sun gods,
Valdor and Aldan,
The brother suns.

Then he added a new verse of his own.

Delighted with his namesake,
With his namesake true,
Valdor smiled upon the Bard,
The Bard of Dalvador,
The Bard of the great sun gods.
Valdor sent his sister,
His incomparable sister,
His luminous sister goddess,
To wed the noble Valdoria Bard.

"Hey!" Jannor yelled. "That isn't part of the song."

Eldrinson laughed and continued. His voice was warming up, so he decided to stretch it a bit. He would begin in his deepest range, a low bass, and work through several octaves, taking the melody higher on each line, until he ended at the highest tenor notes.

The clouds had come to the ground,
Come to cover the land,
Cover the land in snow,
In blue, cold snow.
The clouds had come to the land,
But the suns melted the ice,
Melted the blue ice and snow,
Melted the cold ice of Lyshriol.

The world filled with warmth,
Filled with a golden warmth,
A lucid golden warmth.
It brought forth the people,
The Lyshrioli people,

> *It brought the golden people,*
> *Golden people into the light.*

He hit a note on "light" one octave above what Roca called middle C and let the word soar, holding it for as long as he had breath. Then, with a smirk, he dropped down two octaves and added a new verse.

> *The suns brought light to their kin,*
> *Golden light to their kin,*
> *Light to their namesake,*
> *Their namesake true:*
> *The glorious Valdoria Bard.*

A snort came from the hollow where Jannor had set up his bedroll, followed by a laugh from farther away. Eldrinson settled back, pleased with the song, pleased with the night, and pleased with the company. Then he thought of why they had come here and his pleasure faded.

The stars came out and wind whistled through the Backbone like spirits calling. Eldrinson thought of the ancient warrior Rillia, namesake of the Rillian Vales, who had shot his arrow into the night sky and cracked the Double Gourd into the Blue Moon and the Lavender Moon. He had long ago realized the tales of the Lyshriol gods and goddesses were probably myths. He wasn't sure about the sun gods, though. Roca shimmered like sunlight and she had come from the sky. Yes, he knew about Skolians and stars and astronomy. Even so. The suns might have sent Roca to him. Just to be safe, to make sure they didn't take her away again, he performed the proper rituals to them once in every octet of days, lighting guardian flames in bowls of oil set on a stone pedestal in the woods, with gem-bubbles floating in the oil.

He fished the air syringe out of his travel pack and made sure it was set for his medicine. Then he checked the comm in its handgrip. No messages. He pressed in Roca's private code and waited. A moment later, the syringe pinged and the holo of a tiny bell appeared in the air next to the miniaturized screen that wrapped around its grip. He flicked his finger through the bell.

"Eldri?" Roca's words came out of the comm. "Is that you?"

He warmed at her voice. "Greetings, Wife."

"How are you?" She sounded worried.

"I'm fine, love."

"How is Denric?"

"Sleeping, I think." It was a good guess. He had already decided not to mention they had split up. Denric might call her and tell her, or ISC might let her know, since they were keeping track of the searchers by satellite, but he didn't want to be the one to say it. She would worry too much. He loved her for caring about his health, but he had no need of coddling.

"Any word on Shannon?" he asked.

"Nothing, yet." She sounded tired. "We searched over the Backbone and Ryder's Lost Memory."

"Ah, love," he murmured. "He will be all right."

Her voice caught. "He's so young."

"I don't think he feels that way."

"We will find him."

Eldrinson knew she spoke as much to reassure herself as him. "Yes, we will. And he will be fine."

"Sleep well," she said.

"You also."

He flicked off the comm, then leaned against the rock wall and closed his eyes, as worn-out from worrying as from the long ride.

Eventually he slept. He dreamed that Brad Tompkins came to him, concerned about an inexplicable power surge in webs of energy that crisscrossed the planet. Eldrinson became aware of a hole of darkness. He would fall into it forever, suffocating, *suffocating.*

The power spiked.

Eldrinson woke with a start. Sweat was running down his neck despite the chill air. He shuddered, unable to clean out the sour memory of the dream. *It's only a nightmare.*

He wished it hadn't felt so real.

8

Beyond the Backbone

Shannon awóke with tinted daylight filtering over him, dim and cool. He rolled painfully onto his back, under a canopy of bubbles, some flat and others inflated, all clustered above him. A lyrine snuffled. Turning his head, he saw Moonglaze licking up the multicolored glitter that had gathered in drifts around the glasswood columns of the trees.

"Moon?" Shannon's voice didn't chime this morning. His words came out rough and rusty. By Rillia's arrow, he was hungry! He grabbed a handful of glitter and poured it into his mouth. It tasted like flinty dust and had almost no nutritional value, but it was better than starving. After several handfuls, though, he couldn't force any more down.

Shannon struggled to his feet and limped to Moonglaze, his legs stiff. His bladder-sack hung from his travel bags. He had to ration his water; he had no idea when he might find more up here. But he was so thirsty, he drained the sack before he realized he had finished.

Moonglaze pushed his nose against Shannon's shoulder.

"I know," Shannon said. "I could have planned this better." At least Moonglaze seemed in reasonably good shape.

As he tended the lyrine, he pondered his situation. He didn't like to analyze, but his reluctance to do so had landed him in this mess. If he turned back now, it would take a day to reach the outlying hills of Rillia, longer to find a village or farm. He hadn't seen any streams on his way here, which meant he probably wouldn't on his way back, either. Water had to be here somewhere; these trees couldn't survive without it. He could probably manage another day without more supplies, but much longer and he would be in trouble. The higher he went, the farther he was from assured food and water. If he continued for another day and couldn't replenish his supplies, he would be too far to make it back to Rillia in time.

Shannon didn't want to turn back. He hated giving up. Besides, people might be searching for him. If he went to Rillia, he could run into them. They would take him to Dalvador, where he had no place. They could call it epilepsy from now until the suns fell out of the sky, but he knew his behavior had invited demons to attack his father. His love for his family had kept him home when the urge to wander prodded him onward. Now he knew the truth: denying his nature only hurt the people he loved. It was time he found his own kind. If they didn't exist, he had to know. He *needed* the Blue Dales, even if he had to live there alone for the rest of his life.

"What do you think, Moon?" he asked. "Turn back or keep on?"

Moonglaze whistled at him.

"What, you think I can't find my way out of my own house?" He laughed amiably. "I might be better at it than you think." He motioned northward, where the forest grew even more densely, some of the glasswood trees close enough that a boy could touch both if he stretched out his arms. "You see the way those grow?"

Moonglaze watched him with one large, silver eye, his head sideways. Shannon motioned at a line of trees. "Those arcs all curve to the northeast. They do that when they're following runoff patterns. I'll bet you anything we'll find a lake or river that way."

The lyrine regarded him first with the one eye, then turned his head and watched him with the other. Then he snuffled.

Shannon laughed. "So be skeptical. I'll show you." He wasn't as certain of finding water as he claimed, but it seemed a good bet.

He mounted the lyrine and started off, following the arcs of trees, ducking his head to ride under their tubule branches. Dusty spheres floated through the forest and burst when they hit other trees, Shannon, or Moonglaze. The lyrine plodded through drifts of glitter. Shannon soon fell into a trance, brought on in part by fatigue, but more because he liked to stop thinking when he rode.

Gradually a burbling penetrated his daze. Water sounds. He didn't have to guide Moonglaze; the lyrine was already heading in that direction.

"Good Moon," he rasped. His voice had lost its lilt.

The trees soon thinned out. Then Moonglaze walked into a small hollow. Water trickled over a stone ledge about Shannon's height and gathered in a bowl formed by overlapping plates of rock, smooth and eroded, with long, narrow cracks. Trees grew around the tiny pool and on the ledge above it, mostly emerald and sapphire glasswood, though a few ruby trees poked their branches through the bubble foliage. A patch of lavender sky was visible above them, a deeper, more vivid hue than down in the plains.

Shannon jumped off Moonglaze even before the lyrine came to a stop. He dropped on his knees by the pool and scooped up handfuls of water. He drank so fast, he choked and almost vomited it up again. Coughing, he sat back on his haunches. He took a deep breath and wiped the back of his hand over his face, smearing his cheeks with more glitter. Then he drank more slowly and slaked his thirst.

Shannon rested by the pool, then washed himself and tended Moonglaze, cleaning away as much glitter and sweat as he could manage. Then he searched the hollow. He found a nest of puffle-wogs, small animals in yellow shells that fit the palm of his hand. He disliked killing them, but they were edible and even tasted good. He cracked their shells with his dagger and devoured his fill, relieved to appease his hunger. When he offered Moonglaze some puffles, the lyrine gobbled them up and snuffled a hearty approval. Shannon had read in one of his holobooks that horses only ate plants. Lyrine were much less picky; Moonglaze had no qualms about killing small animals for food.

After filling his bladder-sack with water and his travel

bags with puffles, Shannon swung up on Moonglaze and rode back into the forest, headed north. The ground slanted steeply but the trees were thinning out.

So he climbed farther into the mountains with no clue what he would find—if anything.

Sunlight on his face woke Eldrinson. He opened his eyes to a lavender sky framed by the rock overhang. Night Charger and several other horses stood a few paces away, nibbling at silver-blue reeds that sprouted around bluestone boulders by the trail. Jannor was holding a reed-hemp pouch for his lyrine while the animal drank.

Eldrinson crawled out and stood up, stretching his back, working out the kinks. Ah, yes. He inhaled deeply, filling his lungs with sweet, pure air. Two of his men were packing up their bedrolls and preparing to ride, and the fourth was cleaning his sword.

Jannor looked up at him. "So, sleepy head, you woke up."

Eldrinson ambled over to him. "A fine morning to you, too."

Jannor smiled and went back to tending his lyrine.

After greeting Night Charger and making sure all was well with him, Eldrinson took a trail cake from his bag and walked to the ledge beyond the cliffs where they had slept. The trail sloped steeply down from his feet, stark with gray and blue stone, but in the distance it leveled out into lush hills carpeted with silvery-green reeds. The Rillian Vales spread out beyond in a pretty haze of patchwork fields brightened by bubble crops in gem colors.

The five of them were soon on their way. As they rode, Eldrinson mulled over the past few days. In the clarity of this morning, everything looked different. He forced himself to admit the truth; he had pushed Soz and Althor away because he was denying how much he feared they would suffer or die far from home. It seemed impossible either of them would ever have a family or a life such as he knew. Perhaps he was simplistic in what he wished for them, but his family gave him joy. He wanted that for them, too.

He had been wrong to accuse Althor about Shannon.

Whatever confusing relationship those two had, Althor would treat his brother with honor. In his anger and fear, Eldrinson had spoken words he could never take back. What if Soz or Althor died or became prisoners of war? Their last memory of him would be the moment he banished them from their home.

Eldrinson knew what he had to do. First he would convince Shannon to come home or else make sure the boy was safely escorted to the Blue Dales. If Shannon's instincts drove him to the home of his ancestors, he had to go, but he was too young to do it alone, especially the way he had left, with no plans or preparation. He could end up injured, starving in some desolate place. Eldrinson had to make sure the youth had proper gear and riding companions.

After that, Eldrinson would return to Dalvador, contact Soz and Althor, and apologize. It wouldn't be easy; he had the same problems with their choices now as before. Nor did he like Kurj's influence over them. But he had sworn to himself even before they were born that he would love them unconditionally, always, forever. They were adults now, regardless of what Skolian law claimed. He had to accept their decisions even if he disagreed with them so vehemently that it made him ill.

The day was warming as they descended into the fertile hills. It would all be set right again. Soon.

The flyer rumbled overhead, its engines loud, which probably meant it was cruising at a low altitude. Shannon reined Moonglaze to a stop, hidden under the trees. He twisted around and twitched open his travel bag, which hung against the lyrine's side. Inside, lights glowed on the jammer, a chunk of equipment about the size of the hardened bagger-bubbles Shannon and his brothers used to play stub-ball. The lights were all green, which meant the jammer was operating as expected, hiding him from sensors.

The rumble faded. Shannon spurred Moonglaze onward and resumed his cautious journey. Unlike in the Backbone, he had no trail here to follow. The lyrine picked his way over fallen glasswood columns and around rocks half-buried in faded glitter and crushed bubbles. He kept going north, always higher into the mountains.

It was afternoon when Eldrinson and his men reached the Rillian Vales. Short, stubby reeds covered the rolling hills. The plants produced little fruit, but the scant bubbles they did grow were larger than the tiny reed-bubbles in Dalvador. Rather than iridescent in hue, these glimmered translucent blue. Barrel vines dotted the hills with big, robust bubbles, red, blue, and violet. The sky arched overhead, clear and vast, as lavender as the filmy spheres on water-flute plants. Night Charger trotted through the lovely countryside, his violet coat shimmering in the sunlight. Jannor rode at Eldrinson's side, but the other men ranged through the hills, always searching for clues that Shannon had come this way.

Eldrinson knew they would probably make the best time if they rode out of these foothills and didn't turn north until they reached the flatlands. Now they were descending into a secluded valley. Hills rose up on either side and cast shadows across the land, bringing a chill.

A flash to the north caught his attention. Several riders on stocky gray lyrine were approaching them. He slowed down, his hand dropping to the hilt of his sword. The peoples of Rillia and Dalvador had always been friendly, but it didn't hurt to be careful.

The group was an octet plus one, eight riders around an imposing figure on a dark lyrine. Two men came in front of the central man, two to his left, two to his right, and two behind. The formation suggested the central man commanded great respect. However, the octet fanned out as they approached Eldrinson and his four men. It disquieted him; for a friendly approach, they would remain with their leader. This maneuver had a long tradition in Dalvador, Rillia, Tyroll, possibly even among the Blue Dale Archers. It symbolized caution, perhaps a prelude to hostilities. Eldrinson couldn't see why these strangers would respond this way, unless they had mistaken him for someone else.

Few lyrine were as fast as Night Charger; the mounts his men rode didn't have the same speed. Nor did they know this territory. It was too late to run, anyway; the newcomers were surrounding them, hands on the hilts of their sheathed swords. His muscles tensing, Eldrinson reined Night Charger to a stop. Jannor and the others surrounded him, a four-point bulwark separating the Bard from the octet closing in on them. No one had made any overtly hostile moves. Yet.

Their leader rode forward on a mount as large as Night Charger. He was one of the tallest men Eldrinson had seen among his people, about the same height as his son Vyrl, who at six-foot-three towered over his friends and father. Men native to Lyshriol rarely grew so large. This person was clearly Rillian, however, with violet eyes and yellow hair streaked with lavender, worn in a shaggy mane to his shoulders. He held the reins with four-fingered, hinged hands.

The man's finely chiseled features hinted at an arrogance Eldrinson had never associated with people in Rillia, however. His men were rangier than most Rillians and darker in the wine-color of their hair. They could be from Tyroll.

The tall man reined to a stop. "Good morn."

"And to you," Eldrinson said warily.

The man looked them over. "You've come through the Backbone."

Eldrinson hesitated. The stranger spoke Trillian, the language of both Rillia and Dalvador, but it sounded wrong somehow. He couldn't pinpoint why. His instincts warned him against revealing their true purpose. "We're from Dalvador. We're headed to a wedding in the town of Rillia."

"Indeed." The stranger continued to appraise him.

Eldrinson suddenly realized why the man's speech bothered him. No vibrato. No lilt. When Lyshrioli women spoke, their voices chimed. For men, it was more of a rumble, a deep vibration. It happened several times a sentence, unless they deliberately suppressed it. Why this man would hold his back, Eldrinson didn't know, but given that a flat tone indicated wariness, fatigue, or hostility, he didn't like it.

More uneasy now, Eldrinson kept track of the other men

in his peripheral vision. They had gathered on all sides, blocking escape. If they wished to take his group prisoner, they could probably manage. But why would they do so? They looked neither poor nor desperate. By custom, the people of Rillia offered hospitality to visitors from Dalvador, and vice versa.

They didn't seem to recognize him. He didn't know if it would be to his advantage or disadvantage to reveal his identity as the Dalvador Bard, arguably its highest authority, though his people had few governmental hierarchies compared to the convoluted, arcane structures of his wife's people. His men would take their cue from him; if he didn't reveal his identity, they were unlikely to give it away.

Eldrinson spoke carefully. "A fine morn to ride."

"So it is." The man continued to study him, ignoring everyone else. Then he made an odd sound, almost inaudible, a groan. Eldrinson wasn't even sure he heard it. The stranger didn't look uncomfortable; he came across as relaxed, even blissful. Something was wrong here, very wrong. This man evoked his nightmare from last night, that terror of falling into blackness. The day no longer seemed bright nor the air warm.

Courtesy seemed advised. "Might I ask who I am speaking with?" Eldrinson asked.

"You might, my dear empath," the man said.

A chill went through Eldrinson. He was aware of Jannor at his side, edging his lyrine in closer. How did a complete stranger know he was an empath? He rarely if ever talked about it, even to his closest friends. It made people uneasy. He was both a telepath and an empath, and they feared it meant he knew all about their thoughts. He didn't; psions only picked up moods, and it didn't happen with regularity. Much more rarely, he might catch a surface thought if it was strong enough. Of his men here, he had told only Jannor, years ago. This stranger shouldn't have known.

Eldrinson didn't believe the man was Rillian. Too much didn't fit. Yes, he had the right appearance. But he had too many other differences. He didn't even try to hide them. It suggested he believed them to be natives who lacked enough knowledge about offworlders to suspect he came from elsewhere than Lyshriol. But how could a Skolian be here? A ship couldn't land without permission the Ruby Dynasty and clearance from the Skolian military. The orbital defenses prevented unauthorized visits, and he had heard nothing about permissions for someone such as this.

He thought of his syringe. ISC had provided him with an advanced model for this trip. Its warning systems could bring in help if he ran into trouble. He didn't even have to activate them; they monitored his condition and transmitted updates to ISC if they judged that he needed aid.

Eldrinson feigned ignorance. "I don't recognize this word, empath." He was aware of his men drawing closer around him.

"No matter." The false Rillian smiled, his assumption of superiority obvious. To his men, he said, "Our friend from Dalvador will come with us."

Eldrinson spoke quickly. "We must be on our way."

"People are expecting us," Jannor said. His lyrine stepped restlessly, causing Eldrinson's mount to shake its head and whistle.

"Then I expect they will wonder why you've vanished." The stranger spoke as if he didn't believe them—or didn't care. "Come. Let us go."

Eldrinson stayed put—and the strangers drew their swords, the blades whispering out of their tooled sheaths, glinting in the sun. He reached across to his right hip with his left hand and pulled his own sword, slow and easy, a demonstration rather than a threat. He heard his men pulling out their weapons, metal scraping on leather. This had become a challenge, still not overt hostilities, but close now. He couldn't imagine Rillians taking such a stance; this party had to be from Tyroll. He didn't dare let them know they had caught the Dalvador Bard. Avaril Valdoria led the Tyroll forces—Avaril, his cousin, who had coveted the title of Bard all his life.

Eldrinson narrowed his gaze at the false Rillian. "You fear us truly, that you need an octet of men to threaten five of us."

"I fear none," the man said. "Least of all an empath."

Eldrinson motioned at the challengers around them with bared swords. "Apparently enough to believe you need these."

The stranger laughed, a cold sound. "Your attempts to have my men disarm are transparent." He pulled on his reins, guiding his restless lyrine to turn around. Then he rode away, ignoring Eldrinson and his men, his back to them as he moved out of range. The stranger's octet remained in a circle around Eldrinson and his group. He sensed no pity in them; they would obey their leader even if that meant harming visitors from Dalvador.

Night Charger stamped under Eldrinson. Jannor and the other Dalvador riders were agitated as well. Their lyrine surged forward, then stepped back, constrained and restive, the five of them backed into a star formation, facing their eight opponents.

"Disarm," one of the Tyroll men said.

Eldrinson tried to read the man's impassive expression, but his features and eyes revealed nothing. He was simply doing his job. The riders sat on their mounts, Eldrinson and his men facing outward, the Tyroll warriors facing inward, all with swords drawn. One of the Tyroll men tossed his sword in a circle, flipping it neatly through the air and catching the hilt.

Jannor swore under his breath.

Eldrinson spoke in a low voice. "Looks like we'll get our tournament sooner than expected."

The man who had flipped his sword prodded his lyrine forward, moving with a contained energy that made Eldrinson think of a geyser ready to erupt. Night Charger snorted and lowered his head until his horns pointed at the approaching animal.

"Easy, Night," Eldrinson murmured, intent on the approaching Tyroll warrior. Sweat ran down his neck and soaked his shirt. He had no mail, no shield, no bow, arrows, or spear. He hadn't expected trouble; indeed, he should have no reason to worry. ISC ought to be keeping track of his actions. They were always telling him, when he chafed at their surveillance, that they had a duty to protect the Ruby consort. Roca stood second in line to the Ruby throne, after the pharaoh's firstborn son; someday Roca could conceivably become pharaoh. They watched her consort as stringently as they watched her. It wasn't just the syringe; they had put monitors in his body to alert them in emergencies.

Nothing had actually happened yet, so perhaps their alarms hadn't triggered, but surely they had ways to tell if he faced potentially mortal danger. It would do no good for them to arrive after this Tyroll person ran him through with a sword; he would be dead before they showed up. Yet he saw no sign they had concerns. Maybe Roca's people weren't as advanced as they insinuated when they subtly, or not so subtly, denigrated his "primitive" culture.

His concentration narrowed to the angular man coming at him and to a second closing in at an oblique angle. The first man lifted his hand, a gesture so slight that Eldrinson almost missed it—but the Tyroll octet responded, lunging at the Dalvador warriors.

Eldrinson had no time to think; he immediately parried a swing from the man who had given the signal. As they fought, the second warrior closed in, forcing him to defend against two of them at once. He was aware of Jannor at his right side, battling two other swordsmen. A lyrine's haunch crashed in Night Charger's hindquarters, staggering him—

One of his men died.

Eldrinson screamed as a sword lanced through the man's chest. His empath's mind felt it as clearly as if it had happened to him. After so many years as an empath, he had enough experience in combat to keep fighting, but this death caught him even more than most. In past battles, he had at least been prepared. Now he wavered and one of his opponents slashed his sword arm. With a grunt, Eldrinson struggled to recoup, to focus on his challengers.

Another of his men died.

"*NO*." Eldrinson strained to parry, but his blade felt as if it had doubled in weight. Blood ran down his left arm and soaked his shirt. One of his opponents raised his sword. Eldrinson tried to counter, but he couldn't move his injured arm fast enough. It felt too heavy—

A third man in his group died.

Eldrinson shouted in fury and heaved up his sword. It struck the blade of his attacker hard and the recoil vibrated along Eldrinson's arm to his shoulder. He felt nothing except a curious deadness in his arm. No pain.

Not yet.

His two opponents worked together with practiced efficiency, attacking from both sides. He was faster than either of them individually, but he couldn't keep up with his sword arm injured. One of the men whipped his blade toward Eldrinson, distracting his concentration. Eldrinson tried to block the thrust, but he only deflected it. His attacker's sword plunged toward his chest—

Another sword hit the blade of the Tyroll warrior and sent it flying. Eldrinson whipped his head around to see Jannor's triumphant grin. In that instant, one of Jannor's attackers slashed in close. In nightmarish slow motion, Eldrinson saw the sword slide into Jannor's chest, straight through his heart.

Jannor stared at him with a startled look, as if he didn't believe a pleasant morning's ride could end this way. Then slowly, so very slowly, he toppled from his lyrine. His dying moment shattered Eldrinson with more force even than the other deaths, as if his own heart broke open. He cried out, barely aware of a Tyroll warrior knocking his own blade from his hand. Warm liquid ran down his arm and dripped off his fingers. He raised his uninjured arm to defend his head, knowing a blade would slice down to hack him apart.

The blow never came.

After an eternity, Eldrinson lowered his arm. His injured limb hung by his side. He stared dully around. Four of the Tyroll men lay crumpled on the ground, unmoving—as did his four men. The other warriors had surrounded him. Bile rose in his throat and an ache spread through him that had nothing to do with his injury. He had brought these men to their deaths, men he had fought beside, fathers with families. And Jannor. His lifelong friend, dead, because of him. In the same way that the pain in his arm was finally registering, so the grief in his heart made itself known.

"Well fought," a languid voice said.

Eldrinson turned his head. The false Rillian sat on his giant lyrine a short distance away. He had a strange blissful expression and a look of possessive satisfaction that scared the hell out of Eldrinson.

"You should have killed me," Eldrinson said, his voice flat, with a hatred that gave it an intensity far beyond his usual timbre. Night Charger stepped nervously, ready to run. "For I'll never rest until I've exacted payment for what happened here."

"Indeed." The stranger seemed perversely gratified. "It does truly grieve you to lose these friends of yours."

Eldrinson said nothing.

One of the Tyroll men dismounted and picked up Eldrinson's sword. Gritting his teeth, Eldrinson held still while another man removed his sword belt. A third took the travel bags off Night Charger and draped them over his own mount.

The false Rillian rode over, surveying Eldrinson as if he were a valuable acquisition. His men took up formation around Eldrinson, creating a barrier between him and their leader, a coward either so confident of their abilities or so unconcerned for them that he had ridden away while they did battle.

"What do you want with me?" Eldrinson asked.

The man's gaze never wavered. "You please me."

Eldrinson had to make a conscious effort not to clench his jaw. "Does it please you to tell me your name?"

"I suppose. We will be together for some time."

Eldrinson knew otherwise. It couldn't be long before ISC

found him. This trespasser would be no match for the forces that protected Lyshriol.

Then the man said, "I am Vitarex Raziquon."

Eldrinson froze.

Raziquon.

It was a Trader Aristo name.

9

The Tent

Roca stared out the window by her copilot's seat, scanning the countryside below. Cultivated patches alternated with forests in a quilt of landscape. The holoscreens in the flyer would let her see the land up close, but she kept looking through the window as well, too agitated to stay still. The longer it took to find Shannon, the worse her apprehension. He had been gone two days now. He could be injured, lost, out of food or water. If only he would turn off the jammer. The orbital positioning system could pinpoint someone on the ground to within less than a centimeter. They also had the flyer and two other ISC shuttles searching. Why the blazes couldn't they break through the jamming field Shannon had set up? It was ISC equipment. Surely they knew how to neutralize their own gear.

"Still nothing," Brad said.

Roca turned to see him studying the screens in front of his pilot's seat. He indicated several drifting red blips where the Backbone Mountains met Ryder's Forest in the north. "Those are riders on lyrine."

Roca sat up straighter. "Could it be—" She stopped when she saw the glyphs flowing across the bottom of the screen, giving statistics from an implant in the body of one rider.

"That's Denric. The other four riders are probably half the octet that went with him and Eldri."

Brad's forehead furrowed. "I wonder why they're headed south."

"Eldri should be with him." She had felt uneasy all morning, though she wasn't certain why.

"They probably split up." Brad glanced at her. "They can cover more area that way."

Roca felt as taut as a drum pulled tight. "Eldri had a seizure last night, the worst in years."

Brad spoke quietly. "This is probably the worst stress he's experienced in years."

Even more than in war. Losing his children was worse to Eldri than going into battle. He could face armed men without flinching, but the thought of injury to his family devastated him. Even with that, last night had been extreme. She rarely discussed his condition with anyone: it was private. But Brad had known him even before her. He was one of the few people who had seen Eldri have seizures.

"This isn't the first time we've suffered family crises," Roca said. "He hasn't had an attack that severe in over a decade."

"Perhaps his treatment needs to be changed," Brad said.

"He sees the port doctor regularly." Roca shifted in her seat. "Eldri always downplays his health problems. It's his damn pride."

"Dr. Heathland would know if he was covering up."

"I suppose." Jase Heathland was the fifth doctor ISC had sent to Lyshriol to care for Eldrinson. They had finally found someone savvy enough to know when Eldri was avoiding the doctor and personable enough to put the Bard at ease. Her husband cooperated because he didn't want the seizures to return, but he loathed seeing doctors. Heathland was the only who could get past all that with him, and he took no guff from the royal consort. Eldri even seemed to like him.

Brad rubbed his chin as he examined the holomap. "Denric must have gone through the Mirrored Pass. If Shannon went that way, he could be a day's ride into Ryder's Forest now."

Roca's frustration welled. "We've been over Ryder's five times."

"We could do it a hundred times and miss him." Brad motioned at the mountains towering in the north, covered by an endless stained-glass sheen. "He could ride for days through that forest and never see the sky. Which means we won't see him unless he turns off that damn jammer."

Roca stared at the holomap, brooding. The peaks of Ryder's Lost Memory rose up, taller and taller. Beyond them, the Blue Dale Mountains reached even higher, blending into a haze, capped with blue snow. Above them, Aldan was a dark amber orb eclipsing the large gold disk of Valdor.

"He's there," Roca said. "In those mountains. I'm certain of it." She wished she could go back and redo her last conversation with Shannon. "I knew he was lonely, but I didn't think he was angry at us."

"It's hard to know." With a rueful wince, Brad added, "At his age, I drove my parents to distraction, always staying out late. I'd get so caught up in making gadgets, machines, whatnot, I'd forget the time." His voice gentled. "Shannon's reasons may have nothing to do with anger at you or your husband."

Roca recalled the scene in the courtyard with Althor. "People think empaths know exactly how other people feel. But that's not true. I could sense Shannon was upset but not the reason." Empathy was a curse as much as a gift. It hurt more to know a problem existed when she didn't understand why. She had learned at a young age to block moods. It was their only defense against the mental onslaught of other minds.

Shannon had fled it all, to the lonely northern mountains.

Eldrinson knelt by the pole in the tent, shifting position, easing the strain on his arms. One of Raziquon's men had pulled his wrists behind his back and tied them to the post, holding him tight against the violet glasswood column. He had tried every method he knew to free himself, with no success. The rope tightened and readjusted the knots every time he loosened them. Roca would call it a "smart-rope," a cable with some technology that gave it rudimentary intelligence.

He sagged against the pole, his head drooping forward. His arms ached so much, he had to bite the inside of his mouth to keep from groaning. Blood saturated the sleeve of his left arm from the wound he had taken. Although Vitarex's people had treated the gash, which wasn't deep, they had done nothing for the pain. But that paled next to his grief over the loss of his men. He couldn't comprehend how an Aristo had infiltrated an orbital system that ISC claimed was the best in the Imperialate. They were supposed to protect the Ruby Dynasty. How had one of the monsters fooled those purportedly matchless defenses? Eldrinson wanted to shout his disbelief, that an Aristo was loose and masquerading as a Rillian.

It had been hours since Vitarex and his men had reached this camp in a secluded valley far from any settled area, hidden in the wild country. They had traveled all day, always west. Every step took him farther from Shannon, who must have gone north. When Roca and Brad realized he had disappeared, they were unlikely to look for him here, but surely the satellites in orbit could find him.

The tent flap shifted, crinkling, and one of Vitarex's men entered. He glanced at Eldrinson, then quickly looked away. He went to a table across the tent and poured a glass of water from a red glasswood pitcher there. The blue liquid glimmered as it flowed into the red cup. Eldrinson's mouth suddenly felt parched, intensifying his discomfort. They had already given him water, but it wasn't enough.

"Ahh . . ." The exhalation came from the entrance.

Vitarex was standing just inside the entrance. The Aristo took a stool there and carried it up to within a few paces of Eldrinson. The Tyroll man gave him the water, then bowed and left the tent. Vitarex sat back, regarding his prisoner with curious arrogance as he idly held the goblet. Eldrinson met his gaze steadily. With hatred.

"You don't like me," Vitarex said. He sounded drugged.

Eldrinson didn't answer.

Vitarex shifted languages. "My presence exalts you."

Eldrinson froze. *Gods almighty.* Vitarex had spoken *Highton,* the language of the ruling Aristo caste. Eldrinson had learned it at the same time he learned Iotic and Skolian Flag, primarily because Kurj hadn't believed his stepfather could master any languages the royal family spoke. They all knew Highton, just as the Aristos probably all learned Iotic. Know your enemy.

Vitarex wasn't even trying to hide his heritage. Then again, why should he? Almost no one in Dalvador had ever heard Highton. Vitarex had no reason to assume otherwise of Eldrinson. At least he prayed not. Otherwise this monster would realize the truth, that he had caught a member of the Ruby Dynasty.

In the past, Eldrinson had always thought ISC was demented in the way they obsessively secured any and all images of him and kept them off the interstellar meshes. Now he was more grateful than he could ever say. Vitarex hadn't recognized him.

Thank Rillia he hadn't worn the ISC med bracelet and had sent Denric away with the offworld supplies. Or most of them. The syringe was in his travel bag. Vitarex's men had taken the bags, so they probably had it. The syringe resembled blue glasswood; he hoped they wouldn't bother Raziquon about an apparently harmless tube. Now if he could just find a way to get it without Vitarex knowing.

"You have no idea," the Aristo lord was saying in Rillian, his voice more normal now. "You empaths feed us."

"Us?" Eldrinson asked. Were there more Aristos here?

"You wouldn't understand." Vitarex waved his hand. "It is genetics. Magic, to you."

"What magic?" If he kept Vitarex talking, perhaps the intruder would let slip some clue about how he had infiltrated the Lyshriol defenses.

"It has to do with a brilliant man." Vitarex's words dripped condescension. "A confused, brilliant man. Hezahr Rhon."

"I don't know who you mean," Eldrinson lied. He had

learned the history from Roca. Centuries ago, Hezahr Rhon had established the Rhon project. He had two intents: to develop Rhon psions, the most powerful empaths and telepaths known; and to make them less vulnerable to the onslaught of emotions around them.

That noble goal had become the worst tragedy in history.

"Rhon was a geneticist," Vitarex said.

Eldrinson pretended ignorance. "A what?"

"Ah, well." He smiled benignly. "It is too complicated to explain."

Eldrinson gritted his teeth. "I'm not slow in the mind." He didn't have to fake his annoyance; he had plenty of practice dealing with Roca's people.

"So you can understand genetics, eh?" Vitarex's eyes glinted. "Rhon altered several of the mutated Kyle genes that create psions. Understand, Dalvador man?"

Eldrinson didn't answer.

Vitarex laughed. "I didn't think so. But I will tell you. Rhon intended to help empaths shield their minds against emotions. But instead he created the most exalted form of life ever known." He touched his chest. "Aristos."

Eldrinson snorted. "I see nothing exalted here."

Vitarex's expression hardened. With a deliberate motion, he slapped his prisoner across the face. Eldrinson grunted as his head turned and hit the pole behind him. His eyes watered and his vision blurred. It was several moments before he remembered to breathe; then he heaved in a shuddering gasp. As his vision cleared, Vitarex's face came into focus. The Aristo emanated bliss, from his half-closed eyes to his radiant expression. Eldrinson clenched his teeth.

Vitarex slowly opened his eyes. "It is pain, you see. Physical. Emotional. Any kind." His voice became almost inaudible. "It is transcendence."

Bile rose in Eldrinson's throat. He understood far better than Vitarex realized. Aristos were anti-empaths. When they detected pain from their victim, their brains protected them by shunting the signals to their pleasure centers. They called it transcendence. He had heard they sought it with obsessive cruelty, but until this moment he hadn't really understood what that meant.

"So you see," Vitarex murmured, "it is why I need you."

Eldrinson shook his head, then gulped as pain radiated out from where it had struck the pole. "You don't need me."

"But I do." He sighed now. "Empaths project their responses more strongly than other people. It heightens the effect. The stronger the empath, the more I transcend." He lifted his hand, palm up, as if offering Eldrinson a gift. "When you make it possible for me to reach that exaltation, it exalts you as well."

Eldrinson was too queasy to answer. Vitarex and his ilk might believe themselves more than human, they might even have built an empire based on that belief, but as far as he could tell, they were nothing more than sadists. For all that he had learned their history, it had never seemed real until this Highton lord sat before him, his face smooth with ecstasy while Eldrinson endured the pain in his body—and his heart. Those men who had ridden with him, fought with him, and died with him, they had wives, children, hopes. All gone now.

With Vitarex so close, Eldrinson felt that suffocating sense of cavity from his dream, the crushing darkness. In that place where most people had the capacity for compassion, the Aristo had nothing. Eldrinson teetered above that abyss, falling into its lightless void. His nausea surged. Vitarex had come for his family, the Ruby Dynasty. Each time the fear hit him, it struck with renewed force. Why else would the Traders go to the extremes it must have taken to infiltrate ISC defenses on a world that otherwise had nothing to offer a star-faring civilization? The Aristo surely had the backing of ESComm, or Eubian Space Command, the Trader military; it was the only way he could have infiltrated the defenses here.

"What are you thinking?" Vitarex asked. "Emotions flow across your face. Fear? Yes. But more, I think." He tilted his head. "What must it be like for you, eh? An empath on a world of mundane minds."

"I don't know what you are talking about," Eldrinson said.

"You must sense your differences."

"How would you know more about me than I do myself?" Over the years, Eldrinson had learned a great deal about his abilities, but if Vitarex believed him ignorant, he wasn't likely to suspect he had captured Roca Skolia's royal consort.

"I can feel the presence of an empath," Vitarex said. "Just being near you, I transcend at a low level."

Eldrinson clenched his fists behind his back. "What do you want with me?"

Vitarex settled himself on his stool, his boots braced against the hard-packed dirt. "I have bestowed a great honor on you."

"And what might that be?"

"I have decided to allow you to be my provider."

"That means nothing to me," he lied.

"My personal slave."

"You can't." It surprised Eldrinson how calm he sounded. "It is against the law."

"No matter."

"What makes you think my friends won't find you?" Eldrinson asked, curious in a morbid sort of way. "They are well armed and numerous."

Vitarex waved his hand. "I have means to hide. When I finish here, we shall leave." He smiled benevolently at Eldrinson. "You may come with me."

Like hell. "Finish what?"

"You come from the Dalvador Plains, yes?"

"That's right. I'm a farmer in Starlo Vale."

"Have you ever been to Dalvador? The capital?"

If Eldrinson hadn't already known Vitarex wasn't Rillian, that last sentence would have given it away. No one called the village of Dalvador a "capital." His people didn't even have the concept. The only reason he knew its meaning was because Roca had asked him a similar question several decades ago.

"I rarely travel," Eldrinson said.

Vitarex leaned closer. "Have you heard of Roca Skolia?"

Hearing his wife's name from this man filled him with anger. It took a great effort of will to appear unaffected. He *had* to respond like a farmer from Starlo, not the husband of the woman Vitarex dishonored merely by mentioning her name. "The wife of our Bard has a similar name."

Vitarex wet his lips. "Have you seen her?"

"The likes of me don't mingle with them." He hoped Vitarex knew too little about Lyshriol to recognize that lie. Social stratification didn't exist here. Everyone mingled. Eldrinson's children played with the other children in Dalvador. People came to him when they wanted a bard or judge, but they otherwise treated him like any other farmer. He was the closest the Dalvador Plains had to a leader, just as Lord Rillia was the closest they had to a king in all the settled lands, but they didn't think in terms of class. Any distance that developed between his family and his people came about because he had married a woman that the Lyshrioli believed descended from the sun gods. He knew about social classes from Roca's people, and he had heard Trader hierarchies were even more stratified. Vitarex wouldn't expect a low-level farmer to associate with the Ruby Dynasty.

"They say she is a great beauty," Vitarex mused.

Eldrinson bit the inside of his mouth to keep from responding.

Vitarex was watching him closely. "You have seen her, haven't you? You find her lovely, eh?" An oily smile spread across his face. "Tell me, farmer, do you covet her?"

"Go to hell," Eldrinson ground out.

Vitarex laughed. "Ah, well, I imagine many men want her." He stretched his arms. "I shall have her. Perhaps some of her daughters, too." He rubbed the back of his neck. "I suppose I could also take the men. They would fetch a high price."

Eldrinson had never hidden his emotions well, but he managed now, knowing the lives of his family could depend on his control. He *had* to hide his rage, lest he reveal himself to Vitarex. He didn't know which would be worse, if Vitarex captured another of his family or if the Aristo realized he already had a Rhon psion and escaped Lyshriol with him. It didn't seem possible Vitarex could take them away, but he shouldn't have managed to trespass here, either. The irony didn't escape Eldrinson, that he had demanded Soz stay at home so she would be safe, yet he was the one the Traders captured.

When he didn't respond, Vitarex yawned. "Intellect isn't one of your strong points, is it?"

Eldrinson spoke dryly. "Bravery isn't one of yours, is it?"

"I could execute someone for speaking to me with such insolence." Vitarex's voice was languid, probably deceptively so.

"The coward's solution." Eldrinson hoped he was gauging Vitarex as well as he thought; otherwise he might have just invited his own death.

"Is it now?" The Aristo smiled coldly. "Tell me, what are you trying to provoke me into doing?"

What indeed? Eldrinson needed a way to signal Roca and Brad. He couldn't achieve much tied up; but if he could get out into the open he might have a better chance.

"I've a proposition for you," Eldrinson said.

"Do you now?"

"Entertainment." He thought fast, making it up as he went along. "A sword competition. You've surely heard of them. Two men fight until one is disarmed or admits defeat. Winner takes on the next challenger. The rounds go on until only one is left." He lifted his chin. "Take a chance. Set me against your men."

"What a strange idea." Vitarex laughed. "You do intrigue me. Where I come from, providers have none of your spark."

"I can best any single fighter you have." The claim was bravado, given his injured arm, but he could probably manage a few bouts.

"Is that so?" Vitarex tilted his head. "Where would a farmer learn such skills?"

Eldrinson pretended astonishment. "You don't know?" Let this Aristo think he had just made a cultural mistake.

Vitarex flushed. "I asked a question. Answer it."

"I qualified to train for the army." Any boy with talent and discipline could learn swordplay in Dalvador. It did tend to be children of better-connected families, the closest they had to a highborn class, but it wasn't restricted. Boys came from all over the plains to train. Similarly, girls came to become Memories. The Lyshrioli were illiterate; they had no concept of written language. Memories were their depositories of knowledge.

"You won't defeat my men," Vitarex said. "I handpicked them for their expertise."

"Afraid I will win?"

The Aristo considered him. "What do you think you will get out of this?"

"The chance to move." He didn't have to act when he grimaced. "It hurts."

"I know," Vitarex murmured. "I can feel it from all over the camp." He stood up. "I will think on your suggestion." With that, he strode away, out of the tent, and set its entrance flap swinging.

Eldrinson exhaled. Vitarex was too confident, too sure of himself. He truly believed he could capture Roca, even more of the family, and take them from Lyshriol. Eldrinson had to stop him.

How, he had no idea.

10

HeadQuarters City

Diesha mesmerized Soz. Its tiny white sun glinted like a bright stud hammered into a pale blue sky. Near the horizon, the sky turned red from dust stirred into the air. The colors left her breathless. Despite the vast red deserts around the port, everything seemed *bluer* here than Lyshriol, even the sunlight itself, as if someone had put a blue filter over the red world.

ISC maintained the planet for military purposes. Althor had landed at the Red Mountain Starport on the edge of HeadQuarters City, or HQC, a major ISC command center. They had none of the holdups civilians endured in the commercial port outside the city; indeed, the personnel here expedited their arrival with efficiency and courtesy. A port official personally escorted them through customs and registration. It didn't hurt that their party included a Fleet colonel and J-Force pilot, even if Althor was still a cadet. Neither she nor Althor identified themselves as Ruby Dynasty. Even if they had been inclined to do so, which they weren't, Tahota advised against it. Ruby heirs revealed as little about themselves as possible.

Now they stood inside the terminal at a curved desk staffed by a person rather than an EI, a polite fellow in a blue uniform. The white Luminex desk glowed, and silvery mesh components glimmered in its surface. It all unsettled Soz; rather than the upholstered furniture and stained-glass hues of her home, everything here was streamlined and polished. The spacious room had two walls of polarized dichromesh glass that looked out over the teeming, geometric tarmacs of the starport and the towers of HQC beyond, sharp against the red sky. The blue carpet under Soz's feet rearranged its fibers every time they took a step. Probably it cleaned itself when no one was looking.

She was too light.

Her body had developed on Lyshriol, which had stronger gravity than there. Diesha made her light-headed, dizzy. She stumbled when she walked, mistiming her steps. Even just standing felt odd. The world didn't *pull* enough. When she handed the officer a mesh-card with her documents, her arm came up too fast and too high. Embarrassed, she lowered it to give him the card. He nodded with courtesy and clicked the plex square into a slot on his desk.

The air smelled strange. Here in the port, everything had a sterile scent. Dry. Parched. Lyshriol smelled so much more alive. Both worlds had been terraformed, with atmospheres agreeable to human life, but a wide variation existed within those parameters. Diesha had a lower oxygen content than Lyshriol. Although she didn't feel short of breath, she could tell the difference. Lyshrioli air tasted richer.

This place sounded odd, too. She had spent her life in a culture with no urbanization. Most people lived in rural areas or villages. The largest city, Rillia, had a population of only ten thousand. No machines. Her mother had introduced technology, yes, but it was discreet, blending with the natural ambience of Dalvador. They almost never heard engines or the hum of compressed air, only chirps and trills of the scant wildlife. Humming-flits rustled in the air; tin-beetles tapped on walls; swords clanked in the courtyard as boys trained. Those were the noises of life. Here in the climate-controlled port, HQC rumbled outside, and its surging power vibrated through her.

This wasn't her first trip offworld. She had traveled with her mother years ago on trips to Parthonia. Roca hadn't wanted to leave her small children while she attended Assembly. Before marrying Eldrinson, she had won election as a delegate and risen in its ranks until she became the Councilor for Foreign Affairs, a member of the powerful Inner Circle. Soz had grown up watching her mother as a political powerhouse in the gigantic, tiered amphitheater of the Assembly.

Some of Soz's siblings never traveled. As a toddler, Shannon had cried even when Roca took him into orbit. So she reluctantly left him home. Now they were grown and no longer went with their mother, except eight-year-old Kelric, who loved to travel. Soz had wanted to continue, but her father had discouraged it. She had never doubted he loved her, but that only made it hurt more when he rejected her dreams.

As Althor gave his mesh-card to the officer, Soz straightened her back. She had to stop brooding. She had made her choice and she would accept the consequences. She gazed out the polarized windows at Diesha, with its chrome glitters and parched sky.

The time had come to face her future.

* * *

The days blended into a haze for Shannon. If he thought about it, he remembered he had run away from home three days ago, but mostly he rode in a trance of hunger and thirst, dimly aware of the thinner air as he went higher into the mountains. His head throbbed. Trees up here were stunted, their colors dulled.

When Moonglaze whistled, Shannon surfaced from his daze. "Are you tired, Moon?"

The lyrine answered with a low sound, more an exhalation than a true whistle.

Shannon sighed. "Me, too." His stomach ached and his throat had gone dry, but he didn't want to give up. He reined in the lyrine among a cluster of trees and checked his bags to verify the jammer continued to work. He could turn it off, but he wasn't that desperate yet.

He slid off the lyrine and sagged against its side. Moonglaze bent his head around to nuzzle his shoulder. Shannon scratched the lyrine's neck where the hair grew in thick curls, and Moonglaze snuffled in appreciation.

"I wish we had more to eat than glitter." He was so sick of the stuff, just the thought made him nauseous. He had enjoyed the puffles yesterday morning, but they were long gone.

Shannon sank to the ground. He had no idea if he had reached the Blue Dale Mountains. He saw no dales and nothing looked blue except the snow crusted on the trees. This part of the country had even less wildlife than down in the plains. Although Dalvador had relatively few animals compared to what Shannon had read about other worlds, small creatures flitted through the air or scampered in the reeds. Whatever lived up here hid itself well. Too well.

"Moon," he said. His parched mouth didn't work well.

The lyrine snuffled.

"We might die of thirst and hunger."

Moonglaze looked down at him with one large eye.

"I could turn off the jammer." They might not be looking for him, given the trouble he had caused. They ought to just let him leave. He knew his parents, though; they would probably search even when they shouldn't.

Shannon lay on his back and gazed upward. Tree tubules crisscrossed above him, blue, green, deep red. In the plains, where trees grew tall and hale, their jeweled colors glowed. Here, they looked as tired as he felt. He had eaten almost nothing for two days. The sparse snow, saturated with glitter, did little to slake his thirst. He couldn't continue this way. If he turned back now, it would take three days to reach the Rillian Vales, maybe longer in his weakened state. The pool with the puffle-wogs was closer, but he wasn't sure he could find it again. Even if he turned off the jammer, he had no guarantee anyone would find him. With a surreal calm, he comprehended that he really could die.

"Moonglaze," he whispered. "We have to go back."

The lyrine edged closer. He surveyed Shannon with one silver eye, then turned his head and looked at him with the other eye. He whistled, high and urgent.

"I'm all right," Shannon said. "I'm not dying." At least, he didn't think so. He had a curious floating sense, as if his mind had detached from his body. He should get back on Moonglaze and search for that pool. The lyrine might find it; he had an amazing sense of direction, better even than Shannon, who took to the wilds with ease.

Shadows under the trees darkened. The suns would be sinking behind the mountains, always doing their orbital dance around each other. He contemplated their celestial mechanics until he no longer felt hungry. He was part of the fading sunlight.

His mind sailed over the mountains, leaving his body behind.

Vitarex reclined in a lounger in the tent, watching Eldrinson. His servants waited on him, a young man and woman, a married couple from a distant village. He didn't treat them like staff, though; he acted as if he owned them. They averted their eyes from Eldrinson when they passed him. His aching arms were still bound to the pole behind him, but he had managed to shift into a sitting position.

The woman set up a black lacquered stand next to Vitarex's lounger. The man poured wine into a goblet of green glasswood and set it on the stand. They bowed to Vitarex, an odd gesture Rillian people normally never used. The Aristo waved his hand, dismissing them, all the time watching his prisoner. They withdrew silently from the tent.

Eldrinson had a hard time concentrating; the ache in his arms and legs had worsened until he could hardly focus. He had spent over a day tied here. He could move a little, enough to stretch his legs, but that put more strain on his wrists.

Vitarex sipped his wine. He had that blissful look Eldrinson had come to hate this past day. One Lyshrioli day, three octets plus four hours; he counted the moments, knowing he was probably off in his estimate, but needing something, *anything*, to distract him from the pain.

"A sword," Vitarex said. "You may have a sword."

Eldrinson stared blankly at his tormentor. "What?"

"For the competition." Vitarex took another swallow of wine. "You may have a sword. And the clothes you are wearing."

"You want me to fight?"

"Yes, I think so." Vitarex smiled. "I will tell my men to go easy with you."

Hope sparked in Eldrinson. If he could get outside, he might have a chance to warn Brad and Roca or the ISC shuttle. "I'm stiff," he said. "I can hardly move. It won't be entertaining for you if I fall over."

"Perhaps." Vitarex tasted his wine. "Very well. I will have you freed now. The competition will take place this evening. You can have until then to recover your mobility."

Thank Rillia's Arrow. Eldrinson barely kept the gratitude from flooding his voice. "All right."

Vitarex's gaze hardened. "Understand me, empath. If you speak one word to anyone during the competition or give any indication that you are other than my honored guest, I will have you quartered alive and send your remains to whatever family you have. And when I am done with you, I will start on them."

Eldrinson didn't doubt he meant it. He wondered what rot-worm had spawned Vitarex. Apparently no one here except the young couple and Vitarex's bodyguards knew what the Aristo was doing to him. If the men in camp learned the truth, they might help him; to treat a Dalvador visitor in this manner would appall most any Rillian.

However, if these men followed Vitarex, they had sworn loyalty to him, possibly even by the Ritual of the Blade. Although the ceremony had become less common since the war ended five years ago, men continued to vie in competitions, keeping fit for any skirmishes they might end up fighting. They might support Vitarex even against a Bard. Or they might come from Tyroll. Vitarex's bodyguards had murdered Eldrinson's men with no provocation and no sign of remorse.

"I will say nothing," Eldrinson said.

"Good." Vitarex tapped his long finger against a gold leaf embedded in the lacquered stand. A bell chimed. A moment later, the young woman who served him entered and bowed.

Vitarex waved at Eldrinson. "Free him."

The woman nodded, her face composed, but Eldrinson sensed her disquiet. As she approached, her mood jumped out to him: distress at his pain, confusion about the situation, fear of Vitarex. From her whispered comments to her husband, Eldrinson knew she hesitated to refuse the Aristo. She and her husband had sworn fealty to him. They owed him their loyalty. And he paid well, in semiprecious stones; without that income, their family might starve and they would be unable to build a house where they could live instead of sleeping in the forest. It wasn't her nature to go back on an oath, nor did she want to endanger her family, but she was finding service to Vitarex miserable. Eldrinson's pain dismayed her.

She knelt by him, her violet eyes downcast, and fumbled with the ropes knotted around his wrists. He gritted his teeth as pain shot up his arms. She kept struggling with the knots until finally he groaned, his eyes tearing up from the agony. Her alarm washed over him. She was so upset, her hands shook.

Vitarex sighed.

The woman let go of the knots and turned to the Aristo. She spoke in a soft voice with no chimes at all. "I cannot free him, Lord Vitarex."

Lord? Eldrinson gritted his teeth. Only Bards carried the title "Lord," and he didn't believe for one instant Vitarex was a Bard. He might be a lord among Aristos, but if he insisted his staff call him "Lord" here in Rillia, he was putting himself on the same level as the Rillian Bard, a grave insult. True, Lord Rillia was a terrible singer, but no one ever mentioned that nor let it affect their respect for his leadership.

"How odd," Vitarex murmured, watching Eldrinson. "It seems your bonds don't want to come off."

Eldrinson knew the semi-intelligent ropes were resisting any attempt to loosen them. He met Vitarex's stare. "Coward."

"What was that?" Vitarex asked politely. "I didn't hear it."

Eldrinson regarded him steadily. "I said you are a coward. It is easy to torment a bound man."

The Aristo's eyes glinted. "You should learn more respect."

Eldrinson desired only to learn how many ways he could punch that superior look off Vitarex's face. He clenched his jaw and held back his words, lest the wrong ones come out and defeat his purpose. When he had control over his anger, he said, "I can't fight anyone tied up this way."

"I suppose not." Vitarex extended his long finger to the lacquered stand and tapped its scrolled border.

The cords around Eldrinson's arms fell away. He froze, expecting a trick. When nothing happened, he lowered his arms with great care. Pain stabbed his muscles anew, and he squeezed his eyes shut, struggling not to cry out. Vitarex was a fool to consider giving him a sword. With half a chance, he would turn it against the Aristo.

Eldrinson opened his eyes. The young woman was kneeling at his side. "Are you all right?" she asked.

"Enough!" Vitarex said. "Come here, girl."

The woman rose to her feet and went to stand before Vitarex, her hands folded before her body, her gaze averted. He considered her, his eyes narrowed, and for one sickening moment Eldrinson thought he intended to make her kneel. He felt the Aristo restrain the impulse and stay in his guise as a Lyshrioli man. Eldrinson doubted Vitarex realized how powerful an empath he had captured or he would have guarded his reactions better. Or perhaps he just couldn't fathom how an empath could read moods.

"Pour me some wine," Vitarex told her.

She bowed deeply to him. Then she crossed to a table where they kept the wines in bottles of vivid, stained-glass colors. Eldrinson began the laborious process of stretching out his legs. He wanted to groan as aches stabbed through his knees, but he barely even grunted. Damned if he would let Vitarex hear his discomfort.

The woman brought Vitarex his wine, a ruby-red liquid in a blue goblet. He idly waved his hand. She apparently understood the gesture, for she moved around and took up a position behind the lounger, standing, silent and waiting.

"So." The Aristo drank his wine as he watched Eldrinson. "Think you will be ready to fight this evening?"

"Yes." Eldrinson doubted that were true, but he didn't intend to give Vitarex any excuse to tie him up again.

"Ah, well." Vitarex rose languidly to his feet and stretched his arms. He turned to the woman, towering over her. "You will tend to his needs. See that he is fed and rested."

She nodded. "Yes, milord."

Eldrinson wanted to snort. Milord indeed. No one here used that title. He knew it only from Roca. Her people called him all sorts of strange things, including "Your Highness," as if he were in the mountains, "Your Majesty," which made him want to laugh, and "Milord," which perplexed him. Apparently he was "Your Highness" as Roca's consort and "Your Majesty" as the purported King of Skyfall. He had given up trying to make them stop and just answered to whatever they felt was appropriate.

After Vitarex left, the woman came back over and settled gracefully next to Eldrinson. "I'm sorry."

"It isn't your fault." This was his first chance to speak with her alone. Perhaps she would help him—

Eldrinson froze. *Ah, no.* An all too familiar queasiness spread through him. His fingers twitched. *Not now . . .*

". . . wrong!" The woman cried. "Please, what's wrong? Can't you hear me?"

"Wha—?" Dizziness rolled over Eldrinson in waves. He was disoriented, nauseated, confused. And so very tired.

After a moment his head cleared enough for him to think. The young woman was leaning over him, her face flushed and concerned. He must have experienced a seizure, a minor one he thought. He just blanked out during the small ones and stopped responding. He knew only because people told him; he never remembered the seizure himself, though he could feel it coming on. The small ones caused no real injury, but they served as a warning.

Apprehension swept over him. Gods, don't let it start again. It had been years since he had suffered any serious problems. The big seizures, the generalized tonic clonic attacks, had stopped altogether. He rarely even had the small ones. Yet in the past few days he had suffered one of each. Yes, he had been under strain, but this wasn't the first time. In the past, he had ridden to war, been injured and in pain, fought with adrenaline pumping, and had no attacks. The treatments for his epilepsy no longer seemed to be working as well.

Eldrinson spoke raggedly. "In my travel bags—there was a long tube . . . ?" He needed his air syringe.

"I don't know." She seemed close to tears. "A guard has your bags."

"Do you know which one?"

She shook her head. "I'm sorry, Goodman Shannar."

"Shannar?"

"This is not your name?"

He started to tell her, then stopped. *Eldrin* wasn't a common name, and people knew the Dalvador Bard was called the son of Eldrin. He said only, "You just surprised me. How did you know?"

"You spoke it in your sleep. I asked if it was your name and you said yes."

He suspected he had been having a nightmare about Shannon being hurt. Her misunderstanding protected him. Vitarex knew his prisoner might give a false name while he was awake, but people didn't lie in their sleep.

She indicated a pile of rugs across the tent. "Would you like to rest?"

Eldrinson nodded, grateful. He had hurt too much to sleep much, and when he did manage to doze, he dreamed of Shannon trudging through snow saturated with dusty glitter, plowing on and on, his hair tangled, his body gaunt. He didn't know if the nightmare came from his condition or if he had picked up his son's distress. Was Shannon wandering, lost and hungry, dying? The pain caused by that thought went far deeper than any ache in his body.

Surely they had found Shannon by now. ISC knew how to nullify a jammer field. They had done so the last time one of his sons absconded with one of the blasted things. Vyrl had "borrowed" a jammer when he ran off with Lily. A battle cruiser in orbit had finally penetrated the shroud it created, but that had taken over a day, more than long enough for the two young people to marry. ISC had improved the design since then, but surely they also improved their techniques for neutralizing it. They *had* to find Shannon. The boy was off in his own world too much to plan such a trip properly. He could end up lost or fallen down a cliff or starved.

As for himself, it frightened Eldrinson that no one had come for him. They had to know he was missing. Denric had expected to meet him yesterday and they were supposed to check in with Roca and Brad regularly. Was Denric all right? Foreboding grew within him. For Vitarex to remain undetected here, he needed equipment far more sophisticated than the small jammer Shannon had stolen. The Aristo's shroud probably covered a far wider area, possibly even extending into the mountains. ISC could counter their own equipment, but they had less knowledge of Aristo technology. And Shannon could be anywhere. If he was within range of Vitarex's shroud, ISC might not find the boy even if he turned off his jammer.

Eldrinson became aware someone had spoken. He realized his eyes had unfocused, blurring the room. He turned his attention outward to find the woman watching him with concern.

"Goodman?" she said. "Can you hear me?"

He shook his head, though he heard her now. He couldn't keep his body upright anymore. With a sigh he lay down on the carpet that covered the floor of the tent.

The woman rose and padded out of view. He closed his eyes, content to lie still, so relieved to stretch out that he could almost ignore how much he hurt. Her footsteps rustled as she returned, and she laid a rug over him, warming his body. He tried to thank her, but he didn't have enough energy to speak.

Eldrinson slipped into the welcoming oblivion of sleep.

11

Blue Dales

The Dieshan Military Academy had stood in the foothills of the Red Mountains for over two centuries. Desert bordered it to the north and south, and in the east the towers of HQ City lifted into the red sky. Soz and Althor strode up the wide, white walkway to the academy entrance, to those famous soaring arches supported by columns three stories high. Its crenellated watchtowers reminded Soz of home, though on Lyshriol they fought with bows and arrows instead of intelligent missiles and antimatter beams.

The stark white stone glittered, accented by black marble borders on the windows in the face of the building. The age and grandeur of the place felt tangible. She had seen it in holos, memorized every detail, read all she could, but none of that seemed real now. This was no holo. She had reached the academy.

Althor walked at her side dressed in his Jagernaut blacks, the trousers, pullover, and boots of their everyday uniform. The cadet's insignia flashed on his shoulders.

He caught her looking at him and grinned, his teeth a flash of white in his gold face. "So what do you think?"

"It's incredible." The words hardly did justice to what she felt. She paused as they reached the bottom of the stairs that led up to the colonnade. The steps stretched out on either side of them all the way down the building, white and brilliant in the harsh sunlight. Fifty people could have walked these stairs abreast. She and Althor started up, crossing a threshold that existed as much in her mind as in the real world.

They entered the academy through a massive pair of arched doors that swung slowly inward in response to Althor's slight push. Although the doors looked antique, wood and stone with no visible mechanism, they swung far too easily to be moving purely on their own momentum. Soz thought she heard the hum of an engine, but it was almost inaudible.

Inside, a few meters on the left, a woman in Jagernaut blacks stood behind a white console-podium. She was speaking with a young woman about Soz's age, taking ID it looked like. This was the second time Soz had noticed a human touch in the automated city, both cases dealing with military personnel. It bemused her; she had always thought of soldiers as the tougher side of humanity, making their way in less humanized, less hospitable areas than the loved ones they protected. That certainly described warfare on Lyshriol.

Here in HQC, though, the reverse seemed to be true; the more deeply involved a person was with the military, the more humanized their treatment. Perhaps it was an attempt to keep a balance, to account for the inhuman conditions of the war they fought. The definition of "less hospitable" changed in space, describing combat fought by machines at accelerations that would obliterate unprotected humans. Battles spread across vast areas of space and throughout the shadowy information universes created by the meshes that spanned the stars.

Althor waited with Soz behind a glowing white line to the left of the entrance. When the woman behind the console finished with the other girl, she sent her on into the building and motioned to Soz and Althor.

As Soz and Althor walked forward, Soz inhaled deeply. Even the air here seemed laden with history and tradition. Actually, it was rather dusty. She bit her lip. What if they had no records for her? Tahota said DMA had approved her admission, but in Soz's experience nothing ever happened among her mother's people without endless and onerous documentation, none of which she had even begun, let alone sent to Diesha.

When they reached the podium, the woman spoke briskly. "One at a time, please." She nodded to Soz. "You can wait behind the line."

"We're together," Althor said. It apparently wasn't a typical response, given the way the woman frowned at him. Before she could say more, he clicked a small disk out of his gauntlet and handed it to her.

With an impatient huff, the woman scowled at him. When he just met her gaze, she shook her head. But she did snap the disk into a slot on her console. The flat holoscreen in front of her glimmered and holos appeared, flowing through the air, going by at the wrong angle for Soz to make out details. They looked like hieroglyphics in Skolian Flag, a structured language developed as a common tongue by the many and varied peoples of the Imperialate. Then a set of more elegant glyphs appeared. Those she recognized: Iotic. It was spoken as a first language only by the noble Houses and Ruby Dynasty.

The woman stared at the holos, her mouth opening, her face flushed. When the display faded, she looked up again. Her frown had vanished. She spoke in a subdued voice. "You may proceed." She made no attempt to verify their identities. No questions, no checks, nothing.

Althor nodded, seeming subdued himself. He took the chip she handed to him and clicked it into his gauntlet. "Thank you." To Soz he said, "Come on. Let's go."

Soz wasn't sure what had just happened, but she doubted it was routine. She hurried to catch up with her long-legged brother as he strode out into a huge lobby. Its domed ceiling curved so far overhead, their entire house at Dalvador could have fit inside here, even its towers. Fluted columns bordered the lobby. White tiles patterned the floor, and also the insignia of the Skolian Imperialate in blue and gold, several meters across, the silhouette of an exploding sun within a circle.

"Wow." Soz gaped at the place as they walked. "It's even more impressive in real life."

"It's supposed to be." Although Althor laughed, his voice had an odd, edgy quality.

Soz stopped gawking. "What's wrong?"

"That disk had our identities on it." After a moment he added, "Including that we were Kurj's heirs."

Gods. "No wonder she let us through so fast."

"I don't want special consideration."

Soz agreed. Their dynastic family name was Skolia, but she wouldn't use it here. She would loathe having people believe she gained admission through nepotism rather than merit. No one would recognize the Valdoria name. "Don't tell anyone."

"I don't." He lifted his hands and then dropped them. "It doesn't help. He comes to the academy sometimes. As soon as we're together, everyone knows we're related."

Soz could see what he meant. It wasn't only that he and Kurj looked so much like each other, but also that they looked like no one else. Their kin ties were obvious. The same wasn't true in her case. She didn't resemble Kurj at all. Perhaps no one would guess the relation.

"Has it caused you problems?" she asked.

"People are more careful around me than they should be." He tapped his finger on his gauntlet. "I won't use that chip again."

"Neither will I."

Her brother grinned. "You can't. I have it." When she glared, he smirked. "I'm older, Soz. Got seniority."

She crossed her arms and turned her head away rather than deign to accept that answer.

Althor laughed. "You're too easy to bait."

"Pah."

"Soz, look."

Curious despite her intent to be aloof, she looked. An archway stood ahead of them, leading out of the lobby. "What about it?"

"That's where new cadets go."

A thrill went through her, followed by alarm. "Me."

"Yes." His teasing smile faded. "I have to use another entrance." He drew her to a stop. "From here on, you're on your own."

Suddenly she wasn't annoyed at him anymore. "Thank you for coming with me. And for being my support."

"I don't know, Soz." Although he tried to appear dour, mischief danced in his gaze. "DMA might not thank me, after you whip through here like an exploding antimatter plasma."

She laughed and grabbed him in a hug. He embraced her, laying his cheek on top of her head. They stood that way for several moments and then released each other.

Althor gave a self-conscious grin. "Good luck, eh?"

"You, too." She glanced toward her entrance, feeling as if an invisible cable were pulling her.

"Go on," Althor said. "I'll see you."

Softly she said, "And I you, my brother."

They went on then, each to their own doorway into the universe of ISC, the massive interstellar machine that someday one of them—and only one—would command.

* * *

"Come on. Drink." The voice ran over Shannon like liquid, with such a lilt and so many chimes, he barely understood the words. "Drink," it coaxed. Cool, smooth pottery touched his lips.

He tried to swallow. It didn't work. He tried again, and a trickle of water ran down his throat. Relief spread through him, and a certain satisfaction. Opening his eyes, he looked up into the silver irises of a man with a pale, almost translucent skin. White-gold hair framed the man's face. He looked like a—

Blue Dale Archer.

"Hai!" Shannon sat up with a jerk and knocked the man's arm. The glazed jug spun out of his grip, splattering water as it flipped through the air and thunked into a drift of old glitter.

"Ah, no!" Mortified, Shannon grabbed for the jug. Or tried to grab. His arm just barely lifted, sluggish and heavy, and then dropped back again. Dizziness swept over him and he swayed. Before he embarrassed himself by toppling over, though, someone grabbed him and eased him to the ground.

The man with the white-gold hair moved aside. Another took his place, exactly like the first, except he had longer hair, down to his waist. A third appeared, his face next to the second. He could almost have been a twin to the first two, except somehow he looked like a girl. He—she?—had a small nose and a fey quality about her face. Her eyes slanted upward, fringed with long lashes. The other two crouched behind her, studying him.

Shannon squinted at them all. He was fairly certain the first two were men, but they were smaller than he was and less muscled. For the first time in his life he experienced what his brothers must feel all the time, being larger, heavier, and less graceful than the people around him. It was an odd experience. Pleasant, though.

He tried once more to sit, struggling to pull himself upright. The Archers moved closer, nudging him back, pushing on his arms, his shoulders, his legs. It took all three of them to hold him down. Bewildered, he closed his eyes, too tired to fight. Then he opened them again. The Archers remained.

"You're real." Shannon's voice came out in a rasping whisper. He was lucky these people had found him; otherwise, he might have died. Except he had never believed in luck. He wet his lips and spoke again. "You've been following me, yes?"

They spoke among themselves in low tones, their melodic voices flowing over him like sparkling water. He barely understood their dialect, though he felt certain that if he could listen a little harder, a little longer, it would become clear. He tried sitting up yet again, and this time he resisted their attempts to stop him, even weakened as he was by lack of food and water. He picked up the blue-glazed jug and peered inside. It still had water. Holding it up, he turned a questioning look toward the Archers.

"Drink," the man with long hair said, his voice chiming.

Relieved, Shannon put the jug to his lips and tilted back his head. The water went down his throat smooth and cool, a blissful respite from his thirst. He drained every drop. When he finished, he lowered the jug and took a deep breath. His fascinated audience watched, kneeling around him, staring with their tilted silver eyes.

"My greetings," Shannon said. His voice cracked. He didn't know whether to laugh or cry. He had dreamed all his life of finding the Blue Dale Archers, but he had never believed it would happen. Yet here they were. Whether or not they would accept him was another question altogether.

The second man, the one with waist-length hair, spoke slowly. "Why are you here?"

"Searching for you," Shannon said.

"Why?" That came from the first man.

"To find my own kind."

"You are not one of us," the second man said.

"You are too big," the first one added.

The third Archer spoke. "Your eyes are wrong." She touched her eyelashes. "They glitter."

"They do?" That surprised Shannon. His siblings had metallic eyelashes, inherited from their mother; in comparison, his hardly glittered at all. Compared to these people, though, he supposed his were unusual.

"Is that why you hid from me?" Shannon asked. If he hadn't gone into a trance, making them think he was dying, he suspected they would have remained hidden.

"You are a stranger," the second Archer said.

The first one added another comment, but it sounded like a melody of chimes rather than words.

"Say again?" Shannon asked.

"You are not welcome here," the first man said.

That felt like an arrow into his gut. Shannon answered with difficulty. "I am not welcome among my people. If you refuse me, I have nowhere to go."

"You are exiled?" the woman asked.

"I caused my father to banish my brother." Shannon wanted to stop, but the truth needed telling. If they accepted him, it would be despite his shortcomings, not because he hid any wrongs he had done. "I left then."

They regarded him with unreadable faces. The long-haired man asked, "How did you cause your brother's exile?"

Shannon wasn't all that clear on it himself. "I went to talk with him one night."

They waited. The second Archer studied Shannon with what might have been a frown, though their faces were so ethereal it was hard to read their emotions. Nor could he sense their moods well; he hesitated to lower his mental barriers with strangers.

When it became clear Shannon would say no more, the long-haired Archer said, "Why did this lead to banishment?"

"I am unsure," Shannon admitted.

"Is your father a Blue Dale Archer?" the first asked.

"No. He is from Dalvador."

"Ah." The woman inclined her head. "The people of Dalvador and Rillia are odd." The others nodded, apparently accepting this as sufficient explanation for the behavior of Shannon's father.

The first Archer spoke too fast for Shannon to understand.

"Again?" Shannon asked.

The man spoke more slowly. "If your father is of Dalvador and your mother has eyelashes that glitter, why do you look like a big Archer?"

Shannon smiled. Big indeed. "One of my father's ancestors was an Archer."

"Who is your father?"

"The Bard of Dalvador."

A murmur went among them and they conferred together, their voices soft and lyrical. Shannon caught a few words, but they spoke too fast for him to pick up much.

Finally the first man said, "The Dalvador Bard is an important man. As his son, will you not be the next Bard?"

"I am the sixth son."

"Ah." They seemed satisfied with that answer. A second or even third son might entertain some prospects of inheriting a portion of his father's work or his mother's land, but a sixth was unlikely to receive much of anything.

"Have you a name?" the Archer with long hair asked.

He hesitated. "Shannon."

"Shannon." They murmured his name together.

He waited, uncertain. His family had never understood his hesitation to reveal his name, and he had difficulty articulating why. To give a name was an implicit appeal for acceptance, one neither casually offered nor taken.

The Archers sat watching him. Unease prickled Shannon. Then the first one said, "I am Tharon."

A man's name. Shannon inclined his head in greeting.

"I am Elarion," the long-haired Archer said.

Another man's name. Shannon nodded, disappointed, though he didn't analyze why.

"I am Varielle," the third said.

His pulse leapt. A woman. He suddenly felt shy.

"Can you shoot a bow?" Tharon asked.

"I have some small skill." Shannon had bested every one of his brothers, even his father, as well as all the other boys.

"Yet you have no bow," Elarion said.

Shannon blinked. Of course he had a bow. He had strapped it to his travel bags.

It finally struck him what was missing. Moonglaze. He looked around the woods, frantic. "Where is my mount?"

"It went in search of water, we think," Elarion said. "That is why we came to help."

"He guarded you for many hours," Varielle said in her musical voice. "He tried to awaken you. Finally he left."

Perhaps he had been in worse shape than he realized. "Do you know where he is now?"

Tharon answered. "We were not here when he left. We were hunting. When we returned, you were alone. We stayed to see if you would awake. When it became clear you would not, we awoke you."

Anger at himself sparked in Shannon. He should never have put Moonglaze in that dilemma, uncertain whether to stay with his rider or seek help. Had the lyrine headed back to the Rillian Vales? He wouldn't realize that Shannon would die long before he returned with aid.

A disturbing thought struck Shannon. A shattering thought. Moonglaze had the jammer. If he had left, then nothing hid Shannon now. Yet no one had come for him. His family had stopped searching. Or perhaps they had never begun. As much as he knew it was right and proper that they let him go, deep inside he had believed they would look for him. He had secretly thought they would want him back despite everything.

Just as suddenly, hope stirred. Perhaps he hadn't been free of the jammer long enough for anyone to find him. "How long since my lyrine left?"

"Two circles of the suns," Tharon answered.

His hope died. It took three and a half hours for the suns to complete an orbit. He had lain here for seven hours. If his parents had been searching with ISC help, which they surely would do, they could have located him in an hour without the jamming field to hide him. He could think of reasons it might have taken longer, but seven hours was too long to justify.

They weren't trying to find him.

Tears gathered in Shannon's eyes. He truly was exiled. The father he loved, the man he had looked up to all his life, who had loved him for so many years, would no longer see him. Why should the Dalvador Bard harbor a son who brought demons against his own father? It was right Shannon had gone, but nothing could stop his grief. The tears ran down his cheeks.

The Archers watched, their beautiful faces unreadable. Even so, it felt right, more bearable than the compassion his family would have shown when they had loved him. He would never recover from this. Perhaps someday he would learn how to bear the loss, but he couldn't see how right now.

"Come." Tharon extended his hand. "We must feed you."

Shannon grasped the offered hand and let them help him stand. When Varielle put her arm around his waist so he could lean on her, his heartbeat increased. She felt slight against him; for the first time in his life, he felt strong and large.

"You must recover your bow," she said. "A man cannot be an Archer without one."

Shannon bit his lip, unable to respond, caught with an emotion he didn't understand, both joy and sorrow all rolled together. He could neither call himself an Archer nor a man, having never used his bow except for practice or hunting for his own recreation, nor had he yet to enjoy his Night of Moons, the coming of age ritual for young men and women. Yet with her words, she accepted him into their group, however small it might be. He would become a Blue Dale Archer, one of a dying breed.

It was all he had left.

12

The Cliff

The academy dormitories were set in a quadrangle to the west of the main buildings and the training fields. The dorms where the cadets slept and ate were more modern than the academy proper. Soz entered hers through tall doors of dichromesh glass polarized to mute the intense sunlight. Inside, she walked down a spacious hall peering at her mesh-card. Directions scrolled on its surface, informing her to cross a white and chrome lobby, wherever that was. She looked up just in time to keep from running into a column with hologlyphs announcing the dinner menu tonight in the canteen.

She did see the lobby beyond it, though, an open area with displays of historical objects like ancient Jumbler guns or gauntlets worn a century ago by early starfighter pilots. After wandering through the lobby, she entered a common room with blue couches, white walls, and holo murals of the pale Dieshan sky, sometimes blue, sometimes hazy red. She kept going, squinting at the mesh-card, with a glance up every now and then to keep from running into unyielding objects. Beyond the common room, she entered a long hall with murals of the Dieshan desert that were darkening, their time of day apparently set to match the actual day outside.

She found the room she sought, fourth on the right.

Soz stood before the door, contemplating. Its mural showed the Redstone Cliffs in the mountains above the academy. She hesitated, uncertain what to expect inside. Had her roommates arrived yet? Supposedly DMA chose the four of them for compatibility, based on their psychological profiles. Even so. They had only her preliminary exams and those nebulous Assembly dossiers Colonel Tahota mentioned. Soz felt unprepared.

"You going to dawdle there all year?" a curious voice asked.

Soz spun around. A young man stood behind her, his dark hair curled haphazardly on his forehead, very nonregulation. He could wear it long enough to pull back in a queue, as she would do, or he could cut it short. Having it stick up in appealing curls wasn't in the rules. He had spoken Skolian Flag, the language they would all use here, since they came from so many disparate backgrounds.

She put her hand on her hip. "Who are you?"

He laughed, his dark eyes crinkling. "I'm the person who lives in that room you're staring at with such ferocity."

Her cheeks flamed. She had known male and female cadets might be assigned to the same rooms, but she hadn't expected it to happen to her. They all knew fraternization meant expulsion from the academy. Why the blazes they bunked men and women in the same quarters if they didn't want them to misbehave was beyond Soz. Well, almost beyond. In combat, they would have to live, fight, and survive together. They had to get used to it now, when their lives didn't depend on how well they dealt with the situation.

Even so. She couldn't live with this person. "You can't be my roommate."

"I might not survive it, eh?" His grin flashed. "With a glare like that, you could incinerate me."

Glare indeed. She hadn't even used a mild one. "You hardly look burnt."

"I have state-of-the-art heat shielding. You can land me from orbit and I won't burn up."

Soz couldn't help but laugh. "Sounds useful."

"It is." He offered his arm. "I'm Jazar Orand."

She extended her forearm, grasping his elbow while he grasped hers. "Soz," she said. "Soz Valdoria." She liked him, mainly because he wasn't cowed by her glare. It scared off most people in Dalvador, except Ari, but she was thoroughly fed up with Ari, who hadn't even said good-bye.

"Greetings, Soz." He indicated the door. "You do the honors."

"All right." She pressed her thumb into the lock and the door slid open with a hum. It relieved her that it responded; it would have been mortifying to go through all this with Jazar and then find out the door wasn't keyed to her fingerprints.

Soz walked into the room. Well. So. Two bunks stood against the blue wall next to her, one on top of the other, each covered with a dark green holo quilt, and another two stood against the opposite wall. Four desk-consoles took up most of what little space remained, top-notch stations of white Luminex, with screens, comms, displays, and flat areas where they could study. The outline of four narrow lockers showed in the wall to her right; to the left, the bathroom door stood ajar, revealing a tiny cubicle beyond. What caught Soz's attention most, though, was the room's sole holo mural, the brilliant image of a Jag fighter soaring above the Red Mountain starport.

She motioned at the mural. "That's gorgeous."

"Yeah." Jazar grimaced. "It makes up a little for the rest of the room."

"Ah, well." She walked inside. "We're the lowly novices. We should be grateful they let us sleep indoors."

"You mean you don't know?" His eyes gleamed as he followed her. "We have to camp out on the track every other night."

"You laugh now," Soz said darkly. "Just wait. If you get one demerit, they'll make you clean spamoozala." Even the best filters couldn't completely counter the endless plague of junk mesh-mail, commonly known as spam-ooze or just spamoozala. Sometimes humans had to get into the cesspools created by overworked EIs and clean out the junk.

"Gods." Jazar gave her a look of horror. "I know you five minutes and already you threaten me with a fate worse than—than catching the flu."

"No one catches the flu." That wasn't absolutely true, but it was so rare that she hardly recognized the word.

He flopped down on the lower bunk bed next to the door. "I caught a cold once."

Her mouth opened. "No." She went to the opposite bunk and sat on the lower bed. "You're making that up."

"It's true. It was a mutated strain. None of my nanomeds caught it."

"What was it like?"

"Miserable. The station master quarantined me in our house."

"Station master?" That intrigued her. "Where did you live?"

"Habitat. It's called Taurus-delta, after the Taurus star system. It orbits the fourth planet, a gas giant."

"You grew up on a space station?"

"That's right. This is my first time on a planet." He reddened. "I mean, I've visited planets before. I just never lived on one."

"It's my first time living away from home, too." The word clanged in her mind. Home. She no longer had a home.

Voices came from outside. They passed the room and went on down the hall.

"Are many other novices here yet?" Soz asked.

"More by the minute," Jazar said. "I was one of the only ones yesterday, but they've been pouring in today."

"Good." Remembering home dimmed Soz's mood. She felt oddly uneasy when she thought of her father. Something was wrong. It had to be an effect of the way she had left home. Except . . . somehow that explanation didn't seem right.

The voices were coming back this way. They resolved into two people speaking Skolian Flag, a man and a woman.

"The number must be wrong," the woman said. "Mine says you're one of my roommates and this is my room."

Jazar gave Soz a mock wide-eyed look and mouthed *Invasion!* Before she could reply, two people appeared in the doorway: a sturdy young man with black hair pulled into a queue at his neck, black eyes, and dark skin; and a lean young woman with a round face and a cap of red hair that wisped around her face in another nonregulation haircut. The girl carried a duffel over her shoulder.

"Heya," Soz said.

"Heya," Jazar said.

"Are you both assigned here?" the woman asked.

"Seems so," Jazar said.

"Looks like it," Soz said.

The four of them all regarded one another. Then the youth with the queue said, "I'm Obsidian."

The woman motioned at herself. "Grell."

Jazar grinned. "Hey! Greetings, Grelling. Obsidian. I'm Jaz."

Soz smiled. "I'm Soz."

"Heya, Soz, Jaz," Obsidian said.

Grell gave Jazar an unimpressed look. "No one calls me Grelling."

"Fair enough," Jazar said. "You two our roommates?"

"I think so." Obsidian lifted his mesh-card. "Someone put the wrong room on this. It already has four people."

Soz brought up the names of her roommates on her card. "Mine lists you, Grell, Jazar, and me."

Jazar was studying his. "Same here."

"Mine, too." Grell gave Jazar a wicked grin. "It says Grell, Obsidian, Sauscony, and Jazzing."

"Jazzing?" Jazar smirked. "You know, I learned some Earth languages. In English, 'jazzy' means you're ultra to the redshift."

"Only in your dreams," Grell said.

Soz blinked, baffled by the slang. She kept quiet about her lack of savvy; no need to give herself away as a rube.

Obsidian snapped his card. "I should go get this fixed." He nodded to them. "Jaz, Soz, Grell. Got it."

"See you," Soz said.

With a wave, Obsidian took off, striding out into the corridor.

Grell strolled inside and hefted her duffel on the bunk

above the one where Soz was sitting. "So you two are Soz and Jaz. Sounds like twins."

"Soz." Jazar nodded to her with approval. "Good name."

"Jaz." Soz flashed a grin. "I approve."

Grell snorted. "I'm glad you approve of each other."

"Soz approves of you, too," Jazar said.

"And why is that?" Grell asked.

Soz motioned at Jaz. "Because you gave him a hard time."

Grell laughed. "I'm good at that."

"I don't know about this," Jazar said. "If you're both always this hard on me, my life is going to be rough."

"It won't be that bad," Soz said. "You get to room with the two smartest novices in the entire class."

Jazar snorted. "Modest, too."

"The three smartest," Soz said, smiling.

They set about moving into their room then. Her duffel had already arrived; she found it stowed in one of the lockers. Soz left her comment about smart novices as a joke, but it was actually true. She and Obsidian had the top scores in the incoming class. This morning she had grown bored waiting for the EI Clerk of the Novices to complete her formal registration, so she had wandered into a public console room and entered the academy mesh. Splitting open its security had been easy, at least compared to hacking the ISC orbital defense mesh at home.

About once a year, Colonel Corey Majda, commander of the Lyshrioli orbital defenses, would send an irate message to Soz's parents, informing them that ISC security had caught their wayward daughter fooling with secured meshes again and would they please do something about this. For Soz, a grave session with her parents and Majda would follow, where they sternly admonished her misbehavior. Soz always tried to look contrite, but she never fooled anyone. Then they would make her go work at the starport, cleaning mechbots, which was truly vile.

She always behaved herself after such a session. All would be quiet for many octets of days. But the bug of curiosity would keep nibbling at her, and soon she would start poking the ISC systems again. In her childhood, it had all been a game, but more recently she had begun to see why it troubled Colonel Majda, as she better learned the significance of the ISC "toys." They were part of a system that protected an interstellar empire, and her ability to compromise them posed a threat to security. She made a suggestion to Majda then: *let* her infiltrate the system so they could patch the holes she found. To her surprise, both her parents and Majda considered it a good idea. Once they started using her as a consultant, everyone had been a lot happier.

Soz intended to behave at DMA, follow orders, walk a straight path. She wanted to do this right. In addition to her insatiable curiosity and constant urge to push boundaries, she also had a pronounced sense of right and wrong. She appreciated better now that splitting open mesh systems wasn't a game. Besides, she had heard the rumors; for all that DMA cadets were notorious for cracking academy webs, rumor also claimed the brass always caught and disciplined the offenders.

She really did intend to behave. But she hadn't been able to resist splitting open the academy mesh that had statistics for the incoming class. She learned a great deal, including that she and Obsidian had the highest scores on exams designed to measure eight types of intelligence: memory, pattern recognition, visual perception, mathematical, emotion, artistic, verbal, and creative. Most DMA cadets scored high in emotional intelligence: empaths generally did and every cadet had to be a strong empath. Soz had high scores in every category except artistic, which didn't surprise her. Obsidian easily topped her there, and to a lesser extent on the verbal. Words had never been her strong point, either. Grell and Jazar were top-notch as well. DMA had put four of its best novices together. She hoped it was done for compatibility and not to set them competing against each other.

Soz also discovered she wasn't the only novice with notations in her record for challenging authority. Many of the novices had individualist tendencies. Some might think it an odd trait to select for at a military academy, but it made sense to her. Jagernauts were the rebels of ISC, the pilots who faced the enemy solo, part of the unique Jag-pilot brain that neither machine nor human alone could match. Together, they formed a weapon unlike any other used in human warfare, one that relied on more independence, more sheer cussedness, than any other unit in ISC.

It was the only way they could survive.

Eldrinson tested the heft of his sword. He hinged his hand, folding it lengthwise so his four fingers could grip the hilt, two from either side. It felt the same as always; if Vitarex or his men had tampered with the weapon, he detected no hint of that. His sword arm felt stiff, but the gash hampered his movements less than he expected, at least so far.

He was grateful he hadn't brought his best weapon on this ride. Roca's people had constructed a sword for him, designing it from a nano-doped alloy according to his specifications. Vitarex would recognize it as forged from a technology far more advanced than anything available to a typical Lyshrioli native. It also had diamonds, sapphires, and amethysts in its hilt, a wealth no farmer would carry on his belt. Fortunately, he hadn't expected to need a sword. He had brought one more out of habit than anything else. This was a practice weapon, well forged by the blacksmith but obviously a product of this land and culture, with no adornment other than the spice-dragon's head molded into the hilt.

Vitarex didn't seem to notice his prisoner's clothes were of a finer cut than most farmers wore. Eldrinson suspected his rustic garments were so much rougher than the elegant apparel Vitarex associated with aristocracy, the Aristo couldn't distinguish the subtle differences between them and the clothes of a less well-appointed farmer.

Four men guarded Eldrinson, the surviving half the octet that had captured him two days ago. They brought him to a clearing in the endless forest that covered the wild lands northwest of Rillia. This camp had about fifty men, their tents scattered through the trees. Some wandered over as Eldrinson warmed up, and he kept discreet watch on them

the wind was blowing enough to deflect an arrow, but none of that mattered to a laser or projectile gun.

No matter. This remained his best choice. He kept climbing, praying death didn't tear him apart.

Except Vitarex didn't shoot him—he shot the bluff.

The entire cliff face exploded. Eldrinson flew backward amid a shower of debris and torn reeds. He had one curious moment where he soared peacefully through the air.

Then he hit the ground.

The world collapsed on him, rocks pounding his head and shoulders. A long stone slammed against his eyes and he screamed as the world went dark. Boulders crashed on his legs. He was lost in a swirl of noise, tumult, and pain.

Gradually the noise lessened. Pebbles showered over him, then nothing. Everything remained dark. He could hear nothing, feel nothing, move nothing. He floated. His mind rose into the sky. Looking down, he saw himself crumpled beneath the broken remains of the cliff. Large boulders covered his legs, and his body lay twisted at an odd angle relative to them. Other rocks had hit his face. He felt sympathy for the dying man below, but he didn't want to stay here. He drifted up . . .

A tall man knelt next to the body. Unease stirred in Eldrinson. That man—who was he? Vitarex. The Aristo pushed back his sleeve, revealing some sort of offworld gauntlet. He removed a slender tube and pressed it against the neck of the dying man . . .

". . . come on, *breathe*." Vitarex's voice came through the fog in Eldrinson's mind. "I order you to stay alive."

Eldrinson would have laughed at the absurdity if he hadn't been in such agony. It crashed in on him, all that pain in his legs and back. Unbearable, it was *unbearable*.

"Gods," Vitarex whispered. "Just how strong a psion are you?"

Other voices came to him, faint, hard to decipher. Someone pressed a cool object against his neck. It hissed like a syringe. He wanted to float back into the air, to escape this terrible pain, not only in his body, but also knowing that if his children were ever captured by Aristos, they could suffer this way. That knowledge was far worse than the agony in his legs.

Another hiss from the syringe. His thoughts grew hazy. He slipped into oblivion.

13

First Echo

An invisible fist punched Soz. She had been jogging with Jazar in an easy, steady rhythm. Now, suddenly, her legs buckled and she collapsed on the mountain trail. She felt as if someone had socked her in the stomach, on her legs, even in her eyes. The world went dark.

Jazar dropped down next to her. "Soz! Are you all right? What happened?"

Her sight slowly cleared. Bewildered, she sat up. Her legs hurt far more than they should have even if she had run for hours instead of just the thirty minutes she and Jazar had gone today. The pain receded, but she couldn't rid herself of a terrible foreboding.

"Something is wrong." She climbed to her feet and took off again, gritting her teeth against the ghosts of pain in her legs.

Jazar caught up with her. "Did you hurt yourself?"

Soz glowered at him. "Pah." She was hardly likely to hurt herself with the easy physical regime here.

He blinked. "Pah?"

Relenting, Soz said, "I'm fine." Now that she was getting the hang of running in this low gravity, it hardly strained her at all. So why had she fallen?

"Remind me never to make you angry," Jazar said.

"Why not?"

"When you glare at me like that, I think you'll flay me alive." Mischief flashed in his eyes. "Might be fun."

Soz smiled. "You'll never know." She wasn't up to bantering with him, though. Someone who mattered a great deal to her had just suffered. The strongest empath couldn't pick up emotions farther than a few kilometers away, and even that was rare; the fields produced by the brain fell off too rapidly from the body to detect much beyond a few hundred meters, and then only if the sender was a strong psion. As far as she knew, that narrowed the candidates for what she had sensed to Althor. Had he been hurt?

As they jogged, Soz spoke into her wrist comm. "Althor Valdoria." Jazar glanced at her, but said nothing.

After a few moments, the comm buzzed. Soz toggled receive.

Althor's voice came out of the mesh. "Heya, Soz."

"Heya. You okay?"

A pause. Then he said, "Sure. Why?"

She noticed his hesitation. "I just wondered."

"You sound out of breath."

"I am not," she answered, indignant. Jazar laughed.

"You running?" Althor said.

"That's right. Are you sure you didn't hurt your legs?"

Another pause. "How did you know they were bothering me?"

"I felt it."

"I guess I ran too hard yesterday. I had some muscle spasms." His voice lightened. "You going to feel sympathetic pangs for all my aches and twinges, sister dear?"

"I hope not," Soz grumbled. He sounded all right, tired certainly, but otherwise fine. "Take care of yourself."

He laughed amiably. "I will. See you at dinner."

"See you." Soz toggled off receive.

"What was that all about?" Jazar asked.

Soz shook her head. "Nothing, I guess." She didn't feel reassured but she didn't know why.

She and Jazar were running through the mountains above DMA, following a rocky trail packed hard from all the cadets who had run here. They came around a loop and headed down to the training fields. Other cadets were return-

ing from their morning run and gathering on a quadrangle
below. Soz and Jazar came down the last of the trail and
sprinted across the fields to the quadrangle. They joined the
other cadets, falling into formation, four lines of eight each,
a total of thirty-two novices. The spelling of their names in
Iotic glyphs determined their place in the pattern. Soz
thought it anachronistic that the academy used Iotic when
everyone spoke Flag, but it had always been that way here
and you never argued with tradition at DMA.

She took her place in the third line, next to Jazar. Grell
stood a few places farther down, watching them. She winked
and lifted her hand in greeting, then turned her attention forward before their instructors could catch them goofing off
during formation.

So they waited, the entire incoming class, every one of
them a psion, their group winnowed down to thirty-two out
of several thousand applicants. No one spoke; being caught
talking during roll call earned demerits, which could land
you webtech duty or cleaning up the onerous holo-junk messages that flooded the meshes.

Pale blue sky arched overhead and hot wind blew across
them. The spacious grounds extended all around, training
fields with synthetic surfaces that mimicked various types of
terrain and obstacle courses that went on for kilometers.
Here in the center, they stood in a plaza tiled with large
squares of white stone and the ubiquitous insignia of the
J-Force. Two of their instructors, Jagernaut Secondary Foxer
and Lieutenant Colonel Stone, were at the front of the formation, but Soz couldn't tell what they were doing. It looked
as if they were waiting for someone. She tried not to gawk.
The moods of the novices washed over her like an ocean,
their minds too well guarded for her to pick up anything specific, just a general sense of anticipation and intelligence.

They remained that way for a while, longer than usual,
enough that Soz grew restless. Why the holdup? She looked
to the side and saw the anomaly: someone was going down
the first line, hands clasped behind his back, his tan uniform
bright in the sunlight. A gold someone. A gold giant. The

blood drained from Soz's face. It was Kurj. He had come to see the new crop of novices.

He went along each line, pausing often to speak with cadets. When he reached the third line, he walked slowly along it, nodding to the novices as he passed. He towered over them, seven feet tall, a massive figure with metallic skin, hair, and eyes. He had lowered his inner eyelids, shielding his eyes with a gold barrier that appeared opaque, but which he could apparently see through just fine.

He stopped in front of Jazar. "Name?"

Jazar stood up straighter. "Jazar Orand, sir!"

"Where are you from, Cadet Orand?"

"Humberland Space Station, sir."

Kurj considered him. "How do you find living on a planet?"

"I like it, sir." Sweat ran down Jazar's face.

"Good." Kurj inclined his head. "Carry on, Cadet."

"Sir! Yes, sir." Relief flickered on Jazar's face that his first interaction with Skolia's mighty Imperator had been benign.

Kurj stepped over to Soz. She stood as tense as a board, her jaw clenched, her gaze directed forward. Kurj stood in front of her, his mind guarded much the way he guarded his eyes, with an opaque shield that revealed nothing.

"Name?" he asked.

"Sauscony Valdoria, sir." She didn't add the last name they shared. *Skolia.*

"So, Sauscony Valdoria." His face was unreadable. "You think you have what it takes to be a Jagernaut?"

"I've no doubt, sir." She felt strained with him, but at least this was better than their usual conversations. This one was supposed to be strained, whereas usually they were trying to behave like brother and sister.

"You have no doubt?" He looked her up and down as if he were measuring her worth. "Quite a boast."

Why these questions? He was the one who had sent Tahota to fetch her.

"What makes you so sure?" Kurj asked.

Soz paused, uncertain. He hadn't done this with any other novices. "I did well on my tests, sir."

"Did you now?"

"Yes, sir." He knew that.

He took his hands from behind his back and crossed his massive arms, straining the gold cloth of his uniform with his gigantic biceps. "You think tests make one damn bit of difference when your life is on the line? The Traders don't give a whistle in hell how fast you can solve math problems."

Soz looked straight ahead. When she realized he was waiting for a response, she said, "Yes, sir."

Everyone had gone eerily quiet. Their instructors, Foxer and Stone, were standing back. They exchanged glances and Foxer shook her head slightly, her forehead furrowed, making Soz wonder just how far off this was for typical behavior when Kurj viewed the novices.

Kurj was still watching her with that that grueling intensity. "You think you're ready to fight Traders?"

Soz didn't bristle. "No, sir."

"You think you're ready to be a Jagernaut."

"Yes, sir."

"Today?"

"No, sir."

"Why not?"

"I need to train." Soz wondered what he was after.

"That's right." He stood there, massive and uncompromising. "You aren't ready, Cadet Valdoria. Get cocky out in space and you die. You understand me?"

"Sir! Yes, sir." Perhaps he came down hard on her to toughen up his heir. It wasn't necessary. She knew she had a lot to learn. She had never doubted that. She looked forward to proving herself.

Kurj finally went on to the next cadet. Soz remained still until he had gone a ways down the linc. Then she let out a breath. She glanced at Jazar, and he mouthed *gods almighty*.

No kidding, Soz thought. She wondered if Kurj had greeted Althor that way when her brother first showed up at the academy.

After Kurj finished meeting the novices, he moved off to one side with Foxer and Stone. Soz had looked up the bios of all their instructors. Foxer was a former Jagernaut pilot. She had graduated from DMA thirty-eight years ago, taking her commission as a Jagernaut Quaternary, the same rank Althor and his classmates would have when they graduated this year. After ten years, Foxer had advanced to Tertiary. Twelve years later she received her promotion to Secondary, among the highest ranks in ISC. Most Jagernauts retired as Quaternaries or Tertiaries—those who survived. Only a few stuck it out to become Secondaries. Almost no Jagernaut Primaries existed, a rank roughly equivalent to an admiral in the Imperial Fleet or a general in the Pharaoh's Army.

Kurj had been a Primary before he became Imperator.

Dayamar Stone wasn't a J-Force officer, but a lieutenant colonel in the Advance Services Corps. The ASC had begun on the world Raylicon as naval units that went ashore as advance scouts or foot soldiers. When the people of Raylicon regained air and space travel, roughly four centuries ago, the ASC became an independent interstellar force, the advance scouts for planetary landings. DMA commissioned Jagernauts, but it drew its faculty from all the ISC services, including the Pharaoh's Army, Fleet, and ASC. Jagernauts often acted as defenders, escorts, or commandos for the other branches of ISC and were expected to develop familiarity with all of them.

Kurj, Stone, and Foxer stood a distance away from the novices, conferring about saints only knew what. Finally they came back, and Kurj went to stand before the front line of cadets. Soz wondered what was up. A trickle of sweat ran down her neck and soaked into the collar of her jumpsuit, which lacked climate controls and any other comforts that might have made life easier.

Kurj stood in front of Obsidian and spoke. Obsidian answered with what sounded like "Sir! Yes, sir!" Soz couldn't tell for certain what he said from so far away, but given that they spent all day long responding with those words, it was a good guess. When Obsidian set off jogging toward one of the training courses, Soz understood; they were to do demonstrations for the Imperator.

Obsidian ran hard around the oval track and jumped the various gates, bars, barrels, and other obstacles set along the way. He tended to slow down between the gates, but he made reasonably good time. When he finished, he jogged back to his place in line. Kurj spoke to him a moment and Obsidian drew himself up straighter, pride on his chiseled face. Soz would have to ask him tonight what Kurj had said. From Obsidian's response, she gathered it had been positive.

It went that way over the next half an hour or so, Foxer or Stone walking with Kurj down the lines. The Imperator stopped often, sometimes at their suggestion, other times on his own, and called on cadets to demonstrate their abilities on the training fields. Finally he reached the third line. Soz stared straight ahead, but she could see him in her side vision. He was headed toward either her or Jazar. Closer. Closer, now—and he passed Jazar. Damn.

Kurj stopped in front of her, with Stone on one side of him and Foxer on the other. The opaque shields of his inner lids covered his eyes.

"So," he said. "The cocky cadet."

She waited for him to ask a question.

Kurj motioned toward an obstacle course about half a kilometer away on a southern edge of the DMA grounds. "Think you can run that one? The Echo?"

Soz peered across the fields. She hadn't tried the Echo, but she knew about it, having read everything she could find on these fields during her minuscule free time when she wasn't studying or training. It was a difficult course, one that required skills her class hadn't tackled yet. To do it well, she needed the physical augmentation that cadets received their third year at DMA. She wasn't sure if she could finish the course, but she didn't want to lose face in front of Kurj or her classmates.

"I can give it a good try, sir," she said.

"A good try." His voice had an edge. "Is that what you will do in combat, Cadet Valdoria? Give it a good try?"

Soz tried not to stiffen. "I'll do my best in all situations, sir."

"Good. Go." Kurj motioned toward the course. "Show me."

"Sir! Yes, sir." Soz took off, jogging toward the course.

"Cadet." Kurj's voice rumbled behind her.

Soz swung around, wondering if she had violated some rule. She didn't think so. Every other cadet had responded in the same way when Kurj sent them to run a course.

Her brother was watching her with a closed expression.

"Yes, sir?" Soz asked.

"I want you to run the course in eight minutes."

What? Soz stared at him. The record time for that course was over nine minutes, and that by a senior who had spent four years training on it. No way could she come close to that record, let alone beat it by more than a minute, especially given her unfamiliarity with the gravity on this planet. Yes, she could run now without mistiming her steps or stumbling, but jogging a mountain trail and executing the Echo were two very different matters.

Secondary Foxer started to speak, but Kurj held up his hand, stopping her. His posture, body language, facial expression—nothing showed any sign of his relenting. "Well, Cadet?" he asked Soz.

What could she say? "I'll do my best, sir."

"See that you do." His voice brooked no excuses. "I hope your best is good enough."

"Sir! Yes, sir." Soz waited a moment, but he said no more. So she set off toward the Echo. Eight minutes. Hell, maybe he wanted her to create a few new universes, too. And she had feared he would show her special consideration. Right.

At least she felt good now, her muscles warm from her workout this morning, her body healthy and fit. She veered toward the entrance to the Echo, a simple dirt path. As she reached it, she started her wrist timer. From her research, she knew the path hid numerous sensors that would evaluate her stride, weight, pulse, brain waves, and any other data it could glean as she ran along its length.

Soz didn't run down the path. Instead she went along the narrow bar that bordered it, moving fast to keep her balance on the precariously curved surface. The less the Echo knew about her, the less effective its obstacles. It could still glean information with her running along the bar, but it wouldn't be as accurate. Every small advantage she gained would help.

A vaulting horse blocked the end of the path. Soz jumped back onto the path and ran hard. She leapt into a vault, her palms hitting the horse as she flipped over it like a gymnast. It was an awkward flip. She hit the edge of the path when she landed and tripped, losing time. Then she caught her balance and sprinted for the scaffolding, a multistory structure of metal struts that resembled the climbing gyms her father had built for her when she had been a small girl.

At the thought of her father, Soz felt dizzy. Her sight clouded over until she couldn't see. She had tried these past days to push away thoughts about her exile; now, it hit hard.

As her sight cleared, she ran harder, hit with a drive more intense even than her usual determination. She *had* to master this course, every course at DMA, every demand they threw at her, so she could go out and defend her family against the Traders. Why it hit her so hard *now,* she didn't know, but it pushed her to sprint faster than she would normally have done this early in a course.

Soz reached the scaffolding and jumped up, grabbing a bar. It immediately bent, trying to throw her off, the mesh components in its structure acting with rudimentary intelligence. She compensated, grabbing new bars as the ones she held sagged, vibrated, and jerked. She made it to the top, but when she tried to cross the scaffolding, the bars shook until she lost her balance and slid down among them, into the lively center of the structure. They bent and rebounded like kinetic echoes, throwing her this way and that. Soz swore, grasping at the chaotic pipes. The harder she tried to regain her grip, the more entangled she became.

Pah. She tried the opposite approach and let her body go limp. The scaffolding quieted a bit, but she fell faster, hitting crossbars on the way down. She managed to grab one, wrenching her arm as she jerked to a stop. Instead of climbing the scaffolding, she went through it, scrambling as fast as possible, trying to outrun the echo. The bars hummed and vibrated all around her like crazed tuning forks. She barely kept her grip.

In desperation, lest she lose her hold, she slowed down. The echoes eased. Finally she reached the end and threw herself out of the cursed thing. She hit the ground hard and set off running. The path bucked under her, trying to throw her off balance, but it had trouble judging her stride, probably because she had evaded its sensors at the beginning. She lost more time but she managed to stay on her feet.

She was approaching the lake, a pool with oil covering its surface so it resembled a mirror. If she hadn't looked up this course, she would have plowed through the water, covering herself with oil. Instead, she tried running around the edge of the pool, staying on the stone lip. She could see herself in the water, a sort of visual echo. Keeping her balance on the uneven edge proved almost impossible, though. Her foot slipped and hit the water, sending out an oily ripple. She started to fall, but she was going fast enough that she reached the other side of the pool before she lost control. As she toppled sideways, she tucked and rolled, but her arm still hit the rim of the pool. She grunted as pain stabbed through her elbow.

Tired now, Soz climbed to her feet. She wanted to walk and probably would have, except Kurj was watching. For all she knew he wanted to prove that the heir the Assembly had forced him to choose, the daughter of a man he hated, wasn't up to the title. Soz had no idea what he thought, given how well he guarded his mind, but it killed her to know that her estrangement from her father came as a direct result of her new status. She would be damned if she let Kurj add insult to that injury by humiliating her on the Echo.

So she kept on, too proud to falter before her indomitable brother. She approached the aural labyrinth in a stumbling run. It rose up before her, an enclosed maze of tunnels and passages that echoed, making it hard to judge direction. It didn't matter. This was an old configuration, one posted for cadets to study. Soz had memorized the maze for the heck of it. She kept running, pushing herself hard, gasping in the thin air. It took only moments to clear the maze, but she came out staggering.

The rebounders crashed and bounced ahead of her, a series of gates that operated in complex patterns, snapping open and slamming closed again. She had a vague idea of the timing that would let her traverse the rebounders without hitting the gates, but her body wasn't responding well now. Only sheer orneriness kept her going. She was too damn stubborn to drop.

Soz dodged and feinted as she reeled through the clanging gates, but they caught her anyway, over and over, slamming closed on her body. The only reason she didn't fall over was because they hit her from both sides, holding her up. She gritted her teeth and kept going, the endless gates bouncing, snapping, bouncing, snapping. After an eternity she found herself before the last one, her chest heaving, her body aching. Twice her height and as thick as her body, the black portal thundered open and smashed closed. She recalled the key to this one; it opened and closed five times, rapid fire, then paused for a few seconds before repeating the pattern. When the pause came, she stumbled through and out into the sunlit stretch of sand beyond.

As Soz collapsed onto the sand, she hit the stop panel on her timer. Sweat was running into her face. She lay sprawled, gasping for breath. After several moments, she rolled onto her back and saw Stone standing above her, his face creased with concern. He offered her a hand.

Soz took his hand and pulled herself up, acutely aware that Kurj was waiting at the edge of the sand trap, watching, always watching. She dropped Stone's hand and squinted at her timer. Gods. Fourteen minutes and forty-three seconds. That was truly appalling.

"Cadet Valdoria." Stone spoke quietly. "You may return to the formation."

"Sir." Soz heard how tired she sounded. "Yes, sir." She couldn't read him well; like most officers who worked with

Jagernauts, he knew how to guard his emotions. At least he didn't seem dismissive of her paltry effort here.

Soz turned to Kurj and saluted tiredly, raising her arms straight out from her body, her fists clenched, her wrists crossed. He nodded, his eyes hidden behind their gold shields. Dismissed, Soz set off at a walk, skirting the edges of the Echo.

It took her ten minutes to trudge back to the quadrangle where the rest of the cadets waited. Everyone was staring at her. Well, how the blazes was she supposed to break an academy record on a course she had never done before? She glared at the first cadet she passed and the girl averted her eyes. When Soz reached Jazar, she glowered at him for good measure. To her surprise, he smiled.

"What are you smirking about?" she muttered. She knew Stone and Kurj were coming back, but she didn't think they would hear her from so far away and she doubted they bothered to monitor cadets in the quadrangle. "I didn't break the damn record."

"No. But you completed the course."

"So what?"

"After you left, Foxer told Imperator Skolia that no cadet in the last ten years has ever finished the Echo on their first try."

Whoa. *That* hadn't been in the specs. Damn Kurj. He had set her an impossible task, knowing she would fail. It served him right that she had finished the course.

Stone and Kurj were crossing the quadrangle now. Foxer called an order and the cadets fell into a new formation, shifting their four lines into two columns. Then they marched across the plaza to a wing of the academy building. Although Soz was recovering her wind now, her legs ached. Despite the pain, she refused to limp.

They entered into one of the large common rooms, with tables where cadets could sit and socialize in their nonexistent free time. The paneling on the walls was genuine wood accented with holo-panels of landscapes that showed scenes of Diesha and the academy. Very attractive. Too bad none of them ever had time to enjoy the place.

Kurj was standing behind a console on one side of the room, speaking with each cadet as he or she filed by him. Soz had never realized he took such an interest in the incoming class, but she supposed it made sense. The Jagernauts would be his elite pilots, officers with rare talents, crucial to ISC operations, the empaths who melded their minds with their ships to become human weapons. He would want to meet the novices, see who was who. He took the time to talk to each person. As she drew nearer, she heard him asking about their homes, families, simple facts that transformed a stranger into an acquaintance. A known quantity.

When Soz reached his console, she stood stiffly, aware of the mess she presented compared to the other cadets, her face sweaty, tendrils of her hair hanging out of her braid and curling wildly about her face, her foot covered in oil, her clothes torn and crusted with sand.

Kurj's inner lids came up for some reason, so she could see his eyes, with their gold irises and black pupils. He spoke quietly. "Still think you're ready for the academy, Valdoria?"

She met his gaze defiantly. "Yes, sir."

"You failed in the mission I set you."

Screw him. "Yes, sir."

"Why then, should I let you stay at this academy?"

Foxer was staring at Kurj with undisguised shock. It gave Soz a modicum of satisfaction. She spoke evenly. "Because I'm the first novice in ten damn years to complete the Echo on my first try."

One of his eyebrows quirked. "So you are."

Soz waited, wondering what the bloody binges he wanted.

"How is your father?" he asked.

So. They came down to the chase. "I don't know, sir."

"Why not?"

She spoke flatly. "He disowned me."

That clearly caught him by surprise. "Good gods, why?"

Why do you think? She was painfully conscious of everyone listening. "For coming here."

He let out a long breath. Then, incredibly, he said, "Soz, I'm sorry."

She didn't know what she had expected, but that wasn't it. Her voice almost cracked. Almost. But she held it steady. "So am I." That barely touched what she felt.

He spoke in an unexpectedly gentle voice. "Dismissed, Cadet."

Soz saluted and went on, out of the common room. The other novices watched her with curiosity. She hid her turmoil. Bad enough she had failed Kurj's test in front of everyone; now she had admitted her exile as well. The Echo didn't matter compared to the scab Kurj had picked off her emotions by asking about her father. His sympathetic response confused her. Apparently the mighty Imperator wasn't as much of an impassive machine as he would have people believe.

They had time for lunch now, but Soz had no desire to go to the canteen with her classmates. Instead she went to the dorm. In her room, she dropped into her bunk and lay on her back, too exhausted even to change her clothes. She stared at the bottom of the bunk bed above her.

"What the holy hazoo was that all about?" a voice said.

Soz turned her head to see Grell sitting on her bunk across the room, her newly cropped red hair sticking up the way it did after she had exercised, making her look like an urchin.

"Hazoo?" Soz blinked. "What is that?"

"I dunno," Grell admitted. "Everyone says it back home. And you're avoiding the subject. What happened with Imperator Skolia?"

Soz mentally shuttered her mood. "It's nothing."

Jazar appeared in the doorway. "Nothing?" He came inside and touched the wall panel, closing the door. "I've never heard of him going after a cadet that way."

Soz wondered what her father would do if he knew she was bunking in the same room as two men. Probably have heart failure. He would never believe the truth, that they never violated the ban against fraternization. As if cadets had either the time or the energy even to look cross-eyed at each other, let alone misbehave.

"It's a long story," Soz said.

Grell leaned forward. "He acted like he knew you."

"Unfortunately," Soz muttered.

"You mean he does?" Jazar looked alarmed.

Soz wished she could hide somewhere. "Yes."

"How?" Grell asked.

Soz didn't want to go into it, so she said nothing.

They weren't letting her off that easy. "Why did he bring up your father?" Jazar asked.

"They don't like each other."

Grell watched her with concern. "Do you think Imperator Skolia means to force you out of the academy?"

"No, I don't think so." Soz put her forearm over her eyes, wishing she could disappear. "He just doesn't want me to think I'll have an easy time of it."

"Why would you think that?" Jazar asked.

"It doesn't matter," Soz said.

"Soz, come on," Grell demanded. "Give."

"Nothing to give."

"I've never met anyone who knew members of the Ruby Dynasty," Grell said. "Don't they intimidate you?"

Soz couldn't help but laugh. She lowered her arm and sat up, taking care with her bruised torso where the rebounders had pummeled her body. "They exasperate, drive me crazy, and fill my life with light, but no, they don't intimidate me."

Both Grell and Jazar looked at her, waiting.

Ah, hell. "Imperator Skolia's father knew my mother."

"Really?" Grell's eyes danced with excitement. "How?"

Dryly Soz said, "They were married."

It took them a while to absorb that. Finally Jazar said, "Gods almighty."

Soz glared at him. "You start treating me like I'm some sort of something, I'll toss you into the Echo."

"Some sort of something?" He smiled. "Soz, ever the poet."

Grell spoke slowly. "If you have the same mother as the Imperator, that would be Roca Skolia. Unless she has another life the public has never heard about, that means your father is the King of Skyfall."

Soz groaned. "The planet is *not* called Skyfall. It's called Lyshriol. Skyfall is the name some sleezy resort planners gave it. And my father is not the king of an entire planet. He's not even the king of part of a planet. He's a singer."

"Oh, gods," Grell said. "Holy hazooing gods. *You're* a member of the Ruby Dynasty."

Soz couldn't help but laugh. "*Hazooing?* Where do you get these words?"

"I can't believe it." Grell didn't look as if she knew whether to be horrified or thrilled. "My roommate is a Ruby heir."

"Grell, enough." Jazar was watching Soz closely, his smile gone. He spoke quietly to Soz. "Your father disowned you for coming here?"

Soz just shook her head. She couldn't talk about it. "Don't tell anyone who I am, all right. Swear. Both of you."

Jazar didn't hesitate. "Sworn."

"No one?" Grell asked. "Not even Obsidian?"

"No one," Soz said. "I'll tell him if it comes up."

"All right." Grell sighed. "I swear."

Jazar grinned, his handsome face lighting with the flash of his teeth. "Heya, Soz, you're a princess."

"I'll princess you." Soz gave him her most formidable scowl, the one that made the youths in Dalvador blanch and avoid her. Either that, or they tried to kiss her, like Ari at the lake, which had never made a lot of sense to Soz, but had been fun. It would have been a lot better if he hadn't immediately hopped off to kiss some other girl. If she ever saw him again, she would be tempted to heft him over her back like the last time.

Jazar didn't look the least bit intimidated. He came over and sat next to her on the bunk. "Can't, Soz. You have to be female to be a princess."

"Go sit on your own bunk," she growled.

"I can't," he said sensibly. "It's above yours. If I went up there, how would we have this wonderful discussion, with you grousing and glowering at us so mightily?"

"Grousing!" Soz reached back on her bed, grabbed the regulation pancake that DMA claimed was a pillow, and whacked him over the head with it. Grell laughed and threw her own pillow across the room. Within moments, pancake pillows were flying through the room amid laughter.

It lasted about two minutes before the clarion for afternoon classes blared, cutting through their tumult. Grell stood in the middle of the room, her arms full of pillows, including Obsidian's, the only one of them who had been sensible enough to eat lunch.

Grell sighed. "Time to get back to work."

"I guess so," Soz said. She enjoyed their company despite their having spent the last two minutes hitting her with pillows. These two people shared her dreams in a way no one at home ever had, except perhaps a few of her brothers, but they had been constrained by the differing expectations for men and women there. Besides, they were, well, her brothers. She loved them even at their most exasperating, but it wasn't the same. She had never had friends like this. It eased the ache inside, the knowledge that she had given up a part of her family to come here, a part of herself.

But the loss could never be replaced.

14

The Price of Silence

Shannon rode into the Blue Dale camp with his companions of the last five days: Tharon, a gifted archer who could bring down a floating sphere from a hundred paces; Elarion, whose white-gold hair reached to his waist; and Varielle, who was surely the most fascinating woman alive.

She was an unparalleled Archer. She bested him at every shot, bested all of them, even Tharon.

Shannon's thoughts turned to Varielle often. Perhaps it was because she was the first woman he had met like himself. He might have reacted this way to any female Blue Dale Archer. He doubted it, though. She fevered his dreams.

No one seemed to realize he was only one octet plus six years of age. He was large for an Archer, and the youthful cast of his face made no difference here; they all had a fey, childlike quality to their appearance. They treated him like an adult. He hoped Varielle saw him that way. She had half an octet of years on him, maybe more.

The days passed in bliss for Shannon, helping him forget why he had fled to the Blue Dales. It disturbed him greatly, however, that he couldn't find Moonglaze. He had always loved the lyrine, and now Moonglaze had become his family. His only family. Without the lyrine, he had to ride with one of his three companions. Today he sat behind Varielle on her silver mount, his arms around her waist. He held her close and she made no objection. Her head brushed his chin, and the temptation to nuzzle her hair as if he were her lover was almost too much to resist.

He would have been content in the moment-by-moment, except for the dreams that plagued him, nightmares of agony in his legs and back, always in darkness. He would awake sweating and terrified, unable to rise from where he slept in the forest, rolled in a blanket. Each time it happened, a compulsion urged him back to Rillia, an urge that grew stronger each day. But without Moonglaze, he had no means to ride anywhere except with the Archers.

It astounded him that his companions let him accompany them. The Blue Dale Archers had hidden so well that everyone in Rillia and Dalvador believed them extinct. Yet these three accepted him. He didn't know how to express what it meant to him, but they seemed to know. They lived in a wash of emotion, letting feelings pour over and through their minds. They weren't empaths, but they came closer to that state than anyone he knew except his family. He felt right with them. They were bringing him home. That made it all the more wrenching that he would soon have to leave them.

Shannon had no wish to return to Rillia. But he had to go. The dreams grew worse each night. Somehow he needed to find another lyrine. When he did, he would head back to the Vales.

Varielle shifted in front of him, and he rested his chin against the back of her head. She felt small in his arms, her hair glossy on his cheek. Visions played in his mind of her floating in a pool, her body bare and glistening with water. He wanted her, but he was afraid to let her know, so he just used this excuse to hold her in his arms.

Varielle leaned back, her head on his shoulder. "You have much strength."

That made Shannon feel taller. He didn't know how to respond to such a compliment, though, so he said only, "You should meet my brothers." Immediately he wished he had kept his mouth shut. Women always found his brothers handsome. He had never envied them their conquests before, or at least not too much, but now his jealousy surged. Better Varielle never meet them, especially Del, who had dallied with half the girls in the village.

Blue mist swirled through the dale below them, curling around the stained-glass trees and drifting past tents. Melodies trilled in the air. After several moments he realized the music came from voices calling and children laughing. People were all around them, hidden in the fog. Silvery figures darted from tree to tree, following them, almost invisible in the fog.

"We are causing a stir," he said.

"Not us." Varielle leaned against him, her eyes closed, her hands loose on the reins. "You."

Shannon winced. "A good one, I hope."

She laughed, a melodic sound. "The women will envy me."

A sense of fullness swelled inside Shannon. He kissed the back of her head, savoring her soft hair, like silk under his lips.

The trail leveled out and tents shrouded in mist appeared

on either side, as blue as snow. The eerie beauty of the place seemed steeped in magic, ready for spirits to step out of legends and come to life. A group of riders formed out of the mist and came toward them. They rode silver lyrine, smaller than a war mount like Moonglaze, more the size of the lavender or blue lyrine most people rode in the Dalvador Plains.

The leader of the group sat tall on her mount, head lifted, her silver eyes surrounded by a nest of lines, her translucent skin creased, her hair silver rather than white-gold. Her authority permeated the air.

They all reined their mounts to a halt and gathered in a restless cluster of lyrine. The leader gazed at Shannon with no welcome in her eyes. She spoke to Tharon, her phrases a ripple of music. Shannon had grown more accustomed to the Archer dialect these past few days, enough to pick up some of their words. The Elder castigated Tharon for bringing a stranger into camp.

Tharon answered in elegant phrases, composing an image that startled Shannon. He described Shannon's persistence, his kindness to the lyrine, his prowess with a bow, his quiet nature. The Archer spoke of "the music of Shannon's ken, the flow of his moods, the sight of his heart." Shannon understood little of what that meant, but the phrases had a symmetry that felt right.

The Elder's demeanor softened toward Shannon. She spoke to him, slowing her voice so he could better understand. "Is your lyrine a giant animal with a dark coat?"

Shannon straightened up behind Varielle, still holding her in his arms. "Yes. A purple coat. He is a war lyrine."

"He came here." This seemed to impress the Elder. "He acted as if he wished us to help someone. We did not know who."

Shannon's breath caught. The great animals such as Moonglaze rarely gave fealty to humans. Although Moonglaze had accepted him, he hadn't realized the lyrine would make such an extreme effort to save his life, even searching out the legendary Blue Dale Archers. Their help would have come too late if Tharon and the others hadn't already found Shannon, but what mattered was that the lyrine tried.

Shannon inclined his head to the Elder with respect. "I thank you for sheltering Moonglaze."

"Moonglaze?" she asked.

"The lyrine." He didn't say "my" lyrine. Moonglaze belonged only to himself.

"A fine name for a fine beast," the Elder said.

Shannon hesitated, unsure of protocols. Varielle was simply waiting, silent in front of him. She hadn't tensed in his arms, though, which boded well. He hoped. Nor had any of the Archers challenged him for riding into camp with his arms around one of their women. He wished he could hold her for hours, days, many nights. But he couldn't stay.

"May I see Moonglaze now?" he asked.

"If it is him." The Elder guided her mount around. It stepped with graceful agitation, like a wraith cloaked in the swirling blue mist. They rode through the camp with the octet of Archers who had accompanied the Elder and now kept watch on Shannon. The fog muted sound.

They soon reached the last of the tents. Among the widely spaced trees beyond, a small herd of lyrine stood in a cluster, most of them nibbling at patches of stub-reeds. They resembled the mist, silvery and slender, indiscernible until Shannon was almost upon them. One stood out from the rest, a huge animal and powerfully muscled, with a dark violet coat. Joy surged through Shannon. He slid off Varielle's lyrine and landed on the ground with a thump.

Moonglaze lifted his head.

For an instant the lyrine remained still. Then he whistled a long cry to the air, resonant and powerful. He shook his head and walked among the other animals. Many of them stopped grazing and moved aside to let him pass. As Shannon went forward through the herd, several of the lyrine studied him, first with one silver eye, then turning their heads to look at him with the other. Animals in Dalvador did the same. They could see with both eyes at once, looking forward, but when they wished to scrutinize an oddity or uncertain phenomenon, they observed it from all possible views.

Apparently satisfied that he posed no threat, they went back to nibbling the reeds. Shannon and Moonglaze met in their midst, and Moonglaze snuffled at him, pushing his nose against Shannon's shoulder. Shannon put his arms around his neck and laid his head against the great lyrine. Moisture gathered in his eyes. Moonglaze whistled and curved his head around, gently butting him. With a laugh, Shannon released the lyrine and stepped back. Moonglaze considered him with one eye, then turned his head and gazed at him with the other eye.

Shannon smiled. "Making sure it's me?"

The lyrine whistled, a chastising note. Shannon scratched his neck in that place the lyrine liked so much. With a snort of approval, Moonglaze lowered his head and went back to grazing.

"He loves you," a fluid voice said.

Shannon turned with a start. Varielle stood a few paces away.

"He accepts me," Shannon said. "I wouldn't presume more."

"You should try presuming more," she murmured, coming forward. She stopped in front of him and looked up into his face. "You will go now, won't you?"

Shannon wished he could stay. It burned inside of him. But he could only nod. "I'm sorry. I must."

"I don't understand." She motioned around at the camp. "You came looking for Archers. Here we are."

He spoke unevenly. "I have dreams. Nightmares. They drive me. Something is wrong, very wrong."

She laid her palm against his chest. "I will go with you."

"I also," another voice said. Tharon also came forward, leading his lyrine, with Elarion at his side.

"I, too," Elarion said.

Shannon's voice caught. "You honor me. But why?"

"We have seen your worry, your restless slumber, your darkened eyes in the morning." Elarion's voice drifted with the mist. "We have also seen your ken of the Dales. You are part of us. We will go for a ways with you."

Shannon wanted their company; indeed, he longed for it. They made him feel complete in a way he had never experienced in Dalvador. But guilt tugged at him. He had no idea what he faced. "You have your home here."

"Our home is the forests." Varielle's words chimed. "We never stay in one place."

So it was true, Archers led a nomadic life. It was probably why they were so hard to find. "But you never go to Rillia." It was a guess on his part, but probably a good one given that Rillians never reported any definitive sightings of the Archers.

"We may go only partway," Tharon said. "Tomorrow the camp rides. We will travel with you for a while. Then we will see."

Shannon inclined his head. "I will be glad for every day we spend together. I would miss your company."

Varielle's pale lashes came down halfway over her tilted eyes. "And I yours."

Shannon suddenly felt warm. He wanted to take her into his arms, but he held back, in part because they had an audience but also because he feared she would reject him.

The Elder and her retinue had remained on their lyrine, back on the path, half-hidden by the drifting mist. Tharon raised his hand, indicating them. To Shannon he said, "Join us for a meal."

"I would like that," Shannon said. "Thank you."

So they gathered for the evening, preparing for a new day when they would ride to Rillia.

Eldrinson's universe had shrunk to a pallet, to darkness—and to pain.

He could see nothing. He lay in darkness, unable to rise. The boulders had crushed his legs, pulverizing the bones. His backbone remained intact, but it was no blessing, for it meant he could feel. The agony in his broken body never stopped. At times it eased, but later it would surge again. The first day

Vitarex had knocked him out with a sedative, giving him a merciful oblivion. He had awoken here, in the tent, laid out on a pile of rugs. And here he stayed, unable to move, hating what he had done to himself, hating Vitarex even more.

He wasn't sure how much time had passed. A day? Two? More? He had suffered several grand mal attacks and numerous minor seizures. The convulsions worsened his injuries. None of it mattered to Vitarex. He deliberately left Eldrinson untreated so that he could transcend.

A shuffle came from nearby. Eldrinson thought someone was kneeling by his pallet. "Who is there?"

A woman answered. "It is Jaliesa."

Relief spread through him. Jaliesa was the wife in the young couple who served Vitarex. She had been tending him since his fall from the bluff. Her touch soothed and her care eased his pain. He spoke in a low voice. "Have you talked with Tarlin yet?" She hadn't been certain who Eldrinson meant.

"I know who he is now," she whispered. "I will speak to him when I can."

"Please help me."

She spoke raggedly. "I will try. But I cannot betray Lord Vitarex. We have sworn our oath to him."

Eldrinson gritted his teeth. "He's a monster."

Instead of answering, she said, "Here, Goodman. Drink." Something scraped, perhaps a lid, and the tantalizing smell of broth wafted around him. As his mouth watered, Jaliesa lifted his head and set a jug to his lips. He pushed up on his elbow, flinching at the pain it sparked in his legs. Holding the jug with his other hand, he drank deeply, grateful for the succor of its soup. When he finished, he lay back down on the pallet, on his back, exhausted by that slight activity. As Jaliesa took the jug from him, a rustle came from the direction of the tent entrance.

"How is he?" Vitarex said. His footsteps approached.

Bile surged in Eldrinson. And loathing.

"He is stronger today," Jaliesa said.

"Why don't you ask me?" Eldrinson asked harshly. "My legs may not work, but my throat is fine."

"Indeed." Vitarex was nearer now, right next to him,

maybe crouching at his side. A hand touched his forehead. "Your fever has receded."

Eldrinson pulled his head away. He hated that he had to depend on Vitarex for his every need. "I'm fine."

"Milord," Jaliesa said. "May I speak?"

"Go ahead." Vitarex made no attempt to hide the pleasure in his voice as he transcended.

"Will you not fix his legs?"

"I cannot."

"But surely such a great lord as you can do anything."

Eldrinson wanted to vomit at Vitarex's "greatness." But he knew Jaliesa believed flattering the Aristo would produce the best results. She was probably right.

"I haven't the resources to mend such damage," Vitarex said.

Liar, Eldrinson thought. But he feared the Aristo told the truth, that his body was so broken, even offworld medicine couldn't fix it. He knew too little about their technology. He couldn't even hope for treatment, lest a medical exam give away his identity.

"He is such a valuable po-po-possession." Her voice scratched with no lilt at all. It didn't surprise him that she stumbled on the last word; the idea of one human owning another was anathema to his people. "It is a shame that someone of your magnificence must lose one of such value."

"This is true," Vitarex acknowledged. "But in his condition, it would be difficult to take him when I leave here." He sounded as if he were speaking more to himself than to Jaliesa. "I must take—certain others when I go. I can't risk the success of our departure by including someone this injured. Were he healthy, that might be different."

"But he will die without your help," Jaliesa said.

"I am sorry. I wish I could take him." Vitarex sounded as if he meant it. Eldrinson even believed him. What the Aristo regretted, though, was losing such a good provider. Eldrinson knew he had only to reveal himself and he would live. Vitarex already realized he was a strong psion. The antiempath couldn't read him well enough to recognize his full strength, but if he gave Vitarex more cause to wonder, the Aristo would investigate. The moment he revealed his identity, however, Vitarex could leave Lyshriol, having gained one of his targets, a Rhon psion.

It would endanger all of Skolia.

Eldrinson didn't really understand how it worked, why Rhon psions were so important to the Skolians, but he believed what they told him. Their description of the Aristos had been true, even understated. Roca's people claimed if the Traders captured a Rhon psion, it would give them advantage over ISC, enough to conquer Skolia. He didn't really fathom why the Skolians had instantaneous interstellar communication and the Traders didn't or why it was so important. He knew the words, but the science remained an enigma. He understood the result, however; if the Aristos captured any member of his family, they would have the key they needed to achieve such communications. And then the Imperialate would fall.

To protect his people, he had only to remain silent—even if it meant his death.

15

The Message

The academy had libraries of every type, including virtual reality arcades where students could experience their studies firsthand, soundproofed chambers where they could listen to texts, console rooms where they could jack into library meshes, and traditional stacks with books in shelves. The paper books were exhibits only; they were too valuable to use. It was far easier, anyway, to obtain information from consoles or holobooks.

Soz had two preferences: the virtual library that made her

studies seem real and the traditional library, which reminded her of home. Tonight she chose tradition. She adored the vaulted ceilings in the library and the intricate carvings, all those ornate scrolls and scallops on the columns, around the windows, even on the legs and edges of the long tables where cadets could spread out their materials. The library was really a museum, but a student could apply to look at the books if they agreed to a voluminous set of regulations for how they treated the tomes. Soz had applied her first day. She loved to browse the shelves of old books, astonished by their paper bindings and inked script.

Today she sat ensconced in an armchair with her legs up on a table and a holobook in her lap. She wasn't studying, though. She was thinking of home. The old-fashioned atmosphere here stirred memories of her youth. No building like this actually existed on Lyshriol, though; a people with no written language had no use for libraries. Their records were kept by women known as Memories, those rare scholars who had holographic recall. The anthropologists who studied Lyshriol believed Memories descended from genetically engineered humans who had colonized the planet five millennia ago during the Ruby Empire.

History had always intrigued Soz. Five thousand years ago, during the Stone Age, an unknown race of beings had come to Earth. They took away a small population of humans and stranded them on the world Raylicon. Then they disappeared, leaving no explanation, no justification for their actions. Some historians believed a calamity had befallen them before they could complete whatever project they had begun. Whatever the reason, they left the humans with almost nothing. Primitive, terrified, and bewildered, the humans struggled to survive.

Their abductors left behind one clue to their origins, the ruins of three starships on the shores of the Vanished Seas. From those ships and their libraries, over the centuries, the people on Raylicon gleaned enough knowledge to develop star travel. Using technology they barely understood, they went in search of their lost home at a time when humans on

Earth were still living in caves. They never found Earth, but they built the Ruby Empire, scattering its colonies across the stars.

With such a shaky foundation, the empire lasted only a few centuries. Then it collapsed, stranding its colonies. A Dark Age followed on Raylicon, continuing for several millennia. During that time, many of the stranded colonies failed. The few that survived backslid into more primitive conditions.

Lyshriol had been one such colony.

Gradually the Raylicans rebuilt their civilization, this time from the ground up, ensuring they understood what they created. When they finally regained the stars, they split into two empires: the Eubian Concord, also called the Trader Empire, which based its economy on the sale of human beings; and the Skolian Imperialate, ruled by an elected Assembly that considered freedom a fundamental right of all humans.

Eventually the people of Earth developed space travel. They were in for a shock when they reached the stars: their siblings were already there, building empires—two thriving but irreconcilably opposed civilizations. The Allied Worlds of Earth became a third power. Although a smaller civilization than the Trader Empire or Skolian Imperialate, the Allieds were strong enough that conquering them would take more resources than either Skolia or the Traders could spare, given the constant threat of war between the two mammoths. So the three interstellar powers maintained an uneasy coexistence.

Scouts from Earth rediscovered Lyshriol. They christened the planet Skyfall because its blue snow looked like the sky fallen to the ground. That referred to Earth, though, rather than Lyshriol, which had a lavender sky. Earth ceded its claim to Skolia when they realized it was an ancient Ruby colony, but the infernal Skyfall name had stuck.

The Ruby colonists had terraformed Lyshriol five millennia ago. No one now knew why chemicals saturated the biosphere, turning the water, the snow, even the clouds blue.

The planet had no axial tilt and an unnaturally circular orbit. Lyshriol had probably been moved there, a feat of astronomical engineering beyond any modern civilization. No one knew if the colonists had engineered the phenomenal recall of the Memories or if it had developed later. Nor did they know why Lyshrioli people had four-fingered hands or seemed incapable of literacy. The answers to those questions had vanished during the Dark Ages.

Soz had some trouble adapting to Diesha. The heat and dry air bothered her. The sixteen-hour days were shorter than the twenty-eight-hour cycle on Lyshriol, and the length of the night varied relative to the day. Usually she slept too little, skipping every other night. Although she understood, in theory, why most worlds didn't have equal days and nights all year long, it felt strange to live in such a place.

"Don't go to sleep," a deep voice rumbled.

Soz looked up with a start. Althor was leaning against a nearby column, his black trousers and pullover a sharp contrast to the yellowed wood. He had dark circles under his eyes.

Soz smiled at her brother. "Where did you come from?"

"The dorm." He walked over, dropped into another chair, and swung his booted legs up on the low table. "I've a midterm tomorrow in Quantum Inversion."

"Good stuff." Soz approved of any subject related to star travel. She hadn't yet studied the quantum theories of relativistic inversion, but she looked forward to it.

He grimaced and rubbed his eyes. "I'm seeing equations in my sleep. I'll be glad when the class is over."

"You look tired," she said.

"I'm all right."

"It's the air here," Soz grumbled. "Not enough oxygen."

"It doesn't bother me much anymore."

"I guess I'll get used to it." She motioned at her legs. "They hurt. I don't know why. I've never had any problem before."

He leaned his elbow on the arm of the chair. "Probably the different gravity."

"It's lighter. That should make things easier."

"Your body still has to adjust." His forehead furrowed. "That's an odd coincidence, though. I've been having nightmares that my legs are broken."

Soz regarded him uneasily. "A while back, I collapsed on the trail. Something felt really wrong. I thought you might have been hurt, except you said you were fine."

Althor's grin flashed. "Thinking about me knocked you out. Admit it, Soz."

She snorted. "Pah."

He gestured at her holobook. "What is it you were pretending to study while you were daydreaming?"

"I was not daydreaming." Soz glowered at him. "I was contemplating life."

He laughed, a throaty, full sound. "I hope life comes out of that all right."

Soz couldn't help but smile. She flicked her finger through a holicon on her holobook. Chemical formulas formed in the air. "It's for my chemistry class. Boring, boring, boring."

"You don't like chemistry?"

"I like it fine. I just know it already." She snapped her fingers through the holicon and the chemicals disappeared. "I asked if I could take the final tomorrow."

"Tomorrow?" Althor stared at her. "That chemistry class is a second-year course. How can you be taking the final less than a month into your first term of your first year?"

"The brass put me in there." She rubbed the back of her neck, working at the stiff muscles. "I just do what they say and go to class. Most of the courses are boring. My instructors already let me test out of Biomech and Neural Science."

He looked alarmed. "Novices don't do that."

"Why not?"

"Because those classes are killers."

"Yeah, right."

Exasperation flashed across his face. "Would you please slow down? The rest of us can't keep up."

Soz smiled. "I thought I daydreamed too much."

"That, too." When she laughed, he settled back, relaxing.

"So what are you taking instead of Biomech and Neural Science?"

Soz actually wasn't sure. So far the "class" had been odd. They sat around and made up scenarios for Trader attacks and then countered them. It fascinated her, but she had seen no texts or syllabus. "Just something called Military Science."

Althor blinked. "They put you in a think tank?"

She wiggled her fingers at him as if she were casting a spell. "We do virtual reality simulations where the Traders are winning and then we figure out how to hex their ships."

He was no longer smiling. "Soz, listen to me. Most cadets never see those classes. Only the best upperclass cadets, the ones ISC expects to become leaders. Those aren't games you're playing."

Soz shifted her weight. "Some of the scenarios are wild. I'll tell you about them sometime."

"You can't. You must know those classes are secured."

"Well, yes. But you're my brother. An Imperial Heir."

"It doesn't make one bit of difference." He spoke quietly. "Just because you're smarter, tougher, and better connected than most everyone else here, that doesn't mean the rules apply any less to you than to everyone else."

"I know that."

"Maybe if you knew it better, you would get fewer demerits."

Well, hell. How did he know about the demerits? She got them all the time, try as she would to follow regulations. "I don't know what you're talking about."

"Right." He cocked his eyebrow at her. "You don't have more demerits than any other student in your class."

"How would you know if I did?"

"I talk to people."

"Too much." She crossed her arms, trying to be forebidding. The effect was marred when it knocked her holobook off her lap and she had to grab for it.

"Heya, Soz," a cheerful voice said. "Throwing things?"

Flustered, Soz looked up to see Grell, her roommate, coming around Althor's chair. Grell glanced idly at Althor, then did a double take and froze. "Sir!" Grell saluted, her arms out and crossed at the wrists, her fists clenched.

"You don't have to salute me here," Althor said mildly. "The library is a free zone."

Grell lowered her arms. "Sir! I'm sorry, sir."

"Oh for flaming sakes," Soz said. "He's just my brother Althor. Sit down, Grell." DMA regulations required novices to salute upperclass cadets, but the instructors had ruled libraries exempt after juniors and seniors began using the rules to bedevil novices, making it impossible for the younger students to study.

Grell sat down. "My apologies, sir."

Althor smiled at her. "It's no problem."

Grell blushed and averted her gaze. Soz wasn't sure what flustered her roommate—Althor's upperclass status, his sinfully good looks, or his resemblance to Kurj. She scowled at him just for good measure, but he only grinned.

"How do you like DMA?" he asked Grell.

She looked up. "It is an honor to be here, Your Highness."

Soz inwardly groaned. It had taken days to convince her roommates to treat her like a normal human. Living together helped; the glamour fast disappeared when you woke up every morning with bleary eyes just like everyone else or stumbled in covered with sweat after a workout. But here was Grell treating Althor like some glorious prince of the empire. He was, actually, but that made it no less irksome.

Althor smirked at Soz. "You know, contrary to your opinion of brothers as a lesser life-form, we're actually human."

Soz reddened. "I never said lesser."

Grell was watching them, intrigued now. She motioned at the four gold bars on Althor's shoulders. "So you're a senior?"

He turned the full force of his dazzling grin on her. "For you, I'll be anything."

Grell blushed, and this time Soz did groan. Mercifully, Althor just grinned. As the three of them talked, Grell relaxed, and Althor soon had her laughing. Soz said very little. She was growing angry, but she didn't want to ruin their good time.

Finally she stood up. "I better go. I'll see you around."

"It's still early." Grell sounded disappointed.

"I have droid duty." Soz winced. A pox on whoever dreamed up the concept. They weren't even real droids. She had to clean the mechbots that tended the academy grounds. By the time she finished her shift tonight, she would be covered in oil and dirt, and exhausted, but she would still have to finish her chemistry, since she had spent her free time daydreaming.

Althor looked amused. "Lovely job."

Soz gave him a quelling look. "It isn't funny."

He didn't look the least quelled. "Just how many demerits do you have?"

Soz picked up her flat-pack, stuffed in her holobook, sealed up the pack with far more force than she needed, and slung it over her shoulder. To Grell, she said, "See you tonight." Then she stalked off. She knew she shouldn't treat them this way, but anger drove her away.

She had almost reached the library entrance when Althor caught up with her. "Soz, wait." He put his hand on her arm and pulled her to a stop. "What's wrong?"

Too furious to answer, she just shook her head.

He drew her into a secluded alcove behind several shelves of books. "Why are you angry at me?"

"You were flirting with my roommate."

"So?"

"It's fraternization."

"What fraternization?"

Her anger surged. "You can't date her, Althor."

"For flaming sakes, we were just talking."

"You're both cadets."

"I won't be for much longer."

Soz clenched her fists. "Grell is my friend. She doesn't deserve for you to lead her on."

"What makes you think I was leading her on?"

"Oh, come on, Althor. You aren't interested in her. Not the way she thinks."

His expression tightened. "How the blazes would you know what interests me?"

"You going to ruin some woman's life by marrying her, is that it?" Her voice grated. "Condemn her to a life of disappointment just so our father will let you come home?"

His posture went rigid. "It's none of your business."

"No, none of my business." She lowered her voice. "It's none of my business that Kurj treats me like a smart-mouthed, cocky cadet he has to cut down to size when I'm the best damn novice here. It's none of my business that I can't seem to prove him wrong, because maybe I *am* a damn smart-mouthed, cocky cadet. It's none of my business that we talk for hours in that think tank about invasion, and that under their veneer, our instructors are scared to death those scenarios will come true." Her voice cracked. "One of these days I'll go out and fight Aristos, defend my people, my family, maybe even lose my life, and damnit, my own father won't even answer my letters."

Althor exhaled. He said, simply, "Yes."

Her anger fizzled. "Why am I mad at you? You did nothing wrong. You never do. You're perfect. The golden boy, literally. Except you gave Father a little shock." She spoke tiredly. "Maybe you're right. Maybe we should try to be what he wants. I hurt him so much. I hate knowing that. What does it mean to defend those we love if we lose their love in the process?"

Althor laid his hand on her shoulder. "He never stopped loving us. That's why he's so upset. He doesn't want us to give our lives in combat, especially in a war he can't understand."

She rubbed the tears gathering in her eyes. Had it been anyone except Althor, she would have left then, unable to let her vulnerability show. He more than anyone understood the pressure of being Kurj's heir. But how could they talk when that pressure created a barrier between them, the knowledge that Kurj would choose only one as his successor? He set brother against sister, and it created a rift she didn't know how to bridge. They could no longer trust each other with their concerns, lest it tempt one to use that knowledge against the other in this forced rivalry.

A thought came to Soz, one she hated but couldn't deny. Kurj had assumed the title of Imperator through the death of their grandfather, Jarac, the previous Imperator. Had Kurj set her and Althor against each other because he feared they would otherwise turn against him, coveting his power? Jarac had died when Kurj joined him and the Ruby Pharaoh in the Dyad that powered the Kyle web.

Kurj had made the Dyad a Triad.

The Kyle web existed in Kyle space, a universe outside of spacetime. Any strong psion could access the web, but only the Rhon could power it. Without the web, ISC would lose the communications that tied the military together as an interstellar force and Skolia as a civilization. Without the Dyad, there was no web, and without the Ruby Dynasty there was no Dyad.

The Dyad consisted of two Keys—two Rhon psions: Kurj, the Imperator, and Dyhianna, the Ruby Pharaoh. The Dyad before them had been Soz's grandparents, the previous Ruby Pharaoh and Imperator. When Kurj joined them, the power had surged catastrophically. Unable to support three such incredible minds, the link had overloaded and destroyed Jarac. In trying to create a Triad, Kurj had instead killed his predecessor and taken his title.

Lahaylia had died several years later of old age, after a life of several centuries. That left Kurj as one of the most powerful human beings alive, perhaps even more so than the elected leader of Skolia, Lyra Meson, the First Councilor of the Assembly. He commanded the Imperialate military, a war machine with no match except ESComm, the Trader military.

Someday that would all go to either Althor or Soz.

Now Soz found herself staring at Althor, the brother she loved as much today as in their childhood. A wall had come between them. By making them vie for the title of Imperial Heir, Kurj made them into rivals. He had to know they would become warier of each other as the years passed and the stakes rose for the power they had to gain, until someday they might have nothing left but distrust for each other.

Tonight, she and Althor each went their way for the evening, the raveling bond of their kinship repaired for now. But Soz feared Kurj would never choose an Imperial heir, that he would wait for them to make the choice for him. He was wrong if he expected one of them to assassinate the other; she could never harm her own kin. But the war might do it for them. Nothing would remove this wall between them except death itself.

Roca sat at the long table in the breakfast room, her arms crossed on the table, her body slumped, her head hanging down. Footsteps crossed the room, but she was too exhausted to move.

"Councilor?" The voice came at her side.

Roca lifted her head. Brad was standing next to her, dressed in dark trousers and an old sweater, his salt-and-pepper hair curled tightly against his scalp, his dark skin wan with fatigue.

"Is it dawn yet?" she asked. Her words sounded as heavy as she felt. So tired. So very tired.

He nodded, sitting next to her. "Del and Chaniece are loading the flyer with supplies for our search today. The shuttles have already left."

"They have to be out there," she whispered. She fumbled for a blue-glass tumbler on the table.

Brad poured her a glass of water. "We'll find them. I swear it." His voice rasped, though with fatigue or apprehension, she couldn't tell. Both, she thought. Brad and Eldrinson had been friends for over thirty years.

Roca drank deeply, her arms shaking. She held the glass with both hands to keep from splashing out water. In the past fifteen days, since Eldri's disappearance, she hadn't slept a single night all the way through. She paced the castle wall outside for hours, trying to reach her husband with her thoughts, unable to penetrate the static in his mind. He was in pain, terrible pain, but they couldn't find him, neither she nor

Brad nor the children nor the entire damned orbital system. How could ISC have such formidable defenses around this planet and be unable to locate one man and one boy?

"It can't just be Shannon's jammer." She set down her water and sat up straighter, rubbing the small of her back. "ISC should have broken through its interference days ago."

Brad leaned his head against the high back of his chair. "Colonel Majda is coming down again today to talk with us."

"I'd like to do a stint in the flyer first, if we have time."

"We should." Brad stood up, then paused as Roca rose to her feet. "Denric said he would come with us. Del and Chaniece are riding with the army personnel who came down yesterday."

They left the breakfast room and headed out. Neither of them spoke. Roca couldn't voice the dread that grew larger within her each day. Shannon's jammer might have malfunctioned in some incredible manner to cause this disappearance, or some other extenuating circumstances might exist that they hadn't accounted for, but the more time that passed, the harder that became to believe. Only ESComm technology could hide someone this well, even from ISC. But surely the Traders couldn't have taken Eldri or Shannon. It couldn't have happened.

If even Lyshriol wasn't safe, where would she protect her family?

The Blue Dale caravan wound through the trees and stirred up the glitter that piled so deeply here, where humans rarely wandered. They had traveled for days, venturing lower in the mountains, until finally they left the Blue Dales. The closer they approached the Rillian Vales, the more uneasy the Archers became. Even the brighter colors of the trees seemed to unsettle them.

All of the Archers rode, the men, women, and children. They passed through the mist as if they weren't solid themselves. Here in the lower mountains, the fog burned off in the late morning, leaving them unveiled from the sky. It made them uneasy, restless. Vulnerable. Shannon knew that soon they would go their own way, back up into the mountains, and he would follow his insubstantial nightmare alone.

His legs ached constantly now, and though he blamed it on riding for many hours each day, he knew the truth. It came from the dreams that drove him onward, down and down, toward the western fringes of Rillia, those isolated wilds beyond the thriving towns or even the outlying farms.

Elarion rode up alongside him, his silver lyrine large for the Archers but only medium compared to Moonglaze.

"My greetings," Shannon said. He enjoyed Elarion's company. "How are you this morn?"

"Hot." Elarion's long hair swirled around his body and glistened in the sunlight. Tufted ends of his arrows stuck up out of his quiver behind his back. Shannon had previously used bits of glasswood twigs on the ends of his arrows, but the Archers preferred twists of cloth they wove from flexible hemp-reeds that grew in the upper ranges. He had discovered that such twists gave his arrows better balance. He knew from school that on Earth they used "feathers" from birds. Lyshriol had no birds, besides which, he found it hard to believe such filmy material could be useful for an arrow.

Elarion noticed him staring at the arrows. He reached over his shoulder and pulled one out, a long tube of purple glasswood with a razor-sharp point. He offered it to Shannon. "For you."

Shannon blinked, confused. "Thank you."

Elarion smiled. "It is a token. For yesterday, during the archery practice. You shot well."

"You honor me."

"Aiya, Shannon," two musical voices crooned. The trill of sweet laughter followed the lovely sound.

Startled, blushing, Shannon turned around. Two girls were riding by on silvery-blue lyrine, their silver eyes teasing him. They giggled at him and rode on.

"For flaming sake," Shannon muttered. Why did girls always giggle at him? It was as bad here as at home.

Elarion chuckled at his side. "They like you."

He slanted Elarion a wary look. "They bedevil me."

"It is the way always with women," the Archer said good-naturedly. "The tall, handsome stranger comes into their midst and they vie for his attention."

Shannon's face was burning. Elarion couldn't be serious. He twirled the purple-glass arrow Elarion had given him, turning it around and around in his hand as he looked up the line of Archers. Varielle was about seven riders ahead of him, riding alongside one of her friends.

"They confuse me," Shannon admitted.

"Who?" Elarion closed his eyes and tilted his face to the sun, letting his lyrine pick the way.

"Women."

"Ah." Elarion looked at him. "So it has always been."

It wasn't the world's most useful advice, but he suspected it was all he would get from the taciturn Elarion. Varielle remained a mystery. He had thought she liked him, but now that they no longer needed to ride the same lyrine, she often went with her friends, leaving him alone. Just when he thought she had forgotten him, she would seek out his company. But before he could find the courage to take matters further, she would go off again with her friends. She kept him off balance, off kilter. Maybe his initial impression of her interest had been wishful thinking. Why would a woman such as Varielle spend time with a boy? Although he hadn't told her his age, he probably came across as young. His height couldn't hide the truth for long.

"Shannon, bannon," voices chimed at his side. "Sing a song."

He smiled as two small boys rode next to him, both on one lyrine, their small faces beaming, their wild gold hair tousled down their necks and around their ears, their upward-tilted eyes full of silver mischief.

"My greetings," Shannon said.

"Sing the story about the night and dawn," they chimed.

"It would be my pleasure." Shannon had sung earlier for the adults as they rode, so his voice was warm and relaxed. He hummed a few notes, then let a ballad flow out of him, using his tenor range:

Ralcon, god of night,
Spreading stars wide,
Spreading stars through the sky,
The dark sky,
Dark as his eyes,
Dark as his hair,
Dark as the night.

The charmed goddess rose,
The goddess of light,
The goddess of Dawn,
Of luminous new Dawn.

Ralcon, god of the dark,
Of fertile, sensual dark,
He brings the Dawn,
The pearly Dawn,
But lives beyond her light.

While he sang, the boys made appreciative chimes with their voices, like music to accompany him. The melody sparkled among the trees. Other riders had pulled closer as Shannon sang, and now they added rills of approval. It made Shannon smile. He had spent many an hour with his father during his childhood learning to sing. He had so loved those days.

His good mood faded. Never again would his father sing with him.

He talked with the boys for a while, but eventually they rode off to explore the woods, away from adults, which apparently included him. Shannon wished he could go with them. He missed running through the Dalvador Plains.

"You are good with them," Elarion said.

"They remind me of myself." Shannon's mood had turned pensive as he thought of his childhood.

"It is good, the things you tell them."

That surprised Shannon. "What do you mean?"

"It is hard to say exactly." Elarion paused. "Your words have honor. Your ken has music."

Shannon rolled the arrow Elarion had given him between his fingers. Then he reached back and pulled an arrow out of his own quiver, a green glasswood beauty he had carved last night. He offered it to Elarion. "For friendship."

The Archer inclined his head as he accepted the arrow. "May we share it always." He put the green arrow in his quiver and Shannon slid the purple one into his. In Dalvador, it would never have occurred to him to offer an arrow to express friendship, but here it felt right.

A commotion came from farther up the caravan. Shannon leaned over Moonglaze's neck, trying to see through the stained-glass trees. The tip of someone's bow hit a tree-bubble and popped the large sphere, filling the air with glitter that obscured his view. Voices floated back to him, chiming with excitement.

Curious, Shannon urged Moonglaze forward and rode through the veils of glitter dust, brushing it out of his face as it settled over his body. Up ahead, the Elder, Tharon, and several other Archers had gathered around a man on a silver-white lyrine, one of the scouts who had been ranging ahead of the caravan. The trees were too thick here for the caravan to go at any significant speed and still remain well hidden, so they traveled more slowly while their scouts ranged out and kept watch for anyone who might see them.

As Shannon pulled up to their group, the Elder glanced toward him. He thought she would send him away, but instead she motioned him forward. It surprised him. He wasn't someone she normally included in her counsels. His curiosity piqued even more, he nudged Moonglaze toward her, and the riders stepped their lyrine aside to let him approach the Elder. He drew Moonglaze to a stop in front of her and inclined his head with respect.

She spoke in her melodic voice. "You know the ways of the Vales, yes?"

"Fairly well," Shannon said. "I grew up in Dalvador, but we often visited Rillia."

"A man approaches. He appears Rillian. I would ask your help."

"Whatever I can do. As long as it causes no harm."

She regarded him with her silver gaze. "I would ask that you lead him away so that he may not know we ride through here."

Guilt washed over Shannon. They had come this far down in the mountains on his behalf. Now he had put them at risk of discovery.

"I will lead him away," he answered. He wasn't sure how, but he could come up with some ideas.

"You have our thanks." She spoke quietly. "When we are safe, we will make camp. Tomorrow we will return to the Blue Dales."

Disappointment washed through Shannon. He would miss them. But he understood. "The company of your people has been a joy for me."

A smile played across her beautiful, lined face. "And for us. You are a pleasure, young man. You are welcome in the Vales should you choose to return."

Shannon hadn't expected such a testimony from the Elder. "Thank you."

After they bid him farewell, he rode on with the scout, a man about his father's age, lanky for an Archer, with silver hair pulled into a knot at the back of his head, a beautifully carved bow on his back, and a quiver full of red glasswood arrows.

They soon left the caravan behind. The wind rustled the trees and puffer-flies hummed through the air, the only sounds besides the muted passage of the lyrine. After about ten minutes, they came out on a tall bluff that dropped away into a vale carpeted in silver-blue reeds tipped by purple bubbles. In the distance, a man was riding across the vale.

Shannon watched the man. "I know him."

The scout glanced at him. "He is from Dalvador?"

Shannon shook his head. "His name is Tarlin. He's an officer in Lord Rillia's army." He wondered why Tarlin was here alone. Perhaps he no longer had employ with Rillia; the end of the wars had greatly decreased the need for soldiers. They still skirmished with outlaws, but nowadays more often than not they served as city guards or in the retinue of a Bard or his honored visitors.

The scout laid his hand on Shannon's shoulder. "Rillia's speed with you, son."

Shannon clapped his hand over the scout's knuckles. "My thanks." Then he set off, looking for a way down the cliff.

On the western end of the ridge, a tangled woods had grown up its edge, almost to the top. Within the trees, the cliff sloped down into a hill. As Shannon followed a worn path down through the forest, disks crinkled on the trees around him. The bow on his back brushed one and it inflated into a red-jeweled orb, translucent and light.

He came out of the woods into a field of reeds so tall that they brushed his legs even though he sat high on Moonglaze. The other rider was well down the valley, just a small figure now. Leaning forward, Shannon spurred Moonglaze into a run. It was the first time he had given the lyrine his head in days and it felt wonderful. He relished the wind on his face. Reeds slapped at his boots and legs as he closed on the other rider.

Moonglaze lifted his head and whistled, his voice full of exultation, At that sound, the other rider brought his lyrine around, the animal stepping skittishly to the side.

Shannon reined Moonglaze to a stop a few paces away from the other man. "My greetings, Goodman Tarlin."

"Gods almighty." Tarlin stared at him. "Shannon Valdoria?"

Shannon smiled. "It's been a long time, sir."

"It certainly has." Tarlin shook his head. "You're so much older. I didn't recognize you."

"Would you like to ride together?" He could lead Tarlin away from the Archer camp. Shannon indicated the woods that bordered the valley across from the ridge where he had parted ways with the Archer scout. "I'm heading into Rillia."

He expected Tarlin to start riding again, but the other man didn't move. For the first time, Shannon realized Tarlin was shaking. It hadn't been obvious from far away, but he noticed now because the reeds that brushed Tarlin's knees were vibrating.

"Prince Shannon." Tarlin took a breath. "Your father has been searching for you."

Shannon froze. *Prince?* How would Tarlin know he had such a title? He had used the Iotic word; the language of Dalvador and Rillia didn't even have a word for prince.

"You've spoken to my father?" It took all Shannon's control to stop himself from kicking Moonglaze's sides and spurring the giant lyrine to bolt. "Is he nearby?"

"No." Tarlin clenched the reins so hard, his ragged nails dug visible marks into his skin. "He is at a camp deeper in the wilds. He needs help."

"What happened?" The pain in Shannon's legs surged and so did the nausea that had started in his nightmares. Gods, could it be his *father?* "Is he ill?"

"There is a man, a Bard." Tarlin's words tumbled out. "I have never heard of his land. Hollina. But he pays a good wage. I had no one to serve after Lord Rillia disbanded most of his army. This Bard came in peace, looking for men to serve on the city guard for his people. They have too few trained men for a full guard, so he searches other provinces. Your father and I met in a sword competition hosted by this Hollina. I took it as a good omen. But your father whispered to me that he needed help. I didn't know what to do. Although I serve a new Bard, I have known your father for many years. We fought together."

A chill walked up his spine. "Has this Bard harmed him?"

"By Rillia, I didn't know. *I swear.*" Tarlin's face paled beneath the freckles sprinkled across his crooked nose, which had been broken several times. "I made inquiries. A young woman who serves Hollina, she told me. Your father is a prisoner. His—his legs—he is injured. Terribly, terribly injured." His voice cracked. "He tried to escape and the Bard crushed his legs."

"No." The blood drained from Shannon's face so fast that dizziness threatened. "Surely my mother, her people, someone must have found him by now."

"No one has come."

"But how long has my father been a prisoner?"

"Many days. Sixteen, seventeen?"

"This cannot be!" Where was ISC?

"I'm sorry." Tarlin wound the reins around his clenched hand. "The girl gave me a message from him. Find help. She gave me the titles to call any of you that I found, to let them know the message was real. Like prince. He said you would understand."

Prince. Shannon's mind whirled. It was an Imperialate title. His father wanted him to think of his mother's people. To warn them? He had to help, but he feared he didn't have what it took. He had failed at so much, especially where his father was concerned. "Did he tell you anything else?"

"Just another name for the Bard. I didn't understand."

"Do you remember?"

Tarlin took a deep breath. And then he said the name that made Shannon want to cry to the winds and die for his father.

Vitarex Raziquon.

16

The Test

Secondary Iral Tapperhaven ran the Military Strategy class at DMA. Tall and lean, with dark hair cut at jaw length, she spent most of the classes listening as students proposed invasion scenarios by ESComm and countermeasures for ISC.

The walls of the room looked metallic right now, gold and ribbed, but their holoscreens could show whatever Tapperhaven wanted. Soz and the other cadets sat in VR chairs around a glossy oval table, some of them reclined with visors over their eyes, others like Soz with their visors up, operating in "real" space. She was the only novice.

In Dalvador, Soz hadn't had a referent to judge her suitability as a cadet. Doing well on exams told her nothing about living, learning, and working with other students. These were the top of the crop, those candidates the J-Force believed would make the best Jagernauts out of the thousands who applied to DMA and the few hundred who attended. It hadn't taken Soz long to see she fit here, and fit well. She no longer felt intimidated.

She was in her element.

Tapperhaven was proposing a new scenario. "The Traders kill both Dyad Keys. The Kyle web fails. ISC loses communications. The Traders launch a simultaneous attack against several major population and military sites in the Imperialate. With crippled communications, how will ISC respond?"

Soz stiffened, and her hand jerked on the table. Tapperhaven had just proposed that the Traders murdered two members of her family: Kurj, the Military Key to the Dyad; and her Aunt Dyhianna, the Assembly Key. Together, the Dyad powered the Kyle web, Kurj coordinating with ISC and Dyhianna with the government.

"Simulation on channel two," Tapperhaven said. "Activate."

Breathing deeply, Soz lowered the visor over her eyes and started the protocol. She didn't yet have the biomech web in her body that would connect her brain to exterior networks, so the simulation appeared only as a three-dimensional holovid on the inside of her visor. It was extraordinarily realistic, but she remained "outside" rather than experiencing it as reality.

If and when Soz progressed to her third year, the J-Force would begin the complex process of augmentation that would turn her into a cybernetic warrior, enhancing her strength, speed, and reflexes. It took several years for a cadet to receive full augmentation and learn to use it properly. Not everyone managed; some washed out of the academy at that stage, when their bodies rejected the augmentations. Soz's physical exams said she would have no problem, but such tests were never perfect.

For now, she had to be content with a holovid. The simulation placed her in a control chair at the end of a robot arm in the War Room onboard the Orbiter space station that served as one of several ISC command centers. The military spread its centers throughout the Imperialate so that no single strike could cripple the ISC command structure. As an additional safeguard, the Orbiter traveled, never staying in any particular volume of space.

The robot arm could carry Soz anywhere within the War Room. Muted clanks came from other robot arms as they ferried operators through the amphitheater. Below her, hundreds of consoles hummed and flashed with the work of telops, the telepathic operators who linked directly into the Kyle web. Pages hurried from station to station, running errands. It all served as an ISC nerve center, a central node in the vast web that extended through distances measured in light-years.

Kurj sat in a command chair far overhead. It hung like a blocky throne in the Star Dome, which showed a holographic view of space. The gold mesh that encased Kurj's body linked to sockets in his ankles, wrists, spine, and neck. Filaments threaded into his head as well. Add to that his metallic skin, hair, and eyes, and he looked more machine than man, huge and foreboding above the War Room. According to the specs rolling across Soz's display, he was coordinating a flood of data from all over the Imperialate, millions of worlds, habitats, outposts, and ships.

Kurj suddenly vanished from the chair. Alarms blared, aides ran, and consoles blazed with warnings throughout the amphitheater. According to the glyphs at the bottom of Soz's display, the Imperator had just died.

A new message appeared: *Message from Secondary Tapperhaven.*

Puzzled, Soz blinked twice, responding to the summons.

Tapperhaven's voice came over the audio prong in Soz's ear. "Cadet Valdoria, we're altering your feed for the simulation."

Odd. Soz had thought all cadets were supposed to receive the same program. Intrigued, she said, "Understood."

The sim went dark. Then it lightened again. After an instant of disorientation, she realized her view had changed; now she was looking down on the War Room from a higher vantage point. Robot arms still swung through the amphitheater below, but starlight bathed her up here.

Starlight?

Soz looked up. The Star Dome arched only a few meters above her. Incredibly, she was in the command Chair for the War Room. If the Traders had destroyed the Dyad, two other members of the Ruby Dynasty would have to form a new one. It sobered Soz; she and Althor were the only ones with direct military knowledge, and neither of them had anywhere near the experience to command ISC. Nevertheless, if Kurj died, one of them would become the Military Key. The Imperator.

If she was the Imperator in this sim, who was the Ruby Pharaoh? Her mother stood next in line. Roca had prepared her entire life for that position; should the current Dyad fall, Roca could immediately assume her duties as the Key to the Assembly. The same wasn't true for Soz or Althor. If the military title came to Soz now, she would defer command of ISC to the admirals, generals, and primaries who knew the job. It was the only rational choice. But she would remain Imperator: no one but a Rhon psion could act as the Key in the star-spanning mesh that held together the Imperialate. If anyone with less mental strength than a Rhon psion entered the Dyad, it would kill them.

However, Soz couldn't act as a Key just by sitting in a command chair. She had to join the Dyad powerlink that powered the web. To do so, she would have to enter one of the Locks, mechanisms that had survived for five millennia, since the Ruby Empire. No one in these modern times could say how the Locks operated; that knowledge had been lost in the Dark Ages after the fall of the empire, and modern science had yet to unravel the secrets of the ancient technology. This much they knew: the Locks let them access Kyle space, a universe outside of their own.

Tapperhaven spoke in her ear. "The simulation is based on

interviews with Imperator Skolia about his work in the War Room. The assumption is that you have assumed command but are not yet a Dyad Key."

"Understood," Soz said. It limited her options. A simulation couldn't injure her, but the J-Force techs who created this scenario would mimic reality to their best ability, even using wireless links to access her brain, re-creating the experience as accurately as they could manage given that none of them had ever been a Rhon psion installed in the War Room. According to the sim, she had linked to the Chair using an internal biomech web that in real life she lacked. That completed the sum total of her information about this scenario; she was otherwise going into this cold.

Time to get down to business.

Primary Node, respond, she thought—and then jumped as her own amplified thought reverberated in her mind.

The throne's answer rumbled. ATTENDING.

Whoa. The sensation of power felt so authentic, she vibrated.

What is the situation in the War Room? she asked.

OBSERVE. Statistics flooded her mind too fast to absorb.

Sort, she thought. **Prioritize. List the worst failures first.** The flood eased, but it still came too fast for her to grasp anything concrete. A river of glyphs poured across her display, taking up all the room. A better way had to exist to process this. **Do you have sorting routines created by Imperator Skolia?**

NO.

That didn't fit the Kurj she knew. He was obsessive about putting the universe into precise order. **Did he use any?**

DEFINE 'HE' IN THIS CONTEXT.

Imperator Skolia.

YOU ARE IMPERATOR SKOLIA.

Ah. The late Kurj Skolia.

SORTING ROUTINES IMPLEMENTED.

The deluge suddenly transformed into a grid extending in every direction. Each bar contained data about the War Room. Many glowed red, warning of system failures.

Soz scanned the bars, able to read them much more easily than the previous flood. She quickly located the most urgent problems; both the War Room environmental system and a SCAD defense node for a distant battalion were failing due to disruptions in power caused by the loss of links in the Kyle web.

She had too little time to fix both problems; she would have to let one fail. If the SCAD system collapsed, it would affect several battle cruisers. Communications were limping along well enough that the War Room could send vital information to the cruisers, in this case, intelligence about a Trader unit approaching them. But without their SCAD defenses, the cruisers would lose a tactical advantage, putting them at risk. If the environmental system here failed, the temperature in the War Room would become uncomfortable, the air stale, the working conditions difficult.

The decision seemed obvious: fix the SCAD. But she hesitated. The bars turned a deeper red, warning that the failures had begun. She had to act now; otherwise both systems would collapse.

Fix environment, she said.

COMMAND TOO UNSPECIFIC.

Soz blinked the holicon of an arrow over to a lurid red bar in the grid. **Make this green.**

ENVIRONMENTAL CONTROLS FOR WAR ROOM REPAIRED. The bar turned green at the same time that the red bar representing the SCAD system vanished, leaving a ragged gap in the grid.

"Damn," Soz muttered.

She spent the next hour working with the War Room telops to repair systems and contain the chaos. Eventually they brought the SCAD system back up and contacted the cruisers. Two had survived the attack, but the Traders had destroyed the third. Soz gritted her teeth; if this had been real, she would have just killed off hundreds of personnel and destroyed a major ISC command ship.

The display faded into a wash of gold. Tapperhaven's

voice came over the main channel that all the cadets received. "Sim completed. Surface."

Surface. Like submerged vehicles coming up out of the water. Soz smiled wryly. That was apt. She pushed back her visor and blinked in the lights of the VR room. The other cadets were doing the same, lifting visors, rubbing their eyes. Although she didn't know who had played what role in the sim, she could guess based on the personalities and behavior of the sim personnel.

The cadets shifted around in their seats, stretching, rubbing stiff muscles. A murmur of conversation started. Apex Colormock, a fourth-year student, said, "What the hell idiot set up that sim to fix the environmental controls first?"

Soz gritted her teeth. Great.

Another cadet laughed tiredly. "You better hope it wasn't any instructor watching this session, Apex."

Soz wished the instructors had done it. Serve Apex right for calling them idiots. Unfortunately she was the idiot.

"We're running late," Tapperhaven said. "Go over a download of the session tonight, and tomorrow we'll do the analysis."

Relief showed on more than one face that they wouldn't have to dissect their performance now. Soz felt only frustration. That decision had made *sense*. It still did. She was convinced of that even if no one else thought so.

As the cadets filed out of the room, Tapperhaven discreetly motioned for her to remain. Soz went through her holobook as if she were searching for something. It was pride; she didn't want anyone to know Tapperhaven wanted her to stay behind. At least none of the others seemed to realize Soz had made the environment decision.

After everyone else left, Tapperhaven said, "Wait here." She crossed to a door at the back of the room and touched a panel. The door slid to the side—and Tapperhaven left.

Soz blinked. What was going on?

Kurj came through the doorway.

Ah, hell. Soz wanted to melt into the floor. She saluted instead, clenching her fists and smacking her wrists together as she raised her arms straight out from her body.

He returned her salute. "At ease, Cadet."

"Thank you, sir." Soz lowered her arms, but she didn't feel the least bit at ease.

Kurj went to the head of the table and stood with his muscular arms crossed, studying her, the gold shields over his eyes. It never stopped amazing Soz that he could so resemble their mother, yet look so hard and unyielding. His square-jawed face and regular features reminded her of Althor and Kelric, but with a harsh cast that neither they nor their mother possessed.

"Why the environmental system?" he asked.

Soz met his gaze. "If it went out, it would have affected the performance of every person working in the War Room."

His voice cooled. "It certainly affected the performance of the crew on the battle cruiser when the Traders blew them up."

Soz winced. "Yes, sir." After a pause, she said, "Permission to ask a question."

"Go ahead."

"Have you run that scenario with anyone else as Imperator?"

"I've done it myself." His shielded eyes gave away nothing. "Althor has also. Three other cadets this year."

"What did you each do?"

"We all fixed the SCAD, except one person, who didn't make the decision soon enough to save either system."

"Did I lose more personnel?"

He spoke evenly. "I lost thirty-three soldiers. You lost three hundred six."

Gods. She hadn't expected that. "What about the others?"

For a long moment he didn't answer. Just when Soz felt certain he wouldn't respond, he said, "Althor lost three hundred twenty-four. The other cadets all lost more than four hundred. The one who didn't fix either system lost over a thousand."

"Did you do it as a cadet?"

Kurj shook his head. "The first time was a few years ago."

No wonder he had done so well. He came to it with decades more experience. Compared to cadets at her level, she had lost fewer personnel. "I was right to fix the environmental system."

Kurj frowned. "Or lucky."

Her good mood faded. It wasn't luck. He knew that. She couldn't say that to her CO, though, so she just looked at him.

To her unmitigated surprise, Kurj smiled, his teeth white against his metallic skin. "If looks could incinerate, I would be ashes right now."

Seeing him drop his guard startled her more than anything else he could have done. "My apologies, sir."

Kurj pushed his hand across his close-cropped curls. "The problem, Soz, is that to lead well you have to know how to lose. You can't always win. You can't always be right. You lost over three hundred people in that sim, and one of our most powerful cruisers. When you go out into real combat, real people will die."

"I appreciate that, sir."

"No. You don't. You think you do, but you've never really been tried." He came around the table to her. "You're flying through DMA faster than any cadet in decades. Later today Tapperhaven will tell you that we're going to accelerate your biomech surgery. If you're willing, we'll start the operations in a few weeks."

Her excitement leapt. "Sir! Yes, sir! You won't regret it."

"I hope not." Quietly he said, "Because I'm not sure you're ready."

Would he never be satisfied? "What more do I have to do to prove myself?"

"Survive when you aren't right. Lead after you fail. It is a far more difficult task."

Soz had no answer for that. She would do what she could, always, regardless of whether or not she won. And he was wrong if he thought she had never lost. She had already failed her family. To come here and be his heir, she had given up her home and turned her back on the father who had loved her unconditionally all her life. Until now. What else did Kurj want her to lose? The whole damn war, which Skolia supposedly wasn't fighting anyway, because it had never been declared, but which nevertheless killed thousands of soldiers every year?

Kurj was watching her face. She felt his mind nudge hers, but she kept her mental barriers strong.

"You want to fight the Traders," he said.

"Yes, sir." Why else would she be here?

"Kill them."

"If necessary."

In a low voice he said, "Obliterate them."

"I just want to defend my people."

He spoke softly. "The day will come, Soz, when you'll want to wipe the universe clean of any trace the Aristos ever existed, when you'll want to see every one of them die a long, painful death."

Soz stared at him. Never had he revealed so much of what lay behind that formidable metal surface he presented to the public.

"When that day comes," Kurj said, "I need to know I can trust your judgment. I need to know that the cocksure Jagernaut who obliterated the competition at DMA will act like an officer and not a juggernaut bent on revenge."

Soz didn't know where to put this. She had no referent to understand. "I will always act in the best interests of ISC. Personal revenge has no place in my duties."

"You say that now." Bitterness edged his voice. "We never stop paying the price. You, me, Althor, all the Rhon. You've spent your life in a bucolic paradise. But that is over. You are an Imperial Heir. Skolia will take everything you have, tear you up, spit you out, and leave you crumpled, but you have to drag yourself up and try again. No one else can do it. If we don't serve as Keys, the Imperialate will fall." His words ground out. "You hate that I've pitted you and Althor against each other. Well, know this: only a handful of Rhon psions stand between trillions of people and enslavement by the

Traders. Learn that. Live it. Breathe it. Then come back and tell me that you're ready to be my heir."

Her anger quieted. "I can't know what you've endured. I can only guess. But I'll do my best not to fail."

He spoke tiredly. "It's all that any of us can do."

Soz hoped her best would be enough.

"Please." Eldrinson whispered in the darkness, lying on the pallet. He felt Vitarex's presence in the tent. The Aristo spent hours here, like a healer sitting vigil, except no sane healer would crave the agony of his patient.

"You can't take me when you leave here." Eldrinson spoke past the pain that had been his companion now for days. He no longer knew how many seizures he had suffered or what additional damage they had done to his legs. "Let me die."

Vitarex answered from deeper in the tent. "I've no wish to see you die. I would take you with me if I could. But I cannot." Frustration darkened his voice. "I can do nothing until the ODS stops all this extra activity of theirs."

Eldrinson's pulse leapt. ODS? Vitarex would assume the acronym had no meaning to his captive. But he knew. Orbital Defense System. ISC was searching for him. He said nothing, schooling his face to impassivity, knowing how close he skimmed to the edge of discovery.

A rustle came from across the tent. "Come," Vitarex said.

The entrance flap scraped open and footsteps entered. Eldrinson picked up dismay from a familiar mind, the young man who served as a valet and cook, the husband of the woman who tended him. From the crinkling of cloth, Eldrinson guessed the man was bowing to Vitarex.

"My honor at your presence, Lord Vitarex," the man said.

"Indeed," Vitarex said. "Go fetch the men who helped me capture this man. Have them bring his belongings."

"Yes, sir." More footsteps, and the flap rustled again.

For a time Eldrinson lay, turning his concentration inward to help him deal with the pain. His world had narrowed to the surges of agony. After a while he became aware that Vitarex was speaking with someone else.

". . . anything else in his bags?" Vitarex asked.

"Just his pipe," a man said.

"Ah, well. It is probably wishful thinking on my part." Vitarex sounded as if he were talking to himself. "The severity of his injuries probably makes him seem like a more powerful psion than he actually is."

"Sir?" the other man asked.

"It is nothing," Vitarex said. "You may go."

"Do you want to look at his pipe?"

"No. That won't be necessary."

More footsteps. As the flap crinkled, Vitarex said, "Ah, why not? Bring me his pipe. I might as well take a look."

"Very well, sir." The other man sounded as if he had almost made it out of the tent.

Foreboding grew in Eldrinson. Pipe? He didn't smoke. The man could mean an arrow, but a native wouldn't call it a pipe. Besides, he hadn't brought a bow and arrows.

Then, suddenly, he knew what they meant. Not pipe.

His air syringe.

Gods almighty! He had to distract Vitarex before the Aristo saw the syringe. Eldrinson groaned, which took no acting.

Footsteps padded across the carpet and disk mail clinked. A hand brushed the tangled hair back from Eldrinson's face. "Would you like something to eat?" Vitarex asked. "Drink? Anything?"

"No." What would turn Vitarex's attention from the "pipe"? The Aristo was fastidious to the point of obsession. He had his servants bathe Eldrinson far more than any dying man would need.

"I feel ill," Eldrinson said. "I think—my last meal—I can't hold it."

"Wait." Vitarex sounded alarmed. "I will have someone bring a pot and washcloth. No, I'll go myself." His mail clinked and his footsteps receded. Eldrinson breathed out in relief; he hadn't thought the Aristo would want to see him vomit. Vitarex would be gone when the warrior returned with the syringe. Eldrinson could drag himself over, take the syringe, call Roca, and then hide the evidence.

Someone tapped at the tent. Vitarex's footsteps paused and he said, "Come."

The man from before spoke. "Here are his bags, milord."

NO! Just a few more moments and Vitarex would have been gone.

"Very well," Vitarex said. "Show me the pipe."

Eldrinson groaned loudly and began to choke.

Vitarex swore in Highton, the Aristo language. The oaths weren't part of the Highton that Eldrinson had learned from his tutors, but he recognized them anyway. Roca, in one of her more playful moods, had taught him how to cuss in ten offworld tongues.

Vitarex spoke fast. "I will look at the tube later. Right now I need a wash—" The sudden cessation of his words left a gaping silence.

"Lord Vitarex?" the warrior asked.

"Well, well," the Aristo murmured. "It's an ISC-issue medical air syringe. Top of the line."

Eldrinson closed his eyes, a useless habit since he couldn't see anyway. It didn't matter. The game was over.

"An interesting development." Vitarex's footsteps came back to the pallet. "You still planning to be sick?"

Eldrinson said nothing. What was the use? The less he spoke, the less he could reveal.

Vitarex's mail creaked as he knelt. "And why, my dear rustic farmer, would you have a nanomed-enhanced syringe issued by the Imperial Space Command of Skolia? Hmmm?"

"The healers at the port gave it to me."

"Did they now?"

"Yes."

"I could twist your legs to make you tell me the truth." Vitarex spoke in a deceptively soft voice. "But then, if pain drove you to reveal your secrets, you would have done that already, *Shannar.* Or should I say Prince Whatever? Perhaps you are even the Dalvador Bard, the man who married Roca Skolia. Tell me, how is she in bed? Do you like her—"

"Silence!" The shout tore out of Eldrinson.

"So," Vitarex murmured. "You don't like that. I wonder why that might be?"

Sweat trickled down Eldrinson's neck. He answered in the dialect of an uneducated Lyshrioli farmer. "It is wrong to speak of the daughter of the gods that way."

"What gods?" Vitarex sounded amused.

"The sun gods. Valdor and Aldan."

"How about the Assembly Heir, hmmm? Or the Foreign Affairs Councilor of the Assembly? Or a Ruby queen, eh? How would her consort have me speak of her?"

Eldrinson felt as if he were sinking in quicksand.

He expected the Aristo to gloat more, but Vitarex moved instead, standing, it sounded like, from the clinks of his mail. He spoke briskly, apparently to the other man. "I have what I came for. I will be leaving as soon as I verify his identity. It is too dangerous to risk further operations here."

"You are returning to Hollina?" the Tyroll man asked. "Shall we prepare to ride?"

Eldrinson wondered how this warrior could serve a monster who kept a dying, shattered man in his tent.

"Prepare as you need," Vitarex muttered. "I will leave as soon as the next window opens in the ODS."

Eldrinson knew what he had to do, then. He could never let Vitarex take him. He had to finish what the Aristo had started when he shot the bluff.

Somehow, he had to die.

"I'll go alone if I must." Shannon's voice shook with his intensity. "But I can't storm an entire camp alone." He willed the Elder to hear his need. "They will do worse than kill my father. They will torture him for the rest of his life. They will enslave my people. *Your* people. All of us. I swear that what I say is true. I must go for my father. I can't do it alone."

He sat astride Moonglaze facing the Elder, with other Archers gathered around him. They listened without comment, their ethereally beautiful faces cool and unmoved, or so it seemed to him.

"Please," Shannon said. "Help me."

They watched him with their ancient gazes.

Shannon was dying inside. He would go for his father. Today. Tarlin had sped on to Dalvador, riding hard for help. Something had to be wrong with the ISC detection methods. He had turned off the jammer, but no one had found either him or his father. It might be that no one was looking for him, but they would never let his father suffer this way. Whatever hid the Aristo also hid his father.

Tarlin had told him the ugly truth. His father's chances of survival were small, probably impossible. Shannon didn't understand how an Aristo could have violated their home, their haven, but it had happened. What if Vitarex took his father offworld? Shannon couldn't wait for help, not even a few hours. But if he went in alone to the Aristo's camp, they would surely capture him. He desperately needed help.

The Archers wouldn't break their centuries of seclusion for him. Why should they? This was his fight. They had no way to comprehend what it would mean if the Aristos captured members of the Ruby Dynasty, that the Traders would conquer Skolia, including Lyshriol. The lovely Blue Dale Archers would become slaves.

Motion came from behind the rows of the mounted Archers facing him. The lines parted and a rider rode her lyrine forward.

Varielle.

She stopped in front of Shannon. "I will ride with you."

His voice caught. "Thank you."

"And I." Another rider came forward. Elarion.

"And I." Tharon joined them.

The Elder considered them. "You would go with this man who is not of our tribe."

Varielle's gaze never wavered. "Yes."

"Yes," Elarion said.

"Yes," Tharon answered.

For a long moment the Elder studied them. Then she

turned back to Shannon. "Three of my most trusted riders choose your quest."

"They honor me." He waited, his heart beating hard.

Finally she said, "I give my answer now as well."

Shannon knew if she refused him, none of the others would ride. With only four of them, he didn't think they could succeed. But he had to try. Gods forgive him if he ended up causing the deaths of these three who had become his friends.

The Elder said no more, she just sat on her lyrine, until finally his heart sank. She had refused him.

Then she spurred her mount forward. "I will ride with you, Shannon of Dalvador."

His voice caught. "Thank you."

She spoke quietly. "You have dealt well with us. You are one of us, but not. Now you speak of menaces beyond the music of our ken. I will trust the sight of your heart."

Other riders moved forward, joining him, their voices flowing as they discussed these changes in their plans. They soon moved out, half of their fighters with Shannon, the other half remaining behind to protect the caravan.

For the first time in centuries, the Blue Dale Archers rode to Rillia.

17

The Red Haze

They arrived at twilight.

In the growing dusk, they crested the ridge above the wild forest that sheltered Vitarex's camp. They lined up, twenty silvered Archers hidden in mists that curled around the trees and their nodding spheres. In the camp below, a few fires burned, but it otherwise remained quiet. No one expected the Blue Dale Archers to visit.

Shannon rode between Varielle and Elarion. He talked to no one and no one intruded on his reserve. Several times Archers rode alongside his lyrine to speak with him, but they took one look at his face and withdrew. Shannon didn't know how he appeared, but if it reflected his growing pain, their response was no surprise.

He hurt. The agony in his legs had intensified until he could barely endure it. He had to barrier his mind, protect it from the pain tearing apart his father, or he would never be able to fight for his father's life. But if he blocked out the beacon of Eldrinson's mind, he couldn't locate his father in the camp below.

They rode down the ridge under the cover of trees. The twilight had deepened into a foggy darkness with no moonlight to show the way. It didn't matter. Moonglaze knew. Shannon wasn't certain how; he couldn't pick up much in the moods of an animal, even one with the intelligence of a lyrine. But he could tell Moonglaze sensed from him the presence of the man they had come to rescue.

He had turned the jammer back on, hiding from Vitarex now. Archer scouts drifted among the trees, indistinguishable from the shadow-drenched forest. Shannon could see how they had remained hidden for so many generations; they blended with the land, with the trees and the hills, until they were no more than wraiths.

A scout took form out of the mist and rode to the Elder, who was up ahead on her lyrine. When the Elder motioned to Shannon, he spurred Moonglaze forward and joined them. The scout was small even for an Archer, with a braid of platinum hair that hung to her waist. The steel of her gaze belied her fragile appearance.

At the Elder's nod, the scout spoke to Shannon. "Many sentries guard the camp."

He swore softly. A group of travelers gathered together by the prospect of employment had no reason to post more than a few guards, if any. But Vitarex knew better.

"How many?" the Elder asked.

"Enough to complicate our work," the scout said. She

spoke to Shannon. "We can get you into camp. But we've no idea where you should go once you're in."

"As we get closer, I can—I can feel—" He took a shaky breath. "I'll know where to find him."

"Can you lead a party there?" the Elder asked.

"I think so. He is in a tent. But I can't be sure. His pain swamps it all."

The Elder watched him, her face shadowed. "I do not understand this sensing of minds."

"Imagine what you call the music of your ken."

"Yes."

"It is like that, but more so."

"And you will recognize his music when you are near?"

A deep tremor passed through Shannon. "It is no music, now. He screams with pain, though he makes no sound at all."

The Elder's face creased. She motioned Varielle and Elarion forward, then spoke to them and the scout. "Go with Shannon. The rest of us will create diversions."

The scout inclined her head. "So we shall."

Shannon's voice caught. "My thanks."

The Elder touched his shoulder. "May you find him surcease."

"I hope so," he whispered.

They headed through the fog, southward, and his awareness of his father increased. He could barely stay on Moonglaze now, he hurt so much.

A skeetel-puff hummed. Shannon raised his head, trying to see the drifting bubble, a small creature that could fit in the palm of his hand. Its body resembled a tiny version of the stained-glass spheres on the trees. He saw nothing, but the skeetel droned again. With a start, he realized Elarion had made the sound. Other calls came from farther away, eerie whistles he had never heard before. The uncanny cries floated through the woods, moving northeast, and the hairs on Shannon's neck prickled.

A shout came from nearby, then another. He pulled Moonglaze to a stop. When he realized they were by a yellowglass tree, he nudged the lyrine forward, slowly, so his hooves made no sound, and stopped at a purpleglass tree that blended with Moonglaze's coat.

His companions faded into the mist. Shannon hadn't wanted to wait until night, but he knew it was easier to hide, especially in these wilds where mists wreathed the tangled woods after the day cooled into night. But every moment they waited was excruciating. It meant another moment of agony for his father.

The ghost calls beyond the camp drifted away and faded into the distance. Shannon started up again, concentrating on his tie with his father. A tent loomed in the fog, pale and dim, peaked, with large tassels hanging off the edges of its roof. No. Not here. He rode by. His fist curled tightly around the reins. He couldn't bear the pain. He had to shut it off. But when he blocked his mind, his awareness of the Bard receded. He had to release the block or he would never find his father.

The pain returned.

Snoring came from within the second tent they passed, deep and coarse. A man stood by a tree on its other side, his hand on the hilt of his sword, his gaze directed toward the other edge of camp, where calls continued to echo. Shannon and his party passed behind the tent like phantoms of mist.

A third tent formed out of the fog. Shannon froze, becoming so still that Moonglaze stopped. Plumes of condensation rose from the lyrine's nostrils.

Shannon slid off Moonglaze. The other three Archers drew alongside him and Varielle dismounted, but the scout and Elarion remained on their lyrine, bows nocked and ready. Varielle had hers as well, her hand gripped firmly around the molded glasswood. Shannon didn't speak, he just tilted his head toward the tent. She nodded, understanding. Then she touched his face. Until he felt her wipe away the moisture, he hadn't realized he was crying. He hinged his four fingers around hers and she squeezed his hand. Then they moved toward the tent like ghosts in the fog.

No alarms sounded. Shannon hoped his jammer was serving its purpose, hiding them, that this wasn't an attempt by guards here to lull them into a false sense of security. He knelt by the tent. He had hoped they could lift the bottom and crawl under, but its floor joined smoothly to its wall. While he worked to separate the two, Varielle kept watch. He pulled the dagger out of his belt and tried to cut a hole, but it did no good. He recognized the tent cloth; nanontubules threaded it, strengthened the material, and repaired damage.

Finally he sheathed his dagger and stood, his hand on the hilt of his sword. Worried, he motioned to Varielle. They padded around to the front of the tent—and froze. A warrior stood at the entrance, a large man in heavy disk mail with a sword at his hip.

Varielle quirked an eyebrow at Shannon, but he didn't understand. With no more warning, she darted out into the woods, kicking up the remnants of crushed tree spheres.

The guard jerked up his head. "Who is there?"

That was smart, Shannon thought to him. *Warn your enemy that you heard them and that you have no idea who they are, all in three words.* He waited in the shadows. He hoped it didn't alert anyone else.

A wraith flickered in the woods, a beautiful but otherworldly woman. She disappeared with a musical laugh.

"Rillia's arrow!" The man went after her. "Come back here."

Shannon shook his head as the warrior jogged into the woods, leaving his post. This fellow had more bulk than brains. Shannon didn't want Varielle in the way of harm, but she had given him the opening he needed. He edged along the tent to the entrance. Excruciatingly aware that the guard could come back any moment, he lifted the flap and ducked inside.

Pain.

Even with his barriers up, Shannon couldn't block it out. Darkness surrounded him. Someone breathed in a rasp nearby. His suffering filled the tent, unbearable, and yet it had to be borne.

As Shannon's eyes adjusted, he saw a shadowy figure lying on the ground, the only other person in the tent, it looked like. He went over and silently dropped to one knee by the figure. Or he thought he had been silent. The man rasped three words—and nearly stopped Shannon's heart.

"Let me die."

Shannon's whisper shook in the dark. "Father?" He would have recognized that voice anywhere, no matter how hoarse.

"Shannon?" His father's voice cracked. "Gods, no."

"Vitarex didn't catch me." He spoke low and fast. "He doesn't know I'm here. Tarlin found me. I came with the Blue Dale Archers." He felt around the pallet. "I'm going to take you away." Perhaps he could drag his father on these rugs.

Eldrinson caught his arm. "You must escape this place."

"I won't leave you." Tears slid down Shannon's face. He strained to pull the rugs toward the entrance. Had he been one of his indomitable brothers, no doubt he wouldn't have cried. He would have done this all with great power and strength, undaunted. But he was no mighty warrior, he was just Shannon.

"Aii . . ." His father's cry of pain was almost inaudible, but it screamed in Shannon's mind. It dismayed him to hurt his father, but he couldn't go any easier. They had to leave as fast as possible or they would never go at all.

As Shannon dragged the pallet, he asked, "Do you have your air syringe?" He could dial in a painkiller.

"Vitarex . . . took it."

A chill went through Shannon. "Does he know it was yours?"

"Y-yes."

The blood drained from Shannon's face, leaving him cold. He stopped at the entrance and ducked his head outside, verifying the guard was still gone, undoubtedly searching for Varielle, tormented by silvery visions of an elusive wood nymph. It terrified Shannon that she put herself in such danger, for he had no doubt what the warrior would do if he caught her. That she risked herself for his father filled him with gratitude and fear.

He maneuvered the rug outside, his mind blazing with the renewed pain it gave his father. Shannon *felt* his father struggling not to scream. As he towed the pallet around the tent, Elarion and the Archer scout appeared, both on foot, leading their lyrine. Eldrinson lay still, his eyes squeezed shut, his face contorted, his legs hidden by a blanket made from lyrine hair.

Clutching a handful of straps, the scout was pulling a sturdy framework of glasswood poles. While Elarion kept watch, Shannon and the scout painstakingly lifted the pallet with Eldrinson onto the frame and fastened it to the poles. Every slight motion jarred the Bard, sending pain rolling through him and so also through Shannon. Yet incredibly, his father made no sound.

Eldrinson never looked directly at any of them. When Shannon tried to meet his gaze, he couldn't seem to connect. Surely it was because of the dim light out here, where faces became pale ovals in the dark. That had to be the cause. It had to be.

Eldrinson spoke in a low voice. "Son?"

"We must hurry." Shannon wanted to say so much, tell his father of his remorse for all the trouble he caused, of his love, of his grief. But they had no time. He looped braided reed-straps over the rugs, securing the pallet in place.

"Shannon, listen." Eldrinson caught his arm. "If I never have another chance to tell you—"

"Don't say that!" Shannon whispered.

"I am sorry," Eldrinson said. "Whatever I did to hurt you, I am so terribly sorry. I never meant to drive you away. You are my joy." His grip tightened. "I always have and always will love you, my son."

A weight lifted from Shannon. Softly he said, "I have much to apologize for. But know I love you, too."

The scout tied a last strap and stood up. "We must go."

Shannon rose to his feet. "Please take him back to the caravan. Care for him. Help him."

Elarion's forehead furrowed. "You are not coming with us?"

"Shannon, no." His father's voice rasped.

"You must come with us," the scout murmured.

Shannon knew what he had to do. "Go," he told them. "Save the Dalvador Bard. An empire will thank you."

Then he headed back into the camp.

He crept among the tents, seeking a nightmare. He had no trouble finding Vitarex; the darkness of the Aristo's mind threatened to swallow him in its suffocating need. Shannon had gone beyond dismay, beyond anger. He knew only the agony his father endured. Vitarex had done that. The Aristo had invaded their sanctuary. It astounded Shannon that his father still lived. He would never walk again. Nor could he deny the other truth any longer, what had been obvious but he hadn't wanted to acknowledge. The Dalvador Bard was blind.

What burned through Shannon was like nothing he had known before. Flames consumed him, a fire of rage, yet he was cold inside. He crept through the camp, Moonglaze at his side. Condensation curled from the lyrine's nostrils. Shannon had looped ropes into his belt, and the jammer hung in his travel bags. He stalked the cavity of Vitarex's mind. Nothing could hide the Aristo from him. Red hazed his vision until the mists themselves seemed to turn crimson.

In the distance, the eerie calls of the Blue Dales Arches trilled and whistled as if spirits drifted among the trees. They were still drawing away the guards, but Shannon knew he didn't have much time. He had to hurry before one of Vitarex's men came back and caught him here.

He drew near to his quarry.

A tent blocked his way, pale in the fog. Shannon crept along the side. A warrior guarded the entrance, a man who held his sword in his right rather than left hand. It made no difference. Most Lyshrioli were left-handed, but among all the Valdoria princes, only Shannon and Del-Kurj were. Their brothers took after their mother, using their right more than the left. Shannon had spent his life training against right-handed opponents.

Hidden in the fog, he left Moonglaze behind the tent and edged closer, his tread as silent as a Blue Dale Archer, as silent as it had been all those times he slipped from his home and wandered through Dalvador so late at night, he was the only person out, always restless, always seeking what he couldn't find, his own people. So he moved now.

The guard never knew anyone came up behind him until Shannon hooked his right arm around the man's neck and pressed hard. As the guard struggled, he grabbed at Shannon where a left-handed assailant would have caught him. Instead of getting Shannon's hand and wrist, the man's fingers scraped his elbow. All the time, Shannon choked him, holding his own wrist with his other hand, added leverage to cut off the man's air. The guard gave one last strangled grunt and collapsed, unconscious.

Shannon took a ragged breath. He quickly bound the guard, then drew his sword, the blade whispering in its sheath. He stepped closer to the tent, silent in the carpet of crushed glitter, and paused at the entrance, his hand touching the flap. Light leaked around its edges. Nothing but the music of night came to him: the whistle of lyrine; a rustle of wind in the disks hanging from the trees; strange calls in the distance, which only he knew were as the Blue Dale Archers.

Shannon stepped inside.

The light wasn't bright enough to blind him, but he had to squint. A man was sitting at a carved table, his attention focused on a silver and black device that resembled the communications equipment in Brad's starport office.

Vitarex.

Shannon knew. Vitarex disguised himself as a Rillian, his hair yellow and lavender, his eyes violet, his clothes and disk mail authentic. He had even altered his hands into the hinged structure. But nothing would change the Aristo perfection of his face or his aura of arrogance. Without the disguise, he would have shimmering black hair and red eyes.

Vitarex turned his head. He considered Shannon with a bemused expression but no surprise, as if wild-eyed youths broke into his tent all the time. He spoke in Highton. "Well, you're quite the provider, aren't you?"

Shannon's pulse stuttered at the insinuation, that he was no more than a slave for Vitarex to torture. He had no doubt the Aristo spoke Highton to see if he would react; on Lyshriol, only members of the Ruby Dynasty knew the language. Vitarex was probing. He had to have realized Shannon was a psion; just as he recognized Vitarex from the cavity in his mind, so this Trader lord would know him as a psion from the completion his mind provided.

When Shannon said nothing, Vitarex switched into perfect Trillian. "What did you do with my guard?"

Shannon walked forward and raised his sword.

"You can't kill me, Princeling." Vitarex touched a cluster of bubbles engraved in the table. A rumbling buffeted Shannon, so low in pitch that he felt more than heard it. The vibration shook his bones and made his stomach lurch. Distracted, he poked at his ear.

"Amazing," Vitarex murmured. "You shouldn't hear that."

Gritting his teeth, Shannon headed toward him again. The sensation grew worse, but he forced himself forward another step, his sword clenched in his hand.

Vitarex rose to his feet. "I will be leaving soon. With your father." An oily smile spread across his too-perfect face. "You may come with us."

Shannon's temples ached with the vibrations. This was more than just sound. He shook his head, but nothing helped. The room blurred and tilted around him.

"Your balance goes next," Vitarex commented. "The effects you feel come from a tangler field designed to disrupt neural impulses in your brain." His smile turned cold, matching his gaze. "It works particularly well on psions, with all those extra neural structures of yours. The sensations grow more and more unpleasant." Bliss washed across his face. "For you. I'm protected from it."

Shannon thought of what the Blue Dale Archers called the music of his ken, what he had come to realize was the trance he submerged into when he ran through the plains, curled in the warmth of Moonglaze's stable, or wandered in the woods, the trance he had gone into high in the Blue Dale Mountains when Moonglaze thought he was dying. He closed his eyes and blanked his mind, submerging into the trance.

The pain in his temples receded.

Slowly he opened his eyes. Vitarex raised an eyebrow. He appeared composed, but unease flowed from his mind. He had expected Shannon to be writhing on the floor by now.

Shannon took another step. His entire body felt as if it were an improperly tuned musical instrument playing discordant notes. But he kept going. Another step. Another.

Vitarex frowned and edged closer to the table. He tapped another of its carvings and the vibrations rumbling through Shannon's body increased. But for all his discomfort, Shannon felt wrapped in a cocoon that protected him from the worst effects. He didn't know why Blue Dale Archers differed from other Homo sapiens, whether they resulted from genetic drift or a deliberate attempt to breed another type of human, but whatever the reason, the fields of Vitarex's weapon didn't affect him as they would a normal man.

Shannon stepped to within striking distance of Vitarex. He swung his sword at the Aristo, slicing the air at waist level. Vitarex jumped back, more startled than threatened. He hit a high-backed chair and it toppled to the floor.

"You should be screaming in pain," Vitarex said. He sounded annoyed.

Shannon spoke through gritted teeth. "So should you." He wanted nothing more than to flee this pressure on his mind, but he couldn't relent. Nothing would stop him.

"All I have to do is shout for help. My men will be here within seconds."

A lie. Vitarex's men were chasing wraiths and nymphs. But the Aristo wasn't worried. Why? He wouldn't sit here unprotected. True, he had safeguards that would work against most people, but Shannon didn't believe the Aristo had no other options than the tangler. It made no difference. No matter what Vitarex threw at him, he would keep going.

Vitarex folded one arm across his torso, rested the elbow of his other arm on it, and tapped his chin. Then he indicated a finely carved chest a few paces away. "I could go over there and get my EM pulse rifle. I would reach it before you reached me. A projectile from my gun would kill you immediately." He sighed. "But what an unforgivable waste of your glorious Rhon mind."

Shannon had trouble hearing. The tangler was affecting him, it was just taking longer than expected. He swayed as his balance deteriorated. He wanted to close his eyes and concentrate on his trance, but he couldn't risk it with Vitarex so close to the gun.

The Aristo stepped back. Shannon followed—and nearly fell. He had to act fast; soon he would be incapacitated. If Vitarex wanted him alive, the Aristo needed to wait only a little longer to make the capture.

Shannon swept the tent with his gaze, searching for the source of the tangler field. Tapestries hung on the cloth walls, above furniture engraved with glasswood bubbles. Rugs lay several layers deep. Crossed swords hung above the brazier in one corner, and a standing lamp with a rose-glass shade stood by the table. Vitarex was circumspect about his technology; Shannon couldn't locate any source for the tangler. He doubted it was in the table where Vitarex had pressed the carving, but that was his only clue. He lunged and swung his sword, but at the table rather than Vitarex. By now, he had so little control over his body, he missed and hit the standing lamp instead, severing the top from its glasswood pole.

Night enveloped the tent.

The lamp used a more advanced light source than oil. Nothing caught fire. Nor was the darkness complete. Braziers burned in two corners of the large tent, shedding a dim red glow across Vitarex, making him resemble Shannon's conception of the demons he half believed invaded his father's body during epileptic seizures.

Shannon still felt the tangler effects. He took another jerky step, driven by his rage. Vitarex seemed more amused than concerned. He backed up to the chest and threw it open while Shannon lurched the last few paces that separated them. He swung at Vitarex, but he could no longer control his sword, and the Aristo easily dodged the clumsy attack.

Vitarex grabbed a weapon out of the chest.

Shannon knew then that he was going to die. Vitarex wasn't holding a pulse rifle, though; it looked more like an air syringe pistol. Shannon had no time to think—he just let his legs crumple, collapsing as Vitarex fired. The shot missed his chest, but it hit him in the shoulder. Numbness spread down his arm. Clutching his sword, he struggled to his feet only a step away from Vitarex.

"Gods," the Aristo muttered. "What do they feed boys on this planet?" He fired again, hitting Shannon square in the chest. "That ought to stop someone twice your size."

Shannon swallowed. His torso was going numb. He could barely raise his sword, but he managed, clenching it until his knuckles hurt. Vitarex made an exasperated noise and blocked the wavering strike with his gun, knocking the blade out of Shannon's hand. In that instant, when Vitarex's over-confident attention was focused on the sword clattering to the ground, Shannon drew his dagger with his other hand. As numbness overtook his body, he let himself topple forward. He smashed into Vitarex and they fell together, and slammed into the floor. Shannon's breath went out with a whuff while his mind lurched and spun. Vitarex made an odd gurgle that abruptly cut off.

Everything became still.

Shannon was lying half on top of Vitarex with one arm trapped between their bodies and the other flung over his head. His heart pounded in his chest. He didn't know what had happened to his dagger; he was still clenching the hilt, but his fist was flush against Vitarex's chest.

Slowly, Shannon rolled to the side. His hand remained clenched on the dagger and the movement wrenched his arm, yet he felt no pain. His body was numb, but he could move. With a groan, he strained to pull his arm free. After several fruitless seconds, he realized he had to release the dagger. When he relaxed his grip, his arm fell away from Vitarex. Still the Aristo didn't move. His eyes remained closed.

Shannon stared at his hand, the one that had held the dagger. Even in the dim light from the braziers he saw the blood that covered it and soaked the sleeve of his tunic. He pushed up on his elbows and leaned over Vitarex.

No response.

He put his fingers against a vein Vitarex's neck, then his hand in front of the Aristo's nose, seeking a pulse or an exhalation.

Nothing.

It was then that he realized blood was no longer pumping out of the wound in Vitarex's chest. Shannon suddenly felt chilled all the way through, and bile rose rose in his throat.

He had just murdered a man.

His hands started to shake. *Gods help me.* For all that he had trained with a sword and dagger all his life, it had been a sport to him. He had never expected to use the skills in violence. But since the instant he had felt what Vitarex had done to his father, he had thought only of revenge. Now that he had answered that driving anger, now that the red haze was clearing from his vision, dismay flooded him.

"No," Shannon whispered. He dragged himself to his sword, fighting the effects of the tangler field and whatever Vitarex had shot him with. His arms and torso were leaden. He barely managed to pull his legs under him so he was kneeling on the rug. He fumbled his sword into its sheath, and his bloodied hand slipped along the hilt, leaving dark streaks. Then he crawled to the carved chest and leaned against it as he pushed up onto his feet. He swayed, his balance ruined by the tangler. If he didn't get out of the tent now, he might never make it. The guards would discover him with the murdered Vitarex, a mute testimony to his guilt.

He forced himself forward. Step. Step again. It was the longest walk he had ever taken, but finally he reached the entrance of the tent. He could barely push aside the flap. As he lurched outside, he stumbled on the unconscious guard and almost fell. He thought he might be in shock; his mind felt as numb as his body. He staggered through the woods. Any moment a sentry could discover that the spirits haunting this forest were Blue Dale Archers. He had to escape this place, and fast, though he could hardly walk.

A low whistle came at his side and an animal pushed its head into his shoulder. Moonglaze. Shannon gave a choked sob as the lyrine nudged him again, a sign he wanted Shannon to mount.

"I can't," he whispered, sagging against the animal. "Help me."

Moonglaze knelt slowly, folding his powerful front legs under his body. When he had gone all the way down, Shannon dragged himself onto his back and collapsed forward, his arms around the lyrine's neck, his hands clutched in his mount's thick hair.

With a whuff of air, Moonglaze struggled back to his feet. Shannon wanted to scratch his neck, praise him, show his gratitude, but he could neither speak nor move, only hang on. The lyrine walked among the trees with the smooth, silent tread of an experienced war mount. Shannon clenched Moonglaze's hair until the hinges of his hand ached, but he couldn't loosen his grip. If it bothered Moonglaze, he gave no hint, just kept going, his pace increasing as he neared the ridge where they had descended into the camp with the Archers.

As they rode beyond reach of the tangler field, Shannon began to recover his equilibrium. Lifting his head, he peered into the darkness. The camp continued to sleep. A few voices called in the distance, but none here. Anyone close to Vitarex's tent would be affected by the tangler, except perhaps Archers; if Shannon had partial immunity to its effects, a full-blooded Archer probably had even more. At least he hoped so. He didn't want them hurt.

As they climbed the ridge, leaving the camp behind in the fog and the night, Shannon finally loosened his grip on Moonglaze's neck. The lyrine whistled, as close to an expression of relief as he would express. Shannon sat up slowly. Although he still felt clammy and sick, his dizziness had receded. His mind spread into trance state, holding off the guilt that hovered within him. He would soon have to face what he had done, but he had to survive first and make sure the Archers were taking his father to safety—if any safety existed anywhere.

Shannon didn't know how long Moonglaze carried him through the night. He sat with his head hanging down, only half aware of his surroundings. Gradually he became aware of a shadowy figure riding near him in the fog, a darker patch in the darkness. He stiffened, lowering his mental barriers, and reached out with his mind. His thoughts joined a swirling pool of emotion . . .

Blue Dale Archer.

Moonglaze snuffled.

"Shhh." Shannon patted his neck.

The other rider spoke in a low voice. "Shannon?"

"It is me." He hesitated. "Elarion?"

"Yes." The Archer came in closer to ride at his side.

Alarm surged through Shannon, disrupting the precarious calm he had attained during trance. "My father! You must take him—"

"He is safe," Elarion told him, soothing. "He is up ahead, in the caravan."

"The caravan came out of the mountains?" That they had even accompanied him out of the Blue Dales into the less massive range known as Ryder's Lost Memory had stunned him. Never in an octet of eons would he have expected them to enter Rillia.

"Don't you know where we are?" Elarion asked.

Shannon hesitated. During his trance, he had let Moonglaze go where he would, trusting the lyrine. Belatedly, he realized they were climbing more steeply now rather than walking through the rolling hills of Rillia. "Are we in Ryder's Forest?"

"It is Ryder's, yes."

Fear caught at Shannon. "And Varielle?"

"She is fine."

He whispered what he feared most to know. "And my father?"

Silence.

"Tell me," Shannon said. He couldn't bear to know but he had to hear.

Elarion answered softly. "I'm sorry."

Shannon's world seemed to end. "He died?"

"No. He lives."

"Why are you sorry?"

"He is—hurt. We can move him no more. It would kill him." Fear washed through his mood. "We are only a few hours' ride from the Rillian camp. They could still find us."

"Tarlin will bring my mother and ISC." Shannon said it as much to reassure himself as Elarion. "No one on Lyshriol can stop Imperial Space Command." Except they were too late.

If Elarion had doubts about Shannon's claim, he kept them to himself. Instead he asked, "And Bard Vitarex?"

"He is dead."

Elarion let out a long breath. They rode in silence.

A skeetel-puff hummed. Shannon saw nothing, but the skeetel buzzed again.

Then Elarion hummed exactly like a skeetel. Another buzz came through the night, much closer now. Two riders took form out of the darkness in front of them like spirits coalescing in the foggy night. Archers. They joined Shannon and Elarion, and rode at their sides without a word.

Shannon didn't even see the caravan until they were within the camp. The Archers had kept the tents dark and lit no fires. More sentries paced among the trees than Shannon had previously seen in his time with them. He hated that he had brought this danger to them, his newfound people, but he would be forever grateful for their help with his father.

They led him toward the center of the camp. When they stopped before a small tent, Shannon slid off Moonglaze, better able to move now, though he remained stiff and sore. Dried blood flaked off his hand. He swallowed the bile that rose in his throat.

Varielle was waiting at the entrance of the tent, her bow in her hand. She touched his cheek as he came up to them, her gaze solemn. He took her hand and hinged his palm around her four fingers. He couldn't speak. He could barely breathe. She squeezed his back, then let him go. Steeling himself, he lifted the flap and entered the tent. The only light inside came from the dim glow of a brazier in one corner. It cast almost no light over the pallet a few paces away.

His father lay there, unmoving.

18

The Node

Roca raced to the starport, through orb-tipped reeds and the overcast night. Tarlin ran at her side. He seemed stunned, even in shock. He had ridden hard and fast over the mountains, making the journey in less than a day. He could have killed himself thundering through the upper ranges of the Backbone at such speeds.

He had her eternal gratitude.

She spoke into her wrist comm. "Brad, is the flyer ready to go?" She was sprinting so hard, the words came out in gasps. Reeds snapped against her legs.

"Yes." Brad's voice came back sharp and fast. "I'm cold-starting it now."

The reeds thinned out as Roca and Tarlin neared the port. The flyer waited on the brightly lit tarmac, glittering gold and black. Tarlin hesitated at the edge of the field, his face pale. Roca doubted he had ever seen anything like the flyer nor touched a material like the tarmac. But he faltered only a moment and then picked up speed again.

They reached the flyer within seconds, and Brad grabbed Roca's hand as she reached up to him. Without missing a stride, she jumped up into the cabin. Tarlin swung up behind her, his ashen face the only indication he was dealing with technology that had to look like magic to him. Her respect for him went up another notch. Eldri had always chosen his friends well.

"You'll need to strap in," Roca told him as she dropped into the copilot's seat. "The webbing will wrap around you. Don't be alarmed; it's for safety." Even as she spoke, her own webbing was folding its silver mesh around her body. She fastened the catches.

Tarlin lowered himself into a seat set slightly back between the pilot and copilot's chairs. He copied her actions, strapping the webbing around his body. Roca knew what it took for him to accept all this. The Lyshrioli lived the same, year after year; change disturbed them. Yet he never flinched.

The comm crackled. "Dr. Tompkins, this is Colonel Majda on the *Ascendant*. We still don't have a lock on either King Eldrinson or the Aristo Vitarex."

Brad spoke into the mesh. "We're headed out now. Do you have a fix on us?"

"To the centimeter," Majda said. "The shuttles are on their way. ETA in six point three minutes."

"Understood, Colonel," Brad said. "We will meet you at the Archer camp."

Just hearing the word "Aristo" made Roca ill. The Traders had violated her most treasured retreat, the haven for her family. They had brought great agony to her husband. No mercy existed in her now. Vitarex would pay. She was the Foreign Affairs Councilor of the Assembly, her life dedicated to dealing in diplomacy with other governments, including the Traders, but right now she could think of only one thing, that she wanted him to pay long and hard and forever, to suffer the same torments he had inflicted on her husband.

First they had to reach Eldri—before his injuries ended his life.

* * *

Eldrinson floated in a drugged sea. He never lost consciousness, but he drifted in and out of awareness. The pain had receded. The hot beverage these strangers gave him to drink hazed his mind and dulled the worst of his agony.

After many hours, or perhaps only a moment, he became aware of someone nearby. He struggled to focus. A man was speaking, softly, brokenly, tears in his voice.

". . . don't die," he pleaded. "Please. You must live. I beg you." His voice broke. "I couldn't bear it if you died."

Eldrinson tried to speak, but no words came. He wet his lips and tried again. "Shannon?" It was barely a whisper.

"We're bringing help." Shannon's words were ragged and earnest. "Tarlin went for Mother. Help will come."

Eldrinson knew it was too late. His life was slipping away. He was too tired. But somehow, incredibly, he had achieved his goal. He had kept his secret from Vitarex long enough to stop the Aristo from taking him off Lyshriol.

A hand touched Eldrinson's forehead, a hinged palm cool against his fevered skin. "Father, can you hear me?"

"I hear," Eldrinson whispered. "I am—glad you are here." He paused, gathering his energy. "I don't want your mother to see me—see me like this. To see . . . my death."

"You won't die." Shannon brushed back his hair.

"Can't see. . . ."

"We'll fix it," Shannon whispered. "We'll make you better."

Urgent voices came from outside and the scrape of booted feet. Eldrinson's sensitized mind reacted to nuances his ears couldn't yet discern. "No! She must not—see me—"

"Who, Father?" Shannon asked.

The voices resolved into Skolian Flag, a tongue flat and harsh after Shannon's Trillian. Then a woman spoke in Trillian, almost chiming, though she had never learned to make the true sounds. Didn't have the right vocal cords . . .

"They're here!" Shannon's boots crackled as he jumped to his feet.

Eldrinson reached out to stop him, but Shannon's footsteps were already receding across the tent. Rustles came from the entrance, then the scuff of feet and someone's abrupt intake of breath. The sharp odor of the oil Brad used in the flyer cut through the air. Currents moved across his face as people knelt around him, creaking, scraping, clinking.

"Eldri?" A soft palm cupped his cheek. Tears filled her voice. "Eldri, can you hear me?"

He pulled his head away. "Roca, leave me."

"I can't." She was crying now. Her hair brushed his arms, his hands, his face, its clean fragrance painful in a way that no medicine could help. She pressed her lips against his forehead and he wanted to weep with the bittersweet agony of knowing he could never again be the man she had fallen in love with.

Other people were doing things, placing cool strips on his neck, moving blankets from his body, no doubt examining him with marvels of medical technology he couldn't see. A syringe hissed against his neck. He felt Roca's anguish and it tore him apart. Someday their children could be the ones lying broken and tortured, victims of the Traders, and he couldn't stop it from happening no matter how hard he tried, because they had *chosen* to fight and nothing he did, nothing he said would ever stop them. A father had to protect his wife and children, always and forever, but he couldn't, not even in his own lands, and it was killing him more than his shattered body.

He meant to tell Roca to leave. But for the first time in days, forever it seemed, the pain was leaving his body, truly leaving, not muted by herbs but genuinely going away.

"I can't feel anything," he whispered, switching into Skolian Flag for the doctors.

A man whose voice Eldrinson didn't recognize spoke in Flag. "We've given you a neural blocker, Your Majesty."

Majesty. He wished they would stop calling him that. But he was grateful they had stopped the pain.

"Can you heal him?" Roca's voice asked.

Silence followed her question. Then another voice spoke. "We will do our best, Councilor."

"Where is Shannon?" Eldrinson asked.

His son answered from farther away. "Here, Father." The

scrunch of cloth and mail came from Eldrinson's right. Then Shannon spoke next to him. "The doctors will fix everything."

Eldrinson reached out and his knuckles brushed a tunic. Someone grasped his hand.

"I'm right here," Shannon said.

"You saved my life," Eldrinson whispered. "Even more. You stopped Vitarex . . . from taking me offworld. He was ready to leave." Roca and ISC wouldn't have made it in time to stop him.

"I should have never run away." Shannon wasn't trying to hide his guilt-torn emotions. "Then you wouldn't have come after me and he wouldn't have caught you."

Roca spoke in a murmur. "Shannon, no, it's not your fault."

"Listen to your mother." Eldrinson took a breath, determined to put strength in his words. "Had Vitarex not captured me while so many people were searching for you, we would have never known he was here. Until too late." He kept going despite the drugged lethargy overcoming him. "His plan might have succeeded. You stopped that. *You.* Shannon."

Silence followed his words, as everyone in the tent absorbed the implications. By running away, Shannon may have averted an interstellar war.

"But what about Althor and Soz?" Shannon sounded bewildered. "What if they are captured?"

A man, one of the unfamiliar voices, spoke quietly in Flag. "Jagernauts have options. If necessary, we can end our lives using the biomech web in our bodies."

Would it come to that? Would war force his children to commit suicide? Would they die in the cold reaches of places unknown and unimaginable? Nor was it only Sauscony and Althor. Kelric would go someday, when he was old enough. Wanderlust drove the boy. It was too much. Unbearable. Eldrinson rubbed his useless eyes. If only he, too, had a biomech web so he could finish this, for he couldn't live in a universe as harsh and inexplicable as the one his wife's people and their enemies had created.

"Love, don't." Roca brushed her knuckles against his cheek in that way he cherished. "You will get better. Our children will be fine. We will protect Lyshriol. You will see."

He wished he could believe her. But those pretty words meant nothing against the truth.

The white ceiling blurred. Soz lay on her back, aware only of the pain in her legs. It shouldn't hurt this way. The tests all said her body would easily take the biomech. She refused to believe they had been wrong, that her body was rejecting the augmentation.

A blurred face moved into her line of sight. A gold face.

"Kurj?" she asked.

Her half brother raised his inner lids. He regarded her with gold eyes, his usually impassive face creased with concern. "How are you feeling?"

She wanted to say she felt fine, just great. But they had to know. Today she had become among the most expensive and complex pieces of military equipment built by ISC. They had designed a biomech web from her own DNA and woven it into her body. It included many components: threads that linked tthe sockets in her neck, lower back, wrists, and ankles to an internal mesh node in her spine; bioelectrodes that spurred her neurons to fire according to directions from either her node or brain, allowing communication between the two; nanomeds that patrolled the implants, healing and repairing, dispensing chemicals to prevent rejection, and working with the other nanomeds she already carried that maintained her health and delayed her aging. And that was just the start. They hadn't yet given her the operations to increase her speed and strength or the microfusion reactor to supply energy.

"My legs hurt," Soz said. "My sight blurs."

A long silence followed her answer. Too long. She hadn't expected to awaken this way. Doctors and biomech techs should be here, checking on her, testing how her body had taken the web. Although it made sense that Kurj would want to see how she dealt with the operation, he should have come with the doctors. She couldn't see him clearly, only the blur of his face.

Then he stepped away.

Disquieted, Soz probed his thoughts. His mental shields glinted bright and metallic in her mind, like his inner eyelids. She didn't push at his barriers. It would never work. No one had his mental strength. But just as someone with less strength might be more nimble than a heavier fighter, so she had more finesse as an empath than Kurj. She edged around his mind looked for chinks in his shields. She found a hint, something serious, something he didn't want to tell her—

Her father?

Soz strained to focus. What was wrong with her eyes? The operations included no optical enhancements. It shouldn't have affected her sight.

Over the next few moments, her vision cleared. She was lying in a hospital room with a glossy white ceiling and walls which could project holographic images. Turning her head, she saw a long white counter that stretched along one wall and ended in a console molded from seamless curves of Luminex. A multi-tiered, wheeled cart-bot with supplies stood by her bed. No, "bed" wasn't accurate. She lay on a mech-table with embedded components that could recognize tension in her body and adjust as necessary for her needs. Right now it moved subtly beneath her, probably to ease her stiff muscles. A robot arm was folded against the table, silver and chrome, quiescent now but with lights glittering along its length.

Then she realized she and Kurj weren't alone. He stood across the room with Secondary Tapperhaven, the two of them deep in a conference, communicating with the comms in their gauntlets by tracing messages on the screens. Kurj towered over the Secondary. He wore khaki trousers, knee-boots, and a pullover with a single gold line of ribbing across the torso that accented the width of his chest and shoulders. His uniform had no adornment, no medals, no indication of rank anywhere. He needed none. Everyone knew he commanded ISC.

Soz squinted at them. Here she was, just waking up, worried about her father and these changes in her body, and they were over there having a secret conference. She sat up and winced as pain stabbed her legs. The glimmering white sheet fell down around her hips, leaving her in a white med-shift that fortunately was smart enough to keep itself closed in the back. She crossed her arms and considered Kurj and Tapperhaven. Neither had noticed she was fully awake yet.

"Are you done telling secrets?" Soz asked.

Tapperhaven jumped and Kurj glanced up. Soz had no idea how she looked, but for some reason Kurj smiled. "Good evening," he said.

"I wouldn't know about that." Soz slid off the bed and stood next to the cart-bot. Her legs wobbled but she caught the cart in time to hold herself upright. Then she glared at Kurj.

Tapperhaven strode over. "Cadet Valdoria, you should get back into bed. You've just had several major operations."

"Is that an order, ma'am?" Soz asked.

The Secondary spoke dryly. "Yes, Cadet, that is an order."

"Yes, ma'am." Soz pulled herself back up on the bed and sat with her legs hanging off the edge, waiting to see what they were planning. Kurj joined the Secondary, his expression concerned. That worried Soz more than any rebuke he may have given her. He never looked at her that way.

Soz spoke uneasily. "Is my body rejecting the biomech?"

Kurj's inner lids came down to shield his eyes. "No, it doesn't appear so."

What was up? "Is it normal for my legs to hurt this much?"

He spoke carefully. "The pain will pass."

"What aren't you telling me?" Soz's muscles bunched under the hospital shift. "What went wrong?"

Tapperhaven spoke quietly. "The operations succeeded."

Soz had always been a good judge of whether or not a person was lying. It came with being an empath. Tapperhaven had given her the truth—as far as the response went. Soz wanted to insist they tell her, but she knew it wouldn't work if she pushed too hard. She took a calming breath. "Sir, if my father has been hurt, I request you let me know."

She thought he would say nothing had happened or tell her in some taciturn manner that she had no need to know. The last thing she expected was the grief in his voice. "In many ways, Soz, it is easier to deal with you when you are glowering like an irate warrior goddess."

Soz didn't know what to make of his response. "What happened?"

Kurj glanced at Tapperhaven. She nodded, accepting some unspoken command, and withdrew across the room. She took a post by the door as if she were a guard. That disturbed Soz even more. An officer with a rank as high as Jagernaut Secondary wouldn't act in such a role unless this dealt with a far more serious situation than her biomech.

"Tell me," she said, respecful.

Kurj spoke with difficulty, something she had never seen from him before. "Your father has been hurt."

Ah, no. *No.* "How?"

He indicated her legs. "It should be impossible for you to feel what happened to him across so many light-years. But it has affected both you and Althor."

"My father hurt his legs?" How? A fall in the Backbone? A seizure? She had seen him have a tonic clonic attack once, and it had scared the blazes out of her. He had been out of danger for so many years, she had forgotten the severity of his condition.

"I've been in communication with Colonel Corey Majda," Kurj said. "She commands the Lyshrioli ODS." He gave her the information without pause. "The Traders got into Lyshriol. We aren't yet sure how. Majda's people found only the jamming equipment and one comm with off-planet range. ESComm apparently planted one agent and meant to pick him up when he finished his mission. However, they have denied any connection to his presence there, and he covered his tracks too well for us to prove their involvement." He lifted his hands, then let them fall back to his sides. "Soz, I'm sorry. They took your father."

"No!" She heard his words, but she couldn't believe them. *It couldn't be true.* "Has ISC caught them?" Her words tumbled out. "Did he escape? Will he be all right?"

"Yes, he escaped. We don't yet know how ESComm placed an Aristo on the planet." Fatigue came through in his voice. "But your father is receiving the best care ISC can provide."

Soz didn't miss what he left out. "How badly is he hurt?"

"We don't know for certain yet."

"Tell me."

"Soz—"

"Tell me!"

Kurj answered with more regret than she would ever have expected him to show for the stepfather he hated. "He may never walk or see again."

Soz clenched the table until her fingers and thumb hurt, her *thumb,* on her Skolian hand, just like Kurj's hand, so unlike her father's four-fingered, hinged hand. "That must be wrong. Surely ISC can help him."

"We will do our best." Kurj spoke quietly. "I won't deny I've never done well with your father. But I would never have wished this on him."

This was an aspect of Kurj she had rarely seen, indeed, one she doubted most anyone alive had witnessed except their mother. The iron-hard dictator had a human side. Kurj's decades of dealing with the Traders had scarred him so deeply he would probably never heal, but the passage of years had ameliorated his antipathy for the man he had almost killed to prevent his marriage to Roca. His inner demons and outer horrors had made him into the unyielding Imperator, but a human being, an *empath,* existed beneath those hardened layers.

"Will you let me know when you find out more?" Soz asked.

"Yes. Immediately."

A ping came from across the room. Soz glanced up to see Tapperhaven speaking into her gauntlet.

Kurj spoke to the Secondary. "Are they asking about Cadet Valdoria?"

Tapperhaven nodded to him with the extra respect J-Force officers reserved for the Imperator, who had once been one of them. "They want to come in and continue the tests."

"Very well." Kurj gave Soz a dry smile. "You up for being poked and prodded?"

She sat up straighter. "Yes, sir." The sooner she could start to use her biomech, the better. She thought of her father. She had even more motivation to become as deadly against the Traders as possible.

As soon as Tapperhaven spoke into her comm, the door slid open and three people entered. Soz recognized the two in white jumpsuits: Dr. Callie Irzon, the primary biomech surgeon assigned to Soz; and Dr. Tine Loriez, a lanky man with intense eyes, the surgeon who had assisted in the operations. Both had the J-Force insignia on their shoulders, the stylized symbol of a Jag in flight.

A biomech-adept came with them. Tall and long-legged, the woman wore a form-fitting blue jumpsuit of metallic cloth. She had the dark hair and black eyes ubiquitous among the noble Houses. The ID holo on her chest had no name, just the five-star symbol of the House of Rajindia. Soz didn't know her, but she recognized the family. The Rajindia line was ancient, dating back to the Ruby Empire. The House had almost died out on Raylicon during the Dark Ages, but it had rebounded again after the Raylican people regained the stars several centuries ago.

The officers saluted Kurj, clenching their fists and crossing their wrists as they raised their arms out to him. He inclined his head, his eyes shielded by the gold lids he could see through but that appeared opaque to everyone else. "At ease." He indicated Soz. "Your patient awaits."

They gathered around her then, all business. Loriez tapped a panel in the mech-table and a console in the headboard activated.

"How do you feel?" Irzon asked.

"Normal," Soz said. It was disappointing. She had thought she would notice a difference, more strength, an enhanced sense of her body. Something positive. "My legs hurt when I came to, and my vision was blurry. But those problems have cleared up." She was aware of how closely they were all watching her.

Rajindia spoke in a dusky voice. "Activate."

Soz blinked "Ma'am?"

"We activated you," Irzon said.

"Oh. Yes." Soz knew the terminology, but recognizing the words and having the process applied to her were two very different things. It felt strange to hear, as if she were a machine. But it was true. The operations would have taken several days and her recuperation even longer. Someone today had apparently decided she was ready to wake up. So they turned on her biomech.

Soz tapped the table where she sat. "Did this activate my web?"

"That's right." Rajindia lifted the sheet and showed her a long rod along the edge of the table. Blue light glowed within it. "The signal came from these bars. However, they can't switch you off unless it is your choice."

Soz ran her hand over the rod. It was odd and intriguing that her conscious mind responded to signals from this machine. Loriez was at the head of the mech-table, working at the console in the headboard, studying holos of her body that floated in the air. He scrutinized them the way she had seen officers study equipment.

Disconcerted, Soz turned back to Irzon. The doctor was simply waiting, neither checking monitors nor performing any other visible doctor activities.

"Why don't I feel anything?" Soz asked.

"You aren't stiff?" Irzon asked.

"I ache everywhere."

"That's expected." That neither Irzon nor the adept asked about the pain in her legs made Soz suspect they knew what she had discussed with Kurj, and were already examining her for problems.

Soz turned her wrist up to the ceiling and rubbed her thumb over the socket there. The circle was the color of her skin and smaller than the tip of her little finger. She tried to sense a change, a difference, an itch from its implantation. Anything. Leaning over, she turned out her feet so she could see the socket above each heel. Without knowing to look, she wouldn't have noticed them. She sat up straight again and slid her hand under her hair, fingering the socket at the base of her neck. Then she moved her hand down her back, searching—yes, there it was, the spinal socket just below her waist.

The doctors and adept continued to wait while she explored. Tapperhaven had remained posted by the door, and Kurj stood leaning against a nearby wall, his arms crossed, his metallic coloring a vivid contrast to the white Luminex. The sleeves of his pullover strained his large biceps.

"It's odd." Soz braced her palms on her knees. "I don't feel a thing. The sockets aren't even sore." She surveyed her arm, trying to find a seam where the doctors had inserted the tubes they used to thread the biomech into her body. The placement didn't have to be exact; the picotech braided into the threads had enough intelligence to make them weave into Soz's neural system. "If I hadn't known you all had operated on me, I couldn't tell now."

Relief washed across Irzon's face. "Good."

Her response startled Soz. Usually J-Force officers were more reserved about showing emotion, not because they didn't feel it but because they learned fast to guard their moods when they spent the majority of their time with other empaths. Irzon's reaction made sense, though. It had to be excruciating to do such work on the Imperator's heir. If anything happened to Soz, the doctors would lose their jobs, possibly even their freedom. They all knew Kurj was listening, watching, analyzing.

Loriez was studying the holos of her body floating above his console in the headrest of the table.

"How does it look?" Soz asked.

He glanced up at her. "You're a healthy young woman, Your Highness."

Kurj's voice rumbled. "She is Cadet Valdoria here."

Red tinged Loriez's cheeks. "Yes, sir."

Any reminder of her differences here made Soz twitch. Somehow she had to find a balance between being one of Kurj's heirs and being like the other cadets. If Kurj hadn't spoken, she might have done so herself, but that could have caused problems. Given her less than stellar subtlety, she might have ended up sounding disrespectful, and she already had too many blasted marks on her record.

Rajindia gave the impression of calm efficiency, but Soz could feel her underlying strain. None of it showed, though, when she spoke. "We can finish activating the system now, Cadet Valdoria."

Soz sat up straighter. "I'm ready."

Loriez pressed more commands into the console, and the blue rod edging the biomech table flared in brightness. Soz waited, striving for patience, but nothing happened. After a moment, she gave Irzon and Rajindia a quizzical look.

"You can finish it yourself," Rajindia said.

Neither the adept nor the doctors offered any more guidance. Soz closed her eyes and concentrated, settling her thoughts as her instructors had trained her to do in the biomech class she was no longer taking. Perhaps testing out of it early hadn't been such a good idea, after all.

She thought: *Node?*

Nothing.

Soz let her consciousness float. She wished she had Shannon's ability to submerge into a trance. Thinking of him made her tense, which had never happened before. She let the memories of home slip away and just drifted.

Still nothing.

Perhaps she hadn't directed the thought enough. She focused her mind and concentrated harder. **Node, activate.** It startled her how strong the thought sounded in her own mind, as if it were enhanced. Still no response, though.

Her agitation surged. She pushed it down, but the more

she became concerned about being concerned, the more it disrupted her concentration. It was like saying, *Don't think of huge pink fungi.* Of course then she could think of nothing but pink glop.

Node, she thought. **I would appreciate it if you would answer me.**

Please specify the question you wish answered. The thought came into her mind, firm, strong, oddly warm, reassuring in its competence.

Soz sat up with a jerk. "Whoa!"

"Cadet Valdoria?" Rajindia asked. Irzon and Loriez were watching her intently. An uncharacteristic furrow showed between Kurj's eyebrow. Soz grinned at them all.

Here is a question, she thought to the node. **Do you have any properties that distinguish you from any other node created by ISC?**

Your question is rather general. It sounded calm. Pleasant. Efficient. Did you have anything specific in mind?

This is ultra, Soz thought, this time just to herself, without the focus she used for the node. Then she added, **Something that would prove I'm talking to you.**

"Cadet Valdoria?" Irzon asked, her dark eyes alert. "Are you all right?"

"Yes, fine." Soz had no idea how her face looked while she "conversed" with her node. Probably she needed better control of her expressions. She didn't want to go blank or make odd faces. Maybe that was why Kurj so often looked impassive; he had developed that control to a high art.

The node thought, My history parallels that of other nodes constructed by the J-Force biomech technicians. However, I do have more memory than other nodes.

Why more memory? Soz asked.

Your brain has extra capacity. Scientific images of neural structures formed in her mind, along with various stats.

Ultra, Soz thought. To Rajindia, she said, "My node has

extra memory because your tests said my brain can handle it. You think I have inherited some of the genes that give holographic memories to the women called Memories on Lyshriol."

Rajindia inclined her head in acknowledgment. "Your node told you this?"

"You bet."

Irzon smiled. "Congratulations, Cadet Valdoria. You're now a Jagernaut."

"Hardly." Kurj spoke from his post by the wall, his deep voice rumbling like a growl. "She's a first-year cadet."

Soz bit back her urge to point out that her classes and new biomech web qualified her as a junior. She was too pleased with the node to be annoyed at him right now. Besides, she could end up with more demerits.

Know who he is? she asked her node.

Which "he"? According to your sensors, this room contains two human males.

Hey. It could detect the people in the room. She could hardly wait to explore all these new abilities. Their interaction was going so fast, barely a second had passed according to the fuzzy display it was creating in her mind. To Kurj she said, "Yes, sir," in response to his comment about her rank.

"We can begin your training with the biomech web after you've rested," Kurj said. He pushed away from the wall and walked toward her, lowering his arms.

"Yes, sir." She sent her node another question: **What can you tell me about the larger man in this room?** She pushed her thoughts even faster, curious to see how much she could learn in the few seconds it took for Kurj to walk to the table where she sat.

Data flooded her mind: Identity: 99.8 percent probability he is Kurj Skolia, Imperator. Weight: 130 kilograms. Height: 2.13 meters. Chronological age: undetermined from physical attributes but given as 52 standard years in history files. Apparent physical age: 38 standard years.

And so it went, ever faster. Kurj was moving in slow motion now, taking each step through invisible molasses. Soz winced and pressed her fingertips against her temples. The node was flooding her with data, everything from his blood type to estimates of the chemical composition of his hair.

Pain stabbed through Soz's head. "Ah!" She pressed the heels of her hands against her temples. **Stop! You're going too fast.**

"C-a-a-a-d-e-e-t V-a-a-a-l-l-d-o-o-r-r-r-i-a-a-a." Irzon's voice echoed so slowly that Soz wondered if someone had recorded it and was playing it at a delayed rate. She groaned and doubled over, her hands clenched around her head.

`Accelerated mode off,` her node thought.

The pain receded in Soz's temples. Someone put a hand on her shoulder and someone else pressed a medical tape against her arm.

"—happened to her?" Kurj was demanding.

"Her blood pressure and heart rate spiked," Loriez said.

"She started to have a seizure. Too many of her neurons were firing at once." Then he said, "Gods above! Her impulse rate increased for a fraction of a second."

Rajindia spoke. "Cadet Valdoria, can you hear me?"

Soz sat up slowly. Afterimages floated in front of her eyes as if she had looked at a bright light. Irzon was monitoring her with a gold metallic strip she had laid on Soz's left forearm. The tiny holos that glittered above it showed data and images of Soz's brain. Rajindia stood with her hand on Soz's shoulder. Kurj was over by Loriez, dividing his attention between Soz and the holos above Loriez's screen.

"I'm all right." Soz lowered her hands.

"What happened?" Kurj asked.

"Apparently I put the node in accelerated mode."

"You'll learn how to control the modes," Rajindia said.

Loriez looked up at Soz. "According to these scans, you tried to change the speed that neural impulses travel in your brain."

Kurj frowned at him. "Is that possible?" He didn't even

hide his worried look. Today he was showing a whole plethora of moods that Soz had never seen from him before.

"I wouldn't have thought so," Loriez said. "Certainly not like this. But she did it."

"Is it dangerous?" Kurj asked.

"If it had gone on much longer, it probably could have caused brain damage."

"I can learn to control it," Soz said quickly. She didn't want them turning off her biomech. It exhilarated her, despite the headache. She needed to know what it could do, how far she could push it. A whole new universe of possibility awaited her.

"And if you can't control it?" Kurj asked. "Neural impulses are the transfer of chemicals across cell membranes. How could you speed that up?"

"I don't know," Soz admitted. "Maybe something about the extra memory in my node."

Rajindia spoke to Kurj. "We can study the effect to see if it can be handled or eliminated."

He considered her for a moment. Then he spoke firmly to Soz. "You will stay here, under Rajindia's supervision, until we ascertain how and why this happened."

Soz had no objection. If she stayed here, working with the doctors, she would learn to use her web faster. "Yes, sir."

"I mean it, Soz," Kurj said. "Don't push this one. You're risking a lot more than demerits. You could damage your brain. Then where would you be?"

It was a sobering thought. "I'll be careful."

"Good." He smiled slightly. "Remember that when you feel tempted to push this web of yours."

Soz flushed. Kurj knew her too well. "Yes, sir." Then she thought, **Node?**

Attending.

She strove to keep her thought process at a normal speed. **Why did your accelerated mode make chemical changes in my brain cells?**

I haven't completed my investigation, it

answered. However, my initial analysis suggests the effect is due to the unusually extensive neural structures in your brain. Many now also include bioelectrodes that can fire according to commands from you or me. When they began to discharge in accelerated mode, it caused some sort of resonance process.

Soz looked from Kurj to Rajindia. "Do I have more neural structures than most psions?"

"Everyone in your family does," Rajindia said.

"Did Althor have any problems like this?" Soz asked.

"None," Kurj said. "Why?"

"I asked my node what happened." Soz described its response.

Rajindia rubbed her chin. "Imperator Skolia, I'd like to jack her into our training system."

Kurj looked less than thrilled. "It's too soon. She just activated her system. We don't know why it's malfunctioning."

"It's not malfunctioning." Soz jumped in, eager for the training. "It's working even better than we expected, better than I'm trained to handle. I need to learn."

His inner lids came down in opaque gold shields. "Do you make it a practice to contradict your commanding officers, Cadet Valdoria?"

Heat spread in Soz's face. Damn. "Sir! No, sir!"

Kurj spoke into the comm on his massive wrist gauntlet, and Soz winced as he registered another demerit on her record. At this rate, she would spend the rest of her life cleaning mucked-up droids and spamoozala.

Loriez had continued to pore over Soz's stats while Rajindia watched Soz with unsettling intensity, as if she would see into the workings of her bio-enhanced brain. Irzon set her holotape on the cart and picked up a pressure-pulse ring. Although Loriez's console could read Soz's vital signs, the ring provided more accurate data. Soz held still while Irzon clipped it around her arm.

While the doctors worked, Kurj spoke to Rajindia. "Which training system do you want her to try?"

Soz glanced up with a start. She had expected him to deny her permission to work on the systems. Her pulse surged, evoking a discreet beep from Loriez's console. She wanted to jump in with suggestions for her training, but she managed to restrain herself. Kurj might be giving her demerits, but he was still listening to what she had to say. If she pushed any harder, that would change.

"I'd like to try the debriefer," Rajindia said. "It will make it possible for her node to interact with our systems here. We can ask it questions directly and record its responses."

Kurj nodded, the elbow of one arm braced on the forearm of the other so he could rest his chin on his fist while he thought. Soz recognized his mannerisms; he was probably going to agree with Rajindia. Well, good. She had always known Kurj was intelligent.

"Very well." Kurj lowered his arms. "But control the speed of the questions. Keep it all in normal time mode."

"We'll make certain of that," Rajindia said.

He nodded to them. "After she's had a chance to rest, you can proceed."

She was ready now! Soz started to protest, but Kurj raised his eyebrows at her, so she closed her mouth.

Her brother actually smiled, his teeth a startling flash of white in his metallic face. It made him look decades younger. "Rest, Soz. Gather your strength. Your node isn't going anywhere without you."

Good gods. That sounded like a joke. From Kurj. "Yes, sir."

To Irzon, he said, "Keep a good watch on her legs and her sight."

The doctor nodded. "We've had extra monitors on both since she awoke and described her symptoms."

So they had heard Kurj tell her about her father. She stared down at her hands, which were folded in her lap.

"Soz." Kurj's voice was a low rumble.

She looked at him. "Yes, sir?"

He spoke with uncharacteristic gentleness. "I will let you know as soon as I have more news about him."

"Thank you, sir." For now, she would learn her biomech system and learn it well, just as she would master her other enhancements when she received them, as she would ace her classes, meld her mind with an EI, and learn to fly a Jag, until she became the most versatile, hardest, fastest Jagernaut in the J-Forces.

Then she would kill the Aristos who had hurt her father.

19

Windward

As commander of the *Ascendant* battle cruiser, Corey Majda was the highest authority in the orbital defense system that guarded Lyshriol. Now, however, Majda had come down to the planet. She sat with Roca, Denric, and several ISC officers at a long table of blue glasswood. It stretched down the length of the dining hall in Castle Windward, the Valdoria retreat high in the Backbone Mountains. Rafters of green glasswood braced the high ceiling, and glasswood mosaics patterned the walls in mountain scenes. A fire roared in the giant hearth at the end of the hall, its flames taking on the color of its glasswood logs, blue, green, and gold.

Roca missed her other children. She wanted to draw them near during this time of grief, but they were taking care of Dalvador while she stayed up here. The twins, Del-Kurj and Chaniece, were eldest now that both Eldrin and Althor had gone offworld. They would tend the house and look after the youngest children, Aniece and Kelric. They were also seeing to their father's duties, with help from Vyrl and Lily. Her husband considered himself a singer and farmer only, but Roca understood what he didn't acknowledge, that in his own unassuming way, he led the people of the plains. In his absence, his children would carry on for him.

Despite the importance of those tasks, they weren't the true reason the children stayed in Dalvador. Their father refused to see anyone, especially those he loved. His insistence that ISC bring him here instead of to their starships hadn't surprised Roca. Windward had always been his retreat, a place he preferred far more than the alien environment of ships in space. ISC had destroyed a substantial portion of Windward shortly after Roca's marriage to Eldri, when they came to "rescue" her. Although they had rebuilt it to match the old castle exactly, Roca knew Eldri felt it was no longer the same. But he preferred a rebuilt castle to a battle cruiser in orbit, and ISC assured her they could care for him just as well here.

Roca looked around at the ISC doctors arrayed on both sides of the table. In their crisp green or blue uniforms, they seemed so out of place beneath the glasswood rafters and columns. They were taller than Lyshrioli men and women, more angular, darker in their hair and eyes, a sharp contrast the rustic, stained-glass hall.

"Surely you can do something for him." Roca spoke to Jase Heathland, the senior doctor of the team here.

"We can rebuild his legs," Jase said. "But they will be more biomech than natural. He will have to relearn their use, not only how to walk, but how to *think* about walking. The way they receive signals from his brain will no longer be the same." He rubbed his chin, frowning as he thought, his narrow face tanned from his time walking in the plains under the Lyshrioli suns, an unusual effect since most Skolians protected their skin. Jase tended to prefer what he called a "natural" state, which was one reason Eldri could relate to him. The Bard avoided most ISC personnel, but he actually liked Jase.

Jase spoke carefully, as if negotiating a field of broken glass. "Councilor, I'm not sure his mind *can* adapt to the biomech system. The structure of his brain is unusual. It differs a great deal from humanoid norms. Even if we can get beyond that—" He spoke with gentle caution. "Ma'am, your husband must want to use his new legs. He can accomplish nothing if he doesn't have the heart to try."

Roca knew he was right. She had never seen Eldri like this before, so turned inward, so full of despair. He had shut her out of his life. She could watch him on monitors ISC had set up, but he refused to let her come to him, talk to him, even stand in the same room.

Roca spoke softly. "I know." She had no more she could add.

The doctors discussed with her more equipment they needed to bring down to the castle, and how they would set it up. Colonel Corey Majda sat at the table, listening with an intent focus. Tall and dark, with regular features, she had the classic aquiline profile of a Raylican noblewoman. And so she should; the House of Majda was the most elevated of the nobility, second in status only to the Ruby Dynasty. Majda's warrior queens had served the Ruby Pharaoh for five millennia.

As Matriarch of her House, Corey reigned over the Majda financial empire, which spanned many star systems and included some of the most lucrative businesses in the Skolian Imperialate. Her aunt was the one who actually ran their corporations; Corey was a career officer in the military. It wasn't coincidence ISC had chosen her for this post. Not only did she serve as their primary protector, in her position as commander of the orbital defense system, but she also represented the nobility and could present herself in that role to the Ruby Dynasty. A consummate officer, she would carry out her duties regardless, but on a personal level she could have taken insult that Eldri refused to acknowledge her presence. Instead she responded with sympathy and patience, earning Roca's gratitude.

It relieved Roca, too, for Corey could have reacted much differently. This wasn't the first time the Ruby Dynasty had given offense to Majda. Four years ago, Corey's older sister Devon had been the Majda queen. The Assembly sought an alliance between the Ruby Dynasty and Majda for political reasons. After much negotiation, they reached a decision: Devon would marry a Ruby prince. She picked Vyrl. He had been fourteen when they told him of the betrothal—and two days later he had run off with Lily, a girl he had loved his entire life. The resulting mess caused an interstellar crisis. Then Devon shocked them all by abdicating her title to marry the man she loved, a commoner deemed unacceptable as her consort, a government clerk. Corey, her younger sister, had become queen.

Roca winced. In issues of the heart, Skolia had much to answer for with Majda. She herself had committed such an offense decades ago, during the negotiations for her betrothal to a Majda prince. Roca had married Eldri instead. It added insult to the injury that she had chosen a husband considered the antithesis of a proper Ruby consort. Roca would have abdicated for Eldri if necessary, but he was a Rhon psion, which meant he descended from the ancient Ruby Dynasty. Five millennia of isolation had separated his people from hers, so the connection was nebulous at best and some among the Assembly still considered him irredeemably inappropriate. That Roca loved him with all her heart mattered to none of them—except herself.

Now he refused to see her.

Denric was speaking to Corey, his Iotic words softened by the chime of his Lyshrioli vocal cords. "Can't your doctors help my father's sadness?"

Corey answered quietly. "If you mean, do we have treatments for depression, the answer is yes. But your father's case is far more complex." She glanced at Jase. "Dr. Heathland?"

Jase crossed his arms on the table, his green uniform dull against the lustrous blue glasswood. The circles under his eyes gave testament to his unending work on Eldrinson's behalf this last day, since they had flown here from the Blue Dale caravan.

He spoke to both Roca and Denric. "How familiar are you with the genetic history of our ancestors, the first Raylicans?"

"I studied it at university," Roca said. That had been half a century ago, though. "I have some medical knowledge stored in my spinal node, but I would have to sort through it for details."

"I've learned some with my tutors," Denric said. His mop of curly blond hair made him look younger than his sixteen years, but he had always been mature for his age. "I don't know a lot of specifics."

"It's important to Eldrinson's situation," Jase said, using Eldri's full name. "The Ruby Empire colonists were stranded for almost five thousand years across many star systems. Most of those populations were genetically engineered, usually to adapt to their colony world and sometimes, like here—well, we don't know why. And populations can shift even more during five millennia."

"Well, yes," Roca said. "But the same is true of our ancestors on Raylicon."

"Yes." Jase inclined his head to her. "The Raylicans were also separated for thousands years from the peoples of Earth, and had to adapt to living on another world. That alone would cause their population to select for distinct characteristics compared to our siblings on Earth. Our ancestors also learned genetic engineering. They must have been desperate. With such a small population, they didn't have enough genetic diversity to remain viable. So they created that diversity themselves. The result of it all? Humans have split into a range of different classes."

"How is that different from new races?" Denric asked.

Jase turned to him. "The distinctions are greater. Some of the more diverse humanoid strains can no longer interbreed. It makes us different species. They aren't Homo sapiens, technically."

"But the peoples of Raylicon," Roca said. "They're the basis for what we call human, yes?"

Jase shifted his weight in his chair. "Actually, no, Your Highness. The people of Earth are the original humans. We call them Alpha class. Raylicans are Beta class."

As an empath she could sense that he was uneasy telling her that, but she didn't know why. The title he used gave her a good idea, though; as a Ruby heir she was a Highness and as consort to the "King of Skyfall" she was a Majesty. She actually had more power as an Assembly Councilor, but the romanticized legend of her marriage had swamped out the more pragmatic aspects of her life. She wondered how Jase saw the royal family, if he hesitated to correct a simple mistake she made about genetics. It wouldn't occur to her to resent his comment. Most military personnel knew the Ruby Dynasty primarily through Kurj, though. Her son expected the truth regardless of how unpalatable it might be, but his iron-hard personality could make officers reluctant to disagree with him.

Curiosity sparked in Denric's gaze. "I'm not Beta. I remember that from genetics last year."

Jase's posture eased. "Yes. That's right."

"I'm Gamma class," Roca said. She recalled that much.

"Yes." The doctor nodded to her. "You, your father Jarac, your son Kurj, your sons Althor and Kelric, and perhaps your daughter Chaniece, though her DNA is more mixed. The metallic components in your bodies, the extra size and muscle density, and the neural structures that confer such great empathic strength but less mental dexterity than other empaths—it is all part of what we call Gamma."

"It's not common, though, is it?" Denric said. "Not if we don't even all fit into it."

"Beta is the most widely known strain." Jase glanced at Majda. The colonel inclined her head, her upward tilted eyes as dark as ebony. To Denric, Jase said, "Most members of the noble Houses are Beta, like Colonel Majda. Also your grandmother and the current Ruby Pharaoh."

Roca could see where he was going. "And my husband?"

Jase brushed back a stray lock of his hair, which he wore in a cap of loose brown curls just short enough to satisfy regulations. "We know a lot more now than when you first came here, but we've a great deal to learn about the Lyshrioli. This world has at least two classes of humans we've never seen. Maybe three."

She thought of the differences between her and Eldri. "Like the people of Dalvador and Rillia."

"That's right," Jase said. "The most common class by far is the Rillians, which includes the people of Dalvador. The hinged, four-digit hands are probably the most obvious difference. And the unusual hair color, the different shades of purple and lavender." He glanced at Denric. "You're registered as Rillian class, with aspects of both Gamma and even some Blue Dale Archer. Your brothers Eldrin, Del-Kurj, and Vyrl are also Rillian, though Vyrl has a bit more Gamma."

Denric held up his hand and flexed his fingers, all four of them and his sturdy thumb. Then he folded his hand lengthwise along the hinge, bringing his two smaller fingers flush against his larger index and middle fingers. "I was born with a vestigial thumb. The doctors made it whole."

Roca remembered when she and Eldrinson had faced the decision: what would they do about their babies' hands? They had no need to worry for most of the children. Eldrin had a normal Lyshrioli hand, with four fingers and a hinge. So did Del-Kurj and Shannon. Althor, Soz, Chaniece, Aniece, and Kelric had hands like hers, with four fingers, a thumb, and no hinge. But Denric and Vyrl had been born with partial thumbs and hinges, their hands a mix of the two types, functional as neither. For Vyrl, the hinge had been too deformed to reconstruct, so the doctors rebuilt his hand to the human norm, with four fingers and a thumb. For Denric, they fixed both his thumb and the hinge. It gave him advantages of both structures, though having a thumb made it harder to use the hinge.

"Your hands had problems because you aren't pure Rillian," Jase told him.

"You said I was like a Blue Dale Archer." Denric set his hand back on the table, palm down. "But I don't feel that way. Not like my brother Shannon."

"Genetically you aren't as close as Shannon," Jase said. "But you do have some of the DNA." He paused, his face thoughtful. "We know much less about the Archers than the Rillians. We have their DNA, but we've only just met living, full-blooded Archers. They have the same bone structure as everyone else here, but their skeletons are less massive, more airy. Their brains are markedly different from Rillians. Actually, from any other humans we've classified."

Roca thought of Shannon, her distant, otherworldly son. "Archers go into trances easily, yes?"

"We think so," Jase said. "They apparently have less analytic ability than most humans and more emotional capacity. They don't seem to separate their emotions into individual moods. It all flows together for them."

It fit with what Roca knew of Shannon. "They're restless, too. They don't like cities."

"They don't even seem comfortable about the other humans here," Jase said.

Colonel Majda spoke. "You said Lyshriol had a third class."

Jase rubbed his chin. "Possibly the women called Memories. We aren't sure yet if they differ enough from the Rillians to qualify as a different class."

"What about my husband?" Roca asked. She didn't like to discuss her family's private life and genetics in front of these officers, who were at best only acquaintances. Many of them were strangers she knew only by name and their dossiers. But she would do whatever was necessary to heal Eldri's wounds, including those that went beyond his physical injuries.

"Your husband is primarily Rillian," Jase said. "He also shows traits of the Blue Dale Archers, and the Memories, who may be even rarer than the Archers."

Colonel Majda spoke quietly to Roca. "We're learning to understand his medical condition even as the doctors treat him."

"You've all been studying Eldri for years," Roca said. Grousing about the ISC doctors and their tests was one of his favorite pastimes.

"This is true," Jase said. "And we know a lot more than we did twenty years ago. But it takes more than two decades to understand even one new class of humans, let alone three."

Roca tensed. "Are you saying you can't treat my husband?"

Jase spoke with assurance. "We can treat him. But we must take extraordinary care. His brain has many differences. The situation is complicated because as a Rhon psion he also has more neural structures than other people. Add that to his epilepsy and the problems multiply. We don't know how he will respond."

At least Jase was honest with her. She had always appreciated that about him.

Roca turned a cool gaze on Majda. "And my son Shannon?"

The colonel had the decency to look uncomfortable. "My people must hold him at the port. But please be assured he has come to no harm."

Roca wasn't reassured. "When will you let him go?"

Majda met her gaze. "I don't know. I'm sorry, Councilor Skolia. But he murdered a powerful man, one highly placed among the Trader aristocracy. We can't ignore that."

Roc stared at her in disbelief. "You've seen what that 'highly placed' monster did to my husband."

Majda only said, "I'm sorry."

Roca knew, logically, that they had to hold him. But all she could see was Shannon kneeling in the tent where the Archers had brought Eldrinson, tears running down his face as he spoke in jagged, heartbroken bursts to his dying father. She wanted to rage against Majda, against Vitarex Raziquon, against all the Traders who thought they had a right to torture people and destroy lives for their own pleasure, against a universe that would allow such atrocities. None of that would help her husband or son, but it took a conscious effort on her part to hold back the words that wanted to explode out of her.

"When may I see my son?" she asked.

"Anytime you wish." Majda seemed relieved to give a positive answer. "As long as Prince Shannon remains in custody."

In custody. That meant the port. Roca's shoulders sagged. She would go to him, but she couldn't leave Windward until she knew—until she *believed*—her husband would live.

"Can I talk to Shannon through the web?" Roca asked. To

reach the port from here required routing their communications through the ODS, which could be construed as using military systems for private use.

Mercifully, the colonel just said, "Of course."

"Thank you." It would mean a great deal to Shannon to hear about his father's condition from her rather than strangers.

One of the officers, a woman in the gray-green uniform of a lieutenant in the Pharaoh's Army, was studying a screen on her wrist gauntlet. She looked up at them. "Dr. Heathland, I'm getting a summons from King Eldrinson's medical console."

Jase tapped his own gauntlet. "Got it."

"Is Eldri in trouble?" Roca asked.

"It isn't a warning alarm, ma'am." The young woman spoke with reassurance. "His Majesty just woke up."

Jase rose to his feet. "I'll go check."

Roca stood up as well, followed by everyone else at the long table. She and Jase regarded each other across its width. They both knew Eldri had refused to see anyone but Jase.

"Walk with me to his suite," Jase suggested. "We can take it from there."

Roca nodded. "Thank you."

They went to a stairway set against one wall. Four steps led up to a square landing; from there, the stairs turned at a right angle and ran up along the wall, bordered by a fine banister of carved emerald glasswood. Roca walked up them with Jase, remembering all the times she and Eldri had climbed these stairs, starting that first night they dined together in this hall, a meal of bubbles in more varieties than she could ever have imagined, from sweet to tangy to bitter. After rounds of wine, Eldri had taken her up here, to the landing at the top of the stairs. They had stood together gazing out at the hall where people mingled below, laughing beneath clusters of red and green bubbles that hung from glasswood rafters, the hall turned golden by hundreds of candles. That night, she had slept for the first time in Eldri's arms. The memory made her ache. Would he never stand here with her again?

Roca paused on the landing. She could see her son Denric at the table below, talking with Colonel Majda. She had wondered, since the disaster of Vyrl's betrothal to Devon Majda, if Corey would offer for Denric. The Assembly still wanted the Majda Matriarch to marry a Ruby prince, but they had mercifully backed off after the last fiasco, willing to let matters take a more natural course. Denric would be a good choice for Corey, but Roca hoped nothing came of it in the near future. She couldn't bear to have another of her children leave now.

As Corey spoke into the comm on her gauntlet, Denric rubbed the back of his hand over his eyes. Roca knew she might soon do the same if her gathering tears began to fall. She didn't want to cry, not with all these people here, but she didn't know how much longer she could hold back.

Jase spoke quietly. "Councilor?"

Startled, Roca turned to him. "My apologies."

Sympathy showed in his face. He opened the door for her, a purple glasswood portal that seemed to glow from within. It didn't surprise Roca that Eldri had retreated here. The beauty of Windward soothed. Lyshriol had no true wood, but its stained-glass trees were lovelier to her than all the conventional forests on other terraformed worlds. The trees here had probably been an experiment; the Raylican people of the ancient Ruby Empire hadn't had much genetic material to work with in creating life for their new worlds, only a few plants and animals from Earth, along with increasingly misty histories of their ancestral home world.

They followed a corridor where glasswood mosaics graced the bluestone walls with scenes of the mountains. A few showed stylized birds in the sky—except Lyshriol had no birds. Roca suspected they depicted ships that had brought the colonists here. Windward was old, immensely old. The original colonists had probably carved this castle out of the mountains. The Lyshrioli people now had nothing resembling the technology they would need to achieve such a feat or build a castle to endure for thousands of years.

Roca paused at a wall niche with the statue of a female

Archer sculpted out of lavender stone. Dressed in a tunic that came to midthigh, she held a large bow in her four-fingered, hinged hand. Beautiful and leanly muscled, she epitomized the ideal of female power valued during the Ruby Empire, which had been a matriarchy.

Over the millennia, the culture here had shifted. The same genetic anomaly that produced the phenomenal Memories among Lyshrioli women had also included fatal recessives. Thousands of years ago, it had become more pronounced and decimated the female population, leaving women far outnumbered by men. The culture evolved patriarchal aspects then, including the idea that only men went to war. They couldn't risk losing their few childbearing women in combat. Eventually the population reestablished a balance among men and women. The fatal mutations associated with the Memory traits had disappeared, either because all the women who carried it died out or because the gene pool shifted. Few women carried the Memory genes now, but those who did no longer died.

Roca touched the statue of the Archer. Sauscony. They had named their second daughter for this Lyshrioli goddess of war. Had she known how prophetic that name would become, would she have chosen another? No. Nothing would change Soz's nature, nor would she have wanted to see her wild, brilliant daughter constrained.

Jase spoke softly. "Ma'am?"

"I'm sorry. I must seem distracted today." She went with him down the hall, to a stone archway framed with engravings of bubbles. A curtain hung in the entrance, sparkling strings of iridescent beads. Beyond it waited the suite she and Eldri shared here at Windward. Except they no longer shared it. Now she slept in another suite down the hall.

Jase pulled aside the beaded strings, making them clink and rattle together, inviting her to enter. She walked into the circular foyer with a cushioned bench running around its wall. Engraved stone moldings bordered the ceiling. Across the foyer, next to a purple glasswood door, a man sat at a console that hadn't been there before today. Neither she nor Eldri would have tolerated such obvious ISC tech at Windward. Now Roca was deeply grateful they could bring down what they needed to care for him here instead of taking him to the battle cruiser *Ascendant*, that gigantic military city orbiting Lyshriol. It would have destroyed his spirit.

The lieutenant at the console wore a jumpsuit similar to Jase's uniform, with the same insignia on his chest, a green vine curling around a silver staff, all superimposed on a blue sun, the symbol medical practitioners used in all branches of ISC.

Jase went over to him. "How is he?"

The officer saluted him. "Quiet, sir. He dozes, I think."

Jase glanced at Roca, hesitating. She knew why. Would Eldri know if she went inside his room? He had forbidden her, but he slept now.

"I don't think a few moments will hurt," Jase said.

"Thank you," she said softly. Then she opened the door.

Eldrinson drifted in a sea of warmth, his mind like flotsam on his consciousness. He could almost ignore the pain that tugged at his legs. It had become distant, bearable, an irritant. He had slept today sometime after the doctors crowded around him in the Archer's tent. He hoped no one else would talk with him now. He had nothing to say. They had taken away most of his pain. It was enough. He needed nothing else.

He became aware of breathing. His mind glided while he listened. Eventually he said, *Who's there?*

No answer.

It took Eldrinson a while to realize he hadn't spoken. He opened his mouth, closed it, then wet his lips. "Who is there?"

A voice came from nearby. "Dr. Heathland, Your Majesty."

So he was Majesty today. When they referred to him as Roca's consort, he was Highness. Perhaps someday they would make up their minds.

Heathland. The port doctor. He could live with that. He rather liked Jase, though he rarely admitted it. It would ruin his reputation as being impossible for Skolian doctors, which might encourage them to spend more time poking and prodding him.

A fire crackled. The fragrance of burning glasswood scented in the air. The room felt warm, but not overly so. For the first time in days he didn't shiver. That fire was to his left, which was where the hearth would be if he was lying in the bed of his suite at Windward. This mattress felt familiar, the way it sagged a bit. He recognized the fresh, clean smell of the quilt. Relief spread through him, so intense his eyes felt hot. It hadn't been a hallucination. He truly was at Windward.

"How do you feel?" a man asked. He was right next to the bed now.

"Heathland?" Eldrinson asked.

"Yes, it's me." He rested his palm on Eldrinson's forehead. "Your fever has receded."

"I had a fever?" Eldrinson had noticed little else but the pain.

"Very much so." Jase's voice soothed. But something bothered Eldrinson, interfering with the mindless oblivion he longed to reach. Someone was here. Her presence hurt.

"Roca?" he asked. "Is that you?" He couldn't bear for her to see him this way, a crippled shell of the man who had loved, protected, and raised a family with her.

Her words came from across the room. "It is me."

"You must go. I will not see you." It was true literally as well as figuratively.

"Eldri—"

"Go!" He pushed up on his elbow, his face turned in her direction. New pain sparked in his legs. "Leave me." He heard the doctor breathing, but the man didn't interfere.

Roca spoke quietly. "Very well. I will be downstairs if you change your mind."

The door opened, then closed.

Eldrinson almost cried out for her to return. He bit back the impulse and lay back down. Part of him wanted nothing more than for her to lie with him, to hold him in her arms, to give him her beloved comfort. But the thought of her touching his shattered limbs made him ill.

For a while he listened to the doctor breathe. In, out. In, out. Eventually he said, "How long will you stand there?"

"Not too long," Heathland said. "I'm scanning your body."

"I feel nothing." Usually they laid one of those infernal tapes on his neck.

"I can take readings without touching you. They aren't as detailed, though."

"What do your readings tell you?"

Silence followed his question.

"Doctor Heathland?"

Jase spoke quietly. "The bones of your legs are pulverized. You also have a massive infection."

"Oh." He had already known he would lose the limbs. Still, it was harder to hear than he expected. "Will you amputate?"

"Essentially, yes."

"Essentially?"

"We can rebuild them, Your Majesty."

"Don't call me that." He felt about as majestic at a slig-slug worming its way through the bole of a glasswood tubule.

"What would you like me to call you?" Jase asked.

"Eldrinson."

"All right." His gentle voice never changed.

After a moment, Eldrinson said, "How can you rebuild my legs?"

"Do you know what biomech means?"

"No." He had heard the word, though.

"It is a medical technology." The doctor laid a smooth strip against his neck.

Eldrinson grimaced. Jase had decided to use the holotape after all. He resisted the urge to pull it away. "My son Althor uses that word. Biomech."

"Jagernauts have it in their bodies."

"I am no Jagernaut."

"This is true. But we can give you biomech similar to theirs. It will control the structural components we use to rebuild your skeleton."

Eldrinson tried to get his mind around the words. They wanted to give him mechbot legs, like the small creatures that cleaned his house when he wasn't looking. "That is revolting."

Another silence. Emotions leaked past Jase's mental barriers. Eldrinson's response had startled him.

"Why is it revolting?" Jase asked.

"I am not a machine."

"Your new legs would look no different than the old."

Eldrinson didn't believe him. "Would I walk like before?"

"I don't know."

That gave him pause. He had expected reassurances. Healers were notorious for telling you less than you wanted to know, and with more sugar than the news warranted. He wished they would realize how aggravating it was for them hold back the truth when an empath could tell they were pretending. He should have remembered Jase had never been that type. It was another reason Eldrinson liked him.

"Why don't you know?" Eldrinson asked.

"We aren't sure if your body will accept the changes."

"Oh." He wanted to ask more, but fatigue weighed on him. The pain in his legs was increasing and he had exhausted himself, though he had done little more than lie in bed.

"Are you thirsty?" Jase asked.

Thirsty? Actually, very much so, now that he thought of it.

"Yes," he said.

A clink came from the nightstand. Then Jase set a glass-wood tumbler into his hand. Lifting his head, Eldrinson drank the water with relief. When he finished, he let his head fall back on the pillows. Jase took the glass from his hand.

The pain in his legs was growing. Softly he said, "I hurt."

"I can increase your medication."

"Medication?" Eldrinson heard the strain in his voice.

"We injected you with a nanomed species that dispenses a painkiller into your body. Each med carries a picochip. Via a remote, we can tell those chips to increase the dosage they release."

Eldrinson wondered if the words made sense. Twenty years ago it would have sounded like gibberish, and right now it wasn't much better. It was hard to think when he hurt so much. "Can you make the pain go away?"

"I think so."

"Do that. Please."

"All right." Tapping noises came from the nightstand. "You should notice a change soon."

"Good." Eldrinson whispered the word.

Then he lay there, enduring it. He didn't notice a change. The agony went on and on.

Gradually, though, he began to feel detached from the pain. After a while it hardly bothered him at all.

"Eldrinson?" Jase asked. "Can you hear me?"

"Yes." He felt sleepy. "Can't see you, though."

"We can help that, too."

His mind began to drift. "Robot eyes? Click, click, Eldri, you're blinking."

"Eldri?" Now Jase sounded confused.

"Yes?" Eldrinson asked.

"Oh. I see. It is your nickname."

"Only Roca may use it." Eldrinson yawned. "And Garlin."

"Garlin?"

"My cousin. He has a farm outside Rishollina now. You would have called him my regent, when I was young." His eyes closed, though it made no difference to what he saw. Or didn't see. "He raised me."

"Ah," Jase said.

Eldrinson slipped into the welcome oblivion of sleep, where he wouldn't face the horror of what they wanted to do to his legs and eyes.

20

Vibarr

Soz walked down the corridor after class, deep in thought, pondering multilayered Hilbert spaces, including those that created the Kyle universe.

"Cadet Valdoria?" a voice said.

Startled, she glanced up. A novice from her own class was walking next to her, a girl with brown hair and a round face. She saluted as if Soz were an upperclass cadet.

"You don't have to salute me," Soz said.

"Foxer says you're third-year status now."

Interesting. It was true she did have the augmentation that most cadets received in their junior year. And she had tested out of her first- and second-year classes, ending up in third-year or senior courses. But she still roomed with the novices and thought of herself as a first-year student. If Secondary Foxer said otherwise, though, who was she to argue?

Soz grinned at her. "At ease."

The other girl relaxed. "I have a message for you, from Foxer. You've a visitor this evening, during your free hour."

"Oh. Thanks." Then remembering herself, Soz added, "Thank you, Cadet. Dismissed."

The novice saluted and took off, obviously relieved. Soz wondered if she felt awkward, having to treat a former class-mate like an officer. Then she wondered who was coming to visit. She wished it could be her mother, with news of her father. Soz wanted to see him so much. He had almost *died*. It helped a little to know it wasn't only her he had refused to see, but she longed to go home, to end her exile and be with her family. They needed one another now.

Even if her father would have let her come home, though, Kurj probably wouldn't let her go. Allowing an extended absence for travel to another world in the middle of the term would be granting her an exception over other cadets, which he wasn't likely to do.

Lost in her brooding, she ran into a barrier. Soz blinked and looked up. Her roommate Grell was standing there with her arms crossed.

Soz's face heated. "Sorry."

"Heya." Grell lowered her arms. "You going to run me over?"

"I wouldn't dare." Soz smiled. "You might organize Jazar and Obsidian into a commando team and attack me with pillows."

Her roommate's grin flashed. "Good idea."

Grell fell in beside her and they walked together down the marble hall bordered by columns. Other cadets passed them by, talking with each other or lost in thought.

"So how does it feel to be wired up?" Grell asked.

Soz thought of her biomech enhancements. "Fast."

"Rajindia still following you around?"

"No, thank goodness." The biomech adept had grilled her for days after the trouble with the node. Soz had fully intended to take care with the accelerated mode, but Rajindia and Kurj decided on drastic steps anyway. "They took out the extra memory in my node."

"Will you get it back?"

"I think, if Rajindia ever decides I'm no longer at risk of brain damage."

Grell smirked. "What, you mean it didn't already happen?"

"Hey!" Soz swung her flat-pack and Grell ducked, laughing. Several cadets glanced their way. Thinking of her never-ending supply of demerits, Soz resisted the temptation to keep roughhousing. Instead she smiled angelically at a senior cadet who was frowning at her. She didn't know his name, but she had noticed him around. He was tall and well muscled, with a patrician nose and the dark coloring of the nobility.

Grell stopped at Soz's side. "Sir!" She saluted the cadet.

Belatedly, Soz started to salute. Then she remembered the novice who had saluted her. Foxer said Soz was a junior now. According to the convoluted academy rules, that meant she didn't have to salute other upperclass cadets. Or was it only juniors? She squinted at the senior, her flat-pack dangling. Yes, she remembered, she was supposed to salute seniors.

"Sir!" Soz dropped her flat-pack and raised her arms, fists clenched, wrists crossed.

He looked bored. "At ease."

Soz lowered her arms. For good measure, she added, "Yes, sir."

"You realize," he said, "that was worth two demerits."

Ah, hell. Resigned, Soz said, "Yes, sir."

He motioned to Grell. "You may go, Novice."

Grell looked from Soz to the senior. But she couldn't refuse. "Yes, sir." Then she went on her way, with a backward glance at them.

Soz considered him. He had to be a psion, given that he was a cadet here, but she picked up nothing from his guarded mind. She waited, unsure what he wanted.

He indicated a side hall. "Novice."

Soz thought of telling him she was an upperclass cadet now, but decided against it. He still outranked her, besides which, with her questionable tact, it might come out badly. She went down the hall, aware of him behind her.

"In there," he said. "On the right."

Soz turned into a secluded alcove that slanted off from the wall. It had probably once been part of a larger room that had been divided. Now a few crates filled it, stacked against one wall. The way it angled back from the hall made it impossible for anyone to see into the alcove unless they came down the side corridor and stopped to look in here.

Soz didn't like it. She paused next to a pile of boxes and regarded the senior. "Sir?"

He leaned against the wall so that he blocked even the restricted view from the hallway outside. Not that anyone was likely to come this way. "I hear you've got nothing but demerits, Cadet Valdoria."

So he knew her name. Soz scrutinized his uniform, but she couldn't read the tag from where she stood and she had no intention of going closer to him. "No, sir."

His voice turned cold. "Are you calling me a liar?"

"No, sir. You said you had heard I had nothing but demerits. I've also many other things." Then she added, "Sir."

He stepped toward her, his face flushing. "Don't goad me, smart-mouth. You just got yourself two more." He stopped in front of her and braced his palm against the crates behind her back, cornering her in the alcove.

Node, she thought. **How many regulations is this asshole breaking?**

None, it answered. An instructor would probably give him one or more demerits for his behavior, but technically, he hasn't violated any procedures.

"So what do you say, Valdoria?" he asked in a low voice, his body a handspan away from hers. "You going to be on droid duty for the rest of your life?"

"I hope not." To her node, she thought, **It must be against regulations for him to get this close to me.**

In spirit, yes. By the book, no. He hasn't touched you.

If he does touch me, is there any device in this alcove that can record it?

Nothing.

Well, hell. That was convenient for him. Then again, if she couldn't prove his inappropriate behavior, neither could he prove disrespect on her part.

However, her node added, both you and Cadet Vibarr have biomech webs and nodes. Anything you do will be recorded on his node, and vice versa.

So his name was Vibarr. That meant he came from a powerful noble House.

"You hope not?" Vibarr was saying. "I'll bet you've suffered more disciplinary action than all your roommates combined."

Soz saw the trap. Of course. He believed she was a

novice. He didn't know she had a node. He probably assumed he could record her behavior, including any violations, but she would have no record to use against him. Spinal nodes were supposed to be tamperproof, but given his actions, it wouldn't surprise her if he had fooled with his enough to gain control over what it recorded. She had to be careful here and go by the book.

She answered in an even voice. "I don't know how many demerits my roommates have, sir."

He lifted his finger, almost touching her lips. "I haven't registered the four you've earned from me yet."

"Is that so?" Soz wanted to ram her knee into a certain sensitive place he was pushing all too close to her. "I'm sure you will carry on according to proper procedure. Sir."

"I'm sure." He moved his finger down, almost touching her chin. Then he went down to her breasts, still not touching. "What would you say is proper, Valdoria?"

For frigging sakes, Node, Soz thought. **If this isn't sexual harassment, I don't know what is.**

In my estimation, if you brought a complaint against him, with my record of this incident, you could have him put on probation.

It would serve him right. Anyone who misused his seniority this way had probably done it to other cadets as well. But if she made a stir, it could backfire. He came from a powerful family. She did as well, but she couldn't appear to misuse her title. Always it came to this: as an Imperial heir, she was watched more closely. It made no difference that relatively few people knew her identity; those who did would assess and judge her behavior by a tougher criterion than other cadets, except Althor. Hell, Kurj would probably come down harder on her than Althor, given the way he seemed to think she needed it more. She had better damn well make sure she handled this without breaking any rules herself.

Pride also came into it; she was a descendant of the Ruby Pharaohs who had ruled a matriarchy where men didn't even fight. For one of those queens, this situation would have been humiliating. To conflict her reactions even more, she had grown up in a culture where only men fought. It all left her with a tangle of emotions that she herself didn't fully understand.

"Proper procedure is in the regulations," Soz said, answering his question. Lame answer, but she was stalling while she decided what to do.

"The rule book?" He leaned closer. "To survive, every good soldier learns when to compromise, Novice."

Soz gritted her teeth. "Is my survival in danger?"

He tilted his head. "Get too many demerits, and you'll find yourself out of this academy as fast as you can say, 'Well, fuck, I broke the profanity rules.'"

"Yes, sir. You did." To her node, she thought, **You get that?**

`Affirmative. However, if swearing was considered a serious offense, the majority of the cadets here would be in trouble, including yourself.`

"You think you're tough," Vibarr said. "Think again."

"What I think," Soz said, enunciating each word, "is that this goes well beyond the respect expected by lower-class cadets for seniors."

His eyes glinted. "And how would you prove that?"

Soz had to make a decision: tell him about her node and make him back off, keeping the matter discreet; or keep silent and let him hang himself for an expulsion. Convincing him to back off would be safer. If she accused him, the inquiries could be embarrassing and might leave her open to a backlash. Smear campaigns paid little heed to the truth, and she had no doubt Vibarr would spread rumors. But who knew how many people he had misused this way, cadets who might also have opted for discretion rather than risk trouble. That was the problem with DMA; as much as its ingrained traditionalism produced well-trained cadets, it also discouraged any sort of stir, even when the person causing it was in the right.

Stop thinking like a cadet, Soz told herself. *Think like the future commander of ISC.* When put in those terms, the decision was obvious. Vibarr didn't belong at DMA.

"The honor system requires a cadet tell the truth," she said.

Vibarr laughed. "Gods, you're naive."

"I know the regulations. Sir."

"So, what, you going to make trouble, hmmm?" He brushed his lips over hers. "They'll kick you out for fraternization."

Soz jerked her head away. "This isn't fraternization. It's coercion."

He trailed his finger between her breasts, touching now. "You said it yourself. We're bound by an honor code. I've four years of a sterling record to support my word. What do you have? One of the worst demerit records in DMA history."

Soz put her palms against his chest and shoved. "Enough."

He moved so fast, his hand blurred. He caught her wrist and slapped it against the boxes behind her. Soz winced as her arm hit the crates. She tried a move from her martial arts class, but he blocked it easily, with augmented speed and strength.

He pinned her against the crates with his body. "You know, I hear a lot about you being a hotshot. It's time someone took you down a few levels. Taught you a little humility."

Soz spoke through gritted teeth. "What are you going to do, Vibarr? Rape another cadet? What the hell kind of officer are you going to make?" Then she shoved him away.

This time when he came back at her, she had nowhere to duck, so she dropped to the floor. The situation had gotten way out of hand. He had probably expected her to give in right away, trading sexual favors so he wouldn't make her already dreadful record even worse. He had to know he had gone too far.

Vibarr dragged her to her feet. His chest was heaving as he slammed her against the crates. "Take that as a warning. I'm not done with you, Valdoria. Neither is my House."

Soz bit back the retort that burned on her tongue. Hell, he was right, she didn't want trouble. But she had it regardless. He had just invoked his noble heredity in an obvious attempt to coerce her silence. Bringing up his lineage would leave him open to exactly the kind of criticism she would have received if she had hauled out her Ruby heritage. Civilian titles had no place here, nor did they make any one cadet better than the others.

He raked her body with a look of disgust, then spun around and left the alcove.

Soz sagged against the crates, her heart beating hard. **Node, you get all that?**

Yes.

Good. She took a deep breath and walked into the hall. Then she headed to the office of the commandant.

"Gods." Lieutenant Colonel Dayamar Stone sat at the console in his office and stared at the download. "This is hard to believe."

Soz stood at attention behind him, her face flushed as the holographic replay from her node displayed her "meeting" with Vibarr. This was her first time in Stone's office. Usually she only interacted with him on the exercise fields, where he and Secondary Foxer trained the cadets. But he was also in charge of the Infractions Committee. She had decided to come here first instead of going to Blackmoor's office because she was uncertain how to proceed.

Stone looked up at her. "How long have you had your node?"

"Ten days, sir."

"That's not very long."

"Yes, sir." Soz couldn't read beyond his carefully neutral expression.

A hum came from across the room. As she and Stone turned, the door slid open—and commandant Grant Blackmoor stood framed in the rectangular archway. Tall and forbidding in the unrelieved black of his Jagernaut Primary uniform, he towered over her and Stone. Metal glinted on his massive gauntlets. His granite-hard face left no room for doubt about his authority. Soz had often wondered if Kurj put him in charge of DMA because Blackmoor looked like him.

Stone stood up, and he and Soz saluted with alacrity, raising their arms and hitting their wrists together with fists clenched.

"At ease." Blackmoor came inside and the door closed behind him. To Stone, he said, "I received your message." He glanced at Soz, then back at Stone. "An emergency, you say?"

Soz felt like she had jumped off a cliff and was plunging down its face now, wondering if she was going to hit the water or smash into rocks.

"Yes, sir." Stone nodded toward Soz. "Cadet Valdoria has lodged a complaint against another cadet."

Blackmoor's dark eyebrows drew together. "Since when do you need the commandant to settle a student dispute?"

"It's serious, sir. I just finished viewing a record from her node." Stone moved aside, leaving the seat at the console for Blackmoor. "Perhaps you would take a look."

"Very well." The commandant took the chair Stone had vacated and flicked his finger through a holicon above the screen. "I take it the recording is the last one viewed here?"

"Yes, sir," Stone said.

Two holos appeared above the flat screen on the console, each about one hand span tall. The detailed image showed all of Vibarr and the edges of Soz's body that she would see with her own eyes. Vibarr was saying, "I hear you've nothing but demerits, Cadet Valdoria."

So it went. Her face burning, Soz stood behind Blackmoor while the entire record played. She felt stupid. But damn it all, this wasn't the Ruby Empire anymore and regardless of her pride, anyone who abused his power that way didn't belong at DMA.

When the recording finished, Blackmoor sat staring at the screen. Then he stood slowly and gave Soz a long, appraising look. His face remained impassive and he barricaded his mind, so she had no more clue of his thoughts than she would have detected with Kurj.

He turned to Stone. "Have you verified the accuracy of this?"

"I've run preliminary checks," Stone said. "We will do a more extensive investigation, but based on the prelims, I would say the recording is genuine."

Soz stiffened. What did they think, that she would falsify the encounter and somehow download it to her node? *To what diddly damn purpose?*

Blackmoor glanced at her. "Cadet Valdoria, you must learn to guard your mind better."

Soz flushed and tamped down her anger. She hoped they didn't give demerits for her thoughts.

Mercifully, Blackmoor turned back to Stone. "Have you spoken to Vibarr yet?"

Stone shook his head. "I contacted you immediately."

Blackmoor exhaled. It wasn't until he pushed his hand across his brush of gray hair, though, that Soz realized he wasn't as unaffected as his manner suggested. He spoke in a neutral voice. "Cadet Valdoria, you may return to school. We will contact you if we need more information."

Soz stared at him. She masked her emotions, but behind her barriers, she seethed. Another cadet, a well-placed senior, had just broken gods only knew how many rules of their vaunted honor code and they were just sending her away? She kept her mouth shut, though, and acknowledged that she didn't know what they intended. She saluted stiffly, her fists clenched so hard that her knuckles turned white.

Then she left. Dismissed.

Twist. Drop. Grab. Soz gritted her teeth as she wrestled with the Echo scaffolding, her nemesis, this blasted obstacle course Kurj had challenged her to complete in eight minutes when no one had ever managed in less than nine. She couldn't do it in twelve. The scaffolding vibrated, trying to throw her off, and she lost her grip. As she slid through the bars, her knee hit a cross strut and she groaned. She banged her fist on another bar, then caught it as she slid past and yanked to a jarring halt. She hung there by one arm, feeling stupid, with the scaffolding vibrating all around her.

Jaw clenched, Soz scrambled up to a more stable region of the structure, then swung the rest of the way through its crisscrossing bars and dropped down on its far side. As soon as she hit the ground, she took off toward the lake. The syncopated rhythm of her run helped her deal with the plex-turf, which reared under her feet in surges calculated to send her sprawling. Although she had grown more accustomed to the lower gravity on Diesha, she had trouble here timing the intricate dance of steps. With a grunt, she staggered and lost momentum. She had just managed to catch her balance when she reached the oil pool that reflected the dust-red sky, but she was off her stride. With a grunt of protest, she stumbled and plowed into the pool, kicking up turgid swells of oil.

"Ah, hell." If that didn't make a bad day worse. Soz waded doggedly out of the pool and set off running again. Bad idea. Slick with oil, her feet slipped out from under her and she slammed onto the turf. Swearing, she climbed back to her feet, and of course the ground had to heave under her. With her feet and legs covered in oil, she could hardly even walk without slipping.

Thoroughly aggravated, she set off for the echoing maze. She had committed the route to memory, but she had to walk the whole thing. After she left the maze, she strode to the rebounders, the doors and gates that snapped open and slammed shut in a crazy, hyper pattern. No problem. She just waited for each to open and jumped through. It was perfectly safe—except it took forever. By the time she stalked out onto the white sand trap beyond, the timer on her wrist said it had taken her more than sixteen minutes to complete the course, her worst time yet.

"Bloody echoes," she muttered and headed out of the sand onto the field of stubby grass, her feet and legs covered with a layer of gravel and other crud that stuck to the oil.

She was in a very bad mood.

Fields, tracks, and other obstacle courses spread all around, pristine under the burning sun. To her left, mountains jutted up into the sky, riddled with jogging trails. An academy building stood on her right, its white columns bright in the intense sunlight and its arched windows annoyingly dignified. Soz veered away from the main building and tramped toward the dorms. Given how long it had taken her to finish the Echo, she had no time left to practice on any other course, not if she wanted to clean up to see her mysterious visitor.

Back at the dorm, Obsidian was the only one of her roommates at home. He was sitting on his bunk, the bottom bed of the set across from hers. Leaning against the wall, with his pillow in his lap, he was intent on a holobook. Quantum circuits floated in the air. His black hair was out of its queue and falling over his shoulder.

He glanced up and smiled as she stomped into the room.

"Heya, Soz."

She glowered at him and went to the bathroom.

"Nice to see you, too," he called as she closed the door.

Soz braced her hands against the metal sink in the cubicle. She felt guilty for taking her bad mood out on Obsidian. It wasn't his fault an arrogant Vibarr lordling had decided to make her life miserable or that the commandant's reaction bewildered her. Didn't they want details? Maybe they intended to cover up the entire business rather than have a scandal involving an Imperial heir and the prince of a powerful noble House.

She stripped off her workout suit, which had been light blue before she started sweating and was as dark as midnight now. Then she opened the cleanser unit and squeezed inside the stall. As soon as she closed the door, water misted across her. She leaned her forehead against the tiles and closed her eyes while tiny soap-bots in the mist cleaned her body.

After a while she began to feel better. When the unit shut off, she stepped out and pulled on her robe, which hung on the bathroom door along with those for her roommates. She went out in the room and found Obsidian still sitting on his bunk, studying.

"Heya, Oboe," she said.

He glanced up. "You human yet?"

Soz winced. "Sorry."

"What happened?"

No one had told her to stay quiet about the incident, but it was probably better to see what was going to happen with Vibarr before she said anything.

"I ran the Echo," she said.

He gave her a commiserating grimace. "No wonder."

"You shouldn't spend your only free hour studying." She smiled. "Go have fun."

"You know, Soz, not everyone can ace their finals halfway through the term without even studying."

She suddenly remembered Vibarr's words. *I hear a lot about you being a hotshot. It's time someone took you down a few levels. Teach you a little humility.*

"Obsidian?" she said.

He watched her curiously. "Yes?"

"Am I arrogant?"

He laughed easily, with good nature. "You're cocky, Soz. It's not the same."

"Do you ever want to see me taken down a few levels?"

His smile faded. "Who said that?"

"You didn't answer my question."

"No, of course I don't." After a pause, he added, "That's because I know you. But I think some people do."

"Why? Am I that insufferable?"

"No." He closed his book and the holos vanished. "It's human nature to resent people who excel. And you don't, well—"

She waited. "Don't what?"

"You don't hold back."

She crossed her arms, bunching up the sleeves of her robe. "Why should I?"

"I didn't say you should." He shook his head. "Some people are unassuming, Soz. When those people leave you stumbling in the dust, it stings less. And some people aren't unassuming." He smiled dryly. "Rumor has it, that includes just about every Jagernaut alive. You've heard what the rest of ISC says about us."

She squinted at him. "What?"

His laugh spluttered. "You haven't heard?"

"Obsidian! Tell me."

"That we're the most cussed overconfident bastards in the forces."

"Oh. That."

"Yeah, that." He seemed amused by her supposed nonchalance.

Soz had already figured out that Obsidian could see through her, that he knew her insecurities and uncertainties. But he was decent about it and never used the knowledge against her, just as she would never use anything she knew about him or their roommates. They might be brash, but they were also loyal. DMA had known what they were doing when they put the four of them together; although they were all different, they suited well in their abilities and values. It was practice for flying with a Jag squadron, which consisted of four people, often two men and two women.

Soz went to her locker and pulled out an academy jumpsuit, blue again. She changed in the bathroom, then waved to Obsidian and went off to meet her visitor, leaving her roommate with his quantum circuits. She strode through the dorm, down holo-paneled corridors and through the common rooms. She entered the visitors' room—and stumbled to a halt. Gods almighty.

Her father had come to see her.

He was sitting on a white couch across the room, holding a blue geometric sculpture that usually rested on the table in front of the couch. Metal balls rolled around within the glass tubes of the artwork and clinked as he tilted it back and forth. His wine-red hair had swung forward, hiding part of his face. He had on odd clothes, at least for him, a pair of dark blue slacks and a white sweater that accented his broad shoulders.

Soz hesitated. Had her father grown? She didn't remember his legs being that long or his shoulders quite that broad. Her shock faded, replaced by disappointment that it wasn't him, but also by warmth and welcome. She headed across the room.

"Eldrin?" she asked.

He looked up—and it was indeed her brother. Of all the Valdoria boys, he was the most like their father. His handsome face could have been The Bard's at a younger age. He had the classic Rillian hair, wine-red, though the sun had streaked it with gold. Metallic lashes fringed his violet eyes.

"Soz!" He stood up, smiling.

Delighted, Soz went over and embraced him. He felt solid and secure in her arms. She had always liked Eldrin, though she understood him less than many of her other brothers. Of all her siblings, he seemed the most Rillian. He was the eldest, twenty-three, married and a father.

As they drew apart, she said, "I had no idea you were on Diesha." She spoke in Trillian, their native language. They were both trilingual, having learned Trillian, Iotic, and Skolian Flag since birth, but they had always considered Trillian their first language.

Eldrin smiled, seeming both pleased and self-conscious. They hadn't seen each other for years. "I just arrived this morning."

"Is Taquinil with you?" she asked. His son was always a safe subject, a beautiful boy with black hair like his mother's and gold eyes.

Soz never knew if she should ask Eldrin about Dehya, his wife. She couldn't help but wonder how he felt being the consort of the Ruby Pharaoh, arguably the most powerful Skolian alive. The family avoided the subject. To say he and Dehya hadn't wanted to marry was the understatement of the century. That they had come to love each other was an unexpected gift in the convoluted emotional intrigues of Assembly-dictated marriages among the royal family. Actually, "arranged" was far too mild a word. Coerced, more like it. Tricked. Threatened. Inflicted.

By law, cousins could marry. Dehya and Eldrin were a step closer, however; he was her nephew. Legally, their contract was on shaky ground. The Assembly had demanded the marriage anyway, desperate for more Rhon psions. They called on an ancient law from five millennia ago that decreed the Ruby Pharaoh must take her consort from among her own kin, because only members of that dynastic line were exalted enough for such a union. It was a crock and the Assembly knew it, but no one had ever repealed the wretched law.

Personally Soz thought that with all that inbreeding among the ancient dynasties, it was no wonder their empire had collapsed. Yet for all that her family resented the Assembly's efforts to control and breed them, no one denied they had reason. They didn't yet know why, but in vitro methods of reproduction became unreliable for people with the Kyle genetic mutations that produced psions. The more Kyle genes someone carried, the greater the problems. For Rhon psions, who had two copies of every Kyle gene, it was virtually impossible to reproduce by artificial methods.

The Imperialate couldn't survive without Rhon psions for the Dyad, and only members of the Ruby Dynasty were Rhon psions. Soz's parents had ten children, but Roca had struggled with her pregnancies, and the doctors advised against her having more. The Dyad had many heirs now, but the Assembly wanted to ensure a continuous supply, especially given the nature of the training for the Imperial Heir, which included combat experience. However, children couldn't be Rhon unless they received the genes from both parents; it took two Rhon psions to make a third. The solution was obvious, at least to the Assembly: make the Ruby Dynasty interbreed. They picked Dehya because she had less genetic connection to the Valdoria branch of the family, and they chose Eldrin because he and Dehya had the fewest deleterious matches among their genes.

It was still too much.

They should never have reproduced. Their son Taquinil, so beautiful and so brilliant, might never be able to live on his own. Born of two people on the extreme end of empathic sensitivity, the boy was so susceptible to emotions, he couldn't block them at all. He had no barriers against the onslaught. His parents had to protect him with their minds and provide the shields he lacked. His doctors were struggling to learn how they might treat the boy without destroying the magnificent neural structures that made him such an incredible empath, but unless they succeeded, Taquinil could probably never survive on his own. The inexorable flood of emotions could drive him insane.

At Taquinil's young age, it wasn't a problem to be with his parents all the time. But as he matured that would change. His independence could cost him his sanity if the doctors couldn't find a way to protect his mind.

Soz wanted to throttle the Assembly. If they insisted on meddling with the lives of the royal family, the least they could do was go back to choosing spouses from appropriate noble Houses to solidify political alliances. Not that it worked. Her brother Vyrl had certainly had his own ideas when they tried to marry him off to Brigadier General Devon Majda. Soz liked Devon, but she couldn't imagine her married to Vyrl, of all people.

Yet for all her anger at the Assembly, Soz understood; if the Dyad ever collapsed, who would protect the Imperialate? It was no wonder they insisted Kurj begin training his heirs. Without experience, neither she nor Althor could function effectively as the Military Key to the Dyad.

Pain sparked in Soz's head. She winced and pressed her fingers against her temples. Excited by Eldrin's arrival, she had unconsciously jumped her node into an accelerated mode. During her entire train of thought, Eldrin had barely moved, only turned his head slightly. According to her node, less than two seconds had passed. It sobered her to think she could have just damaged her brain if the doctors hadn't pared down the extra memory.

"Soz?" Eldrin asked. "Are you all right?"

Her time sense snapped back to normal. "I'm all right." She gave him a rueful smile. "I've a node in my spine now, but I'm still learning to use it. Sometimes it distracts me."

"I don't know how you can stand to have all that biomech put inside of you."

Soz found it exhilarating rather than intrusive. "I like it."

Eldrin indicated the couch. "Sit with me. Tell me how you are."

Soz settled with him on the sofa, relieved to get off her feet. It had been a grueling day. It was hard to relax, though.

"I'm doing all right," she said.

"Good." Still tense, Eldrin was sitting up so straight, his spine didn't touch the back of the sofa.

Across the room, two novices strolled through an archway, a woman and a man. When they spotted Soz, the man raised his hand. Soz nodded awkwardly, but fortunately they went on their way, leaving her in privacy with Eldrin. No doubt they would raise questions later. What would she say? Oh, he's my brother, His Majesty, Prince Eldrin, the Ruby consort. Yeah. Right.

Eldrin's face relaxed into a smile. "You have that look, Soz."

"Look?" She wondered why her brothers always seemed to find her so amusing. "What look?"

"That 'Oh, Gods, what do I do with these brothers' look."

Soz glowered at him. "You sound just like Althor. I'll have you know that I do consider my brothers human."

He burst out laughing, an incredible sound, like music with rumbling chimes. Soz sighed, delighted. She wished he would sing. He had inherited their father's glorious voice.

"I'm glad you consider us human," Eldrin said. "I've wondered."

"I can't be that bad."

"You're unique." He turned to her, resting his elbow on the back of the couch, one knee pulled up on the cushions, which were shifting subtly to ease his muscle tension.

Soz smiled. "I can deal with unique." He wasn't guarding his mind much, at least not compared to the people who surrounded her here at DMA. Nothing specific came through, but she could tell he was upset, something about their father and his son Taquinil.

Soz hesitated. "When I first saw you, I thought . . ."

He waited. "Yes?"

"That you were Father."

He averted his gaze, his long lashes shading his eyes.

"Dryni?" she asked.

He looked up at her. "I had to leave Taquinil with Dehya. I was having nightmares about what happened with—with

Father." His voice lost its chiming quality. "Which means Taquinil had them, too."

"Hai, Dryni, I'm sorry." Supposedly it was impossible for them to experience what had happened on Lyshriol from so far away, but both she and Althor had suffered effects. Eldrin, the child closest to their father, had probably experienced it even more. Rather than risk Taquinil suffering, he must have come here, hoping distance would at least help the boy, if not himself. Knowing how much Eldrin loved his son, Soz could imagine how hard it had been for him to leave. "Have you felt any effects?"

He spoke in a low voice. "I can walk now. But I couldn't for several days. The doctors found nothing wrong with me. I lost my sight for a while, too."

Soz's voice hardened. "The Aristos who did this to him will pay. I don't care what it takes."

Eldrin pushed back the hair that hung straight and glossy to his shoulders. Soz had always liked the way it framed his face, his bangs often askew like a youth about to get into mischief. Now he looked exhausted. And vulnerable.

"I want vengeance, too," he said. "But it won't bring back his sight or heal his legs."

A rustle came from across the room. Soz looked to see Obsidian headed toward her, his stride firm. Damn. Not now. It wasn't like him to intrude.

At the couch, he hesitated, glancing from Eldrin to Soz. "Heya."

"Heya." Soz motioned toward Eldrin. "This is my brother, Eldrin."

To her consternation, Obsidian bowed. Straightening, he said, "My honor at your presence, Your Majesty."

Soz knew he meant respect, and she appreciated his intent, but if anyone saw him bow that way, they would ask questions she didn't want to answer. "Obsidian."

"I'm sorry to disturb you." He spoke more formally than he ever did in their room. "Commandant Blackmoor wants to see you, Soz."

"Ah, hell," Soz said. It had to be about Vibarr. She turned to Eldrin. "I'm sorry. I have to go."

He nodded, his disappointment obvious. A teasing glint also lurked in his gaze, undoubtedly because the commandant had summoned her to his office. "I will be here for a while. Maybe we can have dinner with Kurj."

Obsidian froze, staring at Eldrin. Soz doubted it would help if she told him that Kurj had acted as a surrogate father to Eldrin during the first months of Eldrin's life, while their mother had been separated from her husband. Kurj actually liked Eldrin and would certainly want to have dinner with him. Soz supposed he might even want her along, too.

"I'd like that," she said, rising to her feet.

"I'll walk out with you." Eldrin stood and inclined his head to Obsidian with a regal carriage that Soz doubted he even knew he had. Although he dressed in modern clothes now, elegant and simple, she would always see him as a boy in the rough leather trousers and a faded blue shirt with thongs lacing it up the front. She smiled at the memory.

They all left then, Obsidian returning to the dorms, and Eldrin headed for the echoing, empty Ruby Palace in the mountains. Soz went to face the commandant of the Dieshan Military Academy.

The first thing Soz noticed about Blackmoor's office was its size. Many dorm rooms could have fit in here. It contained a great deal of empty space. Wood paneled the walls. Genuine wood. On a world with no forests, the expense of such paneling spoke eloquently of the value the J-Force put in the commandant who trained its elite cadets.

A large desk stood across the room. On the wall behind it, a holo of the J-Force insignia dominated the wall, the starfighter seeming to cut through the air. Other holos of academy buildings and the Red Mountains glowed along the walls. Blackmoor was sitting behind his desk, leaning back in his chair, watching her as she entered the room, his face just as unreadable as every other time she had seen him.

They weren't alone. Soz was aware of Kurj as soon as she

entered, though it took her several moments to see him. He stood by the back wall, his skin the same shade of gold as the wood. He was leaning against the wall, his arms crossed, his eyes shielded, like a metal statue.

Soz saluted them both, first Kurj, then Blackmoor.

"Cadet Valdoria." Blackmoor indicated a high-backed chair by his desk. It had the J-Force insignia emblazoned on its back and the ISC insignia on its gold upholstery. "Please be seated."

Soz sat. This felt unnervingly like a disciplinary action on a level far beyond demerits. She thought she had dealt all right with Vibarr, but it didn't take a genius to see it was a touchy situation. Perhaps she had erred or overreacted. She had no way to evaluate it; she had never faced a comparable situation.

Blackmoor considered her from his big chair, which he filled with his imposing frame. "Are you aware of the identity of the cadet you recorded this afternoon?"

It wasn't an auspicious opening. "Yes, sir. He is a Vibarr."

"The oldest child of the Vibarr Matriarch, to be precise. Her heir."

Damn. That gave him a hereditary rank approaching her own. It was unusual for a matriarch to designate her son as heir, but in this modern age, it was no longer unheard of even among the most conservative noble Houses. Dehya had named Taquinil as heir to the Ruby throne, and no one dared question Kurj as Imperator.

Even so. Vibarr's title didn't excuse his behavior. Soz waited to see where Blackmoor intended to go with this. She was aware of Kurj back there in the corner, listening, barely visible from where she sat.

The commandant sat forward and folded his arms on his desk. "I verified your node recording. I concur with Foxer that it hasn't been altered."

The implication that she might fabricate such evidence offended Soz. But she realized that given the identities of the people involved, they had to take every precaution, and that would include verifying the recording. She spoke quietly. "I would never alter it, sir."

His gaze never wavered. "The House of Vibarr has recently suffered the death of several of its elder members. It appears family responsibilities require Cadet Vibarr to withdraw from the academy."

Withdraw? *Withdraw?* They were going to let Vibarr go without a mark on his record. It stunk to the stars. They should kick his sorry ass from here back to the washed-out star system his family owned.

"I see," she said.

"Do you?" Blackmoor studied her. "What would you suggest?"

"He violated the academy honor code, sir, including two breaches that require expulsion: physical assault and coerced sexual contact."

"Expulsion."

"Yes, sir." Soz realized she had clenched the scrolled arms on her chair. She relaxed her fingers.

"And then?" Blackmoor asked.

"Then?"

"That's right." He shifted his weight, a subtle motion, one she wouldn't normally have noticed. Now, though, she had her full attention on him, with an empath's natural ability to interpret body language, gestures, and facial expressions, a skill developed after a lifetime of associating moods with behavior. He wasn't as impassive about this situation as his demeanor implied.

"After we expel the Vibarr heir, what happens then?" he asked. "We have earned the enmity of a powerful House, one whose support has value to the academy."

"Cadet Vibarr dishonored basic principles of our training. What about the honor code?" She drew in a breath to slow her pulse. "As Jagernauts, we must obey it. Why? Because civilian law doesn't apply to us. Isn't that the point, sir, that if we must act contrary to the law in our defense of Skolia, the civil authorities can't prosecute us? But no one is above the law. Our instructors drill that into us every day. We live by the code." She had studied it even before coming to DMA. "Vibarr made a mockery of it. He expected to get away with it because he didn't know I had a node. His record may be sterling, but I'll bet I'm not the first novice he has coerced."

"So you would have him leave."

"Expelled, sir."

"And if the decision harms the academy or ISC?" He waved his hand as if indicating all of Skolia. "We may be governed by the Assembly, but you of all people should realize great power still resides in our supposedly titular aristocracy."

Soz assessed his words as she would a scenario in her military strategy class. "In other words, political pragmatism outweighs honor and regulations."

"Life comes in shades of gray, Cadet. A leader knows how to deal with those shades."

What bothered Soz most was that she saw his point. Blackmoor could also have thrown her own dreadful record at her. He didn't. But that made none of this easier to swallow. Her demerits came from an eagerness to make her opinion known when it wasn't wise or to move forward with more seniority than she possessed. She had never violated the honor code nor acted to harm others. That DMA would let Vibarr escape admitting responsibility for his behavior corroded her respect for the code she had so admired.

Kurj came forward, a behemoth in motion. He fit this huge office. Blackmoor did, too. If Kurj unconsciously chose his top officers to resemble himself, that didn't bode well for her chances as his heir. At the moment, she was angry enough to wonder if she cared.

When Kurj reached Blackmoor's desk, the commandant rose to his feet. Soz followed suit immediately, wanting to kick herself for her slight delay. She was letting her concerns distract her. If Kurj noticed, however, he didn't let on.

He spoke to Blackmoor. "I will see you tomorrow, in the briefing."

The commandant saluted. "Tomorrow, sir."

Kurj turned to Soz. "Walk out with me."

Apparently they weren't done yet. "Yes, sir."

He nodded to the commandant, one giant to another.

Then Kurj and Soz left.

* * *

The sun had just set over the Red Mountains in a blaze intensified by red dust until the entire sky seemed on fire. Soz walked with Kurj through the twilight across an inner sanctum of the academy, a private garden put aside for the commandant's use. Moss designed for low moisture environments carpeted the ground, and beds of well-tended flowers nodded in the dry, hot breezes of the oncoming night.

"You're quiet this evening," Kurj said.

"Disillusionment does that to a person."

"Real life doesn't put itself in a pretty box tied up with ribbons, Soz."

She spun around to him, stopping on the white gravel path. "I never said it did. But letting him off this way is wrong. It's a tacit acceptance of what he did. You're saying it's all right."

His gaze never wavered. "Vibarr was among the top students in his class and little more than one semester away from receiving his commission. He would have graduated with honors. Now he has nothing. He left this afternoon. Yes, what he did to you was inexcusable. But he's paying for it. Why is it so important to you that he also suffer the public disgrace of expulsion?"

"He should have thought of that before he violated the code." She set down her anger and spoke evenly. "He tried to intimidate me with his title so I wouldn't speak up. Now he's receiving special treatment because of that title. That's wrong. You know it."

"Yes, it's wrong." He met her gaze. "Suppose Blackmoor did expel him. And suppose that because of it, the House of Vibarr acted against DMA interests in the Assembly."

"I hate politics." That wasn't actually true; at times they intrigued her. But right now she despised them.

"That's not an answer," Kurj said.

Soz gave him an implacable look of her own. "Yes, we have to make compromises to govern effectively." She took a deep breath. "But every time we compromise our integrity for the sake of politics, we lose something. Ultimately, it weakens the structure of anything we build. Including the military."

He considered her for a long moment. "You're a lot different from Althor."

"Althor?"

"Are you recording this on your spinal node?" Kurj asked.

"Well . . . no. I recorded the session with the commandant. I stopped when you and I started walking through here."

Curiosity leaked past his barriers. "Why stop?"

It was hard to articulate; she had made the decision instinctively. "You're my brother. I guess I put that above you being my CO. One doesn't record their family." She supposed she would if it was in some official capacity, but it hadn't even occurred to her now. She had given him an implicit expression of trust that she hadn't consciously realized she felt until this moment. That knowledge startled her, given all the times she wanted to rage at him when he was driving her twice as hard as the other cadets.

"I'd like to talk to you about something," Kurj said. "But I don't want it recorded."

"I won't. You have my word."

"Good." His gaze darkened. "When I saw that holo of Vibarr harassing you, I wanted to take him apart with my own hands. And if you ever repeat that, I'll deny every word."

Soz would never have expected such a reaction from Kurj. She wasn't the only one offering trust; for him to make such an admission said volumes about his faith in her. He had only her word it would stop here.

"Thank you," she said, as much for his trust as for the sentiment.

Kurj started walking again, his face shadowed in the dusk. "Althor had a situation come up his first year that in some ways parallels yours."

Soz walked with him. "What happened?"

"He found out a senior was dealing phorine to other cadets."

Gods almighty. "Phorine is addictive."

He raised his eyebrow. "You've always been a master of understatement."

"Did he tell you?"

"He should have."

"But?"

"He hesitated because he knew the boy selling the drugs." Kurj shook his head. "So he talked to the dealer himself. He had some idealistic view the kid would stop. Instead, the senior threatened his life."

Soz knew her brother wasn't one to give in to threats. "Then he went to you about it?"

"Not to me. To Blackmoor." His inner eyelids were up now. "It isn't coincidence that some cadets here come from well-placed families or the nobility. That makes for better educations, better preparation, and better connections."

"The dealer came from a noble House?"

"Not a House." He sounded tired. "He was the son of a powerful banking consortium. Any scandal could have had serious financial repercussions for DMA."

Soz grimaced. "Hell."

"That about sums up my reaction."

"What happened to him?"

"He got sick."

"And had to leave DMA as a result."

"Yes."

This sounded even worse than her situation with Vibarr. Cadets lived under intense pressure. A phorine dealer could cut an ugly swath through their ranks. "Althor must have been furious that the senior wasn't expelled."

Kurj gave her an odd look. "He was relieved. He wanted it kept quiet."

Her idealistic view of the honor code was taking a beating today. "That doesn't sound like Althor."

"He claimed it was because he knew the senior. But this kid threatened to kill him. And he meant it." Kurj glanced toward the dorms. "I think Althor knew some cadets who used phorine."

"He should have given you the names." Althor had always had an intense loyalty to his friends, but surely he realized that any psion taking phorine needed help. The euphoric drug affected empaths and telepaths; the stronger the psion, the greater the addiction. Every cadet here was at risk. Far more harm would come to his friends through his silence.

A thought shook her. "He didn't try it, did he?"

"No. The doctors found no trace of the drug in his system."

Soz breathed out in relief. As a Rhon psion, Althor would be brutally susceptible to even a tiny dose. Given the minuscule size of the population phorine affected, very little research existed on the drug outside of the J-Force and a few neurological institutes. She knew about it because she had researched high-level psions while preparing for her DMA prelims. A Rhon psion probably couldn't survive the withdrawal without medical intervention. It would take a strength of will beyond even Althor, who was a remarkably powerful man in both mind and body.

"He wasn't helping anyone by keeping quiet," Soz said.

"I agree." Kurj turned onto another gravel path. "To this day, he insists he didn't know any cadet who used the drug. He passed a lie detector test. If he wasn't an empath, I would believe him."

"He couldn't pass a lie test unless he was telling the truth." Experts considered the tests better than ninety-eight percent accurate.

"Some psions can learn to modulate their brain waves. It affects the test." Kurj slanted a wary look at her. "And if you repeat that, I'll put you on droid duty for the rest of your life."

"My mouth is sealed." She was learning a lot tonight they never taught in DMA courses. "Who do you think he's protecting?"

"I'm not sure." Kurj paced through the twilight, and his atypically relaxed barriers let his frustration leak through to her. "We checked the entire student population. We found two cadets addicted to phorine and one who had tried it a few times. If Althor knew any of them, we have no evidence of that. But it isn't impossible."

"He could be telling the truth."

"Perhaps." Kurj considered her. "What would you have done, if it had been a friend of yours?"

Soz didn't hesitate. "Given you the name." She couldn't imagine doing otherwise, *especially* for a friend. "I would have asked you to get them in treatment as soon as possible."

"That's good to hear."

She scowled at him. "And I would expel Vibarr's sorry butt."

His smile glinted. "You know, Soz, his name came up last year when the Assembly was discussing possible marriages between the Ruby Dynasty and noble Houses."

Soz considered regurgitating her lunch. "Pity for my poor sister Chaniece."

"They weren't talking about Chaniece."

"Well, Aniece is too young, and besides, she wants Lord Rillia." She gave Kurj her most sour look. "And I *know* they weren't talking about me."

His laugh rumbled through the dusk. "If the subject comes up again, I will describe to them your expression as you delivered those words."

"You do that."

His smile faded into something harder to read. It almost looked like affection. "It can be refreshing, you know."

She stared at him, aghast. "What could possibly refresh you about the Assembly interfering in our lives?"

"I meant someone who speaks her mind to me."

Soz suddenly realized she had been glaring at her CO. "I mean no disrespect, sir."

"Right now, Soz, we are just brother and sister."

A confusing emotion washed over her, at least where Kurj was concerned. Affection? Was it possible? It felt odd; they rarely interacted as siblings unencumbered by other responsibilities.

"Family," she said.

"Yes. Family." He spoke in a low voice. "Fodder for the Dyad."

The Dyad. Everything they did came back to that power-link.

The last traces of the sunset were fading and the stars of Diesha glinted in the sky. They walked on, caught in an isolated bubble of kinship, with the weight of the Trader Empire poised outside that tenuous safety.

Soz was beginning to understand the weight Kurj and Dehya lived with as the Dyad. They were responsible for a mesh that served thousands of settlements and hundreds of billions of people. Any telop could use the Kyle web, but only Dehya and Kurj could control it. Dehya created the web and ensured it survived. Kurj used it to build ISC into a deadly machine that even the Traders, with their greater resources, couldn't defeat. He was blunt power: she was subtlety and nuance. He was the Military Key; she was the Assembly Key. They called Dehya the mind of the web and Kurj its fist.

It wasn't enough.

They were exhausted. Two people, no matter how strong or driven, couldn't keep up with the growing, ever-changing demands of a voracious mesh that added new networks at billions per hour. And always now Kurj and Dehya were searching to discover how Vitarex Raziquon had infiltrated Lyshriol. The same thought hung like a specter over them all; if the Traders could violate the Imperialate stronghold of Lyshriol, no place was safe. Soz knew the truth no one admitted, that the Assembly kept quiet, that ISC buried in secured systems. No one spoke it aloud, but it terrified them all. The Kyle web was out of control. If they didn't find a solution, it would collapse under the sheer weight of its success.

And kill the Dyad.

21

Aftermath

The Dalvador winds ruffled Roca's clothes and cooled her skin. Iridescent glitter dusted her body and swirled in the wind, curling up into the lavender sky. Streamers of blue clouds stretched from horizon to horizon, with wisps trailing down from the sky to the ground.

Corey Majda walked with Roca to the starport. The Majda queen gazed around at the countryside. "I'll never get used to how beautiful—and how strange—it is here."

Roca felt too dispirited for talk about the landscape. She spoke in a low voice. "How is he?"

"Prince Shannon?"

"Yes." She rubbed a muscle kink in the back of her neck. "He hardly says a word to me when we talk through the web link."

"He's been through a lot."

"Too much." If Roca could have taken into herself the memories that haunted her son, she would have done it in a moment. But only Shannon could free himself from the prison of his nightmares.

As they neared the port, the reeds petered out into an open stretch of velvety piper-moss. A circular, whitewashed house stood beyond, its turreted roof reminding Roca of an upturned bluebell. ISC had agreed to let Shannon stay in Brad Tompkins's house for his custody. The boy was under military guard, but at least he was living with a family friend.

The door of the house opened as they drew near. Brad stood there in jeans and a gray sweater, his belt slung with a staser. "Roca! It's good to see you." He raised his hand in a wave to Corey. "My greetings, Colonel Majda."

"Dr. Tompkins." Corey nodded with the wariness she always maintained toward anyone from Earth.

Inside, the house charmed Roca as much as it had twenty-four years ago when she had first come to Lyshriol. Although it served as the port office, it was also the home where Brad lived with his Lyshrioli wife Shallia and their four children. Green glasswood paneled the living room, with a rustic bar along one wall and blue doors leading to inner rooms. Throw rugs lay about on the stone floor, which was tiled in pale blue and green squares. Paintings graced the walls, landscapes of spindled mountains cloaked in blue snow, actual pictures rather than holoscapes.

Shallia and the children had gone to live with her mother in Dalvador, about a fifteen-minute walk from the port. Roca knew why they had gone, even if neither Shallia nor Brad would admit it, and she felt a debt of gratitude to them. They didn't want Shannon taken up to the battle cruiser in orbit any more than Roca did. It would traumatize him to be yanked away from Lyshriol, especially now, when his emotions were already so injured. The port was ISC property, so they could hold Shannon here, but Corey Majda would never have let him stay with Brad's family. Roca didn't believe for one moment Shannon was a danger to anyone, and Corey knew it, too. But the colonel always followed procedure. No laughing children filled the living room today, no toys lay scattered over the rugs and tables, and no plump Shallia beamed at them, urging them to have more syrup-filled bubbles. Instead, two guards in dull green-gray uniforms of the Pharaoh's Army stood posted by the walls.

Shannon was sitting in an armchair at a table with a chess set made from green and gold glasswood. He looked up as they entered and then rose to his feet. His silver eyes had a hunted look, with dark circles marring his pale skin. His white-gold hair shimmered in the light from the overhead lamps.

Roca wished she could reassure her son. But he had grown more distant these past years as he navigated the boundary between youth and manhood. He wasn't the first of her sons to withdraw from her during adolescence, becoming taciturn and noncommittal with his mother. The other boys had come out of it after a few years and relaxed with her again. Shannon was in the middle of that time now, struggling to define himself, and she didn't know how to reach him.

He looked so much like a Blue Dale Archer. He wore the clothes they had given him, a moss-green tunic that reached to midthigh, thick leggings that would keep him warm in the northern mountains, and dark green boots. He lacked only his magnificent bow, the quiver of arrows on his back, and his sword with its jeweled pommel. His ethereal beauty, upward tilted eyes, and silver gaze made him seem a creature of myth more than a human boy.

He watched her like a wild lyrine ready to bolt. "Mother."

"My greetings, Shannon." She almost called him Shani, but it felt wrong here. Shani was a boy. She faced a man, the killer of a Highton Aristo.

Her son averted his gaze, his lashes hiding his eyes in a white-gold fringe that glinted.

Hai! He had picked up her thought. She spoke softly, painfully aware of everyone in the room. "I am glad to see you."

"You shouldn't be."

"Shannon," she murmured. Gods, she wished these people would leave. Even under normal circumstances, talking to Shannon wasn't easy. With an audience, she felt too constrained to speak at all.

Brad came over to the chess board and gave Shannon a rueful smile. "I guess I can finish losing this game another time."

"You played well," Shannon said.

"You played better." Brad glanced quizzically at Roca.

"Perhaps you could come back later with Colonel Majda to finish the game," Roca said, hoping he would take the hint. They couldn't "come back" unless they left. Majda wouldn't dismiss the guards, but she might at least take them outside.

"Perhaps we could." Brad turned to the colonel. "Did you still want to check on the landing field?"

"The field?" Corey glanced from Brad to Roca. "Oh. Yes. Let's do that."

Thank you, Roca thought, though Corey wasn't a psion. Now if she could just convince Corey to take the guards, too. When the colonel met her gaze, Roca tilted her head slightly toward the guards. Corey just looked puzzled.

"We could use some help checking the field," Brad said.

Roca could have hugged him. Corey considered him, started to speak, then seemed to change her mind. Instead she turned to the guards. "You two will aid Dr. Tompkins."

The taller of the two scratched his chin, seeming perplexed, which didn't surprise Roca; even if Corey and Brad really were going to check the field in some way, they hardly needed the two lieutenants. But he just said, "Yes, ma'am."

Roca watched as they all left the house. Brad raised his hand to her, then closed the door.

She turned to Shannon. "I'm sorry. About the guards."

"They never intrude." His voice chimed softly.

"Are you all right?"

"Yes. Fine." He rubbed one hand over his cheek in a gesture he had used all his life, since he was a little boy in his crib. It made her ache to see him do it now, for it had always meant he felt scared.

Shannon, talk to me.

He gave no indication he heard her thought, though she directed it with enough strength and clarity to reach him. He had barriered his mind to her, probably to all of them. It broke her heart to see both Eldri and Shannon withdraw this way, shutting out the people who loved them.

"Would you like to sit down?" she asked.

"All right." He settled into his armchair and she sat across the table from him in Brad's chair.

Shannon moved his green chessmen to their squares along his side of the board. "Would you like to try a game?"

Roca touched one of the gold pawns on her side. "Aren't you and Brad playing?"

He shrugged. "I was about to checkmate him."

She wondered if she knew this son of hers at all. "I hadn't realized you could play chess."

He continued to set up his pieces. "When I worked at the port last year, Brad and I used to play after my shift."

Roca had encouraged her children to try part-time jobs here, when Brad allowed. He put them to work maintaining the flyer or monitoring the consoles. It was a good experience beyond their farming chores. They learned what it meant to earn credits they could use to purchase Skolian goods or services. Althor and Soz had spent many hours here. Shannon had been less interested, but he had tried it. Perhaps he had really come to play chess. It hadn't occurred to her to suggest the Earth game to him, but now that she thought about it, she could see its appeal. Although he had trained as a warrior, like her other sons, he had always seemed more interested in strategy than the actual fighting. Chess would intrigue him in the same way.

She set up the gold pieces on her side of the board. If Shannon could beat Brad, he would trounce her; she knew little about chess beyond how to move the pieces, and she wasn't even sure about that with a few of them.

"Gold goes first," Shannon said.

Roca slid one of her pawns forward. "Is ISC treating you well?"

"Yes." He picked up one of his pawns. "Fine."

Roca looked up at him. "Shannon, you have to stop blaming yourself for what happened to your father."

He jerked and dropped the pawn. It hit another chessman and the two statuettes spun off the table. A flush touched his cheeks.

Ai! Roca wanted to kick herself. She leaned down and gathered the fallen pieces. When she straightened up, Shannon was still sitting, staring at the board. His face had gone pale. Roca started to speak, but then stopped, afraid she would only make things worse. She wished she knew how to talk to this son of hers, half man, half boy, half Archer, half Rillian. She felt his mood, strained and uneasy, but it didn't do much beyond letting her know she had to tread with care. Sometimes being an empath made it harder; she could feel when her children hurt, but that didn't tell her how to help.

She put the two chess pieces back on the board. Shannon looked at them for a moment, then set down his pawn in another square. Roca had no idea what strategy to use. She liked the castles in the corners, but her pawns were in the way, a whole row of the little foot soldiers. She moved another one forward.

Within a few moves Shannon was taking her pieces right and left. Another few moves and he had won, neatly trapping her king in one corner.

Roca smiled ruefully. "I'm afraid I'm not much challenge for you at this game."

He continued to stare at the board. "I used to play with Father."

Roca chose her words with care, taking it obliquely this time, as he had done. "The day I met your father, he had come here with his cousin Garlin to play chess with Brad."

Shannon looked at her. "Garlin plays better than either Brad or Father."

Roca smiled. "So Brad tells me." Garlin, Eldri's former regent, lived on a farm some kilometers distant, but he still often visited.

"I can beat Father sometimes. But never Garlin."

"I hadn't realized you enjoyed the game so much."

He shrugged. "I don't play much now. I did more when I worked here."

She wondered if he felt a loss at that. "You could challenge your brothers or sisters."

"Soz is the only one who really knows the game." He looked rather alarmed. "She plays like she's in a war. Even Garlin can't beat her. She doesn't win, she obliterates."

Roca couldn't help but laugh. "I can imagine."

Shannon smirked. "I think Lord Rillia escaped a grim fate."

"Shannon."

"It's true. Besides, Aniece wants him. And she will like being the queen of Rillia."

"What?" *That* caught Roca off guard. "Aniece is too young to have such thoughts."

"She doesn't know that. She wants to marry him."

In truth, Roca agreed that when Aniece grew up she would make a far better match for Lord Rillia than Soz. For all that the marriages of the Ruby Dynasty and other Skolian nobles were often arranged for political reasons, Roca had never been able to make herself insist when her children balked at the plans their elders hatched for their marital state.

She regarded Shannon curiously. "How about you?"

He stiffened. "What about me?"

"I just wondered if you had anyone."

His face turned red. He mumbled, "No," but his thought was so strong, it came to her despite his barriers, the image of a lovely young Archer, a woman with a superb bow made from glowing red glasswood and nocked with a gold arrow.

Roca held back her smile. She doubted Shannon would feel gratified to know his love interest charmed his mother. "Well," she said, setting up her chess pieces for another game. "I'm sure you will meet someone someday."

He made a noncommittal sound and put his own pieces in place. "You can go first," he offered.

Their second game lasted a few moves longer than the first. Roca even figured out what to do with the pieces that resembled warriors on lyrine, what Shannon called "nights" in English, though she wasn't certain why. The game had no "days." In the end he captured her queen, which looked like an ancient Ruby Pharaoh and had a similar level of power in the game. Then he checkmated the Pharaoh's consort, or king.

"Well, that was fast," Roca said.

He grinned at her. "Father used to say that, too."

"Perhaps you could play him when he's feeling better." She spoke with care. "It will give him something to do."

Shannon's smile vanished. He moved his pieces back to

their original positions, then stood up and walked over to the glasswood bar against the wall.

Roca wished she had some magic spell that would tell her what to say. When he had been younger, he had often wanted to talk, but rarely volunteered. If she came asking, though, he spoke with enthusiasm about his thoughts, his dreams, his frustrations, and his joys. Now she had no idea what approach to take. He might open up to her, but if she pushed too hard, she could put him off, too, even antagonize him.

Shannon rummaged under the bar and came up with a pitcher and a large tumbler, neither of which could have originated in Dalvador given the relatively primitive glass crafts here. Many homes had glassware and windows now, though, introduced over the years by Roca's people. Shannon filled his tumbler with blue water from the pitcher, focusing as if it took all his concentration to transfer liquid from one container to the other.

Roca tried to think of something to say. Then she changed her mind and just sat, letting him decide.

After a moment, Shannon said, "He can't."

"He?"

"Father." He stopped pouring. "He can't play chess anymore."

She gentled her voice. "His mind is fine."

Shannon looked up at her. "He can't see the pieces."

"Maybe not. But he could identify them by touch." She wanted him to know his father's life wouldn't end if he didn't recover his sight or ability to walk. "You can carve the board so he recognizes the squares."

Shannon set down the pitcher. He picked up his glass and drank slowly, then put it down again. After another long moment he spoke in a low voice. "I should have gone to him sooner."

Roca's heart ached to see him so troubled. "You didn't know."

"I *should* have known." His hand shook and sloshed the water in his glass. "I felt what happened to him."

"If you should have known, so should I have." She struggled with that guilt. As an empath, she had been certain Eldri was in trouble, but what good did that realization do when it told her nothing more? She didn't know what was wrong or how to help him, only that he suffered. She had raged at her helplessness when they couldn't find him and now guilt ate away at her.

"Somehow we have to make peace with ourselves," she said. "We can say, 'If only' so many ways, but no one can foresee the future."

"I can't find that peace." His voice sounded hollow.

She spoke softly. "It could have been far worse. Vitarex could have succeeded in what he came to do."

"Colonel Majda is furious with me."

"Furious?" Roca had never seen Corey angry about anything.

"She hides it. But I know. They wanted to question Vitarex. If I hadn't killed him, they would have him now."

Roca wanted Vitarex alive, too. Ah yes, she had wanted him to live. But her motives were far less pure. She wanted him to suffer as Eldri suffered, in agony, a horror as drawn out and as brutal as what he had inflicted on her husband. It wasn't a noble sentiment, but it burned within her.

None of that mattered, though, when she thought of her fourteen-year-old son setting himself against a warlord who could have crushed him as if he were nothing. She wanted to rage at Shannon, make him promise never to risk his life that way again.

"It took great courage for you to face Vitarex," Roca said. She wondered if he knew the depth of that understatement.

Shannon shook his head, his eyes downcast. Watching him, Roca knew that the greatest toll exacted in a war had nothing to do with exploded machines or who had better weapons. It was the devastated lives that nothing could repair, not even victory. Her children might recover from the demons that haunted them, but the scars would remain. It made no difference who won; everyone suffered the emotional shrapnel.

* * *

Roca sat with Brad and Corey in the control room located in a short tower just off the landing field. They pulled their chairs inside the curving Luminex console and studied the holo displays. Brad indicated a three-dimensional graph in the air. A series of glowing lines in different colors curved within its cubical area, showing the fluxes and flows of power through various systems at the port.

"There," he said. "Another one."

Roca peered at the graph. The blue curve came to a point, like a thorn. "What is it?"

"A surge in the energy grid," he said. "The one that supplies power to this building and my house."

Roca vaguely remembered him mentioning something like this before. "Is it a problem?"

"We checked it out with our equipment on the *Ascendant*," Corey said. "It's within normal range."

Roca could tell there was more. "But?"

Brad splayed his hands on the console. "It isn't anything as far as we can tell. But if we're going to find out how Vitarex got in here, we have to look at everything." He indicated the thorn on the curve. "This spike is just a bit larger than usual."

Majda moved her hand through another graph floating above the console, the red, blue, and green lines rippling in streaks of color over her skin. "We've found a few more of these spikes in records for the past year. They don't appear to correlate to anything other than normal power variations."

It didn't sound like a promising lead to Roca. "Why did you notice them, then?"

"They're at the edges of the bell curve for fluctuations," Brad said. "About one standard deviation out from the center."

"Oh." It had been decades since Roca had studied error analysis and the subject had never particularly interested her, but she remembered enough to realize he meant the fluctuations were on the outermost edge of what they considered normal. "What will you do?"

"Keep an eye on it," Majda said. "See if we find anything similar anywhere else."

Brad leaned back in his chair. "I'll keep trying to isolate the cause of the spikes."

Keep trying. It seemed to be her internal mantra lately. Roca rubbed her eyes. It felt like ages since she had slept. Every time she closed her eyes, she thought of Eldri lying crippled and blind, alone at Windward; or of Shannon, trapped in a prison of his own making, built from his remorse.

Brad was watching her. "I can fly you back to Windward."

"Thank you. Yes." She glanced at Corey. "And Shannon?"

The colonel spoke carefully. "I've sent a report to HQ, including Shannon's confession and my recommendation that they release him on the basis that he was defending your family and the people here against an ESComm attack."

It was true, Roca supposed. But they all knew that Shannon had acted for one reason only. Vengeance. Although she doubted any court would support criminal charges against him, they had to do everything by the book. A Highton lord had died here and the Trader emperor demanded an investigation. Given that Vitarex had no cause or clearance to be on Lyshriol, the demands rang hollow, but ISC still had to observe the interstellar treaties.

No treaty, however, could heal the wounds of Vitarex's trespass here.

The doctors operated on Eldrinson in the earliest hours of morning, long before the suns offered their light to the sky. Roca sat in the dining room of Castle Windward, unable to sleep, waiting to hear.

For hours.

The sky lightened and the suns rose, both darkened with spots, each slightly elongated toward the other. Roca thought of those suns slowly perturbing Lyshriol out of its orbit, tugging at the world as they executed their never-ending dance around each other. Humans had moved this planet here, but nature would destroy its orbit. Nothing remained stable no matter how hard they struggled to give their universe order.

Dawn usually lifted her spirits, but not today. For twenty-four years she and Eldri had lived together, loved together, and raised their children. Always the threat of the Traders shadowed their lives, but now it had violated their innermost sanctum.

Nothing could undo the events of two nights ago. Shannon had killed Vitarex. No matter how much anyone wished otherwise, nothing would change that truth. ISC would never learn from Vitarex how he had infiltrated Lyshriol. Unless they discovered other clues, they would never know—and so they could never be certain they were guarding against another invasion.

Fourteen hours later, the suns sank behind the horizon. In the dark hours of night, long after most everyone in the castle had gone to bed, Jase Heathland finally came down to the hall. And he told Roca: *it is done.* They had repaired Eldri's legs and eyes to the best of their ability.

Only time would reveal if it had been enough.

22

Commencement

In the year 325 ASC on the Imperial calendar of the Skolian Imperialate, the year 2228 A.D. on Earth, the Dieshan Military Academy graduated its three hundred fifteenth class. The graduates included a tall, gold man—Althor Izam-Na Valdoria kya Skolia, Im'Rhon to the Rhon of the Skolias.

The graduation took place on a windy day in the quadrangle before the arches and columns of the academy. Students sat in chairs set up on the plaza, an area paved with glittering white flagstones and a tiled image of the J-Forces insignia two meters in diameter, a soaring Jag in white, silver, and black. The sun beat down on the assembled crowd, and chimes hanging in the eaves of the academy building clattered in the breezes.

Families and friends watched from risers bordering the plaza. Soz sat with her mother, her brother Eldrin, and his son Taquinil. Eldrin seemed unusually serene today, probably because he was with his son. His peace of mind calmed Soz and shielded Taquinil. Her brother Denric, her sister Aniece, and her youngest brother Kelric sat on the riser below them, restless with excitement on this world they had never before visited. Del-Kurj and Chaniece had stayed on Lyshriol to look after Dalvador, and Vyrl and Lily hadn't been able to come either, with the demands of their farm and children, and Vyrl preparing for his university exams. But the family members on Lyshriol could experience the graduation in a virtual reality broadcast, using mesh links Brad had set up for them in the castle.

For the graduation, DMA had erected a stage at the front of the plaza facing the cadets. Kurj sat in a high-backed academy chair, as did Secondary Tapperhaven, Lieutenant Colonel Stone, and Secondary Foxer. Commandant Blackmoor was at the dichromesh glass podium, speaking to the graduates. The officers made a tableau of strong figures in the sunlight, their uniforms crisp, gold on black, their faces just distant enough that Soz couldn't read their expressions. Were they proud of the graduates? Certainly. But she sensed regret as well. They were taking the pride of Skolia, the smartest and the fastest, the greatest empaths, and sending them to battle, perhaps to die.

Soz's aunt, the Ruby Pharaoh, sat in an academy chair next to Kurj. She wore her hair swept onto her head in an elegant roll. Her black jumpsuit had no adornment except the silver insignia of the Imperialate on her chest. The edges of her body rippled, the only indication from this distance that she was a holo, a creation of light sent through Kyle space and projected here by hidden screens. Rumors of hostilities from the Traders became more widespread each day. The Skolian Assembly didn't want to risk having both members of the Dyad in the same place at the same time, not even on the same planet if possible. So Dehya attended as a virtual simulacrum while she remained on the Orbiter, the governmental center that orbited throughout the Imperialate.

It puzzled Soz that people thought she resembled Dehya. She had even overheard one of her instructors describe her as a robust, sexier version of the pharaoh. Soz just didn't see it. Dehya's hair hung straight to her waist, as black as space, whereas Soz's curled wildly and lightened to gold at the tips. A shimmer overlay Dehya's eyes, a remnant of the inner eyelids from her father, Soz's grandfather. Soz had no trace of it. Dehya had an ethereal quality; Soz felt more like the mythical bull-dragon. Personally, she thought Dehya resembled Shannon. Although he was a Blue Dale Archer rather than a Raylican noble, his face had that otherworldly beauty Soz associated with her aunt.

When it came to intellect, Dehya left her in the metaphorical dust. As an unusually sensitive Rhon psion, Dehya had a brain full of extra neural structures, intricate and convoluted. Psions tended to be smart, but Dehya was in a class with no one except her son Taquinil. Legend claimed the Ruby Pharaoh's mind had gone beyond human. Soz thought it an annoying statement; the pharaoh was human, so how could her mind go beyond itself? Dehya made mistakes like everyone else, forgot where she put her light-stylus, misread moods, became absentminded. But she learned tremendously faster than other people and at an unusually abstract level, especially now with all her biomech enhancements. The few times Soz had pitched wits with her, Dehya had left her so far behind, Soz had felt like a wind blasted by her mind.

The Ruby Pharaoh ruled through the meshes. Dehya spread her mind throughout the webs of humanity until she became the mind of Skolia. And reign she did, regardless of what the Assembly claimed. Soz doubted Eldrin had any true sense of how far his wife's influence extended or how deep it went. If he cared that he was consort to one of the most powerful human beings in the history of the human race, he gave no sign.

Now Dehya and Kurj—the Dyad—sat together, though only one of them was physically here. He said something to her and she smiled. Commandant Blackmoor continued his commencement oration. When he finished, he took his seat on Dehya's other side, and Kurj went to the podium. He spoke only briefly, as taciturn as ever. Then it was time to give out the diplomas. Blackmoor returned to the podium and called the names, and one by one the new Jagernaut Quaternaries came up to receive the antique parchments from Kurj.

When Althor crossed the stage, the audience fell unnaturally quiet. Anyone who hadn't realized before that he had a kinship to Kurj would have no doubt now. They looked like twins, two gold giants, muscled and square-jawed. Kurj handed Althor his diploma, along with the certificates and medals Althor had earned by graduating with honors. Then the Imperator paused, which he had done with no one else.

Breezes ruffled Althor's short hair, making the metallic locks glitter. Kurj laid his hand on his brother's shoulder and inclined his head. Even from so far away, Soz felt Althor's gratification at the unexpected display of approval. He nodded, his face easing into a smile, and Kurj returned the nod. Then Althor went on, down the stage and back to his seat. An exhale seemed to come from the audience, though it could have been only the wind in the arched colonnade.

After the last senior had crossed the stage, the ceremony ended. DMA had graduated another class of elite warriors, sixteen Jagernauts, all that remained of the thirty-six who had entered as novices. Sixteen new weapons joined the ranks, sixteen of the deadliest, most versatile fighter pilots created.

And Soz watched, wondering. When she graduated, would her ceremony suffer the same lack as this one, the absence no one mentioned but everyone felt, the cavity in the foundation of their family and their love, the one person Soz had heard nothing from since the day she left Lyshriol, the one she feared would never speak to her or acknowledge her again.

Her father.

23

A Debt to Vengeance

Gradually Eldrinson became aware of heat on his face. He lay on his back, soaking in the warmth. His legs ached, but only as a distant pain he could almost ignore.

After a while, hunger came. He rolled over and reached to the nightstand for the plate of spice bubbles that the girl Marla often left for him. She was one of the few people he allowed in the room. The other two were Jase Heathland from ISC, and the Lyshrioli healer Channil who had tended Eldrinson since childhood and taken care of Roca during several pregnancies.

Roca. Saints, he missed her. He hadn't seen her face since—well, since before he had traveled across the Back-bone, searching for Shannon and finding Vitarex. He knew she came into his room sometimes, especially when she thought he slept. He remembered the day she had come to speak to him. She had left when he insisted, unwilling, he knew. He lived alone now, without her, without his family. They wanted to come. He felt it. But he had made his decision. No visitors. He longed for them to remember the man he had been, not this broken shell that even the boastful Skolian technology couldn't fix.

He found the spice bubbles and took three. Pulling himself up in bed, he sat against the headboard and crunched the bubbles. They exploded with sweet, spicy sauce in his mouth. Had he been able to see, he could have enjoyed their rose color. He always had before.

After he ate, he rubbed his temples. He thought a seizure had wrung him earlier, but he wasn't sure. Whatever had happened, he must have slept afterward. No sunlight had slanted across his body then but he felt it now. Someone had opened the shutters in the alcove across the room. The suns must be low in the sky, if they could shine through those windows. For a marriage gift all those years ago, Roca had arranged for glass in the openings here and in Dalvador. Now they could open the shutters on the ceiling-high windows without letting in the icy mountain air.

A hum came from the nightstand. Eldrinson hinged his hand around another spice bubble, then felt around until he found the engraved circle he sought on the stand. Holding the ball in two fingers, he pressed the engraving with a third.

Jase Heathland's voice floated into the air. "My greetings, Your Majesty. Did you sleep well?"

Heh. That Jase knew he had slept implied Eldrinson had suffered an attack. Jase always monitored him afterward and buzzed him when he awoke. Losing his appetite, he set the spice bubble back on its plate. He had been fine for so long. But when he lost his sight and legs, so too had gone his freedom from the seizures. His doctors understood it no better than he did, though they made a good show. Perhaps Vitarex had done more damage than they realized. Eldrinson was a psion. His constant exposure to the Aristo's brain might have injured his mind. Jase thought his body had changed over the years, until his nanomeds were no longer effective in fighting the seizures, but Eldrinson couldn't help wondering if the sun gods were punishing him for failing with his children.

Before Vitarex had caught him, Eldrinson had intended to talk to Soz and Althor, to take back his bewildered words of anger from that terrible day when he banished them from their own home. But he couldn't now. He couldn't bear to see anyone, neither family nor friend. He had failed his men as well as his wife and children. Even worse, he knew firsthand what would happen if Althor or Soz were ever captured. His children, his beloved children, would suffer as he had suffered at Vitarex's hand. Or worse.

No.

He couldn't bear the thought. Better to deny them all than to accept a pain that went too deep to endure. If he refused to acknowledge his family, he wouldn't die a little bit more every day trying to understand the terrible beauty of their inexplicable lives. He had nothing left to give them. Let them live free, in the splendor and fury of their new universe, unfettered by their barbarian father.

"King Eldrinson?" Jase asked over the comm.

He mentally shook himself. It was hard to concentrate. He had so few conversations these days. "I am here," he said, knowing Jase would somehow hear, though he was in another part of Windward.

"How are you feeling?" Jase asked.

He gave the same answer as always. "Fine."

"Your legs don't hurt?"

Eldrinson scowled. Why did Jase ask if he already knew the answers? His machines could tell him anything. A man had no privacy anymore. "My legs are fine."

"May I come up to work with you?"

"No." He wasn't up to "physical therapy" right now. The damn exercises didn't work. Neither did the mental exercises meant to help him see. He tried concentrating on his eyes until his head throbbed. When it caused a seizure, he quit. He didn't believe a person could "retrain" the way his brain communicated with his body. His blasted head didn't even connect to his legs. He didn't care how many lectures Jase gave him about biomech threads, neural impulses, and synapses, he knew his brain and his limbs didn't have conversations.

Besides, they weren't his legs or eyes. They were some sort of machines that mimicked being human. He was no longer Eldrinson Valdoria. It was a horrendous thought, as if he had lost parts of his soul. The legs felt like his old ones. Jase and his assistants claimed they had grown more of his own skin to cover the rebuilt limbs. Nor did his eyes feel different. He didn't care. No matter how much they disguised reality, he knew the truth.

"Are you there?" Jase asked.

Eldrinson had the feeling the doctor had been speaking while his mind wandered. "Yes. I'm here."

"Does your head bother you?"

"My head is fine." The throb from earlier today had receded.

Frustration crackled in Jase's voice. "Talk to me."

Eldrinson didn't see the point. "Why?"

"So I can help you heal."

"I'm fine."

"What about your elbow?"

His elbow? "What about it?"

"You bruised it during the seizure. I wondered if it was giving you any trouble."

So he *had* suffered a seizure. It disheartened him that he couldn't even tell anymore. Maybe his mind was disintegrating from these changes. He certainly felt dissociated from everything.

Now that Jase mentioned it, though, his elbow did ache. But he could ignore it. "My elbow is fine."

"Eldrinson, listen." Jase spoke with that inexhaustible patience of his. "We need to do more tests if we're going to understand why you aren't responding to treatment."

"Jase, you listen. You've had forever to do tests. It doesn't work. My mind is flat. My head doesn't chatter with other parts of my body. The seizures have come back. It's time you gave up and went away so I can have peace." He stopped, running out of words.

Silence. Then Jase said, "It hasn't even been quite a year yet. You need more time."

"What time?" Eldrinson wondered if Jase had heard anything he said. "Althor told me that he could use his biomech the day they turned him on." It appalled him to imagine ISC switching his son on like a piece of equipment. "Are you saying some people take a year?"

Jase paused. "Every person is different."

Pah. "You didn't answer my question."

Another silence. Finally Jase said, "No, I've never heard of it taking a year."

It surprised him to hear the doctor admit it. Lately even Jase evaded his questions. "How long does it usually take?"

"It depends."

"That's not an answer."

Jase exhaled. "If it isn't immediate, it usually takes a few days for the person's brain to integrate with the neural threads."

"A few days."

"Yes." Jase sounded subdued. "I'm sorry."

"For what?" Eldrinson told himself he wasn't dying inside, that he didn't care.

"I'm sorry it is taking you longer."

"No, that's not why you're sorry."

"It isn't?"

"No. You're sorry because I will never walk or see again."

"Damn it, Eldrinson, that's not true."

"Come up here where I can sense your mind. Then tell me it's not true."

"Fine." Jase sounded annoyed. "I'll be there, five minutes."

Too late, Eldrinson realized the doctor had maneuvered him into doing exactly what Jase wanted. Eldrinson scowled. "Never mind. I changed my mind. Don't come up."

No answer. Either the doctor was already on his way or else he was pretending he could no longer hear his patient. Eldrinson grabbed a bubble off the plate and crunched down hard, chewing angrily.

Sure enough, his door soon creaked open. A familiar tread crossed the room.

"So you're here," Eldrinson said. "You can go now."

The footsteps stopped near the bed. "Eldrinson," Jase said.

"What?"

"Your wife is in the foyer outside."

"The answer is no."

"I didn't ask a question."

"Yes you did. You want to know if I will see her." Why did

they torment him this way? How many times did he have to say no?

Jase spoke tightly. "I never would have guessed a man like you could show such cruelty."

Eldrinson clenched his fist in the covers. "Go to hell."

"She loves you. This is killing her."

"Get out of here," Eldrinson said. "As of today, I'm no longer seeing you, either."

"I'm your doctor. You can't refuse to see me."

"Yes, well, didn't you know, I'm the King of Skyfall." He couldn't keep down his anger. He hurt inside and Jase was making it worse. "I rule the whole planet. Not that anyone lives on most of it and never mind that someone else actually rules Rillia and Dalvador, not me. You offworlders want me to be the King of Skyfall. Fine. I'll be a king. I order you to leave."

The door from the foyer creaked open, followed by a painfully familiar voice. "And when you've sent everyone away?" Roca asked. "Then what? Will you wallow up here in self-pity until you die of thirst and starvation?"

Eldrinson froze. "Get out."

"No." Then she said, "Doctor, if you would leave us please."

Eldrinson felt rather than heard Jase's stunned silence. The doctor hadn't expected her to come in this way. He said only, "Of course." His footsteps receded across the room. The door scraped on the stone floor and closed again.

"Roca, don't do this." Having her come here hurt too much. He could be nothing for her now. He had always known he was crude, far less than the type of man she could have married if he hadn't been a Rhon psion. He had spent some incredible years with her, but now, faced with what he had become, he could no longer ask that she tie herself to him.

Don't make it so hard, he thought.

It doesn't have to be hard, she answered.

No. He closed his mind to her. "Go, Roca. Leave Lyshriol. Find a man you deserve."

"I don't want anyone else."

"Go," he said. "Don't come back. Ask the people who do Skolian laws. They can make documents to free you."

"Eldri, stop." *Don't say things now you'll later regret.*

I regret it now. But I mean it.

You are a Ruby consort.

Only until your legal people arrange otherwise.

I don't want otherwise.

You shouldn't have come in here.

Don't shut me out. She didn't hide her loneliness; he felt how much it would hurt her if he dissolved their union.

Eldrinson exhaled. He loved his wife more than his life. He couldn't cause this pain. Hell, he couldn't even keep his mental barriers in place against her. He spoke tiredly. "I want you to go. If you keep pushing me, I will divorce you. I'm sorry. But I can't take this." His voice cracked. "Go away, Roca."

"Eldri—"

"Go," he whispered. "Please."

She said nothing more. The door creaked and scraped closed.

He was alone again.

Shannon ran through the plains. Scents of Dalvador came to him: dusty glitter; the tart smell of the crushed reeds that bounced up after he passed; the pungent scents of the hummer-flits that looked so pretty but preyed on darters, the tiny animals that whizzed through the air like needles. Moisture saturated the air here compared to the mountains. A gauzy flock of shimmer-flies dipped on the wind and their iridescent wings glistened in the sunlight.

He ran until he could go no longer. Then he collapsed into the reeds and let them sway above him, hiding him from the sky, the shimmer-flies, and the eyes of any searching parent who might seek him out. No, not parent. Mother. His father no longer wanted anything to do with him.

He rolled onto his stomach and laid his cheek on the flattened reeds. The tubules felt smooth under his skin. He closed his eyes, knowing he should go do his studies. But he no longer cared. His father would have sent one of his brothers out to find him. But Father was gone. Maybe forever.

He was too listless to move. The lethargy had often come over him since he stabbed Vitarex.

Murderer.

Prior to that night, Shannon had never fathomed what it meant to take another life. He knew his brothers Eldrin and Althor had ridden into battle, each when they were only two octets of years. Eldrin had killed three people, one with his bare hands. He came home a hero—and deeply troubled. He lost control of his temper more and more often, turning to violence. In the end, when his rages had threatened even his own safety, their parents had sent him to the Orbiter, where experts helped him deal with his conflicted life and emotional scars. He had also learned to read and write. The Orbiter had been good for him. Finally he had begun to heal.

Too bad the Assembly had ruined everything by forcing him to marry. At least Eldrin seemed happy now. He certainly loved his little boy. Shannon thought of Varielle and ached. He had initially wondered if he liked her because she was the first woman of his own kind he had met. He knew now it was her, just her. But he hadn't seen her since that terrible night he had gone into Vitarex's camp. No one would ever love him now. He would never win Varielle, never have a family, never have children.

He thought of his brother Vyrl, who had married at a younger age than Shannon was now. Vyrl and Lily had so many children, with another on the way. Shannon couldn't imagine it. Nor could he imagine leaving Lyshriol.

Most of all, he struggled to understand Althor, who had slaughtered over three hundred Lyshrioli soldiers with a laser carbine. Shannon knew the remorse his brother had wrestled with after that day. But it never showed. Althor was by nature a warrior; he conquered his inner demons with a success Shannon could never manage. He had worshipped Althor all his life, but he could never be like his warlord brother.

Six years had passed since that day. No one fought battles

on Lyshriol now. Everyone seemed stunned, the armies of Dalvador and Rillia, who had fought side by side, and those of their enemy, Avaril Valdoria, their father's cousin, who hated Eldrinson for inheriting the title of Bard.

Shannon had never met Avaril. Those days of strife had become remote. He had dreaded going to war, and it filled him with immeasurable relief that he wouldn't be expected to ride into battle when he reached his two octets of years. He wanted to wander the mountains, use his bow for bringing down game rather than men, let his emotions blend with the Archers beyond the Backbone, beyond Ryder's Lost Memory, far in the north where the chill winds blew.

Instead he had murdered one of the most powerful men in an interstellar empire, and in doing so, he had robbed his family, this world, and the Imperialate of their chance to discover how Vitarex had invaded this Skolian stronghold. In the end, neither ISC nor the Traders demanded Shannon be prosecuted for Vitarex's death, but it made no difference. Shannon knew what he had done.

For that, he could never forgive himself.

24

Onyx Platform

It was only a blip.

Just a little spike of power in a Dieshan power grid.

The tech on duty noticed and checked the fluctuations in that section of the grid. The spike was in reasonable bounds. He found nothing out of order, so he went on to his other work. He had done this shift for years, taking night duty at the ISC power station high in the Red Mountains West of HQ City and DMA. This grid served only a few defense installations—and the palace they guarded.

He glanced out the window. The palace stood high in the mountains, majestic and otherworldly, with walls of rose crystal. Its onion towers made silhouettes against an intense crimson sunset.

Ruby Palace.

Home of the Imperator.

Half an hour before sunrise, Althor jogged out to the airfield with the other three members of his squadron.

Their Jags waited on the tarmac.

Technically the single-pilot spacecraft were called JG-8 fighters. The name Jag came from "lightning jag," the nickname test pilots had given the prototype, the JG-1. Althor's adrenaline surged when he saw Redstar. His ship. Only he could fly this beauty. Its onboard Evolving Intelligence had become part of his brain and recognized no other pilot.

The four ships waited on the tarmac like alabaster works of art. On the ground, they were elongated, with wings extended. In flight, they could change according to their purpose: spread wings for subsonic speeds; wings pulled in tight for hypersonic flight; rounded shape to minimize surface area during interstellar flight or for stealth or battle. The corrugated hull optimized airflow. Its weapons remained hidden in bays.

Secondary Steel, their squad leader, jogged at Althor's right. An older man with a distinguished record, he had steel gray hair and regular features. This was his last year in the J-Force; soon he would retire and spend time with his grandchildren. Tertiary Belldaughter ran on Steel's other side, strapping on her Jumbler gun. After Althor, she was the youngest member of the squad. Tertiary Wellmark was jogging to Althor's left. She gazed out at the red line on the horizon that presaged the dawn, her chin lifted, her queue of dark hair rustling. They all wore Jagernaut blacks, with silver conduits, studs, and other equipment embedded in the leather and their gauntlets. Their boots thudded on the field and their Jumblers hung heavy and black at their hips.

Althor was the newest of the four, proud to fly with Black-star Squadron, one of the most resourceful squads in the J-Force, though he suspected the Traders used a far less po-lite term than "resourceful." Blackstar had a notorious repu-tation. He intended to make it more so.

His Jag was luminescent in the predawn light, pearly and white like alabaster. As he ran alongside it, he trailed his hand along its tellerene hull, a composite threaded with tu-bular fullerene molecules. Lightweight and fatigue resistant, tellerene retained its strength even at the extreme tempera-tures of hypersonic reentry. Doped with specialized nanobots, it could repair itself better than many materials, which meant the hull showed fewer of the pits, grooves, and other damage ships took on during space travel. Like their pilots, Jags were top-of-the-line.

He stopped and laid his palm against the unmarked sur-face. A prong clicked out. When he pressed his wrist against the prong, or psiphon, it snapped into his biomech socket.

Connection, Althor thought.

`Verified.` That response came from his Jag's EI. Red-star was sentient, its brain inextricably interwoven with his.

The airlock snapped apart. With his enhanced optics, Althor could slow the motion enough to see the outer and inner doors open together. ISC wizards were working on membranes that would act as molecular airlocks, but they hadn't perfected the technology, so Jags used conventional airlocks with two doors.

Althor swung up into the cabin. It was small, only a few paces across, its deck tiled with white squares that shed dif-fuse light. Equipment filled the cabin and bulkhead compart-ments: a cocoon bunk, survival gear, hand weapons, waste processor, environment suit, propulsion pack, all the neces-sities to live—and fight—in space. Alone. Jags had to oper-ate autonomously. A squad could spend days or even months on their own. They were the vanguard, the units that sup-ported the behemoths of ISC, the battle cruisers, the fleets, the multitude of other spacecraft, both manned and un-manned, that made up the majority of the space forces.

The pressure of his boots on the deck activated the cockpit, and it irised open like the shutter on a high-speed holo-cam. Althor squeezed into his pilot's seat, and its exoskeleton folded around his body, encasing him in a silver mesh. The visor lowered over his head and data scrolled across its display. Panels moved into place around him, and their translucent surfaces produced holomaps of space and stats on the Jag. A panel to his right showed a holographic representation of the area outside, with his ship as the last in a line of four. Beyond them, the arches and magrails of the starport soared in the sky, silver, white, and cobalt in the dawn.

Althor barely noticed as the exoskeleton plugged psiphons into his sockets. Redstar linked to him by sending signals through the psiphons to threads in his body, which carried them to his spinal node. They could also use remote signals, but the prongs offered a more reliable connection.

His mind interpreted Redstar's interaction with his node as a voice: Redstar attending.

Acknowledged, Althor thought. He needed no security checks; Redstar knew him. Some of its components had been developed from his own DNA. It was an extension of his brain just as he was of its mind. If anyone else tried to fly the ship, use its controls, or even board without permission, Redstar would lock up every system, trap the intruder within, and notify Althor, or if it couldn't reach him, the nearest J-Force authorities. If Althor ever stopped flying, the J-Force would have to retrain Redstar from scratch. Sometimes a Jag's EI refused to accept a new pilot and they had to transfer a new brain into the ship.

Redstar growled in his mind. Boosting to Kyle space.

Althor submerged his mind into another universe.

Kyle space obeyed the laws of Hilbert spaces, a mathematical formalism known to the Raylicans for millennia, and to the peoples of Earth well before they achieved space flight. Just as a Fourier transform shifted signals from an energy space to a time space, so Redstar had just shifted Althor from real space into Kyle space.

When Althor had a thought, the quantum wavefunction of

his brain changed according to the chemical processes produced by his neurons. In quantum terms, it meant the wave that described his brain evolved as he thought. Humans had known for centuries how to express such waves, but it had taken much longer to achieve the computing power to calculate them.

The waves that described Althor's thoughts at any instant depended on the positions of the particles in his brain. When his mind shifted into the Kyle web, he entered a place where his *thought* defined his "position." The more his thoughts matched those of another telop, the closer together they were in Kyle space. It made no difference if the other telop was near him in the real universe or halfway across the galaxy; they would be next to each other in the web. It made possible immediate communication over interstellar distances.

The Kyle web, popularly known as the psiberweb, spanned the Kyle universe. Its nodes provided gateways from the real universe into the web. Only telepaths could use those gates, and each experienced the web in their own way. To Althor it was a grid, vivid red against a deep black background. The presence of his mind distorted the grid into a peak that resembled the diffraction pattern from a circular aperture, as if his thoughts diffracted through the gateway into Kyle space. Circular ridges surrounded the peak, lower in height, like ripples in a lake when a stone dropped into the water. The peak was his central consciousness, and the ripples were satellite thoughts at the edges of his mind.

An emerald green spark appeared next to him and grew into a second peak, rising up out of the grid. A gold peak appeared next, as close to Althor as the green. Then the blackness itself formed a dark peak, with the red, green, and gold packets arrayed around its powerful shape.

Blackstar Squadron report. That came from Steel, the squad leader, the black peak.

Goldstar up, Belldaughter thought.

Greenstar up, Wellmark thought.

Redstar up, Althor thought. All four pilots were strong psions, but the Rhon power of his mind rumbled compared to the others. In their four-way link, he had to hold back the full strength of his mind so that he didn't overpower the others. Their exchange flashed by in a fraction of a second. They had jumped into accelerated mode and would probably remain with it until they finished this run.

A psicon blinked on Althor's display, a blue circle, the image of a button used to activate the lock on a piece of luggage. He focused on it and a prerecorded thought from Secondary Steel came to him: *The security cloak is operating. Our presence in Kyle space can't be detected by other telops here.*

Then in real time, Steel thought, *Link.*

Greenstar linked, Wellmark replied.

Goldstar linked, Belldaughter thought.

Redstar linked, Althor answered.

In the four months Althor had flown with Blackstar, since his graduation, he had been integrating into the mental link they formed together as a squadron. Their minds felt right to him: strong, intelligent, calm, rational. They had been selected for mental compatibility; otherwise they couldn't function as a unit.

Althor knew he was sitting in his chair, but his perception of reality receded, displaced by his mindscape. He had trained at DMA to operate simultaneously in his universe and Kyle space. Most telops couldn't manage it, which was another reason so few Jagernauts existed. The thoughts of the other squad members murmured in the background of his mindscape. Wellmark was running checks on her Jag, synchronizing Greenstar with the other three ships. Althor had Redstar parallel his systems to hers, and Blackstar and Goldstar joined them in doing checks: nav, cyber, weapons, comm, hydraulics, biomech.

Pain sparked in Althor's head and he pressed his fingertips into his temples. Jagernauts paid a price for their four-way link; to maintain such a strong connection required concentration and resources. The more people in the link, the more it taxed their bodies, minds, and ships, and that limited the size of a squad to four Jagernauts. Nor could humans sustain that boosted connection for long. But when it worked, the squadron link was a miracle. They could communicate anywhere, under any conditions, instantaneously.

Althor smiled, thinking of the Cheshire cat he had read about in a literary work from the Allied classics. He felt that satisfied to be a member of Blackstar. He didn't make a big deal about it, though. Some might say that Jagernauts were notorious for their cocky self-confidence, especially Blackstar Squadron. No reason to swell the already healthy egos of his squad mates.

A psicon appeared in a corner of his mindscape, a smirking cat with Wellmark's features. It lifted its paw and stretched out its claws: *Too late, Valdoria. We know what you think.* It vanished with a self-satisfied pop.

Althor laughed, his voice rolling through the cockpit. He sent his own psicon to Wellmark, an image of himself in the leather armor and disk mail of a Rillian soldier, holding a burnished sword above his head. **You dare to mock the great warrior of Skyfall?**

Wellmark's answering psicon consisted solely of the cat grin. *Hey, a sword and everything. That's some metal stuff you're wearing there.*

It's called armor, you know. He laughed and a pillar of flame erupted from the sword of Althor's psicon.

Steel's thought reverberated in Althor's mindscape. *Engine and thrusters check.* Then he added, *If you two are done rattling your sabers.*

Wellmark sent her grin psicon to Steel.

Althor focused on an engine psicon in a lower corner of his mindscape. In response, displays formed with data for the Jag's thrusters, both the rockets and the photon thrusters they used in deep space. The system checked as ready to go.

Systems initialized and ready, the Goldstar EI thought.

Systems initialized and ready, Redstar thought.

Systems initialized and ready, Greenstar thought.

Blackstar squad initialized and ready,
Blackstar thought.

The tower cleared them for liftoff, and warning lights
flared around their launch pads in the half-light that presaged the dawn. Their Jags leapt into the sky, blasting the
pads, four deadly works of art streaking up and out until they
reached the starred darkness of space, their voracious engines devouring fuel, their pilots protected from the immense accelerations by quasis coils.

When they were well away from the orbiting planets,
Steel thought: *Prepare to invert.*

All set? Althor asked Redstar.

Ready, it answered.

Inversion circumvented the speed of light. They couldn't
go *at* light speed because the ship's mass would become infinite compared to slower objects and its time would stop.
They were like runners whose path was blocked by an infinitely high tree. No matter how much energy they used, they
could never climb over the tree. To reach the superluminal
universe, the Jag added an imaginary part to its speed. Then
it went around the light-speed singularity the way a runner
might leave the road to go around an infinitely high tree. Humans hadn't conquered light-speed, they had snuck around
the barrier.

Invert, Steel thought.

Go, Althor told his Jag.

The universe twisted inside out and disorientation rippled
through Althor. He knew space didn't really twist, but his
mind perceived it that way. The Jag left the real universe and
rotated through an eerie existence where it was part real and
part imaginary. Experts claimed the process could drive a
person insane. Althor didn't know, but he had no wish to
spend any longer than necessary in transition. It was why
Jags pushed close to light-speed before they inverted; they
could "go around the tree" in a tighter circle and so spend
less time in the process.

Inversion had brutally changed warfare. Ships could burst
out of superluminal space anywhere, at relativistic speeds,

making the concept of a front line obsolete. Unaugmented humans couldn't cope with space combat. Defenses developed along with offensive capabilities, and the military managed to protect the settled worlds and habitats of humanity, but no one could watch all of space. Huge volumes remained contested, regions where no clear boundaries existed for Eubian, Skolian, and Allied territory.

Blackstar Squadron was going out today as it had done every ten days for the past six months, to patrol the hinterlands of Skolia, keeping watch, guarding against incursions. Today they headed for Onyx Sector to investigate an unconfirmed sighting of an ESComm scout ship.

Inversion complete, Redstar thought.

Althor exhaled with relief as his mind and body returned to normal. Actually, "normal" was relative; compared to the sublight universe, he and the Jag now had imaginary mass. Of course, relative to his ship he wasn't moving at all, so he didn't notice a difference as long as his real and imaginary parts weren't in flux.

How is my fuel? he asked Redstar.

Positron containment secure. It submerged Althor's awareness into the strange universe within the magnetic containment bottle that held the fuel. During inversion, the bottle drew on the cosmic-ray flux, pulling in high-energy particles. It stored the contents by spreading them through complex space, varying the imaginary parts of charge and mass. As a result, the bottle could carry far more antimatter than if it were confined to real space. The situation was simpler than with people; the trauma of having both real and imaginary parts had no effect on particles. Althor doubted his fuel ever felt like throwing up.

It exhilarated him to be *part* of his ship. He checked various systems: the gamma-ray shields and superconducting grids prevented waste heat from destroying the Jag; the selector culled electrons out of space and funneled them into the interaction area; the fuel bottle leaked positrons into the interaction area; the electrons and positrons annihilated in magnificent bursts of energy, producing thrust for the Jag.

Quasis drop, Redstar thought.

Althor blinked. He hadn't even felt the Jag go into quantum stasis, more commonly called quasis. It protected him against the accelerations of relativistic travel. A quasis field fixed the quantum wavefunction of the ship, including him. They didn't literally freeze; their atoms continued to vibrate, rotate, and otherwise behave as they had in the instant the quasis began, and the atomic clock in his biomech web continued to work. But none of the atoms could alter their quantum state. It meant the ship and everything within it became rigid even to immense forces. Without that protection, the g-forces would have smashed him flat. Apparently Redstar had jumped him in and out of quasis without his even noticing, as they continued to accelerate.

Steel's thought reverberated in Althor's mindscape. *Quaternary Valdoria, check your time. You're future shifting.*

That didn't sound auspicious. **Redstar, check my temporal position relative to the rest of the squad. Am I going into their future?**

Checking, Redstar thought. Stats reeled off in Althor's mind, processed by his node faster than he could think. Yes, you are drifting forward about three seconds relative to them per each minute of travel.

Compensate for temporal drift, Althor thought.

New course plotted, Redstar answered.

The EI displayed its calculations as graphs in his mindscape. If he stayed on his current trajectory, he would drop out of inversion several hours later than the rest of the squad. The problem was due to his Jag having traveled a bit faster than the other ships just before they inverted. When they accelerated close to light speed, their time dilated, or passed more slowly on the Jags than on Diesha. It had only taken a few minutes to invert, but by then the dilation had jumped them about a month into Diesha's future. His speed had been enough to put him a few minutes farther ahead than the others.

However, at superluminal speeds he could plot a path

backward in time. He wished they could reach Onyx Station before they left Diesha, but no one had ever succeeded in thwarting cause and effect. What happened in their reference frame had to be consistent with events in every frame. It might not be the *same* event; an electron traveling into the past from A to B would appear to a sublight observer as a positron going forward in time from B to A. Different events, but consistent. Theorists hypothesized that if a ship came out of inversion before it entered, it would end up in another universe. Unfortunately, no one who had tried had returned to tell the story. For now, the best they could do was leave inversion with no more time passing in the real universe than on their ships. It usually took longer, as errors accumulated; the farther they traveled, the bigger the discrepancy.

If someone on Diesha could have recorded their progress, they would have observed some truly bizarre effects. During inversion, Blackstar Squadron would go into the past for a while to compensate for their jump forward due to the time dilation when they inverted. Sometime before they turned pastward, four Jags had appeared in Onyx Sector. Those ships existed right now. They *were* Blackstar Squadron.

At the same time, four antimatter Jags had appeared, pair-produced from photon annihilations. While the normal ships continued on to Onyx, the antimatter squad flew backward in a time-reversed path, gaining fuel, like a movie run in reverse. The antimatter Jags and the original Jags headed toward each other, meeting in the instant when the originals turned pastward. Then they annihilated, the energy of their mutual destruction balancing the energy used to create the antimatter ships. After that, the four ships already at Onyx would be the only version of Blackstar Squadron left.

The process disconcerted Althor. He was at rest relative to his Jag, so he experienced no strange creations or destructions. He simply traveled to Onyx in an uninterrupted journey, going forward in time and space as he knew it. Yet others would observe Redstar annihilated during inversion and recreated elsewhere—which meant he was annihilated and re-created as well.

The result, however, was consistent for everyone: Blackstar arrived at Onyx Station. They managed it all with an advantage ESComm could never match. Conventional signals traveled no faster than light speed, so inverted ships could communicate only with tachyons, or superluminal particles. Although ISC and ESComm were developing such technologies, neither could yet make tachyons carry reliable information. Too much uncertainty existed in when and where the signals arrived. As a result, ships couldn't coordinate well at superluminal speeds; most squads suffered both temporal and spatial drift. When they left inversion, the ships would be spread out in space and time. The longer they traveled at superluminal speed, the greater the spread.

But not Jags.

Steel, Belldaughter, Wellmark, and Althor linked through Kyle space. Their Jags were nodes on the Kyle web. It gave them immediate communication among themselves and with any node in the star-spanning ISC network, allowing them to coordinate with a precision that thumbed its nose at light speed itself.

Althor checked his connection to the other squad members. They were all monitoring their systems but otherwise relaxing. Travel during inversion was actually rather boring.

Open gate to Kyle space, Althor thought.

Gate open, Redstar answered.

His mindscape reformed into the red grid with the circular peak circled by concentric ripples. Three similar peaks surrounded him, black, gold, and green, the rest of Blackstar Squadron, their ripples overlapping and blending with his. As he cast his thoughts through Kyle space, the peak of his mind changed, decreasing in height here and growing elsewhere. He thought of Onyx Platform and his consciousness shifted through the grid. It reformed near a cluster of nodes that signified several outposts of the platform.

Clock, Althor thought.

An antique timepiece appeared in his mindscape, matching the decor of his home on Lyshriol. It showed him data about the passage of time far more sophisticated than a real timepiece that old could have managed. He was about six minutes ahead of the rest of the squadron.

Commander Steel, he thought. **Request permission to contact Onyx in my future timeline.** If he could link with the Onyx mesh, he would be at least six minutes ahead of when they expected to drop out of inversion.

Give it a try, Steel answered. *But be careful. If you're still in that timeline when we leave inversion, you won't come out with us.*

Understood, sir. At the moment, Althor had some probability of being in the future relative to the squad and some of being in their time. To contact Onyx six minutes ahead, he had to collapse his wavefunction into that future timeline, severing his link with his squad. It was a risky proposition; he might not be able to rejoin his own timeline. He might just drop out of space six minutes ahead of his squad, but that was by no means guaranteed. The farther into the future he ventured, the more he risked. Ships that played too much with spacetime could lose contact with their own universe. At least, that was what ISC believed. No one knew for certain, since those ships disappeared.

To Redstar, he thought, **Drop the Blackstar link and submerge into the Onyx timeline.**

`Disassociating with Blackstar,` it answered.

Althor's link with the other Jags faded. He was still under the security cloak, so he was hidden from all telops except those rare few with a clearance high enough to contact a J-Force unit. Althor had an even higher clearance, enough to make contact with just about any ISC base. He sent his ID codes to one of the Onyx outposts, which showed as a blurry peak in his grid. Then he thought, **Requesting time check.**

Static came from the Onyx Station. In his mindscape, it manifested as ragged, indistinct peaks. *Time ch**) . . . —lete?*

Repeat, Althor thought. **I'm having trouble focusing your timeline.**

Time check *** incomplete, the Onyx telop answered.

That came through better.

How fa—** futureward?

I'm from about six minutes in your past, Althor answered.

Six minute** . . . ooner?**

Can you repeat? He was growing uneasy. The longer he spent in this link, the greater the danger he would lose his squad.

***—*sooner?* The Onyx telop repeated.

You want us to arrive sooner than scheduled?

Yes!

Warning, Redstar thought. I'm losing coherence with your previous timeline.

Damn! Onyx, I'll see what we can do. To Redstar, he thought, **Drop me back to Blackstar.**

Synchronizing with previous timeline. Then: I can't find them.

Althor gritted his teeth. **Can you extrapolate from where they were in space and time and calculate their probable position?**

Yes. But I can't guarantee you will be in the same universe.

Perspiration gathered on his forehead. **Do your best.**

Working. Then: Temporal correction complete.

And?

I find no trace of Blackstar Squadron.

A bead of sweat ran down Althor's temple. **Are you sure about your calculations?**

Some uncertainty exists in them.

Is it possible that—

Contact!

Althor's pulse surged. He wondered if the Jag had simulated its own excitement.

Steel's thought came into his mind. *Althor? Is that you?*

Althor sent him an image of his warrior in armor and disk mail. **Greetings, sir.**

Steel sent back his psicon, a steel girder. *You all right?*

Fine. At least now that he had regained his place in space-time. **I contacted a telop at Onyx.**

Anything interesting?

He badly wants us to arrive early.

Think they're in trouble?

It's possible. Althor thought back to the exchange. **Very possible.**

Steel directed his thought to the rest of the link. *Jags, recalculate our route so we drop out of inversion closer in to Onyx.*

Won't it be risky to reinvert so close to space habitats? Belldaughter asked.

Do what you can to minimize the danger, Steel thought. *But get in as close as you can. The shorter our sublight travel, the sooner we reach Onyx.*

Preparing to reinvert, Redstar thought.

Engage shrouds, Steel thought.

Engaged. The responses came from all four Jags in a light speed pulse of thought. They were in the most accelerated mode possible for the human brain.

In superluminal space, they didn't need shrouds, but in subluminal space, the squad would partially disappear. Blackbody shielding shrouded the hulls and they stopped reflecting light. Holographic surfacing on the ship projected images of the stars as if nothing occupied that space. Other systems hid them from radio waves, microwaves, and ultraviolet probes. They even created false echoes to fool neutrinos, which passed through just about anything.

Invert, Steel thought.

Althor fired the photon thrusters. The only way he knew Redstar went in and out of quasis was by the discontinuous change in speed on his displays. The Jag decelerated in a series of jumps he perceived as a continuous process. The stars jerked forward, converging on a point in front of the ship. Their colors shifted into ultraviolet and disappeared. Blackstar Squadron roared out of inversion in perfect formation—

Straight into a swarm of ESComm warships.

Their shrouds provided a disguise, but every time the Jags accelerated, their exhaust gave away their position. The

Traders knew they had arrived. The attack chilled Althor; Onyx was a major Skolian complex, eight space habitats with millions of people. This was no minor skirmish.

It was an act of war.

Redstar identified the attacking ships: three Wasp corvettes and eight Solos. Although Solos were the closest ESComm equivalent to a Jag, they had no access to Kyle space because they carried no psions. The Traders had only one use for empaths and telepaths: as providers. They used the pain of such slaves to transcend. They considered psions unstable and found the concept of their serving on war craft ludicrous. Even if they had been willing to put them on the ships, they had too few psions to risk any significant number of them that way.

Althor readily admitted psions had a disadvantage; they felt the emotions of their enemies and compatriots alike. Applicants to the academy underwent extensive analysis in their entrance exams to see if they could endure that empathic onslaught. Even so, the suicide rate of Jagernauts was the highest of any ISC personnel. But every loss the J-Force suffered only hardened the resolve of its remaining Jagernauts to protect their people from the Aristos.

Taus incoming, Redstar thought.

Evade! Althor answered. **Release dust.** Tau missiles carried inversion drives, which made them notoriously hard to catch or destroy. If another missile came too close, the tau jumped out of spacetime. Redstar's dust consisted of microscopic bomblets that could protect Redstar and beleaguer the taus enough to slow them down.

Quasis jump, Redstar thought.

Nausea surged in Althor from the Jag throwing him into quasis too fast. A tau had detonated against their hull. The ship couldn't change state during quasis, so nothing could blow it up, but no quasis was perfect. The explosion weakened the Jag. A few more hits and the quasis would fail, leaving him defenseless.

Fire MIRVs, Althor thought. MIRVs, or multiple independently targeted reentry vehicles, were small ships as well as bombs. They used only conventional rockets, so they couldn't invert, but that made them smaller and lighter. He could carry many more MIRVs than taus.

Hurtling through space at relativistic speeds, Redstar released a swarm of MIRVs. They spread outward in a cone at 92 percent of light speed, giving them the energy equivalent of megaton bombs. Stats poured into Althor's node far faster than his unaugmented brain could have absorbed. ESComm taus were catching Blackstar MIRVs. The taus inverted with their captured missiles, reinverted as they closed on the Jags—and exploded both themselves and their MIRV captives in violent bursts of energy.

It could have done serious damage to the squad. However, the jump through superluminal space had thrown off the taus. If ESComm could have controlled their taus while the missiles were going through inversion, the evasive tactics of the Jags might have failed. But the taus came out a fraction of a second too late, after the Jags had shot through that volume of space.

Quasis jump, Redstar thought.

Althor swallowed the bile in his throat. Redstar had veered into such an abrupt course change to evade a tau, the quasis had kicked in to protect him from the lethal acceleration.

ESComm tau detonated to port, Redstar thought.

It missed! He had another few seconds of life. They had already shot past the Onyx stations. Althor brought Redstar around for another go at the ESComm ships. Fighting in space was like jousting in three dimensions, with beams and smart missiles. He hurtled past a Solo at almost the speed of light, their times dilated relative to each other. The Solo registered as a rotating, flattened coin on Althor's holoscreens. It released a tau—

His stomach wrenched as Redstar jumped into superluminal space. He thought, **This is for you, Father,** and dropped out of inversion, his MIRVs blasting ahead of his Jag.

Althor felt his opponent die.

The pilot's terror blasted Althor's mind—and cut off with chilling finality.

`Solo destroyed,` Redstar thought.

Althor groaned and lost his grasp on his mindscape. In a rush of memory, he was sixteen again, above the Plains of Tyroll, that day he had slaughtered an army with one carbine. He had suffered every shattering death. He had been so frightened, so desperate. His father's cousin, Avaril Valdoria, would never give up until he killed his enemy, the Dalvador Bard, Althor's father. So Althor had ended it all. He had ensured that neither his father nor his brothers would ever have to ride in that barbaric war again.

—doria, respond! Are you all right? Steel's voice echoed through the psilink.

Althor swallowed. **Fine, sir.**

Relief came from Steel's mind. *Good work.*

Not good enough, though. Stats about the battle flowed through his mindscape: ESComm had done great damage to Onyx, neutralizing its defenses. To stop the destruction of the stations, Blackstar still had to take on seven Solos and three Wasps.

Redstar had exhausted its supply of MIRVs. Time to joust.

Prime Annihilators, Althor thought. They accelerated antiprotons, focusing the beam through foils where it picked up positrons. Beams were easier to evade than missiles, since they couldn't chase their target, but they offered a better offense against quasis shields; annihilating matter in quasis was easier than deforming it with missile strikes. Althor headed toward a Solo like a knight with his lance ready.

`Warning.` Redstar highlighted part of his mindscape to show an unmanned drone on intercept course.

Fire, Althor thought.

His Annihilator blasted the drone. Its mag-shields deflected some of the antiprotons, but many hit their target. The resulting annihilations created brutally energetic photons, pion showers, and high-energy processes. Particles and radiation tore through the drone. They hit the antimatter fuel bottles, and the drone detonated in a burst of plasma. Part of it vanished with the eerie *sucked away* effect created when real matter collapsed into the complex space within a Klein fuel bottle.

Warning! Blackstar's EI thought. Greenstar has been detected.

No problem, Wellmark answered. As a Wasp raced toward her Jag, she saturated the volume of space around Greenstar with smart dust. Although a Wasp was small compared to most ships, it dwarfed a Jag. Its crew rode in the head and thorax. A stalk separated those compartments from its detachable abdomen, which carried antimatter plasma. Usually a Wasp attacked planets or other large bodies. When jettisoned, its abdomen plunged into its target, drilling its "stinger" in to bury itself. Then it released its plasma and blew its target into smithereens. It could obliterate a Jag a hundred times over, but ESComm wouldn't waste an entire Wasp on one ship. They probably intended these for the Onyx stations.

Solos on approach, Redstar thought. Three ES-Comm fighters were moving in to defend the Wasp.

Althor and Belldaughter, cover Wellmark, Steel thought.

I'm on the Beta Solo, Belldaughter thought. One of the Solos turned gold.

On Gamma, Althor thought. His Solo turned red.

On Alpha, Steel thought. The third Solo turned black.

As Althor went at the Solo, it changed course, cutting him off from the Wasp. Another section of his mindscape registered Wellmark's tau hurtling toward the Wasp.

Fire Annihilator, Althor thought. He and the Solo hurtled by each other, appearing to flip over as they passed, their time dilated relative to each other. They fired at the same instant, their EIs compensating for the relativistic effects that became so dramatic at these speeds.

Quasis jump, Redstar thought.

Althor's head swam from the jumps. The Solo had hit him dead-on and Redstar's quasis system was weakening. The Jag could take only one or two more hits.

One of Steel's taus exploded a Solo, and its pilot's death reverberated in Althor's mind, though less violently than when one of his shots succeeded. He wasn't as focused on Steel's target.

The Wasp caught Wellmark's tau with an Annihilator shot. As her missile exploded, the Wasp went into quasis and remained whole, speeding onward, a rigid body in motion. Althor waited until it dropped out of quasis—and fired both his taus into its abdomen.

Wasp in quasis, Redstar said.

Damn! He had just wasted his only taus.

Then, suddenly, the Wasp's quasis collapsed. Antimatter plasma spewed outward and its abdomen exploded in a swath of destruction that wiped out the head and thorax as well. Althor went rigid as he felt the crew of the Wasp die—

Blackstar exploded.

Wellmark's mental scream ripped through their link, Althor's mindscape went dark, and Belldaughter's cry reverberated over his comm. Althor reeled, his link with the squad shattered. His mindscape tried to reform, sparking with erratic lights, jagged and unstable. Stats poured through it too raggedly for him to absorb. In real space, alarms blared in the cockpit and emergency lights flashed on his controls.

Wellmark's thought cut through the chaos. *Squadron, regroup! Orient to Greenstar.*

Althor's Jag answered when he couldn't. Redstar reoriented.

Goldstar reoriented.

Invert! Wellmark thought.

Althor vomited when Redstar inverted. His Jag hurtled through superluminal space, following a trajectory downloaded by Greenstar to Redstar. His exoskeleton whirred as tiny scrubber bots embedded in its mesh cleaned him up.

Wellmark's thought came raggedly. *Report.*

Althor clenched the arms of his pilot's chair. **I'm here.**

And I. Belldaughter's thought shook.

We have to go back, Wellmark's struggle to project confidence felt tangible in their link. *We only put out one Wasp. If we don't destroy the other two, they will demolish Onyx.*

Althor took a deep breath. Six Solos remained and two Wasps. Their chances of taking out all those ships were slim to none, and they all knew it. But they had to try.

Do either of you have any taus left? Wellmark asked.

I've both mine, Belldaughter thought.

None here, Althor answered. **MIRVs gone, too. I've Annihilators.**

I've two. Wellmark paused for a fraction of a second. *Belldaughter and I will release our remaining MIRVs as we come out of inversion. Althor, cover us with your Annihilators while we go after the Wasps.* She took a breath he sensed rather than heard. *If that doesn't work, we'll all try Annihilators.*

Understood, Althor thought. Belldaughter echoed his reply. None of them could risk thinking about what the loss of Steel meant to their squad. If they survived this battle, they could mourn him properly.

Go, Wellmark thought.

They blasted out of inversion preceded by their last MIRVs. The Onyx stations were firing Annihilators at the Wasps and Solos, but the ESComm ships had disabled most of their defenses.

Wellmark and Belldaughter each went after a Wasp and Althor blasted the Solos that dogged their progress. Redstar hurtled through a complicated evasion pattern with killer accelerations. The quasis jumps made him so ill he could barely think. The ESComm ships followed just as bizarre evasion patterns against his shots.

Quasis jump, Redstar thought. Then: Solo quasis failed.

Althor's beam stabbed the Solo dead on. His forward holomap lit with a flash of light—but it was too much for one Solo—

Got it! Wellmark shouted mentally. *One Wasp down—*

Greenstar exploded.

Althor screamed as his map lit with a burst of light.

Althor! Belldaughter's frantic thought exploded. *Answer!*

Ah—no. The thought tore out of him.

Wellmark!

She's gone. His mind reeled.

We have to keep going.

Yes. He struggled to focus. Five Solos and one Wasp. **The stations can deal with the Solos if we get that Wasp.** The thought ripped out from a torn place in his mind left by the deaths of Steel and Wellmark.

I still have both taus, Belldaughter thought. *Cover me?*

Yes. He hung on to the arms of his chair.

Althor went after the Solos with manic intensity, knowing they surely had pilots more experienced than himself. He was so ill from the quasis jumps that he gave up trying to think and acted on instinct. Redstar backed him up with every evasive maneuver in its memory. Belldaughter hit the Wasp with her first tau, but it went into quasis and survived the blast.

Quasis jump, Redstar thought. Annihilator strike on my starboard hull. It is unlikely I can withstand another hit.

Weapons? Althor asked.

You have enough Annihilator fuel for one more shot.

One shot. Gods. Belldaughter only had one tau left. One more chance with the Wasp. That was it.

Belldaughter. His thought came in jagged bursts. **I'm going to hit the Wasp with my last Annihilator shot.** He couldn't be the only one losing quasis. **I'll weaken its shields. Then you fire your tau.**

If you use your last shot on the Wasp, the Solos will obliterate you.

Doesn't matter. He gripped the arms of his seat. **Redstar, get the damn Wasp.**

Engaging inversion engine.

What the hell? He no longer had the coherence to question why Redstar threw him back into inversion. They dropped out almost immediately—practically *on* the Wasp. Redstar fired and caught the ESComm spacecraft dead on, simultaneously blasting it with relativistic exhaust as they hurtled past.

Wasp in quasis, Redstar told him. Then: Althor,
I took another hit . . .

Althor groaned. Alarms were blaring all over the cockpit,
red lights flashing, displays melting. But even as his mental
grid unraveled, an explosion ripped through its fabric.

I got it! Belldaughter shouted. *I got the Wasp.*

Thank the saints. Althor's response barely registered.

*Gods almighty, Althor invert! Those Solos are coming at
you!*

Tell my family I love them. He knew he had internal injuries, mortal injuries.

Download, Redstar thought.

What? Althor had no idea what it meant. Download what?
His spinal node answered. Download commenced.

What the blazes?

Damn it! Belldaughter shouted. *You CAN invert. You have
one engine left.* Her thought was like hands gripping his
shoulders, shaking him. *Invert!*

Redstar's response came dimly. Inverting . . .
But it was too late.

Althor drew in one final, strangled breath—and passed
from life into death.

25

The Stairs

Eldrinson snapped awake. Before he was even fully coherent, he was pulling himself up, dragging his inert legs
across the mattress. He couldn't see if darkness cloaked the
world outside the windows, but he felt the sense of slumber
that filled Castle Windward. It was night, late night, a terrible, terrible night.

His heart pounded and his pulse raced. He thought he would

explode. Something was wrong. *Wrong.* It crashed through his mind. He pulled himself to the nightstand and reached out to hit the panel that would alert Jase Heathland, his doctor.

Then he stopped. What he felt had nothing to do with his own health. One of his children was in trouble. He knew it without doubt. Jase could do nothing. His dread came from vague impressions, nothing he could isolate or identify. It terrified him; if something happened to Roca or the children on Lyshriol, he would feel it clearly. This came from farther away. Much farther.

Althor. Eldrin. Althor. Soz.

Althor.

"*Althor.*" The name tore out of him. He had tried to repress his dread for his children, to deny they could come to harm, but faced with the certainty that his worst fears had been realized, he couldn't hide. He had to find Althor, help his son, escape the confines of his crippling injuries and blindness. He pounded his legs. "Move. *Move, damn it!*"

His legs did nothing, just as they had done nothing this past year despite endless exercises and tests from Jase and the other healers. Furious at himself and at the refusal of his body to cooperate, he heaved himself to the edge of the bed. He tried to slide off, but he had too little control even for that simple effort. He fell off and hit the floor, his impact cushioned by the throw rug that covered the stone.

Clenching his fist, he struck the floor with his fist, tears of fury in his eyes.

Roca stayed at the blueglass table in the long hall where the staff at Castle Windward ate each day. This early, more than an hour before dawn, the hall was empty. She sat in a high-backed chair, one elbow on the table, her hand supporting her head, her other hand limp in her lap. Tears ran down her face.

A stir came from across the hall. Roca lifted her head to see Jase enter. He came over to her, but then hesitated when he saw her face.

"I'm sorry." He spoke awkwardly. "I didn't mean to intrude."

Roca wiped the tears off her cheeks. "It's all right."

"Do you mind if I sit?"

She indicated the seat nearest hers. "Please."

He settled into the chair. "Can I help?"

Roca felt as if she were dying inside. "No."

"Did Eldrinson do something?"

She gave a shaky laugh. "Would that it were that simple."

Jase's forehead furrowed. "What's wrong?"

"ESComm attacked Onyx Platform. They claim it was retaliation for ISC ships violating their territory and preying on their civilian transports." She spoke leadenly. "They're lying. It is an act of war."

He stared at her. "We're going to war?"

"It would seem so."

"Was Onyx Platform destroyed?"

"No. They lost only a few lives."

"But how?"

"They had help. A Jag squadron arrived in time." Another tear ran down her face. "There were only three casualties. Only three. The squadron leader. The next in command." Her voice broke. "And the youngest squad member. He was just commissioned a few months ago."

Jase went very still. "Councilor Roca—"

She didn't know where to put this grief. It was too big. "Now he lies in a coma. The doctors can't help him. He is brain dead."

His face was ashen. "Althor?"

"Yes."

"Ah, gods, no. Councilor, I—I'm sorry."

"Why must those I love insist on going to war?" The words tore out of her. "What madness drives them?"

"They have courage."

"*Courage?*" Bitterness filled her voice. "They're heroes. Eldrin fought with his bare hands to save men on the battlefield. He was sixteen. My husband endured pain I can't even imagine but he never broke, never told Vitarex his identity. He stopped an Aristo from taking a Rhon psion. Shannon rescued him and faced Vitarex on his own, a fourteen-year-old boy against a Trader Aristo. And Althor. He saved gods only know how many millions of people."

An unbearable sympathy showed in Jase's eyes. "Your children learned their courage from their parents."

"I don't want them to be heroes. I want them to *live*. I want for them long, happy, healthy lives." She was breaking inside. "Instead they leave home to die."

Eldrinson gritted his teeth and pushed up on his elbows. Driven by his anger, by his inability to help those he loved, he dragged himself across the stone floor on his stomach. The throw rug bunched up under him and he yanked it away. He couldn't even relax his fists to grab the floor. He kept pulling, unsure what he was doing, where he thought he could go. What would he do, crawl down the stairs and drag his crippled body to his son in some incomprehensible place? He would die for his children if it kept them safe, but nothing, *nothing* he tried had stopped them from running, riding, flying to their deaths.

When he had seen what the war had done to Eldrin, he had sworn he would never take his sons in combat again. Then Althor had insisted. Back then, Eldrinson had believed it would have been morally wrong to deny his son. A man had to make such decisions. As the Bard and commander of the Dalvador army, he should have been proud his son wanted to ride at his side. Then Althor had changed history. For all that his son had hidden his anguish and guilt from his family, Eldrinson knew how it had crushed him. Eldrinson decided then: never again would he see his children go to pain and death. But they kept insisting on it, and they did it to defend him, making it even worse, that they would die for him, their father, when it should be the reverse.

He kept dragging himself, blinded as much by grief as by his eyes, the hateful eyes that were supposed to see, the legs that were supposed to walk, but that never worked because his deficient, failed brain could do nothing but give him bone-wracking seizures.

His fist rammed into a vertical stone surface and he stopped, breathing hard. He barely felt the scrape where his knuckles had hit. Pressing his palm against the stone, he realized he had reached the bench that ran around the inside of the window alcove. He crawled into the alcove until he reached the place on the bench where he so often sat, either by himself or with Roca.

Roca.

His eyes burned. He had failed his wife most of all, the mother of their children. He grabbed the bench and hauled himself up, sideways to the windows he could no longer see. Putting out his hands, he hit the shutters. With a few moments of fumbling, he opened them. In his youth, he would have felt air blast across him, but now glass filled the windows, a wedding gift from Roca, who had brought light into his life.

Eldrinson stared out the window, his palm flat against the pane. He saw only blackness. He thought of opening it, of letting himself fall out into the abyss these windows overlooked, with the walls of the castle plunging straight down into the chasm that circled Windward. But he couldn't take his own life, not as long as any of his family lived. He could do nothing to help them, but he wouldn't add to their pain.

"See!" He shouted the word. What did he have to do to make his brain accept these false eyes in his head, these false legs on his body? He had become less than human, a creature of technology created by strangers who made it impossible for him to deny the truth, that he was no more than a primitive farmer who couldn't even learn to read and write.

"Walk." He hit his thigh with his fist. "Move, damn it!"

Nothing.

If a heart could have burst from sorrow, his would have done so. But it remained steady in his chest, mocking him with its health even as it broke.

Ever so faintly, light appeared.

Eldrinson froze. He should have seen the sky, the spindles

of the Backbone Mountains, and the precipitous cliffs outside the castle, a spectacular, wild landscape. Instead he saw darkness.

Except . . . for a faint, vague light.

Gradually the light brightened. Shadowy outlines formed within it, a jagged line in the far distance. A strange feeling came to Eldrinson, a pressure slowly building within him, a sensation he couldn't identify except that it *hurt* and he didn't know why.

The sky continued to lighten.

The sky.

The shadowy forms were mountains.

He was watching the dawn.

He recognized this new pain now. Hope. He didn't want to hope he would see, that he would walk, that his children would come home, that he could be a true protector for his wife and family, for if he hoped, it could all be crushed, as this past year had crushed so much within him, both physical and emotional.

Eldrinson watched the suns rise.

The world outside came as blurs of color. He couldn't distinguish the mountains clearly, but he saw their outlines, the contrast between the peaks and the reddening sky. Dawn continued to come, despite his conviction that it would never again arrive. Valdor lifted its gold orb above the horizon with Aldan eclipsing him.

He slid his hand along the border carved into the window frame. The details were lost and colors blurred—but he could see the outline of its engraved vines.

Eldrinson looked around his room. It remained all shadows, dim in the early light. The bed across the room—yes, he could make it out. The door in the wall was shadowy but he could discern its purple color. His mood surged, hard to define, hope and jagged edges, shock for Althor, disbelief for his eyes.

And his legs?

Eldrinson grasped one of the shutters that stretched from the bench up to the domed ceiling high overhead. Leaning his weight into the shutter and clenching his hands around the glasswood frame, he slowly pulled himself up. His legs immediately buckled; all that kept him from falling was his grip on the shutter. He hung from it, gritting his teeth, fighting his frustration.

"Think," he muttered to his brain. "Think to my legs. Jase says I can do it. So do it." Again he put weight on his legs. Again they buckled.

"Walk." His voice cracked. "Walk, damn you." Furious, he pushed away from the shutter and took a step. Immediately his legs folded and he collapsed. He hit the floor hard, barely catching himself on his hands.

Swearing, berating every god or goddess he had ever even half believed existed, he grabbed the bench where he had been sitting and struggled back to his feet. Without taking the time to think, lest he convince himself he couldn't do it, he took a step.

Again he collapsed.

Once more Eldrinson hauled himself to the bench and back to his feet. The room surrounded him, blurry, hard to see, but miraculously visible. He lurched forward in a jerky, uncontrolled step.

Another.

And another.

And he walked.

Eldrinson lurched across the room. When he reached the door, he fell against it, aware of his heart pounding in his chest, his strained breathing, his shaking legs. A shout welled within him, but he held it back, for with the joy came pain. He grasped the doorknob and rubbed his other palm across his face, smearing his tears.

Then he opened the door.

No more words came. Roca had nothing left to say. She sat with Jase at the long table while the traitorous suns rose above the mountains. They lied with their promise of a bright new dawn. Jase started to speak, but she shook her head. She couldn't bear his sympathy.

Who was next? Foolish, angry Kurj. He had lost one of his heirs. Perhaps subconsciously he did it on purpose, afraid Sauscony and Althor would plot against him and gain his title through his death, as he had done with his grandfather. She didn't want to believe it, this hard man who had once been such a loving golden-haired boy. But she was no fool. Her golden child had turned into a military dictator, and no matter how great a leader he had become, he had an iron-cast side capable of atrocities. In that, she had lost him too, lost the miracle child, her firstborn. The war took everything.

"Councilor." Jase spoke quietly. "Perhaps you should speak with someone on the *Ascendant*."

Roca set her hands on the table. "I will talk to no war queens or warlords." As Councilor of Foreign Affairs for Skolia—the civilization that took its name from her family—she had to talk with the military officers, confer, plan for defense. But never again would she see them as protectors, not after they had taken so much from her family.

"They may be able to help," Jase said.

She suddenly realized what he meant. "Doctor, I have no wish to see an emotion counselor."

"I truly am sorry about your son."

"So am I," she whispered.

The door scraped open down the long hall. Denric came into the hall, rubbing his eyes, his yellow curls tousled around his head. He wore his sleep trousers and shirt with a robe pulled over them. When he saw Jase and Roca, he headed down the table.

"A pleasant morn," he mumbled as he sat next to Jase, his eyes half-closed. Drowsily he added, "But no food."

Despite everything, Roca couldn't help but smile. Denric ate everything in sight. She didn't know where he put it all; he had a slender build and he wasn't that tall, but he consumed enough food to feed two men twice his size.

"It's early," she said. "The kitchen staff is probably fixing breakfast now."

Roca didn't know how she sounded, but Denric glanced up abruptly. "Mother, what is wrong?"

She couldn't answer. She wiped her palm across her tear-stained cheek.

Jase spoke. "If you will excuse me—?"

Roca shot him a grateful look. "Yes, certainly."

Denric looked from her to Jase, but said nothing.

They waited until Jase had left the hall. Then Denric said, "What happened?"

"It's Althor."

He went very still. "I dreamed about him last night. I was so relieved when I woke up and realized it was only a nightmare."

"Did you dream he went into battle?"

"Yes." His voice was almost inaudible. "And died."

Another tear ran down Roca's cheek. She rubbed it away angrily, ashamed to show weakness in front of the family that needed her to be strong. But they were empaths. They knew. Putting on a front did no good when those you created it for knew what lay beyond.

"He's in a coma," she said in a low voice. "His brain is dead."

Denric watched her as if waiting to hear it was a mistake. She couldn't say the words he wanted to hear.

"No," he finally said.

No. Such a simple word. As if it could stop reality or run time in reverse and make the present undo itself. But they couldn't. No matter how many times they said "no," they couldn't make it true.

She said only, "I know."

"We should go to him."

"Yes." Roca nodded, so tired. "First I must talk to your father."

His face paled even more. "This will kill him."

"Don't—please don't use those words." She reached toward him. "Promise me, Deni. Promise you will never go to war."

His voice gentled. "After I go to university, I want to teach. I want to go places where they have no schools and make a difference." Light from the dawn trickled in through windows at the far end of the hall and glinted on his eyelashes. "You and Father taught us the importance of our duties to our people. You taught us about honor and integrity. About love and what it means to stand up for those you love. We don't all have to do it through the military. I want to help people learn."

"Thank you." She gave up trying to stop the tears that streamed down her face. "Thank you, Denric."

"If I can—" He suddenly stopped, his gaze shifting to a point behind her.

Roca turned to look at the stairs that led up to the landing where a person could gaze over the hall. The door up there was opening. The arched glasswood portal slowly swung outward—

And left Eldrinson framed in its archway.

He stood there, clutching the frame, staring at them, his face drawn, his blue sleep shirt and trousers rumpled, his hair tangled over his collar. Then he walked onto the landing in careful and uneven steps. Two steps. Three. Four. He reached the railing and grabbed it, hanging on to the red bar of glasswood, all the time watching her.

Watching her.

He saw them.

To Roca, time stopped its beat. She rose from her chair, hope and fear welling within her, together, inextricably linked. She would have run up the stairs and taken him into her arms if she thought he would have let her. But she knew Eldri. His pride would prevent him from accepting anything that looked like an offer to help him down the stairs, those twenty steps that suddenly seemed like a thousand.

He turned to the stairs, clutching the rail until his knuckles turned so white, she could see it from where she stood down here. The staircase ran down the wall to a second landing; from there, it turned a corner and came out, just four steps the rest of the way down. With painstaking care, he let go of the railing and took a step, another, and another, until he reached the top of the staircase. When he put his foot on the first step, Roca's pulse leapt. What if he fell? She wanted to call Jase, but she neither moved nor spoke. If she interfered now, he would never forgive her.

He put his weight on the first step, one foot, then two. Then he paused, his hand clutching the banister. After a long moment, he slid his left foot to the second step, followed by his right foot. Again he paused. Again he repeated the procedure. He descended, one step at a time, stopping on each, using his legs as if for the first time.

He reached the lower landing.

Roca could hold back no longer. She walked forward, taking it slow so he wouldn't think she was running to help. She stopped at the bottom of the steps. His gaze never left her face, as if the universe had narrowed to just the two of them. After so many years of marriage, she could no longer separate what she read from his body language and her empath's sense, but she knew his mood right now: determined but afraid, furious and triumphant, brimming with joy—and drowning in grief.

He came down those final steps, leaning on the banister, slow but never wavering. At the bottom, he stepped onto the floor in front of her and slowly let go of the rail. He stood there his gaze level with hers. Moisture gathered in the corners of his eyes and slid down his face.

Then he pulled her into his arms.

Roca put her arms around his waist and leaned her forehead against his. "Welcome home," she said, her voice shaking. "Welcome home, my love."

26

False Echo

Soz ran.

Her feet pounded the trail through the Red Mountains, hard and steady, faster and faster, until she moved in a blur. With the augmentation to her skeleton and muscle system complete, her speed had more than doubled. The microfusion reactor in her body powered the system. State-of-the-art nanomeds circulated in her body. She was a case-hardened machine.

An enraged machine.

She ran until the sun passed its high point in the sky and began its descent. Her lungs ached, her natural muscles burned, her breath rasped. Still she ran. She would go on and on, forever, until exhaustion deadened her mind and she couldn't think, couldn't remember, couldn't mourn the man who lay in a living death within the ISC hospital only a few kilometers from where she ran and ran and *ran* . . .

A loud hum startled Soz out of her trance. A red panel had lit up on her left wrist guard. It must have beeped several times; the hum was a warning to gain her attention if beeps didn't work. Soz slowed to a walk and touched the panel. "Valdoria here."

"Soz, where are you?" Jazar's voice burst out of the comm. He was no longer her roommate; this year the brass had put her in with the seniors. Jazar and Grell were still together and Obsidian had new roommates, but they had all remained friends.

"What's up?" Soz asked.

"The classes are going to start the final runs. If you aren't here in five minutes, you're late. You miss all those demerits you finally worked off? You're about to get more."

She swore under her breath. "I'll be right there." She was losing her focus. She had to *do* something, take action, fight the nameless Traders who had shattered Althor and her father. What use was it being the best damn cadet at DMA if she couldn't stop the Traders from destroying her family? She felt useless and she hated it.

Soz sped up, but she resisted the urge to run full out again, not wanting to exhaust herself before she started exercising with the other cadets. As she pounded around a curve, the fields of DMA came into view, with the stately academy beyond. She sprinted down the mountain, headed for the lines of cadets forming on the central plaza. When she reached the training fields, she finally let go and raced toward the second-year cadets. Although she trained now with the seniors, who had full augmentation in their bodies, the classes from all four years were gathering on the field. Tradition at DMA gave students who skipped year or more a perk; they could pick which class they joined in such a formation. Soz always chose the second-year students. She reached her place next to Jazar, breathing hard, just as Secondary Foxer called all four classes to order.

"Always early," Jazar said.

She smirked at him. "Hey, I made it."

He grinned. "You're allowed to thank me now." His teasing sounded forced, though. He knew what had distracted her. Everyone knew. It was the specter they lived with every day, in every class, every training run, every exam. They were going to war and they could die.

Foxer glanced at Soz, holding the look a moment longer than normal, but she said nothing. The Secondary called out assignments, sending cadets to the weights, track and field, calisthenics, and obstacle courses. She inflicted Soz with her bane—the Echo. Soz set off jogging toward it with Jazar, whose class was just beginning to work on the obstacle course. She wanted to pulverize the course, but nothing helped, nothing she did, nothing she thought, nothing she studied. She wanted to fight Traders until the stars screamed. Denied that, she was left with running the damn Echo.

When they reached the course, Soz stood restlessly at its entrance, shifting her weight from foot to foot. Foxer had changed the programming again, altering the scaffolding vibrations, the patterns of ground movement, the maze structure, and the timing of the rebounders. It didn't matter. Soz was too angry to care about niceties anymore. She had cracked the training mesh and memorized the new configurations.

When Foxer called her name, she set off hard, her feet pounding on the ground. She sprinted along the edge of the path toward the scaffolding, then vaulted over the pummel horse and flipped up to grab a vibrating bar. She climbed with single-minded focus. Every bar that tried to throw her off became an ESComm warship. Every strut that slipped under her feet became an ESComm soldier. She went up and over, through and down the bars, throwing herself from handhold to handhold, not pausing long enough to feel them shake.

Soz reached the far side and was barely halfway down when she let go. She dropped through the air and landed with a force that would have broken her knees in their unaugmented days. Now they bent at exactly the amount her node calculated she needed to cushion her landing, and her enhanced legs absorbed the force. She barely felt the impact.

She lunged into a run and danced in a rapid-fire pattern on the perplex turf beneath her feet as it rippled and bucked. The hell with the Echo. The hell with DMA. She knew it wasn't anyone's fault, certainly not inanimate objects, but as long as she kept raging, she could outrun the grief, that relentless, unbearable grief.

She didn't bother going around the edge of the pool. It never worked. She always slipped into the oil and ended up coated with the slimy stuff. Instead she jumped. The pool was too large to clear even with her enhanced muscles, so she leapt to the edge, touched down, and rebounded into another jump. Her node calculated the trajectory. She had no time to analyze. She jumped a third time and cleared the pool.

Again she ran the perplex gauntlet. Then she plunged into

the maze. Last night she had cracked the Echo mesh and memorized the new configuration. Tapperhaven would give her endless demerits if she discovered what Soz had done, but Soz had checked academy history; they didn't throw cadets out for hacking the field-training webs. They were disciplined, yes, but not expelled. She was too angry to care. She had one goal: become a Jagernaut. Kill Traders. Nothing else mattered, even if she earned more demerits than any cadet in DMA history. Graduating with honors made no difference. What had it brought Althor? She would do whatever was necessary to survive against the Traders—hack their ship, hack their weapons, hack their forsaken brains.

Soz broke out of the maze and raced to the rebounders. They didn't faze her today; she had also memorized their new sequences. She darted through the smashing gateways, using her augmented reflexes to move faster than she had ever done before. As the last door slammed behind her, she sprinted into the sand pit at the end of the course and came to an abrupt stop, her chest heaving. Several cadets who had already run the course were standing around the trap. A spattering of applause greeted her.

Soz just stood, breathing too hard to speak. Lieutenant Colonel Dayamar Stone was a few paces away, intent on the timer of his gauntlet. The cadets jogged over to Soz, including Jazar, who was grinning.

"Soz!" Jazar clapped her on the shoulder, making her stumble.

"Hey," she said, catching her breath and her balance.

"You broke the record!" He motioned at her gauntlet. "*Look.* You shattered it."

"What?" Soz peered at her timer. She had run the Echo in seven minutes and eleven seconds, pulverizing the previous record of nine minutes forty-three.

"Whoa." Soz blinked at her timer. Then she blinked at Jazar.

"That was articulate." Laughing, he turned as the other cadets gathered around. Soz tried to reorient on them, but she couldn't unwind.

Stone came over and spoke without smiling. "Quite a feat, Valdoria."

Soz saluted him. "Thank you, sir."

He glanced at the other cadets. "Take four laps around the track, then off to the showers."

They saluted and jogged off, but as Soz turned to follow, Stone said, "Not you."

She turned back. "Sir?"

He spoke quietly. "How did you run the maze so fast?"

"Practice."

"What practice?" His voice tightened. "It's a new setup."

"I learn fast."

"No doubt." He met her gaze. "If I find you've been cracking DMA networks, Cadet, I'll have you up before Commandant Blackmoor faster than you can say 'You're expelled.'"

Hell and damnation. "Sir! Yes, sir!"

He jerked his head toward the track. "Go run. Eight laps."

Eight. Soz saluted and took off before he could ask more questions. She caught up with Jazar on his second lap.

He jogged next to her. "What did Stone want?"

"He thinks I cheated on the Echo."

"Did you?"

She slanted a look at him. "If you're going to fight Traders, you damn well better do anything you can to stay alive."

"You didn't answer my question."

"You can't cheat death." She focused inward, drawing on her resources, and had pulled ahead of him before she realized she was using her enhanced speed.

"Soz, cut it out." He sprinted up next to her and drew her to a halt. She could have easily pulled free; as a cadet only a few months into his second year, he had no biomech yet, neither a node nor any enhancement to his body. But she stopped, breathing deeply, ready to take off if he pushed.

"Listen to me." He stood with sweat running down his face and soaking his mesh shirt. "If you crack the Echo, the only person you're cheating is yourself."

"Jaz, don't."

"Let yourself hurt." His voice gentled. "Let go. Be human."

"I don't know how." She choked on the words. "I'm dying inside."

He put his hand on her shoulder. "Give it time."

"Time. Right." She shifted her feet. "Let's run."

They started off again, and she tried to exhaust herself with the exercise. But nothing could fix her broken edges. She couldn't drop her anger and let herself grieve—for if it started, she feared it would never stop.

Kurj sat in a high-backed academy chair at a round table with the Jag insignia enameled into its surface. He looked away, out the arched windows of Commandant Blackmoor's office, into the night. That darkness reflected his mood more than any glossy symbol.

A clink came from behind him, and he turned back as Blackmoor set steaming mugs of kava on the table. The commandant lowered himself into his own chair across from Kurj and folded his hands around the massive gray mug.

"Stone thinks she cheated," Blackmoor said.

Kurj took a swallow of bitter kava. "How?"

"Cracked the field mesh and memorized the Echo."

"Do you have proof?"

"Nothing. She covered herself too damn well."

"Without proof, we can't apply penalties."

Blackmoor frowned. "We can't let it go."

"I know." Steam curled out of Kurj's mug and drifted over the J-Force insignia. "She's hurting."

"We're all hurting. That doesn't excuse it."

"No." Kurj set down his mug. "It doesn't."

"I want her off the honor list."

"With what justification? Cadets aren't the only ones bound by the honor code. If we punish someone without evidence, we're violating it as well."

The commandant thumped the table. "She's one of the best cadets we've ever had, but she's never going to reach her potential if she can't shape up."

Kurj could only nod, too tired to say more. He had so little left for this mess. The Kyle web drained him more each day. That voracious, ill-defined universe absorbed all he had to give and demanded more. It was too much for two people, but he and Dehya *had* to do it. No one else could. Now his brother—his heir—had died. He had known the risk existed, known that the same flame of battle that would forge his heirs as it had forged him could also kill them. He understood Soz's rage. It burned within him as well, but in his case, the fury turned inward, against himself, for he was the one who had sent Althor to his death.

He had only one heir now. And she wasn't ready.

The lights were low in the viewing chamber when Soz entered. A sofa and several armchairs stood around the walls, upholstered in soft cloth, subtle grays and blues. Abstract holoart swirled on the walls, soothing and calm.

Soz did not feel calm.

A large window took up the top half of the opposite wall—and a woman with a cap of red hair stood there, gazing into the room beyond.

Soz stopped, startled. "Grell?"

The other woman turned around. It was indeed Soz's former roommate. "Heya, Soz." Grell sounded subdued. Her face was drawn, with dark circles under her eyes.

Soz joined her at the window. Althor lay in the hospital room beyond. He was stretched out on his back on a floater, a bed with chips worked into its air mattress, giving it an AI brain. It could react to tension in his body, ease muscle strain, dispense nanomeds, monitor his vital signs, massage his body, anything.

None of it helped.

The doctors were still running tests, and until Soz's parents told them to stop, they would continue, convincing themselves beyond every infinitesimal doubt that he would never wake. During it all, they allowed very few people to visit him. Soz didn't want to stay out here. She wanted to sit by his bedside, talk to him even if he couldn't hear, offer comfort. But she had to wait for permission, until they exhausted every hope modern medicine could offer. It seemed so useless, all their vaunted technology. Althor lay there, his eyes closed, his chest rising and falling with each shallow breath, but he never woke.

"He's been like this ever since I came," Grell said. "Every time I come."

"I hadn't realized you and he were . . . friends." Soz didn't know what to say. Had he been seeing Grell? She hadn't even known. Given their argument, she supposed he had reason to keep it to himself.

Grell glanced at her. "Yes. We're—friends."

"I didn't realize."

Grell went back to watching him. "Do you know what he asked me?"

It was easier for Soz to look at her than at her dying brother. "Well—no."

"If I could imagine spending my life with someone as a friend."

Ah, gods. He had really meant to do it, marry a woman so their father would let him come home. "What did you say?"

"I didn't. I never gave him an answer. But I could have said yes." She smiled at Soz. "He's an incredible man. Sweet."

Althor? *Sweet?* "Are we talking about the same person?"

"Well, yes. Of course."

Soz squinted at her. "He wasn't sweet to me."

Grell cocked an eyebrow at her. "Maybe that's because of all the puffle-wogs you put in his clothes."

"I did not put puffle-wogs in his clothes," Soz said, indignant. "It was spiney-wogs." Twelve-year-old Althor had yelped most satisfyingly when he put on his shirt. "He put puffle-wogs in mine to get back at me."

Grell laughed, soft and strained. "He loved you. Even if the two of you didn't always know how to express it."

"Loves," Soz said. "Not loved."

"Soz—I'm so sorry."

Soz shook her head. She couldn't go where Grell had already arrived. Until Althor actually stopped breathing, Soz refused to believe he wouldn't wake up.

Grell spoke awkwardly. "I'm not sure why he was seeing me. But I wanted you to know . . ." Her voice trailed off.

"Know what?" Soz asked.

"It didn't matter to me."

"It?"

"His, uh, preferences."

"Oh." Soz flushed.

"I liked him the way he was."

"Is." *Is.*

"Yes. Is." If Grell had any thoughts about contradicting her, she kept them to herself.

"Could you have been happy in a relationship like that?"

"I think so." Grell smiled crookedly. "Hey, he's an Imperial Heir."

Soz scowled. "Not a good answer." If someone sought her out because of her title, she would flip him over her shoulder and whack him down on the ground. She sometimes suspected that the men feared she would do that to them regardless. It could explain her lack of dates.

Grell smiled. "You should see the look on your face."

"You haven't seen the half of it, if you go after my brother for his title."

"You know me better than that."

Soz exhaled. "Yes. I do." Grell had been trying to make a joke, with about as much success as Soz's jokes. Neither of them would ever win awards for their wit, she supposed.

They stood side by side for a while longer, watching Althor breathe. Finally Grell said, "I've a test tomorrow. I guess I should try to study." She squeezed Soz's shoulder. "See you."

"Right. See you." Soz squeezed her hand back.

After Grell left, Soz continued to watch Althor. *Wake up,* she willed. *Please. Wake up.*

After a while she sat on the couch and sprawled out, slouched against its back, her legs stretched out on the table in front of it, what Earth types called a "coffee" table, though Soz could never imagine having a cup of the strange stuff anywhere, on a table or otherwise.

She dozed for a while, exhausted from running all day and slamming through the Echo. As fatigue leached her anger, remorse set in. Jazar was right. The person she had cheated today was herself. Even if the brass here never proved what she had done, she would know.

The door across the room whispered open. Soz considered waking up all the way to see who had arrived, but it seemed too difficult. She slitted her eyes open to peer at the door.

Shannon walked into the room.

What the hell? How did he get here? Her thoughts tumbled in a rush as she jumped up. "Shani! When did you—"

He turned—and the words died in her throat. How mortifying. She had just called a perfect stranger by her kid brother's nickname.

"Excuse me?" the man asked.

Soz's face heated with her blush. Gods. He was about Althor's age, early twenties. Straight blond hair brushed his shoulders in a style similar to the way Shannon wore his. He had blue eyes, though, and his face had a chiseled look, too unbearably handsome to be real. No one should be that gorgeous. It had to violate some conservation law of the cosmos.

"Uh—sorry." Soz cleared her throat. "I thought you were someone else."

"Are you Soz?"

"Yes." She blinked. "How did you know?"

"You fit Althor's description." He motioned toward her head. "Not many people have hair like that."

"Oh." Apparently this was another of Althor's "friends." It was bad enough he had paramours coming out of the woodwork when she couldn't even get a date, but really, the universe had no justice when her brother had so much better luck with good-looking men than she did.

"Well," Soz said. "So you know me but I don't know you. Who are you?" Then she inwardly winced. Social niceties had never been one of her strong points.

"I'm Chad." He nodded, the formal greeting of a com-

moner to nobility. Either he didn't know people were supposed to bow to royalty or else he didn't realize Althor's full
identity.

"My greetings, Chad," Soz said.

"Althor never mentioned me?"

"Not by name." She had a pretty good idea who he was,
though, given Althor's comments about his "former" friend.
"You're the one who dumped him, right?"

Chad flushed. Then he glanced toward the window. "How
is he?"

"Just about dead," Soz said. "That what it takes to make
you come around?"

He paled, his face strained. Then he went to the window
and looked into the room beyond.

Soz joined him. "How come you never visited him at
DMA?"

"He told me to stay away."

"Why?" she demanded.

Chad slanted a look at her. "Are you his protection
squad?"

Soz crossed her arms. "I know when he's been hurt."

"This is between Althor and me."

"Well, I guess it's stalled then." Maybe she wasn't being
fair to him, but it grated that he would come only when Althor lay in a coma.

Chad started to speak. Then he shook his head. They
stood, neither looking at each other, both watching the hospital room.

"Ah, hell," Soz said. "I'm not handling this very well."

Chad leaned his forehead against the window. "Nor I." In
a low voice, he added, "I never did."

"Let's try again." She forced some cheer into her voice.
"I'm pleased to meet you, Chad."

He straightened up and faced her. "And I you."

Then he smiled.

Whoa. A smile that dazzling should have been rated as a
lethal weapon. It would drop people in their tracks. What a
lovely way to go, though.

Soz cleared her throat. "So." She ran out of words. Even at the best of times, she wasn't great with small talk. When faced with her brother's devastatingly handsome former boyfriend, she had no clue what to say.

Chad's face gentled. "You're exactly like he described."

Soz grimaced. "I couldn't be that bad."

He laughed, his voice full and resonant, like an orator or a singer. "He never said you were."

"Did you, uh, know him long?"

His smile faded. "Several years."

"Why did you wait until now to come back?"

His voice cooled. "What makes you think it was my choice?"

That surprised her. Althor had given her the impression Chad left him. "I had the sense Althor missed you."

"That may be." Bitterness edged his voice. "But it changes nothing."

Soz could tell there was a lot more here. "You guys had a fight?" Then she winced. That was clumsy. But how was she supposed to say it?

"Of sorts."

"What sorts?"

He looked exasperated. "Are you always this blunt?"

Soz reddened. "Well—yes. Afraid so."

He smiled slightly, but it rapidly faded. "I was doing something he disagreed with. He gave me an ultimatum. Stop or he would leave." He exhaled. "I didn't stop. So he left."

Suddenly, with clarity, Soz knew. "It was *you*. The phorine. You were the one he was protecting."

"He told you?"

"You chose *drugs* over my brother?" Soz wanted to hit him. "Gods, you're stupid."

His voice hardened. "You've obviously never taken phorine."

She crossed her arms. "He should have goddamned turned you in."

Chad spoke tightly. "He did."

She saw it in his face then. The betrayal. The shock. The withdrawal. No wonder he hadn't come to see Althor again. She lowered her arms and spoke more quietly. "Did it work?"

"It was a nightmare."

"I'm sorry." She meant it.

It was a moment before he answered. "Yes, it worked. I'm grateful to be free of it. But that doesn't excuse what he did."

"Chad, if you had died or had your life destroyed because he had done nothing, would that have been all right?"

"It was my life to destroy."

"You don't know my brother very well, if you believe he could have walked away from someone he loved and lived with himself."

Chad pushed his hand through his hair, tousling it around his collar. "It didn't seem that way then."

"He told the brass at DMA he didn't know any cadets who used phorine."

"He didn't. I was never at DMA. I'm a civilian." He turned back to the window and pressed his palms against the glass, looking into the room. "He paid for me to stay at the most expensive private clinic on Diesha. Then he turned me in to the civilian authorities. My sentence was either the clinic or prison." He shrugged, trying to look as if he didn't care. "I took the clinic."

"You must be a psion, if phorine affected you."

"Yes. Both empath and telepath."

No wonder Althor liked him. "I'm sorry it didn't work out."

"Your family would never have accepted us anyway."

Soz didn't know what to say. He was right. Nor was it only her family. The Assembly no doubt had an arranged match in mind for Althor, just as they did for the rest of her siblings. Maybe Grell.

For a while they stood together watching Althor. Eventually Chad had to leave. Then Soz was alone with her memories and a life that no longer made sense. In her childhood, she had seen the world in bright, clear colors. Now everything had changed. She could no longer fall back on unconditional ideas of right and wrong. Every time she thought she knew what path to take, she ran into moral, ethical, and emotional roadblocks. Which way? Always the choices came with a price. DMA. Vibarr. Shannon and Vitarex. The Echo. Althor's silence on Chad. Right and wrong made no sense anymore. It had all turned gray.

She laid her palm on the window, wishing she could apologize to Althor for all those spiney-wogs. "Come back," she whispered.

No one answered.

A single light burned in the outer office, gilding the antique moldings on the door frame and the polished wooden desk. Soz paused, uncertain. For some reason, she hadn't expected this place to be empty. It made sense, of course; it was well into evening. The executive officer who usually sat here had surely gone home.

Soz steeled herself and walked to a large door behind the desk. Paneled in gold wood, with brass fittings, the door arched with an elegant severity. Antique severity; it had no pager or access panel she could see. Nothing to do but knock. Taking a breath, she rapped on the wooden portal. Then she waited.

"Come," a deep voice called.

She had gone too far now to turn back. She turned the ornate brass knob and opened the door.

The large office beyond matched the door, traditional and imposing. It wasn't the first time she had been here, but it was the most intimidating. Commandant Grant Blackmoor sat behind his desk across the huge office, his arms folded on its surface, a slew of holosheets in front of him. He looked tired, worn-out, ready to finish his day. From the pile of work, Soz suspected that regardless of whether or not he was ready to go home, he would be here for many more hours. The prospect of full-scale war was keeping more than a few people awake at night. Like about two trillion.

He set his light-stylus on the table. "Good evening, Cadet Valdoria." He indicated a chair by his desk. "Come in."

"Thank you, sir." Soz made the long trek across his office. Her palms were wet with perspiration, but she restrained the urge to wipe them on her jumpsuit. She sat in the chair, on its edge.

Blackmoor watched her with a cool, measured gaze. "What can I do for you this evening?"

Soz knew she had to push ahead with this now or she would lose her nerve. "Sir—I don't know if you heard. Earlier today I broke the record for running the Echo."

His gaze seemed to shutter. "Quite an accomplishment."

"I'm afraid it isn't." She bit her lip, then realized what she was doing and stopped. "Sir." She forced out words that wanted to stick in her throat. "I cheated."

"You cheated." Blackmoor didn't make it a question.

"Yes, sir."

"How?"

"I hacked the field training mesh."

"In other words, you violated the honor code."

"Yes, sir."

His expression hardened. "Tell me why I shouldn't have you expelled immediately."

What if they threw her out? Just because they hadn't done it to other students for similar infractions didn't mean they wouldn't with her. She wanted to say, *You didn't expel Vibarr for harassing me. You didn't even expel a damned phorine seller.* But those cadets had "left" anyway.

None of that mattered, though. Soz had realized it as she watched her brother's living death. She had to live with herself. The fact that others may not have received as harsh a punishment made no difference. She had to learn to deal with the gray or she would lose her way forever.

She said only, "You have the right."

"So I do." He sat considering her. "Valdoria, you aren't the first student to crack the field mesh. And we already had good reason to believe you had done so."

She had no excuses, so she said nothing.

Blackmoor leaned back in his seat, his elbow on its upholstered arm. "What do you think I should do with you?"

Soz met his gaze, knowing her face was red. "Some sort of disciplinary action."

"I'm glad we're in agreement." He rubbed the back of his neck and turned his head from side to side. "I'm taking you off the honor list. You will have a new set of demerits, starting this evening. Your altered status and assignments will be posted on the mesh tonight. Also, you will be on probation for the rest of this year."

Soz nodded, stiff and awkward, but also relieved. At least they weren't going to kick her out. "Yes, sir."

He spoke with a quieter aspect than usual. "How is your brother?"

"He's . . . as well as can be expected." She couldn't say the truth, even if they both knew. As long as Althor breathed, regardless of how much help the machines gave him, she hoped.

"My sympathies," he said.

Soz swallowed. "Thank you."

He glanced at the holosheets scattered across his desk, then back at her. "That will be all."

"Yes, sir." She stood and saluted.

As she turned to leave, she heard him shuffling the holosheets. She had only gone a few steps toward the door, though, when he spoke behind her. "Cadet."

Soz turned around. "Yes, sir?"

"It can't have been easy to come here tonight."

"It had to be done."

"Yes. It did." He exhaled. "Carry on, Valdoria."

"Yes, sir."

She left his office and went out into the night. As she walked to the dormitory, she passed cadets on their way to the library, to study or socialize, as so many students did on a balmy night like this. She wouldn't be joining them any evening soon, balmy or otherwise. Mucking with spamoozala and mechbots would occupy her free time for the rest of the year.

A few people waved at her, and she waved back, but she felt like an interloper. A cheat. A fake Jagernaut. No, they weren't perfect. Yes, they made decisions compromised by the conflicting demands of their lives. But the code of honor had to matter. She had lost sight of that. Stupid, cocky cadet. She would have been tempted to throw herself out of the academy, too.

So she trudged on, headed to her dorm and a year of probation, knowing she could make no more mistakes if she wanted to graduate, to receive her commission, all for the purpose of going out there to live the reality of an on-coming war that had put those dark circles under Black-moor's eyes.

That had killed her brother.

27

Visitors

A walkway circled to the Blue Tower of the castle in Dal-vador under the overhang of its turreted roof. Shannon stood on the walk, shaded by the roof, his hands resting on the sculpted edges of the wall, which resembled stone petals, just as the roof resembled a bell-flower turned upside down. He had studied holos of flowers in school, but he had no de-sire to see real ones in their natural habitat. He couldn't imagine going offworld. It would split him in two, leaving his spirit here while his body went elsewhere.

He had to leave.

He couldn't leave.

His parents were going to Althor. He wanted to go with them. But he couldn't. The ISC doctors had concerns, some-thing about his neural development, that it was going through a growth surge. They claimed that where he went in the next few years would affect its proper maturation. He didn't really understand, and he suspected they didn't, either.

No one had expected it to take over a year for Father to learn the use of his new legs and eyes. They had yet to unravel the differences between the Rillian brain and human norms. Blue Dale Archers differed even more. Shannon's doctors genuinely feared that if he left Lyshriol now, his brain wouldn't develop properly, especially after the shocks of his recent experiences. So he had to stay home.

He and Althor had never truly said good-bye. Maybe his Blue Dale brain was different, but it didn't change his love for his family. The thought of leaving Lyshriol frightened him. But the thought of never seeing his brother again frightened him even more.

In the distance, out at the starport, an ISC shuttle waited on the tarmac, gleaming black and gold in the sunlight. His parents were walking toward it with several other people, their pace slow and careful. Eldrinson took it step by step, leaning on a cane, refusing any aid that hinted at advanced technology. Roca walked beside him, but she didn't offer her arm. Shannon knew why; pride would stop his father from accepting help.

Soon the shuttle would rise into orbit, taking his parents to a battle cruiser. He thought of running to the port, insisting they take him. But they had already said no. He would remain here while they bade Althor farewell.

It hurt more than he could say.

In the greater scheme of star travel, the trip wasn't long, only a few days. They traveled on a Firestorm battle cruiser. The kilometers-long cylinder rotated to create an apparent gravity close to human standard. The ship was a star-faring metropolis. Bronze corridors and gold paths led through a city of coppery buildings and balconies. A sky needle soared in the distance, one of the great spokes that radiated from the center of the cylinder to its rim. Eldrinson doubted he would even have known he was on a ship, except that instead of a sky, it had a curving hull far overhead.

This wasn't his first trip offworld. He went as rarely as possible, but he did travel with Roca every year or so. As such trips went, this was routine. It could have even been pleasant.

It was the hardest journey he had ever taken.

He spoke to almost no one. He spent time with Roca, but no one else. Although he wished they could have brought the children, it relieved him to know they were safe. Except even Lyshriol wasn't safe; his aching legs and blurred sight spoke brutally of that truth.

He rarely tried to walk. Either he had to go painfully slow or else he lurched and fell. But he couldn't lean on people. Alone, with Roca, he could bear the shame of needing help, but every time he looked into her gold eyes, so different from the violet or silver of his people, he remembered his wife came from this fast, cold universe. He knew she loved him. How could he not know? They were psions. But it never changed the truth. Her willingness to settle for less didn't make his deficiencies any less bleak.

The power spiked.

Normally the tech wouldn't have noticed such a slight power surge in the grid he monitored, one dedicated to the desert east of the Red Mountains on the world Diesha. Tonight he had forgotten to bring the entertainment disk he was enjoying with its in-depth exposés on the lives of nobles from the great Skolian Houses, especially Majda and Rajindia. It left him staring morosely and with great boredom at the graphs floating in the air above the console. He had nothing else to do, so he noticed the spike.

With so much free time, he spent half an hour checking various systems, first the defense installations he monitored and then the systems he used to do the monitoring. When he found no problems, he made a note in the record, adding his opinion that the surge was a bit too far out of the usual parameters. He forwarded a copy to the main office. It gave him something to do.

Then he resumed staring wearily at the holomaps and graphs. He had another six hours to fill.

Perhaps more spikes would appear.

Two doctors escorted Eldrinson and Roca into a room with glowing white walls, equipment embedded in every surface and chrome robot arms folded against the bed. It resembled any other bed, despite its glistening white sheets, which no doubt were threaded with technological marvels. But the man who lay there, his gold skin gone sallow, his chest barely moving—no, that couldn't be.

It couldn't be.

Eldrinson was dimly aware of the doctors speaking, but he couldn't hear. It was all he could do to limp forward using his blue glasswood cane for each step, his hand gripped on the carved lyrine head at the top.

He stopped at the bed and leaned his weight on the cane. Althor. His son. Althor's eyes were closed and his body wasted compared to the muscular giant who had visited home more than a year ago. Eldrinson died inside again, as he had so often this past year, remembering how he had sent his son away. If only he could take back those words. But nothing would change the past.

He almost wished he had remained blind, so he wouldn't see Althor's motionless, wasted form. His gold-rimmed spectacles made his vision almost as sharp as before his injuries. An ISC doctor had constructed them after Eldrinson refused to have any more operations on his eyes. Spectacles he understood. He could touch them, hold them, see why they worked. And he could remove them, unlike the changes within his body. He had dreaded the biomech, considered it alien and inhuman, but he would have given anything now, including his own life, if only that technology could have helped his son.

Roca stood at his side. She put her hand over his on the head of his cane. He laid his other hand over hers and they remained at the bedside of their son. Such heroism, everyone told them. The doomed Blackstar Squadron had saved Onyx Platform and billions of people, places and populations Eldrinson could barely imagine. He tried to feel pride in his son's sacrifice, but all he could think was that he would have rather have had Althor alive than a hero.

He had felt proud of his two oldest sons when each insisted on riding into battle with him—and he had hated it as well, fearing they wouldn't come home. What could he say: stay protected while your father goes to war? They were bigger, faster, stronger, smarter, and younger than he. Now, seeing Althor, he wished he had never trained them in swordplay or archery. As primitive as such skills were compared to those of Jagernauts, they had still taught Althor the mindset of war. Perhaps if his sons had never learned to fight, they would have become farmers, like Vyrl, or teachers, like Denric.

Or maybe it would have made no difference. Soz had never trained with a sword, at least not with his permission. She had spent hours with a bow and arrows, but he had never taken it seriously. He should have; she shot like a Blue Dale Archer. But no matter what he tried, encouraging his sons or discouraging his daughter, in the end they each went down their own path, one he would never have wished for them. He had to let them go, and when he did, he lost them.

Althor looked as if he were only sleeping, that any moment he might awake. His metallic lashes lay on his pallid skin. With the weight he had lost, his face had become gaunt, bringing his features into sharp relief. Equipment hummed around him. Although the doctors weren't ready to make a final diagnosis, their emotions about this were too intense, and Eldrinson picked up their moods even through their many mental defenses. They had no hope his son would recover.

Eldrinson gritted his teeth. Machines piloted by nameless soldiers had done this. Althor had never even seen their faces. It seemed so *wrong* on such a fundamental level, so dehumanizing, that it made him wonder if offworlders could be fully human. Perhaps they were all like him now, full of biomech. Walking machines.

Someone touched his arm. Startled, he looked up. A doctor was standing there, a woman in a white jumpsuit. She nodded kindly and indicated a chair by the head of the bed. "Would you like to sit, Your Majesty?"

He very much wanted to sit; his legs felt ready to liquefy. He almost said no anyway, but weariness crept over him. He had been walking only a few days. When he nodded, the doctor stepped back to give him room. He limped to the chair, leaning on his cane, and settled into its faintly shimmering cushions.

Another woman brought a chair for Roca and she sat next to him. He found it difficult to reach out to her, but he felt how much she needed him, and if he was honest with himself, how much he needed her. He put out his hand and she took it, curling her five fingers around his four.

The doctors spoke, phrases of comfort, futile words that meant they had no hope so they offered kindness instead. Then they began, ever so gently, to talk about the decision he and Roca would have to make: How long would they leave Althor on the machines that were keeping his body alive after his brain had died.

Eldrinson stopped listening then, unable to bear any more. He stayed with his wife, the two of them sitting a vigil that would never end.

"She needs training." Lyra Meson, First Councilor of the Assembly, paced across Commandant Blackmoor's office.

Kurj stood by the wall with his arms folded, studying the councilor as she strode past him, then past Blackmoor, who was half sitting on his large desk. Colonel Starjack Tahota, the admissions officer who had brought Soz to DMA, stood on the other side of Blackmoor.

As the newly elected leader of the Skolian Imperialate, Meson had served less than two years. Long and lanky, almost as tall as Blackmoor, she wore crisp blue slacks and a white shirt. Blue tattoos bordered the left side of her face from her temple to the line of her jaw in a curve of interlocked circles, the sign of a powerful family among the mercantile class. With her sharp motions, intense eyes, and shock of dark hair, she exuded energy.

Although Kurj considered Meson a good choice for First Councilor, he had no intention of revealing that opinion. He had never agreed with the separation of power that made the First Councilor—a civilian—leader over even the Imperator. Meson had served in the Pharaoh's Army for twelve years and retired as a lieutenant colonel. Even so, she had far less familiarity with ISC than Kurj. ISC should be the final voice of the government during either war or peacetime. It made no difference to him that most of the civilian government disagreed; he knew what Skolia needed and it wasn't a dithering Assembly.

It disquieted him more, however, that Meson was only forty-three, five years his junior. She had savvy, intelligence, and foresight, but she lacked the kind of experience that could only come with many years in office. A civilization facing the prospect of interstellar war needed a veteran at the helm, not someone who had only recently assumed power. The Traders knew that. It was probably why ESComm had made their move now.

He watched Meson through the gold shimmer of his inner lids. "You won't find any better training for pilots than here at DMA."

Meson stalked over to him. "I have no doubt about that. I mean your sister needs training as your heir."

He regarded her implacably. "If I recall the order that your vaunted Assembly gave me two years ago, I was to choose heirs and have them attend academies for their training." His voice cooled. "Fine. I did it. Now my brother is dead."

She spoke quietly. "Imperator Skolia, I deeply regret the loss you have suffered. I am sorry to bring this up. But it only underscores the unstable nature of our situation."

Kurj knew where she was going with this. As long as his

heirs could work as Rhon telops, in theory they could join the Dyad if he died. But Skolia needed a true Imperator, one capable of holding the title in more than name. If they couldn't succeed as military officers, they had no business being his heirs. However, even the best officers could become casualties; that truth had become an all too brutal reality. He had lost Althor. Soz remained.

"She isn't ready." Kurj said. "If you send her out in a squad, I could lose my second heir." His voice took on an edge. "I don't have any more spares, Councilor."

"I wasn't thinking of a squad," she said.

"Then what?" Blackmoor asked, leaning against his desk. He was at ease with Meson in a way Kurj had never felt with the First Councilor. But then, Blackmoor and Meson belonged to the same political party, the Progressives, which had misguided views about holding elections instead of passing power through hereditary lines. They probably disliked the hereditary nature of his position as much as he disliked answering to a civilian. He had appointed Blackmoor as the DMA commandant because he had been better qualified than the other candidates, but his politics annoyed Kurj.

"Your sister needs hands-on experience," Meson told Kurj. "Procedures, ships, resources, strengths, weaknesses—she needs to learn it for all branches of ISC, not just the J-Force."

A good suggestion. Kurj had served aboard army, fleet, and ASC ships during his training. But he hadn't been so raw. "She's only eighteen."

"She is young," Meson acknowledged. "But these aren't normal times."

"If you're saying we need to speed up her training," Kurj said, "then yes, I agree."

Meson blinked. Kurj supposed it wasn't often he openly agreed with her. She had a tendency to make sense, unfortunately. If she continued to do her job so well, it wouldn't help the Royalist Party, which asserted that Progressive ideas weakened the Imperialate and power should pass through hereditary lines. Although Kurj belonged to the Technology Party, he sympathized with the Royalists.

Tahota spoke for the first time. "Cadet Valdoria doesn't have to stop her DMA training. She can alternate her work here with tours on ships in other branches of ISC. She has time, with her advanced standing." Satisfaction showed on her weathered face. "When I first met her on Lyshriol, I could tell she was going to be one of our best. What a fire in that one! I'm not surprised she's over two years ahead of her class."

Blackmoor snorted. "Yes, well, she's busy now. She spends all her time cleaning mechbots."

Meson cocked an eyebrow at him. "The Imperial Heir?"

Kurj answered dryly. "Especially the Imperial Heir."

"Ah, well." Meson's lips quirked in a smile. "We've all been young and brash."

"Some more than others," Blackmoor said. "However, I concur that she would benefit from the tours."

"I suggest we start with the Fleet," Tahota said. "It's the largest branch of ISC."

"Put her on a battle cruiser for a few months," Meson said. "She can do her classes as a VR student, through the webs."

Roca's Pride is the best in the Fleet," Kurj said. "It also has a Dyad Chair she can study."

Meson cocked an eyebrow at him. "I'm sure she'll appreciate the name."

"Perhaps," Kurj said, neutral. ISC selected names for its vessels from three categories: historical battles, well-known figures, and the royal family. By assigning Soz to *Roca's Pride,* he achieved two goals: putting her on a ship named after her own mother might give her some measure of additional confidence in what was bound to be a difficult tour, and it offered an implicit reminder to the Progressives that ISC had strong ties with the Ruby Dynasty.

Meson nodded to him. "Then it is decided. Cadet Valdoria will begin her new tour as soon as possible."

Full-color holos of a Jag's inversion engine rotated above the transparent screen of the table where Soz was working in the media room. Beautiful, beautiful holos. She highlighted the thrusters in blue, fuel selector in purple, cooling coils in green, the luminous column of the engine itself in white. Her course of Jag engineering was sheer pleasure.

"Look at you," Soz crooned. "Beautiful engine."

A laugh came from nearby. "Maybe if you treated your dates that way, you'd have more success with men."

Soz looked up. Jazar was leaning against a nearby holo table with his muscular arms crossed, straining the weave of his blue sweater. His black hair lay sleek and short against his head.

"My dates aren't as sexy as this engine," she said. Or as sexy as Jazar, though she wasn't thinking about that. Really.

He shook his head, laughing. "You know, I've always wondered why someone as good-looking and well connected as you has so much trouble with men. It's no wonder, if you go around telling your fellows they aren't as sexy as an engine."

She glowered at him. "Did you come here to analyze my love life?"

His grin flashed. "No, but it wouldn't take long."

"Jaz, I *swear*—"

He held out his hands in surrender. "Don't attack."

She glared.

"You have a visitor. A girl. I saw her."

Soz couldn't think of any girls who would visit her. "Where?"

"In one of the common rooms. I asked around. People said she came to see you. I offered to let you know."

She considered him warily. "Jazar Orand, I am sensing ulterior motives here."

"Well, uh—" He scratched his ear. "I was hoping you would introduce me."

"Whatever for?"

"Oh for flaming sakes, Soz, you really are dense sometimes."

"Yes, well, I'm densely not going to introduce you to my mysterious visitor." Apparently this "girl" was older than she had first thought.

"Come on," he coaxed. "Tell her that I'm your great friend."

"Why? Who is this person?"

"I've no idea. She's star-jazzing gorgeous, though."

"Oh, well, that tells me a lot." Soz had never been a judge of beauty in women. Now men, that was another matter. A frustrating matter, but that had nothing to do with this request, which was annoying her far more than it should. So what if he thought this woman was gorgeous. Pah.

"She's gold," he added. "All of her. Hair. Eyes."

That got her attention. Her annoyance surged into hope. She covered it with amusement. "You want me to introduce you, hmmm? Why, Jazar? Going to ask her out?"

He squinted at her. "Why is that funny?"

Soz just smiled and shook her head. She couldn't be certain who had come to see her, after all. She turned off the engine holos and went with him, out of the library and across campus. Inside their dorm, he led her to one of the smaller common areas. As they entered, Soz saw her visitor standing by a window across the room, gazing out at the gardens, a golden woman with lustrous hair down her back and a rose-hued dress clinging to her dancer's body. Soz froze.

Jazar elbowed her. "Introduce me."

Soz slanted him a look. "To my mother?"

His mouth fell open. "She's your *mother?*"

"Yep."

Red flushed his cheeks. "Oh."

Soz smiled. "It's all right, Jaz. You aren't the first to react that way." Inside, her joy warred with uncertainty. What would her mother say to her?

At the sound of their voices, Roca turned around. Her face lit up. "Soz!"

At that moment, Soz forgot Althor, school, demerits, bots, her appalling social life, and this strange business about a tour on a battle cruiser. Suddenly she was back in Dalvador, laughing with her family. Her mother brought suns and warmth. Soz wished she were small again and could run to her for comfort. She couldn't, of course, but seeing Roca meant more than she knew how to say.

"My greetings, Mother." She heard how formal she sounded, as if she had gone back to being thirteen, that year when she had hardly spoken to her parents, answering their inquiries about her life with grunts or one-word sentences, not for rudeness, but because she had needed to separate from them and stop depending so much on them when she felt so uncertain about life.

Soz went to her and then they were hugging. Hotness filled her eyes, but she didn't care. She hadn't consciously realized until this moment that she had questioned whether she would ever see her mother again.

Finally they let each other go. Soz smiled awkwardly, aware of Jazar standing back a few steps. Roca appraised her with a firm gaze. "You aren't eating enough. And are you going to bed on time? You look so tired."

Soz couldn't help but laugh. "Mother, I'm eighteen. Not ten."

Roca's gold-tinted skin turned rosy. "I know that."

Soz beckoned to Jazar. "This is my friend Jaz."

He came forward and bowed deeply to Roca. "My honor at your company, Your Majesty."

Roca smiled at him. "And mine at yours. A friend of my daughter's is a friend of mine."

"Thank you, ma'am." He regarded Soz with a question in his gaze. She felt what he didn't ask. Did she want him to leave?

Soz glanced at her mother, but Roca was guarded in both her mind and expressions. Although Soz enjoyed Jazar's company, she wanted to catch up on news in private—especially news of her father. Realizing how much she missed her mother made her father's absence that much more painful.

Jazar picked up on her unspoken response. He spoke to Roca. "It is a pleasure to have met you ma'am."

Roca inclined her head. "A pleasure shared."

He turned to Soz. "I better go study. I've a test in Kyle space theory."

"Yes. Yes, of course." She sent him a mental glyph of gratitude. "I'll talk to you later."

"Sounds good." He bowed to Roca and discreetly withdrew.

Roca was watching Soz with veiled amusement. "He's charming."

"He's a rogue."

"A handsome one."

"Don't tell him that," Soz said, alarmed. "I'll never hear the end of it."

Although Roca tried to smile, it seemed strained. "Ah, well."

Soz's mood dimmed. "Did you see Althor?"

"Yes." The one word, so full of sorrow, told Soz more than any description of his condition. He hadn't improved.

Roca spoke with difficulty. "Apparently the cortical region of his brain no longer shows any activity."

Soz wanted to back away. "Surely they can do something." She was talking too fast. "Didn't I read somewhere that biomech surgeons on Metropoli developed a nanomed species that repairs neurons?"

Her mother answered gently. "We checked, Soshoni. Gods know, I wish it could be true. But at best, they could repair only a few, nowhere near enough to bring his brain alive."

Soz didn't want to hear. But she knew that even if a way had existed to heal Althor's brain cells, the result wouldn't have been her brother. His personality, his essence, his intellect, his memories—it would all be gone.

"His doctors asked if he had a living will," Roca said. "I didn't know of any. Do you?"

A living will. Soz shook her head, hyperaware of the room, her hair brushing her cheek, the rustle of her uniform, the pulse in her neck. "I don't think he had one."

It was a moment before Roca spoke again. "They want to know if we wish to keep him on the machines."

"Don't take him off," Soz said. "Please don't." A tear gathered in her eye.

"Don't cry." Roca looked as if she wanted to shelter Soz the same way she had in Soz's childhood, offering the haven of her arms whenever scraped knees or imagined monsters darkened her child's life. Roca pulled her close and hugged her, and somehow it all seemed a little better. To Soz, her mother's beauty had nothing to do with her face or her form. It came from within, from a woman whose heart held such warmth for her family. But Soz couldn't run to her now the way she had as a small child. Those days had passed.

Soz pulled back, unable to reveal her emotions for long. "It's good to see you, Hoshma."

"And you, Soshoni." Her mother seemed subdued. "I'm not alone."

"Did Denric come?" He was the only one she could imagine leaving Lyshriol. Next year he would go to an off-world university. Maybe Aniece or Kelric, but they were so young.

"Not Denric." Roca hesitated. "He's in the other common room. He wasn't sure if you wanted another visitor."

Soz realized then who she meant. *Eldrin.* Saints, she was a terrible sister. He was staying up at the palace again, only a short ride by flyer, but with all her droid duty recently, she hadn't kept in touch. She was embarrassed to admit why they had taken her off the honor roll and loaded her with de-merits. Perhaps, knowing how she had left Lyshriol, he thought she didn't want to see him.

"Yes, of course." She pushed back the tendrils of hair curling about her face. "I'd love to see him."

Roca looked relieved, also a bit confused. As they went to the entrance of an adjacent common room, Soz thought about how she would apologize for being so out of touch. Perhaps she should just confess she had been cleaning bots. It would be mortifying, since he would ask why, but better he knew the truth than he thought she had been ignoring him.

They entered a wood-paneled room with antique book-cases and comfortable chairs. Eldrin was standing on the other side, looking at a holo that floated in front of the wall, a portrait of the previous Imperator, Jarac, Soz's grandfather. Jarac could have been Kurj's brother, they looked so alike, with their large size and gold coloring. Jarac had worn his hair longer, though, in a shaggy mane over his collar. In the portrait, Jarac's inner lids were up, showing his gold eyes.

The portrait interested Soz far less than her brother. It worried her how tired Eldrin looked. When did that streak of silver appear in his hair? And why was he wearing spectacles—?

Soz drew in a sharp breath.

It wasn't her brother.

It was her father.

28

Resolution

Eldrinson studied the portrait of his late father-in-law, trying to find the similarities everyone else saw between this man and Kurj. He had never known Jarac; the previous Imperator had died before they had a chance to meet, shortly after Eldrinson married Roca. On a superficial level, he saw a resemblance; Jarac and Kurj had similar coloring, features, and build. But the artist who had done this portrait had captured more elusive qualities, those Roca had often described to him, the gentleness within her towering father, the warlord who preferred peace to combat.

A sharp inhale came from behind him. Puzzled, he turned—and went completely still.

Soz was standing across the room. The flow of time seemed to stop and freeze him in this moment, like a shimmer fly caught in amber. His daughter looked so much like herself, alive and well, her hair curling wildly around her face and her eyes as large as a startled rockhorn deer. Then he saw the dark circles under her eyes, how thin she had become, her stiff posture. She stood as if she wasn't sure whether she should go to him or flee.

His voice caught. "My greetings, Soshoni." He used the childhood nickname out of habit and his pleasure in seeing her, and then immediately regretted it. This was no child facing him, but an adult whose life would be forged in the oncoming war.

She said nothing.

Eldrinson looked from his daughter to his wife, who stood next to her, but he saw no answers in Roca's face. Puzzlement came from Roca's mind and made him fear that she hadn't warned Soz he had come.

"Father." Soz gulped in a breath. "You're—gods above—you're *standing*."

Up until that moment, he had been so tense, he had forgotten that she didn't know he could walk now. Leaning on his cane, he stepped toward her. He slid his cane forward and took another step, so slow, so hard, but none of that mattered when he saw his goal, his wife and daughter standing together. Soz was too thin, her face strained with fatigue, a smudge of dust on her cheek—a truly beautiful sight.

"Hoshpa." Her eyes glistened. "You can see, too."

Eldrinson took another step, leaning heavily on his cane. He wanted to answer, but he couldn't speak with the exertion of coaxing his rebuilt limbs to obey his thoughts in this strange gravity. He had to do this right with Soz, or at least as right as he could manage, and that meant giving his full concentration to his words when he spoke with her.

Soz waited while he took step after slow step and rested in between with his weight on his cane. With her face so gaunt, her eyes seemed even larger than usual, too big for her face. It gave her a haunted quality. He suspected she had learned far more this past year and a half than math and military strategy, perhaps more than she ever wanted to learn.

Finally he reached her. His heart filled with the sight until he couldn't speak.

"Father?" Her voice was low, tentative.

He took a shaky breath. "I practiced what I would say to you for many hours during the trip here. Now it seems I have forgotten everything."

She seemed afraid to smile, to greet him, to say anything at all. Eldrinson understood. He felt the same way. But he had to speak. "If you will forgive my clumsy words, which lurch and stumble as much as my legs—I—I hope—you will always want to come home." He reached out his free hand to her. "You are always welcome, Soshoni."

The tension drained out of her posture. She took his hand and he pulled her into a hug, dropping his cane. For an endless wonderful moment they stood that way, and he remembered all the times he had embraced her when she was younger. A sob caught in her throat, almost inaudible.

"Always welcome," he whispered.

Soz drew back, slowly letting him go, taking care he didn't fall. She picked up his cane and handed it to him, pushing those splendidly disarrayed curls out of her face. Roca stood back, smiling now, giving them space.

"How?" Soz asked, indicating his legs, then looking into his eyes. "The last I heard, you would never walk or see again."

"Ah, well." He shifted his weight, changing his grip on the cane from one hand to the other. "It seems my mind is rather strange. It doesn't respond the way these ISC healers expect. Their healing didn't work. Not at first. Or at second or third, either." He managed a smile, despite the growing ache in his legs. "But I'm a stubborn old barbarian. Eventually it worked."

"I'm so glad." Soz rubbed tears off her cheek. "And you aren't a barbarian."

He tried to smile, but his legs were becoming oddly heavy, a peculiar sensation given how much lighter he otherwise felt here.

Roca spoke to Soz. "You look as if you've had a long day. Perhaps we should sit down?"

Soz's cheeks reddened. "I've been cleaning robots."

Eldrinson frowned. "What for? You came here to be a warrior."

She gave a soft laugh full of embarrassment. "Ah, Hoshpa, they think I misbehave. Can you imagine such a thing? Me, misbehave."

"Quite a concept, eh?" Eldrinson could imagine how unprepared DMA must have been for his whirlwind of a daughter. "Cleaning robots is good for the character, I've heard."

"Then I must have great character," Soz grumbled, sounding more like her usual self. He had long ago realized she had no idea how charming or funny she sounded. He didn't dare tell her; she might take off his head.

The three of them went to one of the couches, slowly for him. Roca came up on his other side, but neither she nor Soz tried to take his arm or otherwise help. They were patient with his pride.

As they settled on the couch, it adjusted beneath them. It would have bothered Eldrinson until he realized its cushions were making his legs more comfortable. It was a relief to relax. He leaned his head back, letting the lively couch ease his muscles.

"Eldri?" Roca's voice came through the haze of his fatigue. "Are you all right?"

"Just a little tired, that's all." He straightened up and turned to Soz, who had sat between him and Roca. "After I've rested, you must show us around this school that has so many robots to clean."

Her lips quirked. "I'll do that." Her voice was stronger now and her eyes brimmed with welcome.

And love.

He had let that get away, this love for his family. He had lost his path. He had never realized he needed to map such a complicated route through the maze of his emotions. Even when he had ridden to war with his sons, he had never genuinely faced their mortality. He had known they would probably survive minor battles, and he had been with them, to fight at their side, their back. Now, seeing Soz here, on a world of red skies, chrome cities, and soaring towers, he knew only relief that she was alive and healthy instead of lying in a hospital room.

He would never have the chance to reconcile with Althor, but he had found his way back to Soz and Shannon. If he had to travel leagues or light-years to see them, he would do so. Whatever it took, he would never again let himself lose the people who mattered more to him than anyone else in the world. His family.

So Eldrinson spent the day with his wife and daughter, and found joy in their love.

Family Tree: RUBY DYNASTY

Boldface names refer to members of the Rhon. The Selei name denotes the direct line of the Ruby Pharaoh.
All children of Roca and Eldrinson take Valdoria as their third name. All members of the Rhon within the Ruby
Dynasty have the right to use Skolia as their last name. "Del" in front of a name means "in honor of."

= marriage   + children by

Lahaylia Selei = Jarac

Dyhianna Selei = [1]William Seth Rockworth III
(separated)

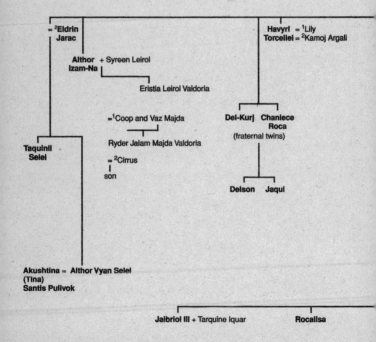

= [2]**Eldrin**
Jarac

Althor   + Syreen Leirol
Izam-Na

Eristia Leirol Valdoria

=[1]Coop and Vaz Majda

Ryder Jalam Majda Valdoria

= [2]Cirrus

son

Taquinil
Selei

Havyrl = [1]Lily
Torcellei = [2]Kamoj Argali

Del-Kurj Chaniece
Roca
(fraternal twins)

Delson   Jaqui

Akushtina = Althor Vyan Selei
(Tina)
Santis Pulivok

Jaibriol III + Tarquine Iquar   **Rocalisa**

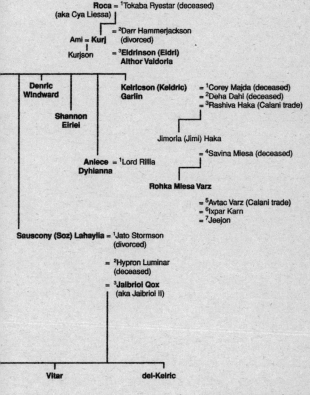

Roca = [1]Tokaba Ryestar (deceased)
(aka Cya Liessa)

= [2]Darr Hammerjackson
(divorced)

Ami = Kurj

Kurjson

= [3]Eldrinson (Eldri)
Althor Valdoria

Denric
Windward

Keiricson (Keldric) = [1]Corey Majda (deceased)
Garlin = [2]Deha Dahl (deceased)
= [3]Rashiva Haka (Calani trade)

Shannon
Eirlei

Jimorla (Jimi) Haka

Aniece = [1]Lord Rillia
Dyhianna

= [4]Savina Miesa (deceased)

Rohka Miesa Varz

= [5]Avtac Varz (Calani trade)
= [6]Ixpar Karn
= [7]Jeejon

Sauscony (Soz) Lahaylia = [1]Jato Stormson
(divorced)

= [2]Hypron Luminar
(deceased)

= [3]Jaibriol Qox
(aka Jaibriol II)

Vitar   del-Keiric

*Genetically, Kurj carries Jarac's DNA

Characters and Family History

Boldface names refer to Ruby psions, also known as the "Rhon." All Rhon psions who are members of the Ruby Dynasty use **Skolia** as their last name (the Skolian Imperialate was named after their family). The **Selei** name indicates the direct line of the Ruby Pharaoh. Children of **Roca** and **Eldrinson** take Valdoria as a third name. The "del" prefix means "in honor of," and is capitalized if the person honored was a Triad member. Most names are based on world-building systems drawn from Mayan, North African, and Indian cultures.

= marriage

Lahaylia Selei (Ruby Pharaoh) = **Jarac** (Imperator)

Lahaylia and **Jarac** founded the modern-day Ruby Dynasty. **Lahaylia** was created in the Rhon genetic project. Her lineage traces back to the ancient Ruby Dynasty that founded the Ruby Empire. **Lahaylia** and **Jarac** have two daughters, **Dyhianna Selei** and **Roca**.

Dyhianna (Dehya) Selei = (1) William Seth Rockworth III (separated)
= (2) **Eldrin Jarac Valdoria**

Dehya becomes the Ruby Pharaoh after Lahaylia. She married William Seth Rockworth III as part of the Iceland

Treaty between the Skolian Imperialate and Allied Worlds of Earth. They have no children and later separate. The dissolution of their marriage would negate the treaty, so neither the Allieds nor the Imperialate recognize Seth's divorce. Both Seth and Dehya eventually remarry anyway. *Spherical Harmonic* tells the story of what happens to **Dehya** after the Radiance War. She and **Eldrin** have two children, **Taquinil Selei** and **Althor Vyan Selei.**

Althor Vyan Selei = 'Akushtina (Tina) Santis Pulivok

The story of **Althor** and **Tina** appears in *Catch the Lightning*. **Althor Vyan Selei** was named after his uncle/cousin, **Althor Izam-Na Valdoria.** Tina also appears in the story "Ave de Paso" in the anthologies *Redshift* and *Fantasy: The Year's Best*, 2001, edited by Robert Silverberg and Karen Haber.

Roca = (1) Tokaba Ryestar (deceased)
= (2) Darr Hammerjackson (divorced)
= (3) **Eldrinson (Eldri) Althor Valdoria**

Roca and Tokaba had one child, **Kurj** (Imperator and former Jagernaut). Kurj marries Ami when he is about a century old. Kurj and Ami have a son named Kurjson.

Although no records exist of **Edrinson's** lineage, it is believed he descends from the ancient Ruby Dynasty. *Skyfall* tells the story of how he and **Roca** meet. They have ten children.

Eldrin (Dryni) Jarac (bard, consort to Ruby Pharaoh, warrior)
Althor Izam-Na (engineer, Jagernaut, Imperial Heir)
Del-Kurj (Del) (singer, warrior, twin to **Chaniece**)
Chaniece Roca (runs Valdoria family household, twin to **Del-Kurj**)
Havyrl (Vyrl) Torcellei (farmer, doctorate in agriculture)

Sauscony (Soz) Lahaylia (military scientist, Jagernaut, Imperator)

Denric Windward (teacher, doctorate in literature)

Shannon Eirlei (Blue Dale Archer)

Aniece Dyhianna (accountant, Rillian queen)

Kelricson (Kelric) Garlin (mathematician, Jagernaut, Imperator)

Eldrin appears in *The Radiant Seas* and *Spherical Harmonic*.

Althor Izam-Na = (1) Coop and Vaz
= (2) Cirrus

Althor has a daughter, Eristia Leirol Valdoria, with Syreen Leirol, an actress turned linguist. Coop and Vaz have a son, Ryder Jalam Majda Valdoria, with **Althor** as co-father. **Althor** and Coop appear in *The Radiant Seas*. The novelette, "Soul of Light" (Circlet Press, anthology *Sextopia*), tells the story of how **Althor** and Vaz met Coop. Vaz and Coop also appear in *Spherical Harmonic*. **Althor** and Cirrus also have a son.

Havyrl (Vyrl) Torcellei = Lilliara (Lilly) (deceased)
= Kamoj Quanta Argali

Havyrl & Lilly's story appears in "Stained Glass Heart," a novella in the anthology *Irresistible Forces*, February 2004. The story of **Havyrl** and Kamoj appears in *The Quantum Rose*, which won the 2001 Nebula Award. An early version of the first half was serialized in *Analog*, May 1999–July/August 1999.

Sauscony (Soz) Lahaylia = (1) Jato Stormson
(divorced)
= (2) Hypron Luminar
(deceased)
= (3) **Jaibriol Qox
(aka Jaibriol II)**

The story of how **Soz** and Jato met appears in the novella, "Aurora in Four Voices" (*Analog*, December 1998). **Soz** and **Jaibriol's** stories appear in *Primary Inversion* and *The Radiant Seas*. They have four children, all of whom use Qox-Skolia as their last name: **Jaibriol III, Rocalisa, Vitar**, and **del-Kelric**. The story of how **Jaibriol III** became the emperor of Eube appears in *The Moon's Shadow*. **Jaibriol III** married Tarquine Iquar, the Finance Minister of Eube. Soz's experiences as a cadet are in *Triad Part I (Schism)* and *Part II*.

Aniece = Lord Rillia.

Lord Rillia rules Rillia, which consists of the extensive Rillian Vales, the Dalvador Plains, the Backbone Mountains, and the Stained Glass Forest.

Kelricson (Kelric) Garlin = (1) Corey Majda (deceased in 2243)
= (2) Deha Dahl (deceased)
= (3) Rashiva Haka (Calani trade)
= (4) Savina Miesa (deceased)
= (5) Avtac Varz (Calani trade)
= (6) Ixpar Karn (closure)
= (7) Jeejon

Kelric's stories are told in *The Last Hawk, Ascendant Sun, The Moon's Shadow*, the novella "A Roll of the Dice" (*Analog*, July/August 2000), and the novelette "Light and Shadow" (*Analog*, April 1994). **Kelric** and Rashiva have one son, Jimorla (Jimi) Haka, who becomes a renowned Calani. **Kelric** and Savina have one daughter, **Rohka Miesa Varz**, who becomes the Ministry Successor in line to rule the Twelve Estates on Coba.

The novella "Walk in Silence" (*Analog*, April 2003) tells the story of Jess Fernandez, an Allied starship captain from Earth who deals with the genetically engineered humans on the Skolian colony of Icelos. The story of Dayj Majda, the prince who was betrothed to Roca in *Skyfall*, appears in the novella "The City of Cries" in the anthology *Down These Dark Spaceways*, edited by Mike Resnick. The novelette "The Shadowed Heart" is the story of Jagernaut Jason Harrick when he survives the aftermath of the Radiance War. It appears in the anthology *The Journey Home*, edited by Mary Kirk.

Time Line

circa 4000 BC	Group of humans moved from Earth to Raylicon
circa 3600 BC	Ruby Dynasty begins
circa 3100 BC	Raylicans launch first interstellar flights; rise of Ruby Empire
circa 2900 BC	Ruby Empire declines
circa 2800 BC	Last interstellar flights; Ruby Empire collapses
circa AD 1300	Raylicans begin to regain lost knowledge
1843	Raylicans regain interstellar flight
1866	Rhon genetic project begins
1871	Aristos found Eubian Concord (aka Trader Empire)
1881	Lahaylia Selei born
1904	Lahaylia Selei founds Skolian Imperialate
2005	Jarac born
2111	Lahaylia Selei marries Jarac
2119	Dyhianna Selei born
2122	Earth achieves interstellar flight
2132	Allied Worlds of Earth formed
2144	Roca born
2169	Kurj born
2203	Roca marries Eldrinson Althor Valdoria (*Skyfall*)
2204	Eldrin Jarac Valdoria born
2205	Prince Dayj Majda runs away ("The City of Cries")

2206	Althor Izam-Na Valdoria born
2209	Havyrl (Vyrl) Torcellei Valdoria born
2210	Sauscony (Soz) Lahaylia Valdoria born
2211	Denric Windward Valdoria born
2219	Kelricson (Kelric) Garlin Valdoria born
2223	Vyrl marries Lilly ("Stained Glass Heart")
2227	Soz goes to Jagernaut military academy (*Schism*)
2235	Denric trapped in Never-Haven ("The Edge of Never-Haven")
2237	Jaibriol II born
2240	Soz meets Jato Stormson ("Aurora in Four Voices")
2241	Kelric marries Admiral Corey Majda
2243	Corey assassinated ("Light and Shadow")
2258	Kelric crashes on Coba (*The Last Hawk*)
early 2259	Soz meets Jaibriol (*Primary Inversion*)
late 2259	Soz and Jaibriol go into exile (*The Radiant Seas*)
2260	Jaibriol III born (aka Jaibriol Qox Skolia) (*The Radiant Seas*)
2263	Rocalisa Qox Skolia born; Althor Izam-Na Valdoria meets Coop ("Soul of Light")
2266	Lilly dies
2268	Vitar Qox Skolia born
2273	del-Kelric Qox Skolia born
2274	Radiance War begins (also called Domino War) (*The Radiant Seas*)
2276	Traders capture Eldrin. Radiance War ends. Jason Harrick crashes on Thrice Named ("The Shadowed Heart")
2277–8	Kelric returns home (*Ascendant Sun*); Dehya coalesces (*Spherical Harmonic*); Kamoj and Vyrl meet (*The Quantum Rose*); Jaibriol III becomes emperor of Eube (*The Moon's Shadow*)
2279	Althor Vyan Selei born

Look for

FINAL KEY

by

Catherine Asaro

Available
December 2005
from Tom Doherty
Associates

"Make it stop, Hoshpa." Tears ran down the small boy's face, and his eyes were swollen from crying.

"It will get better." Eldrin murmured the words, agonized by the anguish of his six-year-old son, Taquinil. "It will get better." He sat on the floor cradling the boy in his arms, rocking him back and forth. He extended his telepath's mind like a shield against the pain that the boy couldn't block with his extraordinarily sensitive mind.

Gradually his mental shields muffled Taquinil's mind. The boy's sobs eased and his body relaxed. After several moments, Eldrin realized Taquinil had fallen asleep in his arms, his head against his father's shoulder. Eldrin breathed with relief. They had made it through another rough spell. He stood up, holding his son, and carried the boy to his room. After Eldrin tucked him in, he sat watching Taquinil sleep. Black hair was tousled about his son's face. Eldrin brushed back the disheveled bangs, and wished he could as easily brush away the boy's night terrors.

Footsteps sounded in the living room of the royal apartments. Startled, Eldrin straightened up. He glanced one last time to make sure Taquinil was peaceful. Then he went out to the hallway. Low voices were coming from the living room at the end of the hall.

Eldrin found Dehya, his wife, sitting on the sofa with one of her doctors. She had slouched down with her head thrown back, her eyes closed, and her long hair disarrayed like black silk. The doctor, Alaj Rajindia, was a dark-haired nobleman. The House of Rajindia provided the military with many bio-mech adepts, the neurological specialists who treated psions.

Alaj was a military expert in the medical treatment of telops, the telepathic operators who used the Kyle webs—the vast mesh of information that stretched across the Skolian Imperialate, tying the interstellar civilization together into a coherent whole. The existence of that mesh depended on the unique abilities of telops, and Dehya was the ultimate telop, the most versatile operator alive.

Alaj was checking her with a scanner. Eldrin hesitated, unsure if he should interrupt. Dehya had been in the webs for two days straight working and also chasing down clues about a man known as Vitarex Raziquon, a Trader Aristo, the sadistic monster in Eldrin's nightmares. Eldrin abhorred that her concern about his dreams added to her exhaustion. In his nightmares, Raziquon was torturing him, blinding him, crippling him, leaving him in unbearable pain, except he had to bear it. But it wasn't *him;* he always awoke in the royal suite here on the Orbiter space station that served as a government center for the Imperialate.

Alaj was speaking to Dehya, "I'm going to prescribe it anyway. Take it. Exactly the dose I give. No more."

She sat up wearily. "I won't take it."

The doctor scowled at her. "You've tied your mind into knots. If you keep this up, you will injure your brain."

"Neural relaxants are dangerous."

"I'll monitor you." He set down his scanner and took an air syringe off his belt. As he programmed it, he said, "The molecules will form complexes with receptors in your neural structures that accept psiamine, a transmitter that interprets telepathic or empathic input. It will block the psiamine enough to relax your mind."

"Relax." Dehya exhaled. "I've forgotten what that is like." She leaned back and closed her eyes. "All right. Do it."

Alaj injected her with the syringe. "It docsn't need long to take effect."

"And tomorrow?" she asked. "When I want more?"

"You'll be fine." Alaj slid the syringe into its case on his belt. "I've given you just enough to release your neurological knots. You may be edgy tomorrow, but you'll think more clearly."

"All right." She already sounded calmer.

"Contact me if you have any problems," Alaj added.

"Hmmmm . . ." Her lips curved. "Good doctor."

"You shouldn't stay alone. Is your husband here?"

Eldrin walked over to them. "Yes, I'm here." He pushed down the tugs of suspicion he felt any time another man came near his wife. "Is she all right?"

"I'm fine." Dehya opened her eyes dreamily. "Just fine."

Alaj looked up at him. "You'll need to tend her. Can you do that? Perhaps I should call in help for you."

Eldrin stiffened. Even after he had been married to Dehya for seven years, her people patronized him. "Of course I can look after her." He hesitated, reluctant to reveal his ignorance but fearing a lack of knowledge on his part could endanger his wife. "What did you give her?"

"It's a Kyle relaxant," Alaj said.

Eldrin had no idea what he meant. "I see."

Alaj was watching him closely. "It's analogous to a muscle relaxant. If you push yourself too hard and too long, physically, your muscles can spasm. Keep pushing after that, and you could do serious damage. You need something to relax the spasm. I gave her the neural analog of that medicine."

Eldrin rarely pushed his body past its physical limitations. In that sense, he didn't know what Alaj meant. But he had seen his father's epileptic seizures. Although his father had been in treatment for years, in his youth he had apparently almost died from the severity of his attacks. Several times Eldrin had suffered similar episodes, not epilepsy, but still an overload to his densely packed, over-developed neural structures. Battle lust. It happened in combat, including the time he had killed a man with his bare hands. Eldrin had been sixteen, a warrior on his first campaign. Later it had happened at school; in a fury born of frustration and guilt, he had used his sword to hack apart a study console as if it menaced his life. He had terrified his teachers and himself.

At his request, the Skolian doctors had treated him so he would never again experience those rages.

"I understand," he told Alaj.

"Good. Just stay with her." He turned to Dehya, who smiled at them both, her black lashes shading her eyes in a lush fringe. Alaj squinted at her, then turned back to Eldrin. "Make sure she doesn't wander off or hurt herself."

"You worry too much, Doctor Alaj." Dehya languorously rose to her feet and shooed him toward the door. "Go on. Go treat some of my nephew's bodyguards. They always looked stressed. Just imagine their lives, guarding him."

Although Alaj smiled, he seemed more alarmed than amused at the mention of her nephew, Kurj Skolia, the Imperator—military dictator of an empire. Eldrin had never seen the Imperator in that light; in many ways, Kurj was like a father to him.

"Call me if you have any trouble," Alaj told her.

"I will." Dehya pushed him out the door. "Go on."

Eldrin watched her, intrigued. She was far more relaxed this evening than was usual for his restrained, aloof wife. He thought of how she had looked up at him through her dark lashes. As he considered her, she turned and smiled slowly. Then she came over and put her arms around his neck.

"My greetings, gorgeous," she murmured.

He grinned and slid his arms around her waist. "You should take this medicine more often."

A shudder went through her. "I hope not."

He didn't want her mood to darken. Bending his head, he kissed her cheek. "It's certainly put you in good spirits."

She relaxed, pliant against him. "Doctor Alaj thinks I need to sleep more," she said softly. "What do you say? Bedtime?"

Eldrin laughed, his lips against her ear. "I think he is a wise doctor."

"Is Taquinil all right for the night?"

His good mood faded. "I hope so." He lifted his head so he could look down at her. "He had another attack. I got him to sleep just before you came home."

"Ah, no. I knew I felt something." She took his hand and headed down the hall. "It's no wonder my mind was in such terrible knots, if he was hurting."

As they reached Taquinil's room, Eldrin heard the boy mumbling in his sleep. Light from the living room filtered into the bedroom. Taquinil was a mound under the quilt, his cheek against the pillow. Even with his son sleeping, Eldrin felt the boy's mental strain.

And yet, as they approached the bed, Taquinil breathed out, long and slow, his body losing its rigid tension under the quilt. He sighed and settled deeper into the covers. Even in the dim light, Eldrin saw the dramatic change as the drawn lines of the boy's face smoothed out.

Dehya sat on the bed, taking care not to jostle her son. When she took his hand, he turned toward her and his shoulders releasing their clenched posture. His fists uncurled and his breathing deepened.

"That's amazing," Eldrin said.

Dehya pressed her lips against Taquinil's forehead. Then she carefully let go of his hand and stood up so she and Eldrin were standing side by side. "He's so peaceful."

"He's a treasure." Eldrin drew her out of the room where they could talk without waking Taquinil. "How did you do that? It's the first time in days I've seen him at peace."

She walked down the hall with him. "I didn't do anything."

"Maybe it's the Kyle relaxant. It affects Taquinil, too."

She came to a stop in the entrance of the living room. "Gods, I hope not. It's nothing Taquinil should ever take."

"Not the drug. He has none of its chemicals in his body." Eldrin smiled as he figured it out. "He's such a sensitive empath. He senses your relief and it affects him." It wouldn't be that unusual; among the three of them, they often affected one another with their moods and health. This was a more dramatic effect than usual, but not unreasonable.

"If that helps, I'm glad." She pulled him close, and her body curved against him. Her voice turned throaty. "We were discussing our own bedtime, if I remember correctly."

Eldrin's pulse surged. This wasn't his reserved wife, the restrained and distant Ruby Pharaoh of the Skolian Imperialate. In the darkness of their bedroom, the ice queen often melted in his arms, but tonight she was heating up before they came near their bed. He pulled her into a kiss, hungry, and he was still kissing her when they stumbled into their room. They fell onto the floater together, and the pillows bounced around them. Out of habit, he and Dehya shielded their minds, giving them privacy from everyone but each other.

Eldrin ran his hands over her slight curves and scraped at the fastenings of her jumpsuit. The cloth crinkled as he dragged the outfit off her body. Then he held her breasts, kneading them, probably too hard, but she didn't object. He stroked her nipples, and they stiffened under his palm. As her breathing quickened, she tugged at his clothes. Soon they were bare skin to bare skin, and he knew only his hunger. He rolled her onto her back and settled on her body, trying to restrain himself so he wouldn't bruise her, though with her delicate skin it was hard to avoid, especially tonight. She was pulling him to herself with an urgency that matched his own.

Later, they lay tangled together in the covers, sated and quiet. Dehya was sleeping on her side, her body pressed against him. Eldrin slid his hand over her hip. He hadn't felt this content in a long time. He closed his eyes and finally let go, unafraid of his dreams. Her neural relaxant had done wonders, her euphoric mood affecting him, too. For the first time in days he fell asleep without fear . . .

Asleep . . .

Dreaming . . .

Mind relaxing . . .

PAIN. Blindness. Such pain! The Aristo hungered for his agony, his grief, his torment. The monster sat on his stool, brutal in his transcendence, and the agony went on and on, inside his body, inside his soul . . .

A scream yanked Eldrin awake. He bolted upright, reaching for a sword he hadn't carried in years. Bleary and dazed, he scrambled out of bed and yanked on his sleep trousers. As he strode for the archway, shrugging into his shirt, another terrified cry broke the night. He ran through the dark, down the hall.

"Lights on!" he called. The hallway lit up as he entered his son's room. Taquinil was sitting up in bed, his terrified face stained with tears.

"It's all right," Eldrin said as he strode to the bed. "It's all right." He lifted the boy and cradled him against his chest. "I'm here, Taqui. You're all right. It'll be all right."

Taquinil buried his head in his father's shoulder and wept, his small body shaking with silent sobs. Eldrin walked from the room, gently bouncing his son in his arms, pacing down the hall to the darkened living room. He searched the silent, darkened suite. No Dehya. It was probably why Taquinil's distress had returned; the ameliorating effects of her relaxed mental state were gone.

"Where is your mother?" Eldrin said, more to himself than his son. Alaj had warned him to look out for her. "Laplace," he said, addressing the Evolving Intelligence, or EI, that served the royal apartments. "Where is my wife?"

A well-modulated voice answered. "Pharaoh Dyhianna left about four hours ago."

Eldrin continued to walk, his head leaning against his son's head. "Where did she go?"

"I don't know," Laplace said. "However, she received a message. Do you wish to view the log of your mesh-mail?"

He stopped by a console in the living room. "Yes." If the mail had come on Dehya's private account, Laplace wouldn't show it to him. But most of her correspondence came over the account she and Eldrin shared.

Taquinil was shaking in his arms with silent sobs, unable even to cry aloud. Eldrin held him close. He didn't want Laplace to read aloud and disturb the boy, so he had the EI scroll through the mail, pausing each one long enough for Eldrin to struggle through the message. Alaj's medical report had come in with specifics of Dehya's treatment and advice that she rest. So why wasn't she resting? Where the hell was she?

Taquinil cried out and his small fists clenched in Eldrin's collar-length hair. "Hoshpa! The man with the bad name!"

Eldrin knew he meant Vitarex, the Aristo in his nightmares, which had spilled into Taquinil's painfully sensitive mind. Eldrin swayed back and forth, murmuring. "I won't let him get you. You're safe, Taqui." On the console, mail continued to scroll by.

"Laplace, stop." He saw the message to Dehya: a major space station had lost many of its primary systems due to a crisis in the Kyle web beyond the ability of their telops to fix. Millions of people lived on that station, and they were losing environmental systems, defenses, even port controls. They couldn't evacuate without launch bays. Dehya had been called in to fix the web before the station died.

Eldrin swore under his breath. He knew she had a duty to help, but when would she ever get to rest? This happened all too often, that she would disappear while he slept, dragged back to her work by her endless responsibilities as Pharaoh. He knew she didn't want to disturb his sleep, but it unsettled him even more to awake alone.

"Was she all right when she left?" he asked.

"She seemed fine," Laplace said.

Eldrin hoped so. He headed down the hall to Taquinil's room.

Make it stop! Taquinil cried in his mind. **Please, Hoshpa.**

I will, Taqui. I'll make it better. Guilt saturated Eldrin. His nightmare had done this. If only he could take his son's torments into himself and free the boy. Dehya had helped; tonight was the first time in days Taquinil had relaxed. But she was gone now, and so was the effect of her medicine. Every time Eldrin fell asleep, he made it worse. He could handle the nightmares; he had mental defenses to mute their effect. Taquinil didn't. When he shielded the boy with his mind, his son was all right, but in sleep, Eldrin lost his ability to provide that protection. He didn't know why he was suffering these nightmares, but he feared someone he loved was in trouble, someone in his family, for they were the only ones whose minds linked strongly enough to his to affect him this way. When he slept, his barriers eased and the connection could intensify. As far as he knew, everyone in his family was fine, yet the dreams continued. Taquinil continued to tremble, his tears soaking into Eldrin's hair, and Eldrin couldn't bear his misery.

He knew what he had to do.

Eldrin returned to the living room and brought up Alaj's medical report. He memorized the details he needed, then carried Taquinil through the master bedroom and into a refresher chamber beyond. Holding his son in one arm, Eldrin took Dehya's personal air syringe out of a cabinet. Normally someone who wasn't a doctor couldn't have a medical-grade pharmaceutical supply in her possession. But as pharaoh, Dehya had a full dispensary, all in a slender syringe that wasn't even the length of her forearm.

Eldrin could have asked Alaj to help Taquinil, but it had never worked in the past and he had lost faith that the doctors could do anything but disappoint his son. It took a Rhon psion to protect a Rhon psion, and the only Rhon in existence were Eldrin's family. He also knew Alaj would never approve this solution. Too bad. Alaj wasn't the one whose son was in agony.

Eldrin entered the prescription Alaj had given Dehya and was relieved to find the syringe had the components needed to prepare the medicine. He wasn't certain about the dose he should use on himself; he was larger than his wife, but she had been in difficulty and he was fine. He settled on the same dose Alaj had given her and injected himself in the neck. He winced as the syringe hissed, not from any pain but because it reminded him of the doctors and their advice against using medicine without supervision. This would be all right. He had watched Alaj treat Dehya, read the doctor's report, and followed it with care.

He put away the syringe and shifted Taquinil to both

arms. The small boy shivered in his embrace. Eldrin paced
through the royal apartments, walking his son, murmuring
comfort.

So far, no effect.

He kept walking, singing now, soft and low, a verse he had
written when Taquinil was two years old:

> *Marvelous bright boy,*
> *Wonder of all years,*
> *Precarious joy,*
> *Miracle from tears.*

He sang it over and over. The night took on a trance-like
quality and his voice rolled like waves on a shore, the endless ocean of waves, lapping, lapping, rocking, soft and
smooth.

Waves murmuring.

Waves rocking.

Rocking.

Eldrin sighed and settled Taquinil more comfortably in
his arms. He could carry his son forever, his beloved son. If
only he could heal the pain, if only he could make Taquinil's
life as serene as his own . . .

Serene?

Not likely. Many words described his life: confusing,
lonely, painfully beautiful—but "serene" wasn't one of them.

It was true, though. He felt remarkably calm.

Taquinil sighed and sagged against Eldrin. Tension
drained out of his body. Immensely grateful, Eldrin closed
his eyes. He wandered through the suit, less focused, aware
of little more than his relief that Taquinil's attack had
passed. It surprised him that the relaxant had acted so fast;
usually this soon after taking medicine, he felt only preliminary effects. He rarely needed any, though; he had top-of-
the-line nanomeds in his body to maintain his health, and he
almost never fell ill. He was only twenty-three and he rarely
thought about growing old, but someday, when it became an
issue, the meds would even delay his aging.

Taquinil began to breathe with the steady rhythm of sleep. After a few more minutes, Eldrin took him to his room and tucked him into bed. The boy settled under his covers, his face peaceful.

Joy filled Eldrin in seeing his son content. Tranquility spread through him. He hadn't felt this good since—well, never. No wonder Alaj had prescribed this medicine for Dehya. His wife deserved peace in her life.

Peace.

Weese.

Geese.

Fly.

Fly away.

The living room swirled in a rainbow of colors. Eldrin didn't remember coming back here. With a satisfied grunt, he dropped onto the couch and stretched out his legs. His body seemed to float. A thought came dreamily to him: he could go outside to the balcony, jump off, and fly over the city. Except he didn't want to move. He felt so incredibly *good.* He hadn't been this happy in ages, maybe never, surely never, nothing compared to this. It was almost too much, too much, too much happiness. *His mind swirled, unraveling in ecstasy, lost to the lovely, glorious night . . .*

Wake up! Father, wake up!

The words in his mind went on, such a dear sound . . .

"Please." The young voice pleaded. "Father, what's wrong? Wake up! Please!"

Eldrin blearily opened his eyes. Taquinil was standing next to him, dressed in pajamas, his eyes wide as he anxiously shook Eldrin's arm. As soon as Eldrin met his gaze, Taquinil made a choked sound and climbed up next to him. Confused and groggy, Eldrin put his arm around his son's shoulders and peered around. He was sprawled on the couch, his body slumped against the white cushions. Light from the Sun Lamp streamed through a window at an angle that suggested it was early morning in the thirty [c] hour cycle of the space habitat's day.

Eldrin sighed. So beautiful a day. He squeezed Taquinil's shoulders. "Don't be scared. I took some medicine last night, that's all. It made me sleepy."

Taquinil curled against his side. "I thought you were sick."

"I'm fine. Really." Eldrin leaned his head back and closed his eyes. The world flowed around him . . .

"—time to eat," Taquinil prodded. "Come on, Hoshpa."

Eldri lifted his head, blinking and confused. Taquinil wasn't snuggled against him anymore. In fact, the boy was standing in front of him, dressed in dark blue trousers and a lighter blue pullover. His shoes peeked out from beneath his trousers.

Eldri tried to focus. "How are you feeling?"

"Fine, Hoshpa." Taquinil looked much calmer.

"Good." Eldrin rubbed his eyes. "Have you had breakfast?"

"An hour ago." Taquinil's forehead furrowed. "You should eat. That medicine makes you too sleepy."

Eldrin sat up and rested his elbows on his knees. He grinned at his son. "You're a delightful sight for your hoshpa's eyes."

Taquinil blushed and smiled. "Come on." He took Eldrin's hand. "I'll make you breakfast."

Eldrin wondered if other people's six-year-olds spoke this way. He had no formal education in childhood development, but he was the oldest of ten children, and none of his siblings had been like this. Taquinil had a boy's voice, but sometimes he sounded more like an adult than some adults. From the effusive comments of the boy's tutors, Eldrin gathered that most children didn't learn to read before they were two. Lyshrioli natives didn't read at all. He didn't know many Skolian children, and Taquinil's handful of friends were older than him, which made it hard to judge. Besides, royal tutors always praised royal children. That had certainly been true for Eldrin, even when he didn't deserve it. He did know that Taquinil could read and write much better than him, and that the boy understood more math than Eldrin would probably ever know. He didn't have a good sense of how far above the norm Taquinil was, but it made him proud to have a smart son.

"My thanks, young man," Eldrin said. As he stood up, the room swirled around him. It had settled down from last night, though, and from his dreams, which had floated in a blissful fog. He let out a satisfied breath. "I feel good."

Holding his son's hand, he went to the kitchen. He walked by the wine cabinet with barely a thought for a drink. And if his head was beginning to ache and his pulse to stutter in odd ways as the medicine wore off, well, that would go away soon, he felt certain.

Surely he had nothing to worry about.